10 JUL 2015

WEDDED *to* WAR

Center Point
Large Print

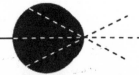

**This Large Print Book carries the
Seal of Approval of N.A.V.H.**

WEDDED
to WAR

Heroines Behind the Lines

Jocelyn Green

CENTER POINT LARGE PRINT
THORNDIKE, MAINE

This Center Point Large Print edition
is published in the year 2015 by arrangement with
Moody Publishers.

Though many of the events in this story are based on
true incidents, characters are either fictional or depicted
fictitiously. Dates of events are given as closely as
possible to their occurrences, though some exceptions
were made to fit the fictional timeline.

The text of this Large Print edition is unabridged.
In other aspects, this book may vary
from the original edition.
Printed in the United States of America
on permanent paper.
Set in 16-point Times New Roman type.

ISBN: 978-1-62899-618-0

Library of Congress Cataloging-in-Publication Data

Green, Jocelyn.
Wedded to war : heroines behind the lines / Jocelyn Green.
pages cm. — (Civil War ; book 1)
Summary: "Charlotte Waverly gives up a life of privilege to serve as a
Civil War nurse and finds herself up against corruption, opposition and
wounded men. This historical novel is inspired by the letters and journals of
one Civil War nurse, Georgeanna Woolsey"
—Provided by publisher.
ISBN 978-1-62899-618-0 (library binding : alk. paper)
1. Nurses—Fiction.
  2. United States—History—Civil War, 1861–1865—Women—Fiction.
  3. Nursing—United States—History—19th century—Fiction.
  4. United States—History—Civil War, 1861–1865—Medical care—Fiction.
  5. Large type books. I. Title.
PS3607.R4329255W43 2015
813′.6—dc23

2015012332

For Rob,
who never made me choose between
following my heart and nurturing my mind,

And for my parents,
who believed I was a writer
before I could even spell.

Contents

A Note on the Sanitary Commission

Anyone who has benefitted from the Red Cross owes a nod of gratitude to the United States Sanitary Commission, the forerunner of one of today's most recognized charitable organizations.

The Sanitary Commission set up supply stations and hospitals, hired nurses, collected donations, sent inspectors to Union hospitals (to evaluate hygiene conditions that directly affected men's health), and taught troops in camp how to cook food properly to prevent the spread of disease. They also organized and staffed a fleet of hospital ships both in the eastern and western theaters of war.

Though it often clashed with the army's Medical Department, especially in the beginning of the war, the Commission saved hundreds of thousands of lives, with the help of an army of women volunteers.

Though *Wedded to War* is a work of fiction, the story was inspired by one Sanitary Commission nurse, Georgeanna Woolsey, whose letters and journals, written 150 years ago, offer a thorough look at what pioneering women nurses endured during these turbulent times.

Act One

THE CALL

IT WAS HARD WORK getting myself acceptable and accepted. What with people at home, saying "Goodness me! A nurse!" "All nonsense!" "Such a fly-away!" and what with the requisites insisted upon by the grave committees, I came near losing my opportunity.

First, one must be just so old, and no older; have eyes and a nose and mouth expressing just such traits, and no others; must be willing to scrub floors, if necessary, etc., etc. Finally, however, by dint of taking the flowers out of my bonnet and the flounce off my dress; by toning down, or toning up, according to the emergency, I succeeded in getting myself looked upon with mitigated disapprobation, and was at last sat upon by the committee and passed over to the Examining Board.

> —GEORGEANNA WOOLSEY, written for the New York Sanitary Commission Fair, 1864

"GEORGY IS MORE EARNEST than ever about being a nurse for the soldiers. *I shall never consent to this arrangement* unless some of her own family go with her."

> —JANE ELIZA NEWTON WOOLSEY (Georgeanna's mother) in a letter, May 1861

Chapter One

New York City
Monday, April 22, 1861

When Charlotte and Alice told their mother they were taking the omnibus down Broadway, they weren't lying. They just didn't tell her where they would be getting off. There was simply no time for an argument today.

Boarding at Fourteenth Street, the sisters paid the extra fare for their hoop skirts, as if they were separate passengers, and sat back on the long wooden bench for the ride.

"This is against my better judgment, you know." Alice's voice was barely audible above the clatter of wheels and hoof beats over the cobblestones.

"Don't you mean Jacob's?" Charlotte cast a sidelong glance at her sister.

Alice twirled a ringlet of her honey-blonde hair around her finger—a nervous childhood habit she never outgrew—but said nothing.

She didn't have to. Ever since she had married the wealthy businessman a few months ago, she had been even more pampered—and sheltered—than she had been growing up. Heaven help her when they reached their destination.

"I'll have you home by teatime and none the

worse for wear." Charlotte's voice was softened by just a hint of guilt. "I promise."

The omnibus wheels jolted over a broken cobblestone, bouncing the passengers on their benches. Releasing her grip from the edge of the bench, Alice raised an eyebrow at her sister. "Just tell me why I let you talk me into coming."

Charlotte grinned. "I've got an idea."

"Why do I have the feeling it isn't a good one?" Alice planted her palms on the bench beside her again, bracing herself against the jarring ride.

"Whatever you do you mean?"

"Do you remember your idea to adopt that lame squirrel we found?"

"I did let it go." And there were more important things on Charlotte's mind. She squinted at the front page of *The New York Times* held up by the man seated across from her. *Washington Still Isolated—New York Seventh Regiment Arrives in Annapolis by Steam—*

"Only after it chewed through five of Mother's best doilies and made a nest in the velvet armchair."

Charlotte turned from reading headlines to face her sister. "I was ten!"

"And I was eight, and still old enough to know better. There were other times, too, like when you chose that outrageous reading on the value of a woman's education to recite for our class at finishing school. Completely at odds with the context of the school."

Charlotte chuckled. "Exactly why it was so perfect! But today's idea is even better. I've found a way to actually *do* something for the war effort."

"And what do you call knitting socks for the troops? Rolling bandages? Doesn't that mean anything?"

"Of course it does. But I mean something else. Something *more*."

Alice's eyes narrowed, but she let it rest as the omnibus slowed to a halt and more passengers squeezed beside the sisters. Any further conversation would soon be drowned out by the cacophony of Broadway.

The avenue throbbed with life, like an artery coursing down the island of Manhattan. Ten days into the war, recruiting offices for the Union army had already cropped up along the avenue, their entrances clogged with eager young men. Between Canal Street and Houston, the street teemed with gentlemen in spats and ladies in silks, their musk colognes and lavender perfumes cloying on the warm breeze. The white marble façade of St. Nicholas Hotel between Broome and Spring Streets dominated the west side of Broadway. In front of The Marble Palace facing Canal Street, porters in their brass-buttoned, blue uniforms opened carriage doors and escorted their elite customers inside, where they would no doubt spend staggering sums on the latest Parisian fashions.

But Charlotte and Alice did not get off at any of these places. At least not today. For just a few blocks south of The Marble House, and just a few blocks east of the German-Jewish secondhand clothing shops on lower Broadway, the steady pulse of polished society gave way to the erratic beat of Five Points, the world's most notorious slum.

Alice squeezed her sister's hand so tightly Charlotte couldn't tell if it was motivated by anxiety or anger for bringing her here.

If Broadway was Manhattan's artery, Five Points was its abscess: swollen with people, infected with pestilence, inflamed with vice and crime. Groggeries, brothels, and dance halls put private sin on public display. Although the neighborhood seemed fairly self-contained, more fortunate New Yorkers were terrified of Five Points erupting, spreading its contagion to the rest of them.

This was where the Waverly sisters got off.

Competing emotions of fear and excitement tugged at Charlotte's heart as she hoisted the skirt of her amber-colored day dress above her ankles and began heading toward Worth Street. "Come on, Alice," she whispered, cocking her head at her dumbstruck sister. A foul-smelling breeze teased strands of hair from their coifs, crept into their noses, and coated their throats. Charlotte had forgotten how the smell of poverty would stick to her skin. Swallowing her distaste, she vowed to scrub herself with sugar and lemon-infused olive oil as soon as she returned home.

Pressing a violet-scented handkerchief to her nose, Alice held her parasol low over her head, blocking out as much of the view as possible as she began walking. "Where are we going?" Her words were muffled, but her discomfort was not.

A disheveled drunk leered at the sisters from a rotting doorway, raising the hair on Charlotte's neck. "The House of Industry. It's just up ahead."

With her parasol in one hand and a fistful of skirts in the other, Charlotte set a brisk pace. As they turned onto Worth Street's littered sidewalk, Alice skirted a child leaning against a lamppost, hawking apples from a broken crate. Charlotte stopped short.

"Maggie?" She reached out and touched the girl's soot-smudged cheek while Alice gawked from five feet away. "It's me, Miss Waverly! I used to teach your mother sewing. How is she?"

Maggie peered up with eyes too big for her face, too old for her nine years. "About the same as usual—only there's not enough sewing to go around, she says—so Jack sweeps the streets and here I am. Say, wouldn't you and the miss over there like a nice red apple?"

"Of course!" Charlotte reached into her dress

pocket and traded several coins for two small, bruised apples smelling of fermentation.

"Charlotte!" Alice gasped while Maggie's dirty face brightened. It was far too much money to spend on apples—especially rotting ones.

"Go on now, Maggie. Give your mother my best."

With "Bless you Miss!" ringing in her ears, Charlotte joined Alice with both apples in one hand, skirt now dragging on the sidewalk.

"Can we hustle, please?" Alice's voice was still muted behind her handkerchief. Charlotte was eager to comply. Virtually every tipsy wooden building on this block—including Crown's Grocery—housed a brothel, and none of them bothered hiding the fact. Bareheaded and bare-chested women stood in doorways quoting their rates to passersby, even in broad daylight—which was a dirty yellow, like a fevered complexion. By the time they stepped into the slanted shadow of the six-story House of Industry, Charlotte noticed she had been holding her breath. The vapors in this area could truly make one sick.

"Ah, there you are!" Mr. Lewis Pease, founder of the charity, had been waiting for them in the shade of the brick building, and now waved the sisters inside, away from the seedy, star-shaped intersection for which Five Points was named, half a block away. "And who is this lovely young woman?"

18

"Forgive me, this is my younger sister Alice—Mrs. Jacob Carlisle." Charlotte and Alice entered the building ahead of Mr. Pease, who closed the door behind them. "She's in town visiting for a spell while her husband is away on business." She set the apples down on the hall stand and wiped her gloves on her skirt.

Pease bowed slightly. "A pleasure to meet you, madam. Mr. Dorsheimer is already here," he added in a whisper just as the visitor's barrel chest entered the room ahead of him. "Ah, Mr. Treasurer. Allow me to make the introductions. Miss Waverly, Mrs. Carlisle, this is Mr. Phillip Dorsheimer, Treasurer of the State of New York and the New York State Military Board. He's here all the way from Buffalo, and we're so fortunate he's making time to meet with us." Mr. Dorsheimer ignored Charlotte's outstretched hand, fading both her smile and her confidence.

Mr. Pease continued. "Mr. Treasurer, Miss Waverly here was the one who suggested we make a bid for the contract. She used to be a sewing instructor here."

Without even the slightest acknowledgment, Mr. Dorsheimer frowned at his pocket watch. "Can we get on with it?" His jowls quivered as he spoke. Charlotte took a deep breath and squeezed her parasol handle. So far, this was not going as she had hoped it would.

A thin smile tipped Mr. Pease's lips. "Yes, quite.

I'd like to give you a tour of the facility before discussing the terms of the uniform contract. Unless you've been here before?"

Mr. Dorsheimer cleared his throat. "Oh, I've been to the Points before, but not here in this building." Of course. Well-to-do New Yorkers often came down to see Five Points for themselves to satisfy a macabre curiosity. "Well, allow us to show you around," said Mr. Pease, leading the way. "This is a fairly new headquarters for us, and we're rather proud of it. This corridor leads to the workshops where neighborhood teens and adults learn several trades. At first we taught only basic sewing, but now we also teach baking, shoemaking, corset making, basket weaving, and millinery. Go ahead, look around."

Mr. Dorsheimer tossed cursory glances into a few of the workshops.

"We have more than five hundred workers currently. Five hundred!" Mr. Pease beamed. "I pay the workers according to what they produce. Sewers can earn up to $2.50 a week—now I know that doesn't sound like much to you and me, Mr. Treasurer, but it's a lot more than needlewomen normally earn. We've also opened a day school for the children so they are educated, fed, and even clothed while the parents work at their trades here."

They walked a little farther and turned into a large open room. "This is the chapel where we hold religious services," Mr. Pease continued. "Of course there is also the Five Points Mission just across the street, whose primary objective is to feed the souls and point them to new life in Christ. The House of Industry began as a branch of the Mission, because I found they had a hard time hearing the Bible when their stomachs were growling. And what better way to feed the multitudes than to teach them a trade so they can feed themselves?"

If Mr. Dorsheimer felt anything, he hid it well in those doughy folds of skin. The palms of Charlotte's gloves began to dampen with sweat.

"One last thing I'd like to show you." Climbing a set of stairs brought them to a well-ventilated floor with spacious dormitories, each with iron beds that termites couldn't penetrate. "We started out housing our worker women, so they wouldn't need to go back to the brothels at night. But now we also shelter dozens of abused, neglected, and homeless children who are waiting for adoptive parents."

Mr. Dorsheimer, winded from the exertion of the climb, did not look impressed.

"These rooms are humble enough, indeed," Charlotte added, "but when you consider many of these people are used to sleeping on the bare floor of a room with no windows and laid out like sardines in a can, you can understand the charm of a bed and some—air, can't you?" Calling it "fresh air" would have been a lie. With human waste collecting in trenches behind most Five Points tenements, no air had been fresh here for decades. At least windows allowed circulation.

Dorsheimer glanced at his pocket watch again, a scowl sagging on his face. "This is all very well and good," he huffed, "but can we get to the bottom line? How much would it cost to give you the contract? I need twelve thousand uniforms, and I need them as quickly as possible."

Mr. Pease turned to Charlotte. "Yes, of course," she said. "We propose a payment from the state's Military Board of thirteen cents per shirt, so that would be a total of $1,560.00. Total." She bit her lip.

"Fifteen hundred dollars?"

Charlotte stole a glance at Mr. Pease. *Was that a lot? Or not very much?*

"Fifteen hundred *sixty* dollars, sir. To be precise. Plus, you'd supply the flannel and buttons," she said.

"I need more than just shirts, miss." Dorsheimer's tone was sharp, biting. "I need trousers, jackets, and overcoats, too, and I need it all in three weeks. Twelve thousand sets. And *you* provide the material. Not me. Do I look like I'm in the garment business?"

Alice's eyes widened into large pools of cornflower blue. Charlotte's narrowed into slits.

"Twelve thousand complete uniforms in three

weeks. I wish I could say we could do that, Mr. Dorsheimer, but you're asking for a huge sum on an extremely short deadline. Not only can we not perform miracles, but I doubt any single company in New York could do a satisfactory job under your specifications."

"I'm sure if we joined together with a few other sewing organizations, we could do it," said Charlotte, swiveling between Mr. Pease and Mr. Dorsheimer. "But we need a little more time to make the arrangements. This contract would mean a great deal to the House of Industry and to the workers in a financial sense, but it would also be a perfect way they could serve their country and their fighting men at war. You could be guaranteed of fine quality products made by conscientious workers."

"Not possible. The boys are going to war, and they need to be clothed."

"Mr. Dorsheimer, please. Consider the greater value of giving a charity the contract. The House of Industry has made a profound impact on Five Points, rescuing people from poverty—and the immorality that sometimes goes with it—and helping them walk a better road."

Mr. Dorsheimer raised a hand to stop her, but she didn't slow down.

"I'm sure you know President Lincoln came to Five Points just last year, just before his Cooper Union speech that launched him toward the presidency. And what did he choose to see in Five Points? Not the brothels or groggeries, but the House of Industry."

"Miss—" He tried again, but she couldn't stop.

"Maggie's mother, and dozens like her, needed this contract. Sir, the good work we do here inside these walls is becoming even more famous than the degradation outside of them. Invest in the House of Industry with this uniform contract, Mr. Dorsheimer, and you'll be getting the products you want and doing society a favor at the same time."

At the end of her speech now, Charlotte caught her breath; Alice stared at her in disbelief. No one said a word until Mr. Dorsheimer jabbed a stubby finger at Charlotte.

"My responsibility, young woman, is to the State of New York, not to your pet project here in the slums."

Charlotte's face burned as she, Alice, and Mr. Pease watched Mr. Dorsheimer trudge out of the building, taking her hope with her.

"It was worth a try, Miss Waverly," Mr. Pease said.

Alice leveled her gaze at Charlotte. "Another good idea, right Charlotte?"

Frustration swelled in Charlotte's chest. "Why? Why would you say such a thing? It was a brilliant idea! It made so much sense!"

"Charlotte, when will you ever realize that not

everyone sees the world as you do? You act so surprised when others disagree with you, when you are the one stepping out of the range of normal."

Charlotte crossed her arms tightly across her waist. "You used to look up to me." Her throat grew tight with the unshed tears of bitter disappointment. "You used to believe in me."

Alice laid a tentative hand on Charlotte's arm. "I believe your intentions are good. But once again, you spoke too boldly. Perhaps if you had not been so vehement with your outburst, Mr. Dorsheimer would at least have considered giving you the contract." Alice sighed, resignation in her eyes. "You must—you *must*—know your place, dear sister, or one of these days, you will stand to lose much more than a sewing contract."

Charlotte opened her mouth to deny it, but could make no reply.

Chapter Two

New York City
Sunday, April 28, 1861

Curling up on the plush cushioned bench inside the parlor's bay window, Charlotte welcomed the bundle of marmalade and cream fur that bounded onto her lap.

"So there you are, Dickens!" Purring vibrated beneath her hand as she stroked his glossy coat. She had named the cat with her favorite author in mind, but quickly realized the little feline was beautiful on the outside but a dickens on the inside. *Probably the way everyone sees me—especially men!*

Still stinging from the news that the uniform contract had gone to Brooks Brothers, Charlotte was in no mood to be courted today. But courting season had arrived with the daffodils, and it would not be put off, even for war. No, courting was serious business. She should know. She had been through ten years of it herself, and not one had produced a suitable match. Still, she couldn't help but assume some of the blame for that.

This year will be different, her mother kept telling her. Perhaps she was right. Even so, by the

26

time Phineas Hastings took his leave of her front parlor this Sunday afternoon, she was more than ready for some solitude.

Charlotte held nothing against Mr. Hastings. In fact, she had respected the law professor ever since she had met him at a guest lecture given by Frederick Douglass at the Broadway Tabernacle. Mr. Hastings was intelligent, charming, educated, and a regular churchgoer. His parents—God rest their souls—had brought him up well. *Not quite as tall as*—She shook her head as if to erase the thought. Comparing every suitor to a ghost from her past served no one.

Importantly, her mother approved of Phineas. A wry smile lifted Charlotte's lips. Little did Caroline know, however, that as soon as she had put an end to Charlotte's work at the House of Industry, Phineas had given the charity a large donation—all the proceeds from a recent lecture he had given—just to cheer Charlotte up. Since then he had made a few more donations, perhaps more to win Charlotte's affections rather than from his own concern for Five Points, but she didn't care. Regardless of his motivation, his generosity to the charity endeared him to her.

In addition to teaching law, Mr. Hastings was one of New York's most well-known crusaders for abolitionism. His fiery rhetoric—and the fact that he had shared the stage with Douglass, even if only for a moment—left her in awe of him from the start. Most men didn't understand why Charlotte attended lectures, but Mr. Hastings had actually seemed to enjoy conversing with her about politics and culture, religion and philosophy. It was what had attracted her to him in the first place. He wasn't afraid of a woman who used her brain.

"Then again," Charlotte told Dickens, "I imagine I would be happier if I just didn't think so much." She leaned her head against the windowpane, her cat still warming her lap. Discontent seeped into her, like the cold air through the glass. Large, wooly clouds sagged in the air, snagging on church steeples and streetlights as they drifted across a grey flannel sky. Every roll of thunder echoed the rumblings of her spirit.

The passionate preaching from the pulpit this morning and the newspaper at her side she thumbed through now deepened her unrest. Since the attack on Fort Sumter almost two weeks ago, New York City had rallied together for the Union cause, but the news headlines did not support the city's optimism. Virginia had seceded on April 16. Troops on their way to Washington were attacked in Baltimore. Southern sympathizers had burned several railroad bridges to prevent Union troops from passing from Baltimore to Washington, and the rioting continued. Col. Robert E. Lee officially resigned his commission with the U.S. Army to lead Rebel troops in the Army of Northern

Virginia. A Southern attack on the Federal capital was imminent.

And she wasn't doing a thing about it.

Sighing, she reached for the Blue Willow teacup on the walnut table next to her, and breathed in the fragrance of orange and cloves. She picked up today's *New York Times* and froze. Without taking her eyes off the paper, she rattled the cup back on its saucer.

CALL FOR NURSING CANDIDATES BY THE WOMEN'S CENTRAL ASSOCIATION FOR RELIEF

Women have not hitherto been employed in military hospitals as nurses. The nursing is done by soldiers drafted out of the ranks for that purpose. . . .

Nursing in military hospitals is a very different thing from nursing in civil hospitals, and still more from private nursing. The class of patients to be nursed, the character of the under nurses, who will always be men, the social isolation of the position, and the absolute necessity of enforcing military discipline, combine to render nursing in military hospitals a service of peculiar difficulty which can only be accomplished successfully by a select and disciplined band of nurses.

The following regulations for selecting

candidates have been drawn up—these regulations being approved by the Hospital Association to whom they were submitted.

Age.—Each candidate must be between the ages of thirty and forty-five years, exceptions being only made in the case of nurses of valuable experience.

Health.—Only women of strong constitutions will be received; chronic disease, or other physical weakness, disqualifying for service.

Character.—Every applicant must present a written testimonial or introduction from a responsible person who can be seen. Only persons of the highest respectability will be received.

Discipline.—A promise of cordial compliance with all the regulations of the service will be required.

Dress.—A regulation dress will be appointed by the board, which each nurse will be required to adopt, no hoops being allowed in the service.

Number of Candidates.—Ten Bands, or a class of one hundred, will now be enrolled, due notice being given in the daily journals when the lists are full. Should a second corps be needed the call will again be published in the papers.

The Registration Committee meet daily

in the Cooper Institute in the Philosophical Rooms, on the fourth floor, between the hours of two and four P.M. They earnestly invite all ladies possessing the necessary qualifications to present themselves for registration.

Those who are fitted by nature and position to engage in this new and difficult work, will render invaluable aid to their country by devoting themselves to its thorough accomplishment.

Signed,

Drs. Elizabeth Blackwell,

Edward Delafield,

J. R. Wood, and

Elisha Harris.

She read the notice again.

Are they crazy?

As the first woman to earn a medical degree in the United States, Dr. Blackwell could be expected to come up with such an outrageous plan to insert women into the men's sphere of work. But there were three other doctors names attached, all highly distinguished men.

Wincing from being in the same position for too long, Charlotte unfolded her legs from under her, sending Dickens to the floor, and began to pace the room, the ribboned hem of her skirt skimming the French rug beneath her feet. Just imagine.

Women serving their country so close to the action! She had read all about England's Florence Nightingale and her work in the Crimean War, but never dreamed such a thing would be possible in this country. They must be desperate for help.

But she was too young, according to the requirements printed in the paper. And even if she were old enough, she would be useless as a nurse. She could scarcely stand the mention of blood, let alone the sight of it, ever since her father's death. And besides, her mother, Caroline, would never allow it. Well-bred women had no business getting their hands dirty, she could almost hear her say. It was the reason Caroline had discouraged her from continuing her work at the House of Industry.

Thunder grumbled outside, and the clouds, finally ripped open from beneath, released their cargo. Raindrops fell fat and heavy on the cobblestones, the rooftops, the carriages out for a Sunday ride, like a drummer boy's steady tapping, calling the men to war.

And the women to opportunity.

Like a bolt of lightning, the call to nurse jolted through her. Her eyes darted around the room, surveying the evidence of affluence to which she was accustomed. Crystal and candlesticks. Heavy velvet draperies. A black marble fireplace veined with gold. Tufted chairs the color of fine wine, a cream and gold chaise lounge, claw-footed tables topped with delicately scented orchids. Gilt-edged paintings on the wall, Roman busts on mahogany pedestals. As a nurse, she would surely trade it all in for the most Spartan of lifestyles. Could she still be a true lady without all of the trappings? Without her hoops and jewelry?

Her fingertips resting on the windowsill, Charlotte stared at the bleary world beyond her parlor as her own desires came into focus. A smile tugged at the corner of her lips as energy coursed through her body like the electric charge in the air outside.

Am I crazy?

She had no loved ones fighting in the war—no husband, no brother, no father. So why did she feel compelled to give of herself in such a personal way to strangers?

Charlotte reached into the writing desk for paper and pen so she could sort out her thoughts in front of her. Instead, she pulled out a small black leather Bible—her father's Bible. It fell open where it was bookmarked, and a single underlined verse jumped out at her. Luke 6:36: "Be ye therefore merciful, as your Father also is merciful."

Yes, her heavenly Father was merciful, and so had been her earthly father. Until it killed him.

Hugging the well-worn Bible to her chest, she rocked back and forth on the edge of her chair, trying desperately to fill her mind with something—anything—other than the memories that came unbidden now.

She was sixteen years old when the cholera epidemic ravaged New York City. The worst breakouts were in the slums. Most wealthy people were in no danger, as long as they avoided the contaminated areas of the city. Ensconced in their brownstone, the Waverly women believed they were safe. Charles Waverly, for whom Charlotte had been named, went to his work as a bank executive on Wall Street at the same time every day, and came straight home. The disease would never touch them if they just stayed away.

Then Charles Waverly didn't go to work one day. Or the next day, or the next. He couldn't even get out of bed, but stayed near the bathroom day and night. Diarrhea and vomiting that sometimes lasted hours at a time sucked the life from his body. Dr. Shaw was summoned and pronounced it cholera.

"How can that be?"

He was barely strong enough to answer his wife. "The new hospital for cholera patients on Orange Street, above the tavern. I visited them to read to them, pray with them."

"You what! But Charles, that's in Five Points!"

"You know as well as I do that New York wouldn't stand for a cholera hospital being built anywhere else. Of course it's in Five Points."

"Those people led harsh lives. Everyone says the disease is God's judgment on them; they got what they deserved. Why would you visit them?"

"We don't get to choose who deserves to hear God's Word, Caroline, or who deserves comfort in their last days. Aren't we to love our neighbors? Aren't these people our neighbors?"

"You called this down upon yourself, then, Charles, and now you have brought it into our home."

"Take the girls to your aunt Mabel's house outside the city. You'll be safe there."

But Charlotte, her daddy's girl, refused to leave her father's side. Someone had to stay with him and care for him. Her mother's pride would not allow him to go to the cholera hospital along with all the slum's worst cases. Charlotte remained and followed the doctor's orders for his care the best she could.

Soon his face was sunken, his teeth and eyes appearing too large for his face. She sat by his side as they bled him, first with leeches, then with a lancet. Time after time, she watched the scarlet ribbon flow out from his veins. The doctor wouldn't stop until her father fainted. Sometimes the bleeding ended after only ten ounces of blood had been drawn, sometimes it went on until twenty-four.

Nausea plagued her nearly every moment, from

the stench of disease, from the sight of his blood escaping his veins, from the palpable fear that all of this misery would not be redeemed, but would end only in death.

Their family friend Caleb Lansing was the only other person who ventured inside the Waverly home during that time, for ever since Caleb's mother had died, making him an orphan, Charles had been like a father to him as well. He helped Charlotte clean up after her father, disposed of the soiled sheets, and scrubbed the floors, since the servants had all deserted the house. He brought food for Charlotte and urged her to eat. He insisted she sleep while he took watch with Charles.

Nothing worked.

Charles continued to decline until his bones pushed against his skin like twigs ready to poke through parchment. His skin turned an unearthly shade of blue, and still they bled him. And bled him.

And still Charlotte watched, with nothing to distract her from her morbid vigil save Caleb's regular visits. Her world shrunk down to the size of her father's bedroom and the bathroom that joined, and it was colored with only a few shades of nature's kaleidoscope. Black: the long nights of watching. Yellow: her father's eyes and teeth. Blue: the tint of his skin. And red: the blood the doctor felt sure was the problem, the blood that had to flee his body, the blood that fell in a ragged crimson stream. The blood that stained her hands, her clothes. Her heart.

Until one day, Charles never woke up from his faint. His agony was at an end, and all that was left was his shriveled-up shell.

The next time Caleb arrived, he had to pull Charlotte off her father's disease-ridden body. Gently, tenderly, he led her to the kitchen, heated water on the stove, and sponged clean her face and hands. He scrubbed the blood and filth from beneath her fingernails and brushed her hair. Her hands trembled as she accepted a cup of tea, sloshing it over the cup's edge and onto her hands. She barely felt the burn.

"What do I do? What do I do? What do I do?" Her mind could form no other thought, and like a child, she repeated herself over and over and over.

"You breathe in. Now breathe out. Breathe in. Breathe out, Charlie," he said, using her father's pet name for her. "You put a bite of food in your mouth. You chew it up, and you swallow it. Even though you won't be hungry, even though you won't be able to taste a thing. You go to bed when it's dark, you wake up when it's light. You clean yourself up and get dressed. These are the things that living people do. And you are still alive."

His words were firm, but tears spilled down his cheeks. "A part of you will be buried with your father. But not all of you has died. You live."

Charlotte did not feel alive. She was numb to everything but grief.

He took her hand. "You live. You live. . . . You live."

She looked at him and realized he had felt this pain before.

"You have to help me," she pleaded.

He engulfed her in an embrace then, and the full force of her grief exploded against his shoulder. Racking sobs shook them both. He didn't let go, even though her dress was stained with a dead man's filth and she hadn't taken the time to bathe in days. Still, he held her, stroked her greasy hair as if it was the softest down.

"I miss him," she choked out.

"I know what he would say to you if he could," Caleb told her. "This is what he said to me when my own mother died: 'Yea, though I walk through the valley of the shadow of death, I will fear no evil; for thou art with me; thy rod and thy staff, they comfort me. . . . My flesh and my heart faileth; but God is the strength of my heart and my portion forever.'"

Finally, Charlotte's shoulders had stopped heaving. She had fallen asleep on Caleb's shoulder to the whispered lullaby of God's Word.

That was twelve years ago.

The room flashed brighter for an instant as lightning cracked the sky, bringing Charlotte back to the present. She focused again on the open Bible on the desk.

Be ye therefore merciful, as your Father also is merciful.

By now her tea was cold, but her heart was on fire. Dickens sat like a sphinx on the writing desk in front of her, watching her with unblinking eyes, as if waiting for her decision.

She couldn't please her mother, but maybe she could please her father. She had to try.

Chapter Three

By morning, the sky was clear, but a new storm was brewing in the Waverly brownstone on Sixteenth Street.

"Why Charlotte, you can't be considering it."

Charlotte glanced at her mother through a cloud of pale fuzz suspended in the air between them, her hands pausing for only a moment from scraping lint for the wounded soldiers. Maybe someday soon, she would be the one to pack lint into some poor soldier's wound. "Yes, Mother, I thought I would at least try."

"But, my dear girl, nursing is a man's job." Caroline's knitting needles clicked to a rhythm of their own.

"I'm hardly a girl anymore."

"Indeed. Twenty-eight—you're a spinster, my dear, and you even have the cat to prove it."

Charlotte's eyelids thinned to a glare as she focused on the lint gathering in her lap. "That's unfair. Dickens was the runt of the litter from our childhood pet. Father said I should keep him."

Caroline waved the rebuttal aside. "You are only lucky that you've kept your youthful complexion and figure. But if you pursue this nursing nonsense, you will degrade your respectability. What manner of man would marry a nurse?"

Frustration wrinkled Charlotte's brow. "Mr. Hastings is known for his strong support of abolitionism, a pillar of the Union cause. I have no reason to believe he will not be supportive of me doing what I can to aid our troops as well."

"You are not married yet. Don't jeopardize your future."

Charlotte sighed. "This isn't about my future, Mother." All of her life, she had been trained and groomed for one purpose—to increase her value as a prospective wife of an upstanding, wealthy man. At Rutgers Female Institute, she had studied mathematics, French, natural philosophy, painting, needlework, drawing, and sacred vocal music. She and Alice had completed courses at a finishing school for young ladies in Philadelphia and had attended classes on church history and biblical literature at New York City's Union Theological Seminary, their father's wish. While she genuinely enjoyed her education, she knew it was intended to increase her chances for a good match. Now it was time to do something for a greater cause.

"Is it too much to think I might have some value for our country aside from marriage and child-bearing?" She knew the question would shock her mother, and almost regretted saying it. Truthfully, she did want to have a family of her own someday, to manage a home, support a husband, and raise God-fearing children. But there was something else inside her she knew couldn't be fulfilled by that alone.

Charlotte set her work aside and swept a fine layer of lint from the braided tunic and full olive skirt of her at-home dress. Rising, she paced the back parlor and fanned herself with her long, piano-trained fingers. Though the weather outside was only a crisp sixty-four degrees, heat crawled up her neck.

The back parlor she circled was hardly recognizable from its previous days. Formerly used by the Waverlys for checkers and singing around the piano, it now resembled a clearinghouse for hospital supplies. The smells of ladies at leisure—rosewater, coffee, almond pastries—had given way to the stronger odors of packing supplies for war: crates of cologne, jams, pickles, tobacco, lemons, and cocoa. A bandage roller screwed into the top of a mahogany table was the centerpiece of the room, and the walls were lined with bundles of shirts, drawers, socks, and handkerchiefs. This parlor was now one of the most popular places for members of the Women's Central Association of Relief to share news while organizing and preparing supplies.

"Charlotte, stop." Caroline set down her knitting and crossed the distance to reach her daughter. She gripped her hands in her own. "You would exhaust yourself. That training program would make a tiresome schedule for you, and I will not allow you to give up your regular French and voice lessons. You know people call you a songbird."

Charlotte's heart squeezed. "I'd rather be a Nightingale. I want to do something useful. I want to make a difference."

"Yes, Florence Nightingale did amazing things for the British army in the Crimean War," conceded Caroline. "But she didn't do it alone. She couldn't have done anything without help from the home front, in fact. Organizing and distributing supplies for the armies is essential! What do you think would happen to our boys if they had no bandages, no clothing, no clean shirts, or soft places to lay their weary heads at night? Isn't the work we do here in this parlor making a difference?"

"Of course it is." Alice stepped in, bearing bolts of flannel. "Who says it isn't?"

Caroline turned, dropping her daughter's hands. "Charlotte wants to be a nurse."

Alice raised her eyebrows. "A nurse."

Isn't it about time for you to go back home? Charlotte clenched her teeth before the unkind thought escaped her lips. Inhaling a deep breath, she tried again. "I really don't see what all the fuss is about. Elizabeth Blackwell, as you well know, is a doctor. And a prominent, well-respected member of society, I might add. She spearheaded the entire Women's Central Association of Relief

43

to make up for the men's lack of services to our nation's soldiers. And the New York Infirmary for Women and Children she started has had great success."

A lopsided smile curved on Alice's lips. "It's a charity, Charlotte. It's busy because it's free, and poor people are always sick. Especially in the slums near her infirmary."

Charlotte spun on her heel, turning her back on her sister while she mastered her tongue and the very unrefined expression of anger on her face.

Slowly swiveling back around, she modulated her tone. "All I'm trying to say is this. In the person of Elizabeth Blackwell, we have a prime example of a woman fulfilling a job—no, a calling—that has previously been strictly relegated to the male sphere. She does her work competently. She makes a difference in the world."

"She is the *only* woman with an American medical degree in the entire country, Charlotte," Caroline said. "Word has it that she used her profession as a barrier to matrimony."

"Oh fiddlesticks!" Charlotte was exasperated now. "Pure mean-spirited gossip! Even if it were true, it's beside the point, anyway."

"You are mistaken, daughter. It is the *entire* point, precisely. A woman should be married, as Alice is, and have children and manage her household. If your husband agrees it is fitting for you to do charity work as well, so long as it does not interfere with your duties at home, so be it. But charity work, or pursuing men's work, is not the primary aim of a young woman."

The silence between the three women reverberated the rumble of marching feet and martial music blocks away.

"Charlotte," her mother began again. "You are swimming upstream with this new-fangled idea of women nurses. You are going the wrong direction."

"I can help," she whispered. "I know I can."

"Child." The quaver in Caroline's voice betrayed her. "That's what your father said when he went to visit that cholera hospital on Orange Street. That's what you said when you stayed behind to nurse him. You were both wrong! Don't you see? You're wrong!"

Charlotte's deep breath was constricted by the corseted bodice of her dress. "I feel like I'm suffocating in here. I'm going to get some air." With a fistful of skirts in her hand, she swept toward the door, leaving a wake of swirling lint behind her.

Before she reached the door, however, Jane stepped into the fray, her starched white apron a flag of forced truce between mother and daughter, at least for the moment. Pale blonde hair crowned her head in a thick braid under her cap, and the roses in her cheeks bloomed bright whenever she sensed tension in a room.

Right now, they were flaming red.

"Telegram, mum," she said, her Nottingham, England, accent flavoring her words. Jane had only arrived in New York two years ago, at the age of seventeen, and had been at the Waverly home ever since. "It's from Albany."

The women looked at each other in confusion before understanding registered on Alice's face. "It must be Jacob. He's there on business, but I don't know what could be so important . . ." She snatched the envelope from its silver tray and ripped it open. No sooner had her eyes scanned the telegram than the paper fluttered to the floor. Her hands shook as she covered her trembling lips. Wide-eyed, Jane quietly left the room.

"He joined the Sixteenth New York Regiment," Alice said, disbelief twisting the words. All color had drained from her face. "Signed up while he was in Albany. Can you believe that? He didn't even ask me. He just did it."

Caroline's lips flattened into a thin, hard line. "Women ask permission from their husbands, dear, not the other way around."

Hot moisture sprang to Charlotte's eyes in sympathy as Alice choked on a sob.

Suddenly, the Civil War was not just a headline in the newspaper, a story from a distant land, neatly constrained to narrow columns of black-and-white typeface. With a single telegram, the war invaded their parlor and their lives. Now it was not just news. It was personal, in living color. And it was terrifying.

"When does he go?" Charlotte gently probed.

Blonde ringlets quivered as Alice shook her head. "I don't know. He just said he's coming home as planned but will be leaving again for training 'soon.' And what about me? I'll be all alone in that big house with just the servants!"

"You know you can stay here as long as you like," Caroline crooned.

"No," said Alice resolutely, looking suddenly years older. "My place is at home."

Not this time, thought Charlotte as she soothed her little sister. *You're coming with me.* She knew better than to say it aloud just yet.

Once Alice was resting comfortably with a cup of tea, Charlotte made her way to the garden behind the house to clear her head. Dappled sunlight filtered through the trees and fell in a lacework pattern on the terraced garden. All the aromas of spring were sharpened in the rain-scrubbed air, lilac blossoms even more pungent than usual. Charlotte carefully perched on the cool stone bench and watched golden daffodils nod their heads in the breeze. Her hoop skirt formed a wide perimeter around her, as if to create a safe distance between her and the world.

When her gaze fell upon weeds crowding the tender shoots of Siberian irises, she felt an

47

irresistible pull to pluck them out herself rather than wait for the gardener to do it. Kneeling on the ground, however, brought her no closer to her goal—yards of fabric and steel hoops were unavoidably in the way.

Bother this contraption! The only way to weed in a hoopskirt, Charlotte surmised, was to lie flat on her stomach and let the hoops flip the skirts straight up at a ridiculous ninety-degree angle to the ground. No, that wouldn't do at all. With a quick glance around the stone wall–enclosed garden to confirm her privacy, she unfastened her skirt from her waist and bodice, stepped out of it and left it in a dejected pile next to the bench.

Unhindered at last, Charlotte knelt in her petticoats and buried her fingers in the soft, damp soil, relishing the musty smell and digging down deep to uproot the weeds that had taunted her a moment ago. She was so absorbed in her tiny patch of earth that she didn't hear the French doors to the garden unlatch.

"Why, miss!" Jane gasped, quickly closing the door behind her. "What can you be thinking, down in the dirt, exposed like that for God and everybody!" She scurried to retrieve the discarded skirt.

Charlotte laughed. "It isn't like you haven't seen all of us in our petticoats before."

"No, miss, true enough, but I'll bet your gentleman caller hasn't."

Charlotte gasped. Thoughtlessly, she brushed a strand of hair off her cheek, smudging the porcelain complexion that was the envy of her peers. "Mr. Hastings! I completely forgot." Charlotte stood, shook the dirt off her undergarments and allowed Jane to help her back into her skirt.

Rushing in from the garden, she ducked into the kitchen and scrubbed the evidence of her unladylike behavior from beneath her fingernails before approaching the tall, handsome visitor waiting in the front hall. One look at his tartan plaid trousers, dark green cravat, frock coat, and top hat told her he had a promenade in mind.

"Aha, so you've taken to painting, I see," he teased.

Charlotte's hands flew to her cheeks, still flushed from the cool May breeze. Indignation creased her face. She did not appreciate his innuendo that she used rouge—only women "on the town" painted their faces.

Mr. Hastings tilted his head and smiled down at her. "Oh, come now. No need to be cross. I think you look beautiful. So beautiful, in fact, that I'd like to show you off on the Broadway Promenade today. What do you say?" His dark chocolate eyes captured hers, soft and inviting.

"Oh, my hair is a mess, I've been out in the garden," she hedged.

"I thought of that." Of course he had. His own jet-black hair was smoothly in place, smelling faintly of pomade, his mustache and goatee neatly groomed, as ever. "Would you do me the honor of wearing this?" He picked up a box she hadn't noticed from the hall table.

"Why, Mr. Hastings—"

"Isn't it time you called me Phineas?"

She cleared her throat. "Phineas. I can't imagine what the occasion is." Hesitantly, she accepted the box from him.

"As the petals are the glory of the rose, the right attire is the glory of a woman," he said with a flourish.

Parting the tissue paper, Charlotte gently lifted out a pert straw hat trimmed with peacock plumes and a band of satin ribbon in a shocking shade of bright green.

"Well?" His voice was eager, expectant.

Charlotte skimmed a finger over the feathers. "It's quite . . . bright, isn't it?"

His low-pitched laughter rippled over her until she couldn't help but join in. "Yes, indeed. These new aniline dyes are the latest rage. No one will miss us."

That much was true. Charlotte managed a nod that she hoped appeared grateful, and excused herself to her dressing room to change into a deep indigo promenade gown with pagoda sleeves and a three-tiered skirt. She hoped it would tame down the peacock feathers in her hat.

Once on Broadway, Charlotte's unlikely ensemble

blended into an eclectic crowd. Coats and dresses of all patterns swarmed around Phineas and Charlotte, the crowd a blur of bright eyes, whiskers, spectacles, hats, bonnets, and caps. Dandies passed by with their hornlike mustaches, kid gloves, thin trouser legs, and patent leather shoes. Smartly dressed ladies in ribbons and silks stepped spritely out of shops, having done their part toward depleting their husbands' bank accounts with the finest Parisian fashions.

The daily afternoon "promenade" on Broadway had the sound of a leisurely stroll about it, but it was impossible to maintain anything less than a brisk pace to keep from getting run over. The booming city's major thoroughfare was a profusion of color and a stimulus of excitement. It was hustle, bustle, and squeeze, like a dance of faltering steps to the offbeat tune of thundering omnibuses and the din of a crowd in a hurry. Charlotte would have preferred a stroll in Central Park, if not for the quieter atmosphere, for the fresher air. The musky scent of Phineas's cologne was soon overpowered, and she was sure her mother and sister would smell on her clothing the horse manure of Broadway when she arrived home.

Phineas, Charlotte could tell, relished being caught in the whirl. His countenance always brightened around luxury and opulence, and here on Broadway, both were displayed en masse in the storefronts lining the avenue. Places like Lord & Taylor and Brooks Brothers usually caught his eye, but today he paused in front of Tiffany & Company, gazing at the dazzling ladies' jewelry displayed on black velvet, with a firm hold on Charlotte's small, gloved hand.

"Phineas." Charlotte tugged gently on his arm. "Did you hear me? I said I'm going to apply to be a nurse."

He swiveled around to face her. "Pardon me?"

"Yes, a nurse. The W.C.A.R. means to train one hundred New York women to serve as nurses for the army—the army doesn't have enough, you know—and I mean to be one of them."

His brow furrowed. "But how would that look?"

"Patriotic," she said, a little too quickly. "Dutiful. Benevolent. Respectable, too."

"Just how would it be respectable to have women mixing with large masses of half-naked men?"

"Phineas, listen to me. The most respectable women—and men—of our class are behind this. Reverend Henry Bellows, Dr. Elisha Harris, Mrs. David Dudley Field, Mrs. Henry Baylis, Mrs. Cyrus Field, Dr. Elizabeth Blackwell . . . all of them." When he still looked unconvinced, she continued. "The army is simply unprepared to handle the magnitude of what is about to unfold on the battlefields. Why not use women who are willing, able, and most eager to serve? Think of it this way. When a doctor or surgeon makes a house call, who takes care of the sick or wounded when the doctor leaves?" She paused. "The women do. The mothers, wives, sisters, sometimes even daughters receive instructions from the doctor or surgeon, clean and dress the wounds, administer the medicines. We are already nurses. This is just moving it to a different setting. Not every soldier's mother or wife will be able to tend their own. Only a select few will fill that role—but we must have training. Do you see?"

"I don't like it. I'm afraid most people won't think about it in the same way. But if you insist on being stubborn about it . . ."

"It is what I want." She pinned him with a determined look. She didn't really need his permission.

Suddenly, a woman in a bright green gown, too low in the neckline for daytime wear, and with a bonnet pushed too far back on her head, sauntered past, leaving behind her a trail of lilac scent so thick Charlotte could taste it.

Charlotte followed Phineas's gaze in time to see the woman look back over her shoulder and throw him a brazen wink and a smile as bold—and sickening—as the heavy fragrance in which she was drenched. Her cheeks were painted. In a flash, Phineas's face flamed just as red, but playing around the corners of his mouth was just the hint of a smile.

Chapter Four

None of it seemed real to Ruby O'Flannery. The noise was deafening, the glaring sun unfriendly to her weak green eyes. Far more used to shadows, she felt as though she had just stepped into a scene in an overexposed photograph. Thousands of people lined the sidewalks, pushed against windows, or streamed out of doors all along the road. New York City's Sixty-Ninth Regiment was marching in full uniform to attend mass at St. Patrick's Cathedral on Mott Street for a blessing from Archbishop John Hughes. It would be the company's last stop before departing for war. Flags of emerald green fringed with gold, the Irish regiment colors, dotted the churning sea of people. The crush of the unruly crowd frightened Ruby; hundreds were attempting to march alongside the soldiers. She had already lost sight of her husband, Matthew, just one bobbing black felt slouch hat among one thousand others.

The tune of the bugles and the steady beat of the drums changed pitch in Ruby's ears as her stooped figure was swept farther and farther away from the marching regiment by the surging throngs of spectators. She could hardly comprehend that so many people suddenly supported what Matthew was doing. She was used to jeers, not cheers.

Ruby and Matthew had arrived at the Port of New York in 1850 at the crest of the mass migration to escape Ireland's Great Famine. While they saw New York as a new beginning, New Yorkers made it clear that the O'Flannerys, along with the thousands of other immigrants who arrived that year, were unwelcome, posting signs on their storefronts reading "IRISH NEED NOT APPLY."

Now, with the joyful shouts of the masses and the steady rhythm of the marching Sixty-Ninth ringing in her ears, Ruby dared to hope Matthew's new opportunity and its guaranteed salary was the answer she had been praying for.

Unable to find a spot inside the cathedral, Ruby leaned against the brick wall enclosing the adjacent cemetery outside and smoothed her dark red hair back into place in a tightly coiled bun. The petite woman had been beautiful once, her parents even naming her for the striking color of her hair. But that was a lifetime ago.

"Hey, hunchback!"

Ruby didn't need to look around to know the brazen child was talking to her. It was true. As an outworker seamstress, unending hours spent bending over her sewing in the poorly lit rooms of her tenement cramped her back and neck muscles so much that she was stooped over even when not working. Her neck bent forward, giving her the appearance either of being in a great hurry when walking or greatly attentive when in conversation.

A ripple of laughter told her that a gaggle of young boys had singled her out as the object of their attention.

"C'mon now, and show us yer arms, tweety!" another boy taunted.

Arms already folded across her chest, she dug her fingers into them as if to keep them from flying up by accident. Like any other hand sewer, her arms had been so trained by holding work up to her eyes that their natural resting position was to bend up from the elbows. The cruel nickname "tweety," she assumed, was based on her hideous resemblance to a bird with broken wings. She made it a habit to carry something in her arms while walking in public to disguise their unnatural bend. Caught empty-handed, she would fold her arms across her chest or prop her fists on her hips, rather than straighten her elbows, which caused great pain.

From around the corner, a Sister of Charity came and shooed the boys away on threat of putting them in the nuns' Orphan Asylum. It would have been a step up for the boys' living conditions, but they scattered anyway.

"Are you all right, my child?" the nun asked Ruby. "Pay those lads no mind. They come from hard homes, you know, with little but the clothes on their backs. You can't imagine the filth and vermin that share those dark, cramped quarters with them." Ruby nodded. She understood more than the nun realized. Those boys were her neighbors at the tenement.

"I'm all right, Sister. Just waiting to see if I can catch a glimpse of my husband before he sets off." Ruby kept her arms crossed. The kind nun nodded and returned to her duties. Taking a deep breath, Ruby lifted her face to the sun. The warmth felt good after another long hard winter. Spring had come again, when she felt like it never would. Of course, this spring was different —this spring had brought with it a war that seemed so far away, but whose fingers had reached up to her city and grasped her neighbors and husband in its mighty grip, pulling them away from her. But the war machine also paid money, for which she was grateful. It had to be wrong to find hope in any aspect of war, but Matthew's steady income would allow her a respite from the life-draining hours she had been forced to keep lately.

An hour later, the Sixty-Ninth spilled out the front doors and began their march directly to the ferry that would take them to Annapolis for their first mission of guard duty. Ruby scanned the uniformed men for a final glimpse of her husband.

The crowd continued to push past her, almost

knocking her down. A strong grip on her shoulder spun her around.

"Don't you have any work to do?" Matthew suddenly stood over her. His brawny form, the evidence of long hours spent building bridges and hauling rocks, stretched the fibers of his ill-fitting Union greatcoat. His blue eyes flashed with their usual intensity, his ruddy cheeks flushed with both anticipation of war and the heat of the packed sanctuary he had just come from.

His absurd question stung Ruby as much as his drunken slaps. She usually worked fifteen hours a day from their dank tenement dwelling, sewing cuffs, buttonholes, and sleeves of bleached muslin for Davis & Company, but work always surged in April as the garment manufacturer rushed summer styles to Western and Southern suppliers. She could easily count on eighteen hours most days this month, earning her between seventy-five cents and $1.50 per week. She knew exactly how much work awaited her and needed no reminding.

"Can't a woman see her husband off to war?" Ruby replied. A rash of heat radiated from her collar to her chin.

Matthew shook his head. "Soon's I get my pay-check, I'll be sending it on home to you, but in the meantime, you are supporting yourself."

Time and pain had chipped away the luxury of common courtesy and kindness, but Ruby knew he wouldn't let his wife go hungry if he could help it.

"This is a new start for us, Ruby." His voice was edged with determination.

And then he was gone, as suddenly as he had appeared, lost again in the formation of soldiers filing down the street on their way to the ferry.

Ruby stood frozen in place. Something about his farewell haunted her. "A new start," he had said. Yes, that was it. That's what he had said when they immigrated to New York, and yet they had still struggled, just in new ways, to survive. That's what he had said when they learned they were going to have a child, both times, and now they had none. Was she still a mother if her children were dead? She pressed calloused and pinpricked fingertips against her eyelids, as if she could close her mind's eye to the horrific images her memory now dredged up. She needed to sit down.

Chin tucked down, Ruby fought her way back to St. Patrick's Cathedral and stepped through the two sets of massive double doors. As the muffled din of the retreating crowd faded, she sank down into the last pew. Her slight shoulders shook with silent sobs that racked her entire body.

Spent at last, she looked up. Stained glass windows on the sides of the church depicted stories from the Bible, while the windows at the front of the nave cast the light in shades of blue and green. Thick, red carpeting created a path from the middle aisle up the stone steps to where the archbishop had said mass a short time ago. The ceiling was so tall her gaze followed it up until it pointed her to the heavens.

Rarely was she in a place this magnificent. Catholic churches, like Catholic immigrants, faced hard times in New York City, too, prompting them to charge an admission fee to enter, and to rent the front pews to the upper- and middle-class as another marker of their wealth. Ruby had been told that the brick wall enclosing the Cathedral and cemetery was to prevent mob violence from anti-Catholics, but she had always thought of it as yet another barrier between her and God.

Today, however, she relished being here. She felt like she should pray, but all she knew from her childhood was the Hail Mary. "Hail Mary, full of grace," she started, slipping to her knees and gently rocking back and forth as she had done as a girl. "The Lord is with thee. Blessed art thou among women and blessed is the fruit of thy womb, Jesus. Holy Mary, mother of God, pray for us sinners, now and at the hour of our death. Amen."

Now, and at the hour of our death, Ruby repeated to herself. *The hour of our death.*

Was it only supposed to take an hour? Just one moment, just one death? For when each of her children had passed from this life, they took pieces of her with them, leaving her with half a heart and a life never to be fulfilled.

Ruby's gaze settled on a sculpture of Mary holding Jesus—not the newborn baby, but the lifeless body of God the Son, just pulled down from the cross. Tears rolled down Ruby's cheeks unbidden as she stared at Mary's stony face. She had come here in search of peace but felt only pain instead.

She hurried from the Cathedral and made her way back to the tenement. For once, she was grateful to be able to turn her attention to the work that awaited her.

Chapter Five

Saturday, May 4, 1861

By the end of the week, Alice was home again at her tranquil estate in Fishkill, seventy miles north of Manhattan, and Jacob was back at her side. For the moment. Charlotte could picture her sister knitting and sewing far into the night to outfit her soldier husband for war.

And what am I doing? Dancing at a ball to honor the newest debutante of society. As if there was nothing better to do. The thought pinched her as much as the whalebone corset cinching her waist to a mere fifteen inches.

She trained her eyes on her dance partner as they twirled through a sea of taffeta and coattails. In the edges of her vision, the room spun in a sparkling, pastel blur of opulence. Charlotte's feet kept time to the polka, but her heart beat to a reveille.

When horsehair bows finally stopped dancing on their strings, the men bowed and women dipped in low curtsies before being handed to the next partner listed on their dance cards.

"You are as lovely as ever." Phineas's mustache tickled her cheek as he spoke into her ear, sending a shiver down her spine. She wore an off-the-shoulder gown of soft white organdy, adorned with a cluster of buttery roses made of silk ribbon in the center of the bodice, and more roses cascading down the multitiered skirt. Her chestnut hair was swept up and crowned with a band of green leaves and a bunch of roses covering the thick knot at the nape of her neck. "You look like an angel in that exquisite gown."

"I'd rather look like a nurse and do something useful for once," she murmured, sure no one could hear her anyway. Phineas walked Charlotte back to her mother and returned to the dance floor to complete a set of eight dancers for the quadrille, without her. Though Caroline sniffed at the empty slot on her daughter's card, Charlotte was content to rest and watch the mesmerizing movements on the gleaming hardwood floor.

"Charlie?"

That voice, so warm and comforting. The faint scent of balsam shaving soap. The name—no one had called her that for years. Not since—

"Caleb! I mean, Dr. Lansing, what a—surprise," she sputtered as her heart constricted in her chest. The mustache was new since she had seen him last, and so was the trace of laugh lines framing his face. But the clear grey eyes were exactly the same. Soft as goose down and piercing as steel, all at once. "I didn't know you'd be here."

His face relaxed into a smile. "Me neither," he admitted, offering her a cup of lemonade as if seeing each other again were the most natural thing in the world. As if a decade of silence between them made no difference whatsoever. "I'm just in town for some lectures on anesthesia at Bellevue Hospital this week. Two of the other doctors at Bellevue were invited to attend this evening but one of them had to bow out when a patient began bleeding after surgery."

Charlotte held up her hand and closed her eyes. "No details, please." Even the mention of blood was enough to make her stomach roil.

"I wouldn't dream of it. Anyway, having no other pressing engagements, I agreed to take his place and come along with Dr. Shearling—that fellow over there jamming too much cake into his mouth. Can't have an uneven number of partners at a ball, you know. Disastrous." He winked, detonating a blast of heat across her face.

Mercifully, Caleb turned to greet Caroline while Charlotte hid her burning cheeks behind her cup of lemonade. It was both sour and sweet on her tongue, but quenched a thirst she only just realized she had. *Like Caleb.* Charlotte nearly choked on the unbidden notion, and resolutely swallowed it along with the cool drink. She couldn't think this way. It was over. She had a suitor. This was crazy.

"Caleb, it's so good to see you," Caroline was saying, kissing both of his cheeks. "Your practice is going well in Connecticut?"

He nodded. "It keeps me so busy I'm afraid I haven't much time for anything else."

Charlotte stole a glance at the fourth finger of his left hand. Still bare. Strange. She thought he'd be married by now. He must be thirty-two years old. But then, she wasn't much younger, and still being chaperoned by her mother. Did he think she was a hopeless spinster? Embarrassment warmed her cheeks. Again.

Caleb sipped his lemonade and turned to watch the quadrille dancers.

"Not feeling up to this one?" he asked her, pointing with his cup.

Charlotte shook her head and willed her voice to sound normal. "Group dances make me nervous. It looks lovely from a distance, but when I'm part of it, I can't help daydreaming about what would happen if I missed a step—or worse, did the wrong step."

"You do realize that most people aren't looking at your feet—can't see them anyway under all those yards of fabric," said Caleb. "They are looking into those caramel-colored eyes of yours." He held her in his gaze for a long moment, his eyes suddenly soft.

"But if I go the wrong direction, no matter where they look, it throws everybody off. Would we all topple into one great heap? How would I recover from that?"

Caroline turned to face her daughter now. "What

on earth are you talking about, child? Go the wrong direction? You were trained in all the dances. Why would you be worried about making a misstep?"

The quadrille music ended, and Caleb took the lemonade cup from Charlotte's hand, placing both his and hers on a nearby table stacked with mounds of small cakes. Not bothering to check her dance card, he placed a hand on the small of her back and guided her onto the floor, his pulse pounding harder with every step.

"Couple dances are more fun than group dances, aren't they, Charlotte?" Caleb kept his tone casual, but his racing heart was not convinced.

As the instruments struck the first few notes of the waltz, Caleb encircled her tiny waist with his right arm and held her right hand in his left. An electric shock coursed through his body at the closeness of her. How many times had he dreamed of this moment? He could barely believe he was holding her again, even if it was at arm's length and not in an embrace.

The music began, and so did their feet. *One-two-three and one-two-three and one-two-three.* His eyes never left her face. He had always thought her beautiful, and had always admired her resilient, compassionate spirit. Now, as a grown woman, she nearly took his breath away. Those luminous eyes, the glowing skin, the full lips forming the bow of Cupid himself. *How in heaven's name is she not yet some lucky man's wife?*

"Am I making anyone jealous?" The question escaped his lips before he could bite back his curiosity.

She peered up at him from under dark, long lashes. "I doubt it."

"Don't be so sure, Charlotte. You don't know the effect you have over a man's heart." His voice turned husky without his permission. He jerked his gaze away from her questioning eyes and struggled to mask the emotion written on his face. But he could not escape the scent of her. The faint fragrance of lemons and rosewater washed over him, and he drank it in. Vivid memories flooded his mind before he could snap back to the present moment.

One-two-three and one-two-three and—"Well, Phineas Hastings signed up for his two dances of the evening already. I'll be dancing with him again next." She pinned her gaze to his shoulder as she spoke.

"Is he the best partner for you?"

"He's the one I came here with."

"That doesn't answer my question. If you make a misstep, step on his toes, if you go the 'wrong' direction, what would he do?"

"Well, he would steer me back to the right way and try to keep leading, I suppose." Her voice was laced with uncertainty.

"What if your stepping out of formation was

actually a step in the right direction? What a shame it would be if you were always confined to a prescribed number and pattern of steps."

Charlotte tilted her head up at him, confusion written on her face. He went on. "Don't you think that instead of yanking you back into place, the right partner would step out *with* you?" He drew her closer—perhaps too close. But he didn't care. And she didn't fight it. He bent his head and spoke softly in her ear. "Daring to believe that another dance, a different dance, could be just as elegant—or even more so?"

Charlotte pulled back just far enough to search his eyes, her breathing rapid and shallow.

One-two-three and one-two-three and one-two-three and one-two-three and—"Don't lead Mr. Hastings on if he isn't the right one for you," Caleb whispered, and the music tapered to a close. "For his sake, and for yours."

Bowing, he pressed his lips to her hand. *And for mine.*

Charlotte curtsied. They both stood tall again.

"I go back to Connecticut tomorrow." He thrust his hands, still tingling from holding her, into his pockets. "And from there, to wherever Uncle Sam sends me."

"You're joining then? To fight?"

"I will be one of Lincoln's seventy-five thousand, but not to fight. To heal. Those soldiers need doctors. It's my duty to help, the least I can do for my country. The Pied Piper is calling, and come what may, I'm on my way."

Charlotte stiffened, a sheen of tears glazing her eyes. Gold flecks in her eyes brightened, as they always did when she was either very happy or very upset. And she wasn't happy. But was she sad? Afraid? Angry?

Caleb didn't want to leave her like this. Not again. "Charlie, I—"

A gentleman with a gardenia in his lapel and suspicion in his eyes ambled toward them now, most likely to claim the next dance on her card. *Phineas?* Caleb, squeezing her hands, said, "Write to me," and walked away.

"Who was that fellow, Charlotte? I dare say he's a sight underdressed for the occasion," Caleb overheard Hastings say.

"An old family friend, that's all . . ."

Caleb should not have been disappointed at her response, after all this time between them.

Raking a hand through his straw-colored hair, Caleb walked back to the refreshments table, completely uninterested in dancing with anyone else.

"Lansing, old chap!" Dr. Shearling was still eating. "Why on earth did you let that marvelous creature go?" He pointed to Charlotte, now dancing in the arms of another man.

A rueful smile played on Caleb's lips. "Believe me, Shearling, I regret it already."

I always have.

Chapter Six

Friday, May 10, 1861

The tantalizing aroma of freshly baked bread wafted out of a nearby bakery and curled around Ruby, following her down the sidewalk. With her empty stomach aching, she tightened her grip on her hope for filling it. In her arms she carried the fruit of this week's labor—a stack of sleeves complete with cuffs and buttonholes, which would be stitched into the rest of their shirts in a factory using Isaac Singer's foot-treadled sewing machine invention, which had recently revolutionized the way garment manufacturers operated. Outworkers like Ruby now hand sewed the detail work, and girls working on the machines did everything else.

Straw into gold, she had told herself as she worked late into the night every day that week. As the miller's daughter spun straw into gold in the fairy tale of Rumpelstiltskin, so Ruby fancied herself in a similar situation—turning cloth into sleeves, which then turn into money. It was a comforting analogy—except when she remembered the consequence if she failed.

A tinny bell clanged as she opened the door to the men's clothing shop, announcing her arrival to the tailor, Simon Levitz. Waddling in from the back room, he leaned against the counter, his protruding paunch of a belly spilling over and resting on top.

"Shoulda' been here shooner." He formed the words around a cigar.

She watched in silence as his stubby fingers rifled through her work, her own hands twisting nervously in the folds of her thin cotton dress.

"Wristbands too long," was his verdict.

"All of them?" Ruby was stunned.

Simon grunted and puffed cigar smoke in her face. "Can't take them." He shoved the pile back at her and said, "Shorten them by one-quarter inch and bring them back."

Ruby knew better than to argue with the man. She had only needed to try it once before he calmly informed her she could quit if she pleased, that women were lining up to get jobs like hers, women who would take six cents a shirt and be grateful for it. She knew he was right. She had no leverage with which to bargain. She would simply have to redo the work.

In the meantime, however, she needed to find money. She had been expecting both her one-dollar deposit to be returned, and the fee for the work to be paid, another dollar. She needed food, but even more importantly, she needed to pay the rent. Her stomach might wait a little longer but her landlord would show no such leniency.

She lifted her chin in resolve. It was time to pay

another visit to the pawnbroker. But first she needed something to offer him.

Once at home, she looked around the humble dwelling. Calling the front room a parlor made it sound more grand than it was: it had a stove, a fireplace, a table, and two chairs in it. The windowless back room held the low bed, a small table, and a few pieces of clothing hanging on hooks. There was a watch, a clock, a few pots, pans, and dishes. Save the broom, the dustpan, and the rags that stuffed the broken windows in winter, this encompassed the entirety of their earthly treasures. She grabbed her best dress and immediately headed out again, bound for the pawnshop.

Since it was Friday and rent was typically due on Saturday morning, she was not surprised to see more customers in line than usual. Pawn business always picked up at the end of the week for this reason. Some, like Ruby, brought their best dresses, or shoes they rarely wore, and would be fortunate enough to be able to buy them back the following week when the cash flow improved. The more desperate ones brought cherished symbols of respectability like watches, books, and wedding rings. The pitiful souls who traded their basic necessities—pots, furniture, bedding— for the ability to eat their next meal were nearest to the end of their options.

Standing in line, Ruby looked around her and

imagined the stories behind each object offered up on the pawnbroker's altar. Within the shadows of a variety of old clothing hanging from the ceiling, there were crimping irons, umbrellas, inkstands, dictionaries, frying pans, rings and necklaces, pincushions, and featherbeds. When her gaze fell on a cradle at the front of the shop, she hoped its former occupant had simply grown out of it, but experience told her that either the parents chose food over the baby's bed, or very likely, the baby had not survived.

"Ruby? That you there?" It was Emma Connors, a neighbor. Emma and her brother Sean, now off with the Sixty-Ninth, had taken in a boarder recently to make extra money. Still, her presence in the pawnshop indicated that money was still tight—at least today. There was no shame in it anymore for them. For most immigrants, poverty was woven into the fabric of their lives.

"Aye, Emma." Ruby managed a rueful smile for her friend. "My work didn't pass today." She gestured to the dress in her arms.

Emma nodded in understanding. "And still no money from the lads, eh?" She lifted her own Sunday dress to show Ruby. "Tell the truth now, Ruby. Times are tight, but aren't things a little more peaceful around the tenement with them gone?" She winked.

Warmth radiated from Ruby's cheeks. A nervous chuckle escaped her lips sounding more like a croak, so out of practice was she with laughter. "'Tis true. I don't hear nearly so much fighting through the walls as I did, and haven't seen a black eye on a lass in weeks."

They moved up in line, and it was Emma's turn to haggle a price for her dress with the pawnbroker. Closer to the cradle now, Ruby took another look at it.

In a flash of recognition, her mouth went dry.

It couldn't be. She shook her head as though to argue with her own eyes. The roughly hewn slats, the humble, simple etching at the head and foot of it. With a trembling hand she reached out and turned it to get a view of the rockers. She released it as if it were burning coal and closed her eyes.

It was no use. The engraving of a four-leafed clover was seared into her mind. The mark had been etched by her father in Ireland in place of his signature, for he, along with most Irish she knew, could neither read nor write. The cradle had held her baby girl Meghan.

Waves of grief crashed over Ruby, the crushing weight nearly bringing her to her knees. Nothing had changed in the rest of the shop—Emma still bargained, a few customers picked over other people's castoffs now for sale or barter. But Ruby felt as if invisible undercurrents swirled around her legs, threatening to pull her down into oblivion.

Meghan. Oh, the joy and pain contained in a

single word. Memories of her and Matthew as teenagers rushed at her.

Matthew had been a *cottier* on her family's farm on several acres of Ireland's most beautiful countryside. In return for his help with the daily chores and with the annual potato harvest, Ruby's father allowed him to build a small cabin on the land and keep his own potato garden for himself. Potatoes were virtually all they ate, but they were satisfied.

Then 1845 had come, and the entire nation's harvest of healthy-looking potatoes turned black with rot within a few days of picking them, right before their eyes. It happened again the next year, and countless people starved to death, despite the few inadequate attempts at relief from the English government. Matthew's and Ruby's siblings worked on a public relief project, breaking apart with hammers large stones that were then used to build a road from nowhere to nowhere. The meager earnings were useless, for there was no food to be found for purchase.

One January day in 1847, sixteen-year-old Ruby paid a visit to Matthew in his cabin just before a blizzard hit. It would have been impossible for her to find her way home in the white-out conditions, and getting lost in the countryside would have meant freezing to death.

"Come, let's stay warm together," Matthew had said, enveloping her in a blanket with himself and huddling on the straw-covered floor together.

Ruby had convinced herself that what had happened next was the result of them falling in love. But Matthew, far less of a romantic, had attributed the act to the combination of a normal eighteen-year-old lad's physical urges and an opportunity.

When Ruby felt the signs of new life in her body, however, Matthew did the honorable thing and married her. After all, Ruby had little in this life except for her Catholic faith, and she already agonized over her lapse in self-control as it was. To have a baby without being married would have destroyed her.

The pregnancy had taken almost more strength than Ruby had in her famished state, but Meghan was born in October, adding one more mouth to feed. Ruby's father doted on the baby more than anyone else, and lovingly fashioned a cradle for her. Truthfully, there was little to distinguish it from the feeding troughs of the animals that shared their cabin. It looked like a nativity-style manger, save for the cloverleaf etching.

"If it was good enough for our Lord and Savior, 'tis good enough for our wee babe," he had said.

Building the cradle was the last thing he did before his skin turned as black as the blighted potatoes. He died of black fever within days.

Meghan's tiny body succumbed to the same pattern when she was just four months old, and she followed her grandfather to heaven.

When Matthew and Ruby decided to emigrate, the cradle came with them, along with the hope it would not stay empty. Fiona had been born while they lived in Seneca Village in New York City, but when they moved into the tenement after their eviction, the cold and the putrid air eventually proved too much for her. Fiona died of consumption when she was three.

The cradle, suddenly the last thing Ruby wanted to see, had been the first thing to be pawned during the next crisis. She had taken care to use a pawnshop well outside their neighborhood so she wouldn't have to see any of her neighbors come home with it one day. The cradle must have changed hands who knew how many times, and found its way back to her. The ghosts of her past, it seemed, were not through with her yet.

Chapter Seven

One by one, women of every form and fashion had been called into the hearing room of the W.C.A.R. Ladies Committee to be accepted or rejected as nurses for the Union army. Charlotte had been told by the waiting room attendant that two hundred women had been examined already today, but only twenty-three had passed. Charlotte sat on the edge of her chair at the association's Cooper Union headquarters, spine straight and feet flat on the floor, as if perfect posture even now might have a favorable bearing on her fate.

"Next!" A voice echoed in the hall, and Charlotte was finally ushered into the presence of two members of the W.C.A.R. Ladies' Committee— Dr. Elizabeth Blackwell, her sister Miss Emily Blackwell, and Mrs. Christine Kean Griffin.

"Name, please."

"Charlotte Anne Waverly."

Charlotte stood as poised as possible, heels together and hands clasped in front. She couldn't help feeling self-conscious as the pair behind the table looked her over, passing judgment already.

There was nothing conspicuous about her

hoopless, navy blue grenadine dress, but compared to Dr. Elizabeth Blackwell's very plain black wrapper with white point lace collar, she felt positively ornamental. Charlotte reached up and deftly plucked the artificial flowers from the brim of her bonnet, crushing and concealing them in her balled fist with an apologetic smile.

"Are you a church member, Miss Waverly?" The first question came from Dr. Blackwell, the principal interrogator.

"Yes, Market Street Church. You may inquire of the Reverend Dr. Ferris there of my regular attendance and involvement." Charlotte willed her voice to remain steady.

"Fine," Dr. Blackwell said. "And do you work, Miss Waverly?"

"I beg your pardon?"

"It is common knowledge that the Waverly family is well off. You have servants, correct?"

Charlotte nodded.

"Well, you will have no servants as a nurse. Are you prepared to take care of yourself and to be without the many comforts to which you are accustomed? To work hard and sleep little, as the circumstance requires?"

"I am not only prepared, but eager."

The committee members looked mildly amused. Miss Emily Blackwell, apparently the chief note taker, scribbled something down with a smile.

"You look to be a very stylish young woman,

Miss Waverly," Dr. Blackwell continued. "You have many admirers, I assume?"

"Just one, but—excuse me, I don't see how this relates to my potential as a nurse."

"More to the point, then. I need to know if you are looking for romance among our nation's young men in their moments of weakness and vulnerability."

"Of course not." Charlotte gasped, feeling her face grow hot. "I would do no such thing."

"So you are satisfied with your beau, then, and do not desire another? You see we really prefer married or widowed women for this position."

"I will say it again." Charlotte strove to regain her composure. "I am not looking for romance, I assure you."

Dr. Blackwell cleared her throat and glanced at the papers in front of her, Charlotte's written testimony most likely among them, before looking up again. "Now then, Miss Waverly, let us be perfectly clear. We are looking for women strong in morals and in body. Nurses will be subject to many disagreeable tasks. Would you help move a wounded man on a litter, if required?"

"Of course."

"Scrub a floor?"

"Indeed."

"Launder blood- and pus-encrusted uniforms?"

Charlotte paused for a half a beat before replying,

"Yes." She hoped it was not a lie, even as she tasted bile in her mouth.

"Would you gently comb lice out of matted hair, wash faces disfigured by shot and shell? Would you pick maggots off of an open sore?" Dr. Blackwell crossed her arms.

Convinced that Dr. Blackwell was trying to scare her away, Charlotte grew hot under her collar, but kept her voice cool. "I would."

"Good. Now as for your discipline. Do you respond well to male authority?"

Charlotte mused that she hadn't lived under male authority for twelve years, but she knew the correct answer. "Of course."

"You realize you would be working directly under and answerable to a military doctor in charge. He may or may not be in favor of your presence, and may decide to make life difficult for you." Dr. Blackwell paused. "In an effort to get you to leave, that is."

"I understand." Charlotte straightened her spine. "And I would not be moved."

An indiscernible expression passed between Dr. Blackwell and Mrs. Griffin. Charlotte prayed her insolent tongue had not just disqualified her.

After a moment of quiet conference between the three committee members, Dr. Blackwell spoke. "You may move on to the Examining Board of the Hospital Committee. Drs. Delafield,

Wood, and Harris will see you in there." She pointed to an imposing paneled oak doorway.

Charlotte's heels clicked along the hardwood floor, every step echoing between the walls and high ceiling, but all she heard was her pounding pulse in her ears.

She entered the cavernous room and squeezed the flowers in her fist, now damp from nervous perspiration. After a pleasant round of introductions, the committee had just two main questions for her. Being satisfied by her answer to the first—"Who is your grandfather?"—Dr. Harris asked, "Have you had the measles?"

"Yes." Charlotte's voice sounded small in the nearly empty room.

"And are you generally in good health? No fainting spells or anything?"

"Perfectly healthy."

"Well done." He smiled, scribbled her name on a chart, left blank the space for recording her age, and reached across his table to hand her a blue slip of paper. She took it and studied the treasure now in her possession. It was signed by Mrs. Christine Griffin and Dr. Elisha Harris below the number 24.

"It's your ticket to the training program, my dear," he explained. "Present it at New York Hospital beginning six-thirty Monday morning. Don't be late."

Chapter Eight

Monday, May 20, 1861

Charlotte had never felt so awake at six thirty in the morning. The hum of two dozen chattering women buzzed through her veins as she stood among them in a meeting room of New York Hospital.

Alice should be here, too, Charlotte thought for the hundredth time. *It only makes sense that she should prepare herself as a nurse if she has any desire to follow Jacob when his regiment goes south.* So far, however, Charlotte's letters had failed to convince Alice. Her place, she maintained, was at her home.

"Ladies!" Dr. Blackwell called the women to attention. "You sound like clucking chickens, but you look like one great big bruise!" The women looked at each other and laughingly agreed. Regulation nursing uniforms not only kept them from wearing hoops, but prohibited them from wearing any color but dark blue, black, grey, or brown.

"I will not be the one to train you during your course, but I wanted to say a few words to you before you begin."

All eyes were on her now.

"Many of you know that since we founded the Women's Central Association of Relief several weeks ago, letters have been pouring in from women all over the country, sharing stories with us of how poorly their soldiers are faring. The flood of correspondence became so overwhelming that we realized our small association, as it currently is, can't meet the needs. But we also realize the needs must absolutely be met."

Nodding heads agreed.

"Dr. Bellows and Dr. Harris left for Washington on May 17 to petition the government to make W.C.A.R. the official United States Sanitary Commission, to 'prevent the evils that England and France could only investigate and deplore,'" she continued. "They are still there. The news has not been good. Dr. Bellows has written to us: 'The War Department regarded us as weak enthusiasts, representing well-meaning but silly women.'" She looked up from the letter and scanned the fresh faces in front of her. "That's you, you know. 'Well-meaning but silly women.'" More than one of them turned a rosy shade of indignation.

Folding the letter and tucking it into the pocket of her apron, Dr. Blackwell sighed. "This nursing corps we have created is what the W.C.A.R. is most known for right now. And like it or not, people are going to be watching us like vultures, ready to swoop in and finish us off if we fail at what we have set out to do. If we fail, I am afraid that women's associations will be discredited and will not be put to use in the war effort. I am afraid that the door will slam shut behind you, and any woman who wants to become a professional nurse after you will have to work twice as hard, or harder, to kick it in again. But most of all, I am convinced beyond any doubt that hundreds of thousands of lives will be lost."

The silence in the air sizzled with tension. Deep concern was etched on every face.

"The army currently has twenty-eight surgeons to care for seventy-five thousand volunteers." Dr. Blackwell let the numbers sink in before continuing. "Twenty-eight. We must do our part, not just to prove what women can do, but because if we don't support the medical department, the Union army will simply not survive. Right now, men are dying when they could be cured with some very basic care and better hygiene. They are dying. As if the wounds of war were not enough, our soldiers are creating their own disease with their lack of personal hygiene and their filthy camps. And it will kill them. Dr. Bellows says that by their recent investigations, one half of the men already recruited will be dead of camp diseases by November 1. I'm sorry to lay this pressure on your shoulders, ladies, but I only do so because I know you can make a difference. You are not 'silly women.' You are brave. Or perhaps foolish, like me."

Dr. Blackwell smiled ruefully at her captivated, confused audience. "Many of you have come to me privately to tell me how eager you are to follow in my footsteps. I might as well tell you publicly, however, that my footsteps have not followed a straight path to get where I am today." She paused. "You've heard the story, haven't you? About how I was finally accepted into Geneva Medical College?"

Charlotte felt her face grow warm. She was ashamed of the rumor, embarrassed to be brought face-to-face with it in front of the legendary Dr. Blackwell.

"It was a joke. The admissions office wasn't quite sure what to do with a woman's application, so they put the question to the student body. The student body was convinced it was a practical joke—who had ever heard of a woman doctor, after all?—so they played along and voted me in. That's all true. You see, I didn't come to be a doctor based just on my skills and credentials. And if I had such trouble getting started, I'm afraid you'll have much trouble being accepted in your positions, as well." The women shifted their weight as Dr. Blackwell spoke.

"I endured prejudice from my classmates and instructors. After I graduated, I was banned from practicing at most hospitals, so I went to France and trained at La Maternité and at St. Bartholomew's Hospital in London. Only after that did I come back and establish the infirmary here, with my sister Emily and Dr. Marie Zakrewska. But here is what you have working in your favor: like it or not, they need you. They need more people to help stem the tide of casualties, and if you are capable, your gender will not matter. In time, they must see that. You will succeed." She nodded, punctuating her words with conviction. "You must succeed."

Dr. Blackwell stepped back now, and Charlotte felt the color drain from her face as the attending physician took over with orientation for their training. *If Dr. Blackwell had to fight so hard to be a doctor, how can I hope to be accepted as a nurse?*

With Dr. Blackwell's words still ringing in her ears, Charlotte was paired with Mrs. Harriet Dowell, another trainee, and assigned to Dr. Winston Markoe's ward.

"No fainting. No shrieking. No tears." Dr. Markoe laid the ground rules as they followed him up to the second floor of the hospital. "Keep a sharp eye, write down anything you don't want to forget, and cork down any of displays of emotions you might feel rising to the surface." Tall and lanky, Dr. Markoe paused at the top of the stairs to allow them to catch up. He looked over the top of his spectacles down the beak of his nose at them with small, close-set black eyes. "Understand?"

Charlotte and Mrs. Dowell nodded.

"Good. Try to keep up. It will do you good to just become familiar with the cases for now. Lectures and more specific instruction will come later."

Dr. Markoe turned and walked briskly to his first patient.

"How are we today, Briggs?"

Briggs didn't respond. He didn't even open his eyes. Dr. Markoe pulled his stethoscope out and listened to his heart rate.

"One hundred twenty beats a minute. Adam Briggs, chronic diarrhea, age nineteen," the doctor said. "What observations can you make by just looking at him?"

"He must have lost a great deal of weight," ventured Charlotte. The boy's skin hung loosely over wasted muscles. His features looked pinched.

"Yes, sixty pounds, at least, have melted off his six-foot frame since the onset. What else?"

"His coloring isn't quite right." Mrs. Dowell squinted at his complexion.

"That opaque clay color comes from the disease," said Dr. Markoe.

Charlotte leaned in a little closer now, hugging her notebook to her chest. "What's on his skin?"

"Furfuraceous desquamation of epithelium."

Charlotte stepped back.

"The poor dear is quite gone with it, then isn't he?" Mrs. Dowell asked. Her son, she had told

Charlotte, had also volunteered and was currently at Staten Island.

"I'm afraid he is. I'm going to open his mouth now." Dr. Markoe pried open the boy's jaws. "Now look at the tongue." He pulled it out.

"Why, it's blood red!" said Charlotte.

"Dirty red, I should say," added Mrs. Dowell. "Like a piece of raw beef you'd get at the market."

"Yes," agreed Dr. Markoe. "An apt description. If you had seen him not long ago, the tongue would have been pale, swollen, smooth, watery, indented on the edges by the teeth, its papillae hardly perceptible. Patients who reach this stage very seldom recover," he added in a low tone. "If he were to speak, you'd notice it would sound weak and feeble, as if you were hearing him from a great distance. You would also notice depression and confusion, which very often accompany chronic diarrhea."

"Well, I should say so! And who wouldn't be depressed about it?" interjected Mrs. Dowell.

"But no delirium, which seems to be the special characteristic of fevers. Of course, the abdomen is also tender. Evacuations from the bowels may occur as often as every fifteen minutes or more frequently than that. Usually it's preceded by gripping pain. The discharges are liquid, and become darker from the presence of blood as the disease progresses. If he is eating indiscriminately, you'll be able to see undigested food in the discharges."

At this Charlotte paused from scribbling in her notebook to put up a hand. "Pardon me, Dr. Markoe, but is it really necessary to tell us all of this? We won't be making the diagnoses ourselves, after all. Just following the doctor's orders. Correct?"

The look in his eyes withered her. "My dear girl, if you cannot handle *hearing* of such things, how do you expect to walk among these poor men? Too weak to reach a toilet, they will need to be cleaned up, sometimes fed, their bedclothes changed. You must begin to think about it scientifically, rather than emotionally, and become accustomed to the sights, sounds, smells of the hospital."

She felt her cheeks ignite in shame and vowed to hold her tongue from that point on. *Eyes open, mouth shut,* she told herself.

"Women nurses indeed," she heard him mutter.

Briggs moaned then, and his eyelids fluttered open. One look into his eyes, and Charlotte's stomach churned. His eyes closed again, and she looked at Dr. Markoe for an explanation.

"Yes, I was about to tell you about that. I have only seen it in two patients in this hospital. It's an ulcer. It grows until it penetrates the cornea and evacuates the humors of the eye. From what I understand from other doctors, no patient has ever recovered who displayed this symptom."

"What can you do for him?" Concern was etched into Mrs. Dowell's brow.

"There is no point in any further treatment. If he were not so far along, we would have given him fresh fruits and vegetables, and given him opiates for the pain. But not now. It's just too late."

Charlotte looked at the boy again, and saw him as a person, not just a medical case. A boy, without even a shadow of stubble on his face. She tried to imagine what he had looked like before he had become emaciated. Before his complexion turned muddy, before his own skin betrayed him in great brown flakes. She was sure he had been hand-some, full of life and energy, and only too anxious to defend his country. She wondered if he had a sweetheart, or if his heart still belonged to his mother or sisters. How shocked they would be to learn he had died before a single battle took place.

"Where is his mother?" she asked, frowning.

"We've tried to find her."

"What will you tell her?"

"Her son died bravely for a glorious cause."

But he wasn't dying for a cause. He was dying alone of a preventable disease before he even shouldered a rifle.

Charlotte couldn't fathom the pain his mother would feel when she learned her son had died without her comforting touch. She reached out and touched his scaly arm, dry and brittle beneath her fingertips. She gently moved her fingers into his palm and felt the slightest twitch of his fingers.

"He knows I'm here?" she asked the doctor.

"It's difficult to say," Dr. Markoe replied. "He is so weak. I'm sure his bed will be empty before too—"

"Shhhhh, shhhhh, Adam," Charlotte drowned out the doctor's words. "It's going to be all right. You're doing fine."

Dr. Markoe shook his head. All three of them knew it was a lie. Perhaps Adam knew it, too, but his body seemed to relax under her hands.

"If you please, we need to move on." Dr. Markoe pushed the spectacles up his hawk-like nose.

"This boy is some mother's son, Doctor, and if what you say is true, he is slipping from this world to the next right before our eyes. There *is* a place for compassion, Dr. Markoe, even in the midst of your scientific observations," Charlotte told him as they turned to leave Adam's side.

Dr. Markoe sighed, deeply, slowly. "Sympathy doesn't save lives. Science does. Efficiency does. If you feel too deeply, it will cloud your judgment, slow you down. I know it's hard for you women to understand—that's why medicine has always been a man's job. But try. So, shall we?"

For the next three hours, Charlotte and Mrs. Dowell followed on Dr. Markoe's heels, examining dozens of patients with pneumonia, fever, measles, rheumatism, tuberculosis, and several others whose symptoms were inconclusive. By eleven o'clock, Charlotte's notebook had several pages of scribbled notes and her head was spinning.

It was time for a lunch break before the afternoon lectures would begin. But before Charlotte was dismissed, Dr. Markoe caught her attention.

"Miss Waverly, a moment, please." She followed him into the hallway outside his ward.

"Yes, Doctor?"

"You're awfully sure of yourself, young lady." His small eyes bore into hers.

"Excuse me?"

"I'm tolerating your boldness because it's your first day of training. But I can guarantee you, if you pass this course, if you actually get placed under an army surgeon, he will be looking for reasons to dismiss you. And you are giving him several."

"I don't understand!" Her spine tingled. She hadn't done anything wrong.

"First and most obvious, you are young and attractive. You'll be a distraction to the convalescent male nurses, to the medical students, and to the soldier patients themselves. And by distraction, I mean they will be tempted to interact with you in ways that will satisfy their hunger for female . . . companionship."

Charlotte looked down, but her voice was firm. "Since I have kept to every regulation of the nursing uniform, I don't know what else I can do to become even less attractive. What else would you have me do, shave my head?"

"Now that's the second thing I'm referring to. Right there. Your quick tongue is going to get you in trouble. I understand your asking me questions in front of the patients because you are in training, and you are here to learn. But did it ever cross your mind that this is an exception, not the rule? If you question the surgeon like this after you're given your assignment, it will appear as if—no, in truth, you *will* be—trying to undermine his authority, as a man, as a doctor, and as a military authority."

Charlotte narrowed her eyes into slits as she looked up at him. "You will forgive me, sir, if I do not understand why asking questions is such a threatening thing. Wouldn't it benefit everyone if I really understood what was going on?"

Dr. Markoe sighed and rubbed the back of his neck beneath the stethoscope cord. "Your father died a while ago, didn't he?"

She blinked. "Yes, twelve years ago, but I fail to see how that has anything to do with this."

"It has everything to do with it, Miss Waverly. You've been without the leadership of a father for quite some time, and you've never been subject to a husband. I understand how this is new to you. But if you want to be accepted as a nurse, you will do as the doctor says and not ask questions.

Asking questions implies that you do not trust the doctor's decisions, his diagnosis, or his treatment. It implies that you could do it better. That he is incompetent. That's grounds for dismissal."

"But how can they do that if I'm given an assignment through Miss Dix?"

"Dorothea Dix is not taken seriously by most men in the army. She has power only to recommend, not to enforce. In other words, she might send you to a hospital for placement, but if the surgeon finds a reason to fire you—or fabricates one—out you'll go. He's still in charge."

Charlotte felt her anger beginning to boil to the surface and fought to retain control of her voice. "What, then, Dr. Markoe, do you suggest I do?"

His mouth tipped up in a smile that didn't quite reach his eyes. "No need to be upset with me, Miss Waverly. I'm just giving you a bit of free advice. You seem to believe that being in this program means you're ready to take charge and do things better. If you don't drop that strong-minded, woman-of-reform attitude, no doctor, and I mean *not one,* will want to work with you. You haven't proven anything yet, and what's more, every step of the way you'll be on the edge of losing what you've gained. If you don't like the sound of that, you might as well go home now."

She remembered the words Caleb spoke to her at the dance. *What if your stepping out of formation was actually a step in the right direction?*

Even if Caleb had been right, she suspected there was truth to what Dr. Markoe said, as well. All nursing candidates had, indeed, stepped out of formation the moment they had applied for the training. But if they were to get much further in this male domain, they would have to tread lightly and watch their step.

And Charlotte would have to watch her tongue.

Chapter Nine

Sunday, June 2, 1861

Phineas Hastings couldn't help humming to himself as his carriage rumbled along Fifth Avenue toward the Waverlys' four-story brownstone on Sixteenth Street. A dozen crimson roses lay on the red leather bench next to him, releasing their sweet fragrance with every jolt and bump over the cobblestones. He had had his doubts about courting Charlotte before, but today his mind was made up. She was beautiful, refined, wealthy, real "upper crust." She was everything he needed.

Phineas pulled his gold watch from his vest pocket and checked the time. Three forty-five. Perfect. Just enough time to pick up Charlotte and get to Central Park for the most popular carriage-riding hour.

He rubbed his thumb over the inscription on the watch's back. *P.J.H.* His father's initials, as well as his own. It was his only link to his father since he'd gone to California during the gold rush of 1849. It was supposed to be pawned if Phineas and his mother ever needed money while his father was gone, but neither Phineas nor his mother could part with it, even when they were getting by on flour and water. Even though his father had never come back, they survived without him. Phineas went from boy to man overnight when he realized it was up to him to take care of himself and his mother. He had done it, too.

His mother had been ready to move into the poorhouse, but Phineas had refused.

"I can take care you," he'd told her.

And she laughed. "Go on, now! You're just a boy, you couldn't possibly!"

But he had. Though it meant working, selling, borrowing, and begging, he had proven her wrong. They had survived, and now they thrived. Thank God that old life was behind them.

Phineas slipped the watch back into his pocket and patted it. His own mother may not have believed in him, but Charlotte did, and that was all that mattered now. A wife on his arm was the only hole he had to fill before achieving the full respect of his peers. It was time. It was past time.

The brass knocker sounded on the front door, jolting Charlotte awake. She was two weeks into her training course at New York Hospital, and though she would never admit it to her mother, she was exhausted. Leaving every morning at six o'clock, arriving home at five in the afternoon, and still keeping up with her music and French lessons was wearing her down. She hurried to the bathroom to splash cold water on her face while Jane answered the door.

When she emerged, there was Phineas at the end of the hallway, his tall figure silhouetted by the sunlight behind him. In one hand, he held his hat by the brim, in the other elbow lay a bouquet of roses.

"Phineas, thank you!" She bent over the roses and inhaled their fragrance before handing them to Jane. "I only wish I were half as fresh as those roses."

He smiled and took her hand in his. "Nonsense! 'Shall I compare thee to a summer's day? Thou art more lovely and more temperate . . .'"

She nodded in appreciation. "Speaking of a summer's day, I can't wait to get out in it."

"Your wish is my command. How about a ride through Central Park?"

"Perfect." Whether he wanted to go to show off his horses or to enjoy nature in the heart of the city, she didn't care. All that mattered to her was that she could sit down in the carriage, feel the warmth of the sun, and try for a fleeting moment to let the sights and sounds of the hospital recede to the back of her mind.

They stepped outside to a sky of robin's egg blue. Charlotte tipped her white-fringed parasol to the side and lifted her face to the sun, closed her eyes and let the golden warmth wash over her.

"I bet your mother would be appalled if she peeked out her window right now," teased Phineas.

"But of course!" Charlotte chuckled. "Anything

that might bring some color to my skin, she's against."

"And anything she is against, you are for. Am I right?"

Her eyes widened as Phineas helped her into the carriage. "It's not my intention to constantly be at odds with her, you know. But you're right, there are many things upon which we disagree. Little things, like the importance of a pale complexion, and big things, too."

"Such as your hospital training." He clucked to his horses and the carriage lurched forward in obedience.

"Such as my hospital training. Yes, exactly."

"Don't be too hard on her for not wanting you to subject yourself to all the rumors. I don't like to think of your name being slandered, either."

"Fiddlesticks. I don't care what people say. I know the truth, and so does she, and so do you. My motives are pure. I just want to help."

He patted her hand the way a father would console a child. "Of course, dear. We all do."

She closed her eyes for a moment and listened to the clip-clopping of the horses' hooves, steady, predictable, comforting.

"Phineas." Charlotte turned to face him. "Why haven't you enlisted?"

He cleared his throat. "New York doesn't need any more fighting men. We've already sent more than any other state in the Union."

She nodded, but the answer didn't resonate with her. The W.C.A.R. had been inundated with applicants for the nursing slots, and that hadn't stopped her from pursuing it anyway.

"Well then, how are you helping?" She hoped the question sounded merely curious, not accusatory.

Phineas stared at her. "Excuse me?"

"You said we all want to help, and I think you're right—I'm going to be a nurse, Alice and Mother are organizing supplies, and I was just wondering if you want to help, what are you doing? For the cause?"

A moment passed, and a shadow darkened his face.

"Too many questions?" Charlotte said quietly. When he still said nothing, she plunged ahead. "Dr. Markoe told me that asking men questions shows that I don't trust them. I'm sorry if that's how I came across. I just wanted to know."

"Wise man." Phineas turned his gaze to the road. "You already know how I feel about the cause. Everyone does—I'm one of the most outspoken abolitionists in the city. If I stir people's hearts for the cause of freedom, if I move them to action to defend liberty and preserve the Union, isn't that enough? I daresay it is. Passion fuels the fight, Charlotte, and I ignite that passion."

"Of course you are right, Phineas. You are an inspiration to all of us." She settled back into the seat and stared straight ahead.

They fell silent as they entered the park at the southeast corner and followed the drive around the pond and through lush green grounds. It was a small slice of Eden tucked within an ever-expanding city.

Phineas slowed his horses down to rest under a canopy of maple leaves and turned to face Charlotte.

"We're stopping?" She looked around.

"Charlotte." Phineas doffed his hat and began turning it in slow circles in his hands. "I want to talk to you about—where we are going."

Ah, so this would be the day. He had her full attention now, but she could imagine what he would say. She had gotten this far with other men before, but never beyond it.

"Charlotte," he began again. "You are the most exquisite woman I've ever met. You're beautiful without trying to be. You're graceful in every movement you make—every tilt of the chin, every turn of your head, every lift of your hand. Every word that falls from your lips is like music. Every step you take is like a choreographed dance. I am completely bewitched. You have cast a spell over me—one that I never want to be broken."

In spite of herself, Charlotte found that her heart was beating faster as he gripped her hands in his.

"Would you do me the honor—that is, would you consider allowing me to provide for you, protect you, and care for you as my wife? I would be the happiest man alive." He opened a small blue box labeled TIFFANY & CO. to reveal a gold ring with a sapphire circled with diamonds.

Charlotte closed her eyes and looked for a vision of the future he was offering to her. For a moment, she considered saying yes. But her conscience would not allow her to accept without telling him her secret.

She sighed. "Phineas. You have been very good to me. I know that if I were your wife, I would want for nothing, for you would provide for my every need, even my every want."

He nodded, but she could tell he was concerned. This wasn't the one-word answer he had been hoping for.

"But I'm afraid I would not be able to give you everything *you* want—what a man deserves to have from his wife."

"What?" Phineas dropped her hands and picked up his hat again, spinning it around and around in his hands. "Whatever do you mean? I would require nothing of you, nothing at all. The responsibility to provide would be all mine! When my father died, I performed my duty to provide for my mother until her passing, God rest her soul, and I long to provide for my wife. Please, let it be you."

"I don't know how to put this delicately." Charlotte bit her lip and willed her voice to be steady. She should be able to do this, she had done it before. "I can't give you—children."

He sat back, staring at her as if she had just spoken a foreign language.

"Children?" he finally said.

"I can't have them."

"You don't want them?"

"No! I *want* them Phineas, I can't have them. My body never—" She searched the sky. How could she tell a man she had never had a menstrual cycle? "My body is not—equipped—it seems, to bear children."

Phineas shook his head. As she watched his face, she could almost see him conjuring up a picture of home and hearth without any babies to rock to sleep or toddlers to bounce on his knee. No child to adore. No daughter to give away in marriage, no son to carry on the family name. No one wanted that.

He would dismiss her now, as every other suitor had.

"Is that all?" He half-laughed the question.

Charlotte's mouth fell open but no sound came out.

"I can do without children, darling. I can't do without you."

His voice was smooth, his words hypnotic. No one had ever said anything like that to her before. In ten years of courting, not one had come remotely close.

"You still want me?" She was incredulous.

"More than ever. Surely you see the depth of my feeling for you now. Be my wife, let me prove it to you for the rest of your life."

A fleeting image of Caleb's face flashed in her mind. *Don't lead Mr. Hastings on if he's not the right one for you,* he had said. But he hadn't said, "Choose me." *Write to me,* he had said. But he hadn't said, "I want you to be mine." No, he had walked away. He wasn't here. If she didn't accept Phineas's offer, another one might never come along. She was four years past the age of spinsterhood. Did she truly want to be unmarried forever?

"You're sure you still want me?" she asked again.

"I've already told you I do! But if you need to hear it again, yes, I want you, and I'll tell you every day as long as we both shall live. I'll give you whatever you want before you even realize you want it. You'll never have to work again." He slid closer to her on the bench.

"I don't really work now."

"Oh be serious! You are working your delicate hands to the bone at the hospital every day." Phineas reached out to touch one of her hands, but she tucked them in the folds of her skirt.

"This is what I want to do, Phineas." She looked him directly in the eyes. "For the first time in my life, I feel as though I may actually have some value to other people. Not for what I look like but for what I do. I am a part of something bigger than myself, saving lives that have been offered to keep our country together!"

"I have tried to be understanding about this new obsession of yours. As a single woman, I imagine you have seen this as an interesting diversion—although a rather morbid one, I must say—to fill up your time."

Charlotte's heart rate quickened at the insult. "This is no game for me, Phineas! I'm not just filling up time. Our country is at war and I want to help win it! I *want* to be a nurse. Don't you see? This is something I have to do."

His brow furrowed. "No wife of mine will be around other men and their frustrated *desires*. I wish you would give this up. With me as your husband, you could have a future ahead of you."

Charlotte lifted her chin and pressed her lips together. "I have always had a future ahead of me, Phineas, whether or not it included marriage. A woman's life is not wasted just because she is unmarried. At least, not unless she spends all of it trying to secure a husband."

Phineas's eyes darted about him. "Calm down."

"I can be calm about a great many things, Phineas, but not this."

His face darkened. He leveled a stony gaze at her, and she returned it, unyielding. Clearly, this conversation was not going as he had planned. Charlotte sighed and looked down at her hands clasped tightly in her lap. "If marrying you means I must give up nursing, I'm afraid I must regretfully decline."

He laughed then, but his eyes were cold and hard. "Afraid you 'must regretfully decline'? My dear, you sound as though you are declining a dinner invitation, rather than ripping my heart out."

But he didn't look heartbroken. He looked like a volcano about to erupt, his eyes smoldering pieces of coal.

She shrank away from him and moved to the end of the seat.

He caught her wrist and gripped it as he would grip the reins of his horses if they were running out of control.

She could feel her pulse push against his hand. Her fingers began to tingle. She gasped.

At the rumble of an approaching carriage, Charlotte slid her gaze past Phineas. "You will remember yourself, Mr. Hastings," she whispered, tilting her head toward the hoofbeats and voices of strangers growing louder. "Let go of me."

He released her wrist then and rubbed his hand over his face. After a moment, she heard him mutter, "Uncalled for." But it was impossible to tell if he was referring to himself or to her.

Act Two

CHANGING TIMES

NO ONE KNOWS, WHO did not watch the thing from the beginning, how much opposition, how much ill-will, how much unfeeling want of thought, these women nurses endured. Hardly a surgeon whom I can think of, received or treated them with even common courtesy. Government had decided that women should be employed, and the army surgeons—unable, therefore, to close the hospitals against them—determined to make their lives so unbearable that they should be forced in self-defence to leave. It seemed a matter of cool calculation, just how much ill-mannered opposition would be requisite to break up the system.

Some of the bravest women I have ever known were among this first company of army nurses. They saw at once the position of affairs, the attitude assumed by the surgeons and the wall against which they were expected to break and scatter; and they set themselves to undermine the whole thing.

—GEORGEANNA WOOLSEY, written in 1864

Chapter Ten

Meridian Hill, Washington City
Friday, June 7, 1861

A log snapped in the fire, sending a shower of sparks under a twilight sky brushed with strokes of pink and gold. Caleb Lansing tugged at the collar of his scratchy blue wool uniform and lowered himself down onto a wooden crate to watch the orange flames dance. He sure didn't need the heat, but at least it kept the flies away as a pot of coffee boiled.

Wiping his glistening forehead with the back of his hand, he looked through the haze of smoke at the rest of the camp, most of them sitting on the ground or on overturned barrels, unwrapping small bundles of hardtack from their haversacks. He pulled out his own, placed it on a flat rock, and rammed a Sharp rifle butt onto it, breaking it into pieces.

"Well, Doc, is it a teeth duller or a worm castle tonight?" A baby-faced private named Hodges dropped down to the ground and reached into his own haversack.

Caleb groaned. "Worm castle." Maggots and weevils writhed through the pieces of hardtack and onto the stone.

"Downright insulting, that's what it is, Doc. A man marches all day under the sun and what do we get for it? All I got to say is, it's a good thing we ain't fightin' yet, or we'd all drop over in a dead faint like a heap of womenfolk. Uncle Sam says 'Fight a war!' but he sure ain't givin' us any help, is he now?"

Caleb chuckled in agreement. "Too hard to chew, too small for shoeing mules, and too big to use as bullets. Utter waste of space, wouldn't you say, Hodges?"

"Darn right, Doc." Hodges scooped up the worm castles, trotted about twenty yards and threw them in the trench.

"Throw that hardtack out of the trenches, private! Haven't you been told that often enough?" Caleb overheard the brigade officer of the day say sharply to the young man.

"I thrown it out two or three times, sir, but it keeps crawling back!"

Caleb didn't advocate insubordination to officers, but he couldn't help laughing at Hodge's very reasonable response. It was a trial to not have decent food when the soldiers were constantly burning up their energy.

It had been another long day of marching and drilling for all but those who had come to see him with complaints of nausea, diarrhea, dizziness, or fever. If he had been in a hospital or at home at his own clinic, he could have offered them lumps of ice or oranges to suck on, but here in camp, that was out of the question. They hadn't seen fresh fruit in at least two weeks. The fruit sent by post from well-meaning mothers and wives was putrid by the time it arrived. So far, he did not feel very effective as a regimental surgeon.

Dinner suddenly over, Caleb poured the coffee into his tin dipper and swirled it in the cup, hoping it would take the edge off his hunger. Hodges had gone off in search of a card game, so for the first time all day, Caleb was relatively alone.

His hand immediately went to pat the pocket of his uniform, assuring himself that Charlotte's letter was still there. He didn't need to see it anymore; he had it memorized by now.

So she was going "out of formation," she said. Caleb rolled the tip of his mustache between his thumb and finger, back and forth, as he mused. He was sure Charlotte's mother would be appalled at any deviation from the norm, and he wondered how that stuffed shirt Phineas Hinges —Hobbs—Happysack—whatever his name was— was reacting to it. He had always known that Charlotte was meant to do more than just look pretty and be petted. But nursing? Why would she put herself in an army hospital, bound to be the bloodiest place on earth, aside from the battle-field itself? Had she somehow gotten past the haunting memories of her father's drawn-out death, or was she punishing herself for being helpless to save his life?

He brought his cup to his parched lips and absentmindedly gulped, as if it was iced tea instead of scalding hot coffee, burning his tongue. Closing his eyes, he ignored the sting in his mouth and allowed his mind to travel back to a time when there was no war on the doorstep, a time when he and Charlotte had been together.

It seemed like a lifetime ago that Charles Waverly had died. Caleb was twenty, Charlotte sixteen. She had looked so lost, so abandoned, and she had asked him for help. Death had bonded them together in a way that little else in life can. He longed to shield her from as much pain as he could, the way a father would protect his child, and called often to check in on her throughout the first year of intense mourning. She grew to rely on him, on his strength, his words of comfort, and he relished it.

What would I do without you? she had often said, and his chest swelled.

When the grey veil of grief began to lift off her face, she looked at him differently with those caramel-colored eyes, the flecks of gold brilliant with happiness. If he could make her eyes shine, it made his day.

Not long after her mourning clothes changed from black to grey and deep purple, he realized his affection for her was not as a surrogate father figure toward a pitiable child, but as a man toward a woman who warmed under his gaze.

The more time they spent together, the more he felt for her. He hoped it was mutual. But when she said, *I need you,* he began to fear that he had simply stepped into the void in her heart left by her father. That she needed him because he was a safe place, he was reliable, as her father had been. The thought needled him until he could no longer sleep at night. He cared for her for who she was, but he had a nagging suspicion that she cared for him just because he was there. He wanted the woman he loved to love him not because she needed him, but because she wanted him, whether he was right there in front of her or miles apart. Would she have loved any man just as much who had happened to be by her side during her darkest days and nights? If Charles could see them from heaven, would he accuse Caleb of putting Charlotte's grief to his advantage by preying on her wide-open heart?

She seemed blind to the spell she cast on him. He had made up his mind not to steal a kiss from her willing lips—she was still so young, by then still only seventeen—but the temptation was driving him mad. Once he kissed her, he'd never be able to think with his head and not with his heart again. He would have done everything he could to convince her to be his, while she was still in a state of grieving for her father.

It wouldn't have been right.

So he chose a path that took him away from her—medical school at Yale College in New Haven, Connecticut—not because he didn't love her, but because he loved her too much to let their relationship simply happen by default. It would have been cheating.

When he wrote to her several months later, just to wish her a happy birthday, she replied that she was glad he had "abandoned" her, that her feelings for him had turned cold. He tried to forget her, to replace her with other women, but none of them captured his heart as she had.

So he studied more than anyone else at Yale, graduated at the top of his class, and worked harder than any other doctor in town. Some had suggested he was burying himself in it, but they didn't understand. With Charlotte out of the picture, it was the only thing that made him feel alive.

Caleb trusted that God had a perfect plan for his life, and assumed years ago that Charlotte Waverly was simply not part of it. Now, he wasn't so sure.

Logs crumbled and hissed in front of him now, and Caleb snapped out of his reverie. On the other side of camp, he could hear strains of men singing "Victory's Band" to the tune of the Southern anthem, "Dixie's Land."

We're marching under the Flag of Union,
Keeping step in brave communion!
March away! March away! Away!
  Victory's band!
Right down upon the ranks of rebels,
Tramp them underfoot like pebbles,
March away! March away! . . .

Caleb sighed. He loved the Union, but singing about treading upon the enemy like they were pebbles smacked of a false confidence the size of New England. These soldiers were as of yet untested, unproven in battle. As a regimental surgeon, so was he, and he knew it.

"Pride goeth before destruction, and a haughty spirit before a fall," he muttered into his tin cup, and swallowed the last of his now lukewarm coffee.

Chapter Eleven

New York City
Monday, June 10, 1861

"My husband is Matthew O'Flannery. He left with New York's Sixty-Ninth Regiment five weeks ago, and I haven't heard from him since," Ruby told the officer behind the desk at the recruiting office on Broadway that had enlisted him.

He looked her up and down. "You're sure he enlisted? Could it be that he just—found an opportunity to strike out on his own?"

"Aye, I'm telling you, he is fighting for your country."

"Not yours, though, eh?" He leaned back and put his hands behind his head, smirking.

" 'Tis more your country than it is mine, sir, as I assume you have been here longer and have an easier time of living here."

"And yet, this is still better than what you left behind in Ireland, isn't it?"

Her face burned, but she bit her tongue. She expected there could be an argument this morning, but this was not the fight she wanted. She hated confrontation as a general rule, but she was so hungry, so desperate for money, she knew she had to stand her ground.

"Look it up, you'll see his name in black and white. Matthew O'Flannery. The Sixty-Ninth. I need to know what happened to his paycheck."

"I don't need to look it up, *lassie*." He leaned forward. "Even if he's with them, I wouldn't expect any money any time soon. The army is regrettably behind in paying its soldiers, but will pay arrears in full as soon as it can."

Ruby didn't know what arrears meant, but she did know about being behind in payments.

"As for why you haven't heard from him about it personally, I could only make a guess." He sneered as he looked over her faded, threadbare dress again. She knew exactly how he saw her, for it was how she saw herself: poor, uneducated, dirty. Unworthy. Well, if she looked the part of a beggar, then beg she would.

"Saints alive, can't your office spare a few dollars? We'll pay it back as soon as the government pays its soldiers."

"Have you considered working yourself, or do you insist upon waiting for money to just magically appear for you?"

Ruby snorted. "Do I look like the sort of person who isn't accustomed to hard work? I work, Officer Jennings, every hour of daylight and then some, and still I am falling behind. I would not have to beg for money if you would pay my husband his wages in the first place!"

"Not my fault."

"I don't care whose fault it is, I am asking for a few dollars to tide me over, that's all."

"It's out of the question. You're not the only person waiting for word or wages from her soldier. Just call it your own patriotic sacrifice. Good day."

Ruby let the door slam behind her as she left the building. Hot tears pricked her eyes as she looked up and down Broadway. Just coming here had cost her precious hours she could have been sewing. A waste of time, only now she was farther behind in her work than before. Her stomach was an empty cavern, and her soul felt just as hollow. She should be praying to St. Jude, the patron saint of lost causes, but her mind couldn't concentrate long enough to find the right words.

Crossing her broken-wing arms across her chest, she turned south and began walking the seventeen blocks home. Putting one foot in front of the other was all she could do at the moment.

"Ruby!"

Ruby turned, squinting into the bright sunshine, shielding her eyes with a shaky hand. She was so hungry she thought she might collapse.

"Ruby! Over here!"

A woman in a bright purple-and-green plaid dress, cut low enough in the bodice for evening wear, waved her over.

"Ruby, you're a mess! What are you doing this end of Broadway?"

The voice belonged to Emma Connors, but this woman looked nothing like her old friend from the Fourteenth Ward. Ruby rubbed the tears out of her eyes and looked again.

"Emma? What happened?" She waved a hand at her dress, her hair, her bonnet. There was no way she could have afforded to look like that a month ago.

"Aye, I got smart, Ruby, that's what happened."

Ruby shook her head. She didn't understand.

"Let me put it to you this way. How much do you make with your needle and thread? On a good week, when your work is accepted?"

"A dollar seventy-five."

"And how much do you pay for your dark, rotting rooms?"

Ruby swallowed. "Seven dollars a month."

"How much do you work?"

"Emma, you know how much I work, it's as much as you. All the time."

"No lass, that's how much I *did* work. Not anymore. Do you know how much I work now? As much as I bloomin' want to, that's what." She threw a wink past Ruby to a small cluster of men who had been watching her. "And do you know how much I make?" She leaned in. "Ten bucks a week for a couple hours o' work. More if I want it."

"What?"

"Come now, Ruby, don't be so naïve. Surely you've thought about it from time to time."

"Prostitution." The whispered word tasted vile in her mouth.

Emma wagged a finger at her. "Don't you be judging me for it either, lass. No money coming in from Sean, not enough from the boarder. Not enough hours in the day to work a fair wage. I was starving, Ruby, and by the looks of it, you are, too. It can't be a sin to survive, surely."

Ruby wasn't convinced. Selling your body was a sin no matter what, and the worst kind of sin, too.

"Just think of it, Ruby. Imagine for a moment that you never have to thread another needle, or prick your fingers in the dark. You never have to wear those rags again, or lack for a meal. No more going to the pawnshop until all your things are gone. No more burning your furniture for firewood. You could get out of the Fourteenth Ward. If you're lucky, you find a nice gentleman who will set you up in your own apartment, keep you fed and well-dressed, and all you have to do is pleasure him when he asks for it. Isn't that worth the cost?"

Ruby felt betrayed. She loved Emma. She didn't want anything to come between them, but this—this was too big to ignore. Ruby felt sick to her stomach, but whether it was from hunger or heartbreak, she couldn't tell.

"You're happy, then?" Ruby searched Emma's face.

Emma's smile sagged as she looked down. "I'm happy that I'm not wondering whether I'll make it through each day." She looked up now. "If only there was a better way to make such good money," she added as she laughed ruefully. " 'Tisn't so bad if you don't think about it much. And if you work on your own, rather than for a madame at a brothel, you can choose your own customers. You learn in a hurry which men to avoid, I can tell you that much." She nodded to a man a few yards away wearing a green-and-gold tartan vest with a camel-colored suit. The green necktie to match was almost as flashy as the color Emma wore. "That one there can be sweet as candy, but if he's had a bad day, he'll take it out on his woman. Have to watch his eyes carefully to see if they are fair or stormy."

Ruby followed Emma's gaze to the gentleman outside Brooks Brothers. He stood a head above the man he was talking to, a gold watch in one hand, the other fist on his hip. His black mustache and goatee were trimmed close to his face, unlike the scruffy facial hair she was used to seeing around the tenements. His eyes were shielded by the brim of his hat, but as she studied his face, she thought she could make out snatches of conversation.

Uniform contract . . . twelve thousand sets . . . not enough material . . . shoddy discovered, she heard the shorter man say.

We'll make it through . . . said the taller man. *Too much money at stake* . . . *Not here* . . .

Of course, of course, the short man bellowed, making every word suddenly clear. *I forgot! The best thing about knowing your way around the law the way you do is—well—knowing your way around the law!* He threw back his head and laughed at his own joke, but the man in the green necktie jerked his head up, glowering, and looked around. His gaze caught Ruby's before she could turn away, and for a moment they appraised each other. His eyes darted to Emma and back to Ruby. His lips had stopped moving, but his eyes told her she should not have been eavesdropping. Goosebumps raised on her skin.

"Ruby?" Emma placed a hand on her arm. "You OK?"

Saints alive, even her nails are painted! "Sorry, Emma," she said turning back to her. "I need to get back to work. I've wasted too much time coming here today." She tilted her head back toward the recruiting office, and Emma nodded in understanding.

"I'm telling you, the only help we'll get is the help we give ourselves."

"Aye, I must not be very good at it, then. I've missed rent for the last two weeks. If I don't have the money by the end of today, I'll be looking for another place, I'm sure of it."

"Let me buy you a dress. Clean you up, fix your hair. You could start a better life."

Ruby shook her head. "If I can just hang on until July, Matthew will come home then."

"*If* he comes home. And what will you do in the meantime? Where will you go?"

"There's only one place left that I can possibly afford."

"You can't go there, Ruby, it'll kill you."

Ruby smiled. "And I'll die just as soon if I don't."

"Mary, Mother of God," breathed Emma, crossing herself. "You have a choice, you know."

Ruby nodded. "Aye. 'Tis Five Points."

Emma shook her head, but pulled a few coins from her pocketbook and pressed them firmly into Ruby's hand.

"Eat, Ruby. I'd break bread with you myself but I've got an appointment coming up. Take care."

Ruby's throat swelled shut as she felt the cold metal in her palm. How could she use this money that had likely been earned with a sexual favor? But her stomach screamed louder than her conscience, and she accepted the gift with a silent nod of thanks.

As she watched Emma sashay down Broadway and around the corner at Spring Street, she caught a glimpse once more of the tall man in the green tie, still watching her. Now he was striding toward her.

Catching up to her, he said, "Fine day for a stroll, isn't it, miss?" His voice dripped with honey as he took her by her crooked elbow. "Walk with me."

"Is there a problem, sir?" Ruby searched his face.

"So, Ruby, is it? You're a friend of Emma's?" He looked at her intently. If she wasn't already suspicious of him, she might have admired the high cheekbones, the straight nose, the strong, square, jaw. Instead, she only noticed that his eyes were the color of Ireland's River Shannon—cold, deep, and dark.

"Aye."

"Noticed you were looking my way a moment ago. Are you . . . in her line of work, shall we say?"

Heat scrambled up from Ruby's collar to her face. "No! I'm a clean and decent woman, I am. I sew."

He stopped walking then and turned to face her directly. "Is that so? How very interesting." His hold on her arm was growing tighter. "So you have an interest in Brooks Brothers, then."

She shook her head. "I work for Davis & Company."

A flash of understanding gleamed in his eyes then, but she had no idea why. What had she said that could possibly interest him? She didn't care enough to find out.

"I'll need to be going now."

"Where might that be? If we're going the same direction, I'll be happy to accompany you there."

"I doubt it, if you don't mind my saying so."

"Try me." Was that a smile? It looked more like he was baring his teeth at her.

Ruby's heart beat faster, her pulse quickened. She felt like a cornered animal.

"Five Points," she said, her thick Irish accent twisting the words so it sounded more like "Five Pints," another name which would have been just as apt for all the freely flowing alcohol there.

"Dangerous territory, miss; I'd watch myself if I were you." He released her arm and tipped his hat to her, and she hurried away from his reach. She only looked back once, and when she did, he was nowhere in sight.

The closer Ruby got to Five Points in the Sixth Ward, the harder it was to find clean footing. South of Canal Street, Mulberry Street soon became all but covered with pools of decaying vegetable matter and mounds of garbage, peppered with horse and pig droppings on every side. The summer sun beat mercilessly down, baking the filth until steaming vapors carried on the breeze, spreading the overpowering stench throughout the neighborhood.

A large brick tenement cast a crooked shadow over her, but the reek of overflowing, putrefying sinks behind it kept her from stopping. Her stomach revolted, and she quickened her pace, holding up her skirt as she went.

"Just pashing through, or are we looking for a room?" Ruby turned her gaze to the shriveled face of a woman in black, hunched over a cane outside a small wooden house. It had shifted in the unsettled, damp ground, like all the other buildings in Five Points, giving it its distinctive drunken look. But it had windows, which meant the rooms would be light, and it was only one story, which meant she wouldn't have to climb stairs in the pitch black.

"I could use a room," Ruby admitted.

"Come in and shee for yourshelf." A gap in the woman's lopsided smile made her whistle as she spoke. She reached up and pulled a strand of Ruby's hair from her bun, and rubbed it between her gnarled fingers.

Inside, once Ruby's eyes adjusted to the dimmer light, she could see that though the house was small, it was clean. The bedrooms each had a bed and a small table. It was enough.

"How much?" Ruby began to open her coin purse.

The woman grabbed Ruby's sleeve and brought it to her nose, inhaling her smell before Ruby could jerk her arm away from her.

"You don't shmell like a Five-Pointer. New here?"

Ruby nodded, but took a step back.

The woman grinned. "It'sh your lucky day," she croaked. "I'll let you shleep here for free—no, I'll even pay you, if you go in on a little bushinesh deal with me."

"What?"

"Like I shaid, your lucky day. At night, I give you a man to shleep with. We shplit the profit. Shee? It'sh the luck o' the Irish."

"I'm a married woman." Ruby's tone was clipped.

"Don't worry! It don't matter! Shee? Eashy money."

"I'm a clean and decent woman, I am, and I'll not be having any of that." Ruby tucked her coin purse away and marched back out into the street.

The farther she walked toward the star-shaped intersection that was the heart of Five Points, the more trapped she felt. She shared the street with roaming, snorting pigs, apple-hawking peddlers, brightly clad prostitutes, gang members displaying their knives, drunks still drinking, a few plaid-panted politicians, and the occasional frightened but fascinated cluster of "uppercrusts" on a slumming party. Barely hidden from the bold stare of the afternoon sun, dance halls and saloons kept up a lively business.

A small woman in black with a white point lace collar stood out against the crowd. She was clean and modest, and though she must have been there by choice, she did not appear any more comfortable in these environs than Ruby did. She was no Five-Pointer either.

"Excuse me!" Ruby called to her, but being heard above the daily pandemonium of Five Points was useless. She hurried to cross the street.

"Excuse me," she tried again. "You're not from here, are you?"

The woman arched her eyebrows quizzically, but a smile danced in her eyes. "No . . . what can I do for you?"

"Why are you here then? If you don't mind my asking?"

She held up a black leather bag. "I'm a doctor. I have an infirmary in lower Manhattan, where I see my patients for free, but not all of them can make it over there. So I make calls over here and do what I can." She handed her card to Ruby: DR. ELIZABETH BLACKWELL, M.D. NEW YORK INFIRMARY FOR WOMEN AND CHILDREN, 170 WILLIAM STREET, NEW YORK, NEW YORK. "Should you ever need a doctor, you come see me. We are less than a mile south of here."

Ruby nodded and tucked the card into the pocket of her dress.

Dr. Blackwell searched Ruby's face. "Is there something I can do for you now?" she asked again.

"Oh no, I'm not sick, I just—" she faltered. Why

had she sought this woman out? "Maybe you can help me. I just lost my tenement in the Fourteenth Ward, and I need to find a place to stay here—it's all I can afford, you see—but I have been having trouble finding a place that's—suitable."

"Not surprising."

"I guess not. But do you happen to have some idea of a good place around here to live? I've seen some signs for basement cellars for just a few pennies a night. Are those any good?"

"They're cheap for a reason, my dear. Spend many nights there and it will whittle away your health until you have nothing left. I can always spot a basement dweller in a crowd. The skin becomes almost corpselike, and the musty smell pervades not just their clothing but their skin and hair as well. The beds are mere pieces of canvas stretched between poles, and the owners stack them two to three tiers deep. They are so crowded—with people and vermin—I wouldn't recommend it."

"What's left?"

"Well, if you don't want to prostitute yourself—"

"Of course I don't."

"Glad to hear it, and longer life for you then. Have you looked into the House of Industry on Worth Street? Just around the corner, just there, you can't miss it. It's a charitable organization that teaches trades to women and houses them, too.

Mostly sewing but other skills now, too, I believe. If you could find a place in there, you'd be safe and well cared for, at least until the end of your course. Good luck," she called after Ruby, who had already seized her hand to shake it and was headed back toward Worth Street.

The Five Points House of Industry cast a long shadow, like a lighthouse above the raging sea. Hoping this place would indeed save her from her personal shipwreck, Ruby took a deep breath, scurried inside, and knocked on the door labeled "MR. LEWIS PEASE, SUPERINTENDENT."

"Come in," called a tired voice.

Ruby pushed the door open and stepped inside. The desk was covered with stacks of papers and books with pencils wedged into the spines. Articles clipped from the *New York Tribune* were pinned on the walls, trumpeting headlines like "Five Points Mission and House of Industry Gems of Moral and Physical Regeneration."

"I heard you take needlewomen here." Her voice sounded small, even to herself.

Mr. Pease leaned back in his chair and took in the sight of her. "Sort of. We take women and teach them to sew, then we find jobs for them."

"Would you have any use for a woman who already knows how to sew?"

"Hmmm." Mr. Pease drummed his fingers on the desk and grabbed a sheet from the top of a stack near him. "Do you have any aptitude for teaching? We have an opening for an instructor."

"I have been sewing for years. I'm sure I could tell others how to do it."

"I couldn't pay you much, Miss—"

"Mrs.," corrected Ruby. "Ruby O'Flannery. My husband is in the Sixty-Ninth, you see, but they haven't paid him yet, and I simply ran out of money and choices."

"Understood." His face, though weary, held no judgment. Maybe he really did understand. "I must ask you, do you have any references? You'll be working with women who have just come from lifestyles of vice and immorality. We at the House of Industry believe strongly that they'll never be able to succeed unless they completely turn their backs on their old habits. We want them to be surrounded only by positive influences so they don't fall back into whatever means of surviving they had relied upon before. This is why we house our workers here, so they can avoid confronting the degrading lifestyles so rampant outside of these walls when it's quitting time. As an instructor, you could be housed among them if you like. So you'll forgive me if I ask for some character references of some kind. Is there someone who would vouch for you? Surely you understand our need to be quite careful about who we allow to move in among these women."

"References," Ruby repeated. The cogs of her

133

mind turned slowly, but she couldn't get any traction. Who on earth would vouch for her?

"What about your pastor?"

"I'm Catholic."

"Your priest then?"

"I—no, that wouldn't work. I've been sewing around the clock for so long, I haven't had time to go to mass." She looked at him to see if he bought her story. "Believe me. This is why I want to be here, instead. I just can't keep working that way. I'd like to go back to church, really I would."

"That may be, Mrs. O'Flannery, but the fact remains that I must have references before I can accept you. Family member?"

"My husband is off fighting. The rest of our family's in Ireland."

"Can you think of anyone else?"

The only person who knew her very well besides Matthew was Emma. "Would a friend count?"

"Well, it's better than nothing. Name?"

"Emma Connors."

"And where can I reach her?"

"She moved. I haven't got the address."

"Does she happen to work somewhere?"

Ruby looked at her hands. How could she tell him that her only character reference was a prostitute? She told him just a piece of the truth, then. "I don't know where she works."

Mr. Pease put his pencil down. "My dear Mrs.

O'Flannery, you realize you are not making this very easy for me. I'm afraid I cannot accept you until I have at least one character reference, preferably two or three."

A knock sounded on the door, and a small woman with mousy brown hair drawn tightly into a bun motioned to Mr. Pease to join her in the hall.

"If you'll excuse me one moment," he said, and left the room. Ruby peered out the window just in time to see a glimpse of a camel suit disappearing around the corner.

By the time Mr. Pease came back in, his face had gone from warm to cold.

"Mrs. O'Flannery," he said, standing over her now. "We have just received a visitor who has informed us that you and your 'character reference,' Emma Connors, are both prostitutes."

"What?" she gasped.

"Then you deny it?"

Ruby sighed. " 'Tis true, Emma has gone that way, but only out of desperation. And I have done no such thing. I've been true to my husband every day of my life, I have."

He crossed his arms and narrowed his eyes at her. She tried not to hate him for distrusting her.

"It's your word against this gentleman's word, you realize."

Her mouth went dry.

"Listen Ruby, I understand that most prostitutes sell themselves because they think it's the only way out. It isn't, but that's how they feel. I don't condemn you for doing that. What bothers me is that you weren't honest about it. You lied about Emma's occupation, and I strongly suspect you are lying about your own. If you had told me the truth, and that you wanted to repent of that lifestyle, I could have accepted that. But if you aren't honest with me, how can I trust you among vulnerable women who have just left that world to try to make an honest living?"

"But I'm not—a—prostitute!" She squeezed the quavering words around the lump in her throat. "*I* am the vulnerable woman trying to make an honest living, I am!"

Mr. Pease hesitated, then shook his head. "As I said, miss. It's your word against that gentleman's." He motioned to the door.

Ruby stood, hurt and fear and anger burning like fire in her veins. "Aye, and the word of a gentleman is always worth more than the word of a poor Irish immigrant woman. Isn't that so?" She paused, relishing the embarrassed look on his face. Was he uncomfortable? Good. "Is he paying you?"

Mr. Pease turned a shade almost as red as her hair, his eyes wide.

"He is!" she cried. "Well, no wonder you won't believe me!"

"No, no." He took a step toward her. She took a step back. "He didn't give me money to turn you away, if that's what you think. Really."

She crossed her arms. "The whole truth, please."

His shoulders sagged. "He's a donor." He rubbed a hand over his face. "Not a major one, but he has given on occasion, and every little bit—"

"I see." Ruby had heard enough. She was no match for money, and she knew it. She left the building, mechanically, putting one foot in front of the other, dragging herself through the muck. She didn't bother holding her skirt up anymore.

Friday, June 21, 1861

Silverware clinked on china plates as the Waverlys and Carlisles sat around Caroline's polished walnut dining table. It was wonderful having Alice and Jacob visit for the week, but the announcement that Jacob's regiment would be moving to Washington at the end of it gave them more than just steak to chew on.

At long last, Alice had surrendered her desire to be home to her desire to be near her husband. On the condition that she take her French manservant, Maurice Fontaine, Jacob allowed Alice to go with Charlotte to Washington. While Charlotte nursed, Alice would offer her help to the Sanitary Commission during the day. Whenever possible, Jacob would visit her in the evenings.

With Alice as Charlotte's chaperone, Caroline finally conceded that Charlotte could go. But her sour expression showed the bitterness of sending a son-in-law and two daughters to war.

"Please try not to worry about us, Mother," Charlotte said as Jane poured coffee for everyone. "We're officially a branch of the government now that Mr. Lincoln signed the bill establishing the Sanitary Commission. And with Reverend Bellows himself as the president of the Commission, I'm sure we'll be in good hands."

Jacob looked at his wife, concern written on his face. "I should hope so, yes." He glanced back at Charlotte. "But didn't Lincoln call the Sanitary Commission 'the fifth wheel to the coach'? I'm afraid that makes it sound quite useless. What is it, exactly?"

"A godsend to the Union army, whether Mr. Lincoln realizes it yet or not." Charlotte sipped her coffee. "More specifically, though, it's an all-volunteer organization meant to support and supplement the army's Medical Department."

"From what I've heard, it sounds more like a bunch of women trying to take *over* the Medical Department," Jacob countered, a twinkle in his brown eyes.

"Not at all. All of the leadership is male. It's true that the members are mostly women, but we're not trying to take anything away from the army. We're trying to add to it. Chapters of patriotic women are springing up all over the country. They look to the Sanitary Commission to know what

138

the soldiers need—socks, bed ticking, blankets, bandages, the list goes on—and where to send them. Without it, can you imagine the waste and confusion? Well-meaning people would send the wrong things to the wrong places and the soldiers would be no better off."

Jacob gave a slight nod. "So where does the 'sanitary' part of the name come in?"

"The Commission will also try to make sure the mistakes of the Crimean War are not repeated here," Charlotte said. "Overcrowding, poor ventilation, bad hygiene all lead to disease in camp before troops ever get to battle."

"So what can the Commission do about it?" asked Caroline, stirring another lump of sugar into her coffee. "Make them follow Florence Nightingale's models?"

Charlotte shook her head. "Not exactly. We can't make the army do anything. We only make recommendations."

"It only makes sense." Jacob leaned back in his chair. "No outside group should have authority over the army."

"But we can at least educate them," said Charlotte.

"And what did you say you'll be doing while Charlotte's nursing in the hospitals?" Caroline looked at her younger daughter.

Alice twirled one of her blonde ringlets on her finger before responding. "I suppose Maurice and I may also bring supplies wherever they're needed, or write letters for some soldiers. I'm not entirely sure, but the important thing is that I'll be near Jacob, and that Charlotte won't be all alone."

"Oh Alice, Dr. Blackwell told me she'd love for you to visit the other New York nurses and tell her how they're getting along," added Charlotte.

Caroline set her cup down and motioned for Jane to bring more. "That reminds me, girls, I just found out my friend Josephine's daughter will be nursing in Washington, too. Louisa Lightfoot is her name. If you see her, I'd love to hear how she's doing so I can tell Josephine. I'm afraid I don't know which hospital she's in, though."

Alice nodded as Jane made her way around the table, refilling everyone's cup with coffee.

"If I had my way you'd all stay right here in New York." Caroline sighed. She suddenly looked much older than her forty-eight years. "Clearly I have no more authority over you than the Sanitary Commission has over the Medical Department. It's going to be awfully quiet around here once they're gone, isn't it Jane?"

Jane's smile lit up her face. "Not to worry, mum. They may be going to Washington, but we'll have a capital time of our own right here."

But by the time dinner had ended and everyone retired to the bedrooms, even Charlotte could not quell the rising tide of uneasiness now crowding out her confidence.

Shafts of moonlight slanted into her bedroom as she pulled a crisp white sheet up to her chin, but sleep eluded her. Thoughts tangled in her mind like the many-tailed bandages she had first attempted to tie.

What if I don't have what it takes? I have failed at so many things already.

She had done well in all her classes and lessons, but had not put her education to good use. She had followed the doctor's orders in caring for her father, but he had died anyway. She went to all the right parties, wore the right clothes, said the right things, but was still a spinster. From some dark corner of her spirit, a little voice told her that she had failed at being everything a refined young woman of means should be.

She glanced at the discarded steel hoops in the corner of her dressing room, shining in the moon's silver light. They had been better than the heavy crinolines, but they had still kept the world just out of arm's reach, and she had resented them for it. Very soon, she wouldn't need them anymore. It was time to try on a new identity, one in which the things that had previously distinguished her as a lady would be forbidden. No more hoops. No more fancy clothes. No more meals served on silver platters, or feather beds and down comforters, or shopping trips on Broadway, or strolls in Central Park. It wasn't that the war had changed her, as much as it had opened her eyes to another way of living.

There was work to be done, and it was time for her to do it. It just had to be a better fit for her than the life she had been squeezed into so far.

But if I fail at this, too, what would be left?

Anxiety needled at her. Throwing off her covers, she tiptoed to her desk, turned the kerosene lamp to a dim amber glow, and opened the letter she had received from Caleb yesterday, written from his camp at Oak Hill, near Falls Church, Virginia. Seeing his handwriting was like hearing his voice, and a balm of comfort to her soul. She scanned the dark grey scrawls on the page until she came to the lines she was looking for.

If you feel you are called to nurse, as I have strongly felt called to put my practice on hold and enter the hard life of a soldier, then we must both strive to be obedient to that calling and leave the rest up to God. I must admit my days are not what I had thought they would be. My rank is assistant surgeon here, and military protocol demands that I must defer to the surgeon who was given the superior title not because he knows more about medicine than I do, but because he had been in the military longer. We disagree often, and I am often given the more menial tasks—supervising bathing, delousing the men, making sure they throw soil in the trenches.

But I remember Colossians 3:23–24, and it reassures me, as I hope it will reassure you: "And whatsoever ye do, do it heartily, as to the Lord, and not unto men; knowing that of the Lord ye shall receive the reward of the inheritance: for ye serve the Lord Christ."

Caring for the sick is surely the work of the Lord, Charlotte. If you are called to it in any way, throw yourself into it with all your strength.

Beneath his signature, he had jotted the references for Isaiah 45:7 and 1 Corinthians 15:58. Charlotte reached for her father's Bible then and looked up the verses, intending to mark them. There was no need. They had already been underlined by her father's own hand.

Closing her eyes, she took a deep breath, inhaling the rosewater scent that permeated her room. *Lord, help me work heartily, as unto You. I can't please my mother, and it's too late to please my father. I don't fit into my own society, so help me focus instead on pleasing You by doing the work You have cut out for me. Amen.*

Her gaze fell then on the card-size photo Caleb had enclosed of himself with his letter. His serious eyes looked into hers from the tiny card in her hands. Those eyes seemed to see her in a way no one else could, even after all these years had separated them.

Guilt curdled her stomach like Dickens's milk gone sour in the sunshine. *I'm so sorry, Caleb. But how could I tell you the truth?*

When he had left, a year after her father's passing, Charlotte was devastated. Then she was furious. By the time she got his letter on her eighteenth birthday, she wanted nothing more than to hurt him as he had hurt her. *I just don't care about you anymore.*

It was a hateful, vicious lie.

Months later, her anger cooled and good sense returned. She wrote him to apologize. But the day she had planned to send the letter, Dr. Shaw came to examine Charlotte. Though she seemed perfectly healthy, the fact that no menses had started caused Caroline concern.

The doctor's pronouncement: "Barren. For some reason, your womb did not develop."

"Is there no hope?" her mother had asked.

"There is always hope," the doctor had replied. "But without menses, there will be no children."

"Time will tell," Caroline said, tears thick in her voice. She squeezed her hand.

Charlotte stashed her letter to Caleb back in her desk as soon as the doctor took his leave. *He deserves a true woman—one who can give him children. And I don't want him to marry me out of pity.* She waited for months to see if her menstrual cycle would begin. Months turned to years until finally, she retrieved her letter and ripped it up. Time had told. Charlotte would never be able to fulfill her female role to its fullest.

No wonder she was ready to try something else.

Tears blurred Charlotte's eyes. It seemed useless to reveal the truth to Caleb at this point, but surely there was no harm in just writing to each other now . . .

Dickens threaded his way between her ankles, warming her bare skin. His low purring the only sound in the room, a lullaby to Charlotte's ears. The promise of sleep beckoned to Charlotte now from her own inviting bed. She would write to Caleb tomorrow, after the clarity of thought that comes with a good night's rest. But first she pulled out a pair of scissors, snipped a lock of chestnut hair, tied it with a piece of yellow ribbon, and slipped it into the envelope.

Chapter Twelve

Washington City
Tuesday, July 2, 1861

Rumpled and stained with axle grease and soot from their eight-hour journey to Washington City, Charlotte Waverly and Alice Carlisle stepped off the train at the Baltimore & Ohio Railroad Station, Maurice tumbling out behind them. A whoosh of steamy, foul-smelling air rushed up to meet them from the opened doors to the street, like hot, moist breath on their faces. The stench of horse droppings and rotten fruit was so thick in the air they could taste it. The avenue outside the station teemed with people, horses, carriages, and hacks, all of whom seemed either oblivious or resigned to the paste of mud and manure on the unpaved streets below them.

"Shine your boots with Union polish for half a dime!" called out small Negro boys, while white boys hawked newspapers.

"*C'est invraisemblable*! And this is the fine capital of the great Union?" Maurice wrinkled his nose.

Grabbing Alice by the hand, Charlotte wove her way through other passengers who had disembarked just as dazed and damp, until she broke through to the line of cabs. Maurice hailed two hacks to carry them and the trove of supplies they had brought for the boys from Caroline and her friends: towels, old sheets, soap, cologne, oil silk, sponges, a small camp cooking stove, and a spirit lamp. "Treasury Building, please." Charlotte directed the driver to the headquarters of the Sanitary Commission, and they were soon lurching forward, trying to break free of the surrounding mayhem.

"Oh please," Alice interrupted, "couldn't we have a quick tour of the city first?"

Charlotte nodded, much to the driver's delight, and he cracked the reins on the broad backs of his horses.

The tour of the capital was disappointing, if not downright depressing. The "city of magnificent distances" sprawled out in every direction, with long stretches of shanties, taverns, and vacant lots between a few marble buildings looking wholly out of place in the swampy city: the Capitol, the General Post Office, the Patent Office, the Treasury, the Executive Mansion, and the Smithsonian Institution.

"This does not seem like a national capital to me!" Maurice's voice was edged with disdain. "These city planners of yours, have they not taken any cues from Paris?"

Charlotte wished she could disagree with the cheeky Frenchman, but the city was undeniably less than grand. The Capitol building was unimpressive, a blunted, unfinished dome against a washed-out sky, scaffolding holding up the skeletal frame with a metal crane perched on top. Even the marble wings on the old sandstone Capitol building were so new they had no steps yet. Littering the grounds were columns, blocks of marble, keystones, carvings, lumber and iron plates, workmen's sheds, and depots for coal and wood. Rather than a stately symbol of a proud and steady country, it looked instead like an ambitious plan still under construction but with no certainty that any sense of order would ever prevail. Perhaps it was a fitting symbol of the nation, after all.

The unfinished stump of the Washington Monument was surrounded by grazing cattle awaiting slaughter to feed the army. Fish and oyster peddlers cried out from the corners, hawking their wares, while flocks of geese waddled on Pennsylvania Avenue and hogs of every size and color wallowed in the mud from Capitol Hill to Judiciary Square. In some neighborhoods, people still emptied slop and refuse into the gutters, and dead animals into the city canals. Carts of night soil were trundled out and emptied into the commons ten blocks north of the White House.

By the time they arrived at the Treasury Building, one of the very few buildings of any stature in Washington, Charlotte and Alice had seen enough of the city to satisfy their curiosity, but they hadn't seen a single hospital.

"Please wait here until we know what to do with those boxes," Charlotte told the hack drivers as she dropped the fare into their leathery palms. "Maurice will keep you company."

Charlotte and Alice climbed the wide stone staircase of the building, craned their necks to follow the tops of the portico's granite Ionic columns, and entered the imposing front doors.

Inside, however, they found the Sanitary Commission's headquarters barely marked, and not nearly as regal as they had expected. It was a single room with a single table nearly overflowing with papers. A pair of crutches leaned against the wall.

"May I help you?" said a small-boned, delicate-looking man who compensated for his receding hairline by letting his black hair flow to his shoulders. "I'm Frederick Law Olmsted, General Secretary of the U.S.S.C." He rose to greet them, but favored one of his legs.

"Charlotte Waverly and Alice Carlisle." Charlotte presented a letter. "You must have received a letter from Dr. Blackwell already, but here is another copy. Reporting for duty, sir."

"Ah! Fellow New Yorkers, welcome, welcome!"

"I knew your name sounded familiar." Alice's eyes brightened. "You're the landscape architect of Central Park, aren't you?"

"The very same."

"My favorite part of the city, by far!" Charlotte beamed, feeling as though she had just met a kindred spirit. "It is just what New York needed. And if I may say so, if you weren't already occupied with the Commission, I would say you would have your work cut out for you beautifying this city, too! It sorely needs a skilled hand."

"It does that." Olmsted motioned for them to sit. "Built on a swamp, with Potomac flats, formerly used for a sewage outlet, just behind the president's house—it's a ghastly mess. But for now, it's home."

"Indeed," said Alice. "We brought boxes of supplies for the Washington hospitals, only—we didn't see any. Did we miss them?"

"So you noticed." He winced. "Not having enough hospitals is an omission on par with not having enough doctors and nurses. For now, the Medical Department is fashioning existing buildings into hospitals—former hotels, buildings at Georgetown College, even government buildings. I'm afraid they aren't suited for the functionality a hospital requires, but it's all we've got. I trust you will be flexible and can improvise as necessary. That includes, at least for the time being, keeping those supplies with you wherever you stay until I can get some more storage space here. I'm staying at Willard's Hotel, on the corner there, but it's quite full. I recommend the Ebbitt House, just across the street."

"Of course," said Alice. "Where will Charlotte be nursing?"

"I leave that to Miss Dix," he said. "Dr. Blackwell had an arrangement with her that we must respect. Dr. Blackwell supplies the nurses to Miss Dix, and Miss Dix supplies the nurses to the army. You'll need to see her next. Corner of New York Avenue and Fourteenth Street. You might even catch a glimpse of the Seventh New York—the Kid Glove Regiment, they're called here—while you're out that way. Lincoln is reviewing the troops today."

"Thank you, Mr. Olmsted." Charlotte ran her hands over the wrinkles in her skirt in vain. "The hacks we hired at the station are waiting for us outside, so we'll be on our way."

"Please don't pay those thieves any more than you have to. I'll send my carriage with you instead."

By the time the sisters arrived at Miss Dix's house, their hair clung in damp wisps to their necks, and a film of dust and sweat coated their faces. Their dresses stuck to their skin. Even if they had changed their clothes before coming, the five-mile journey across town would have wilted them back to the same state of perspiration they were in now. They waved their fans in front of them, but succeeded only in stirring up hot sluggish air.

Maurice waited in the carriage with the horses in a patch of shade while the sisters marched up the steps and rang the bell. A maid in a crisp white hat and apron answered the door to Miss Dix's house and made no effort to disguise her disapproval of the wrinkled women standing on the doorstep.

"We are here to see Miss Dix," said Charlotte, "about the nursing positions."

"She isn't expecting you." The words were laced with scorn. "And if she isn't expecting you, she won't be seeing you." She began to close the door.

"Has she received her fill of qualified candidates, then?" Charlotte shot back, fully aware that their appearance didn't work in their favor. "There is no more need for women who meet her regulations and have actual training from an actual hospital? My, what good fortune she has!"

The door paused before clicking in the latch.

"My sister has a letter from Dr. Elizabeth Blackwell." Alice's tone was softer than her older sister's, but still firm. "We have only just arrived in town, and apologize if we needed to make an appointment, but since we are here, won't you let us in to see her? It need not take long."

A muffled voice sounded from the other room, and the door opened wide to them. The maid's face reddened only the slightest bit as she ushered Alice and Charlotte into the parlor where

Dorothea Dix sat ramrod straight on a velvet-covered armchair.

"Do sit down," said Miss Dix, after they had introduced themselves. Her black hair was parted in the middle and gathered tightly into a small bun at the nape of her neck. A stiffly starched black dress covered her thin body from the hollow of her throat to her wrists and ankles, the skirt spreading over her knees and spilling onto the floor in an inky puddle.

Charlotte and Alice perched on the edge of a settee, backs straight, ankles crossed, matching the posture of the almost gaunt figure in front of them. So this was the woman who had marched on Washington the very day of the Baltimore riots, when the war was not yet a week old. This was the woman who bent Lincoln's ear and told him in no uncertain terms that he needed help, and that she was the one to give it to him. The woman had pluck.

"You have references?" It was a flat voice, but not shrill.

"Yes, here is my letter from Dr. Blackwell." Charlotte extended the precious paper to her.

Miss Dix scanned the paper, then handed it back. "There must be some mistake."

"I beg your pardon?" Charlotte's heart jumped into her throat.

"I believe I was very clear in my stipulations for my nurses. And if Dr. Blackwell is amused by sending an unqualified candidate, I'm afraid the joke is on her, because I will send you right back where you came from."

"Miss Dix, be reasonable, and tell me what the problem is," said Charlotte.

"The problem, my dear, is that my rules have been ignored by one of my own sex. I am used to not being taken seriously by men, but I must admit I expected more from another woman."

Charlotte shook her head, unable to comprehend the problem.

"Miss Dix, I have been trained for four weeks at the New York Hospital under the direction of the Women's Central Association of Relief, which spawned the United States Sanitary Commission." Miss Dix's mouth twitched in an indulgent smile, but Charlotte continued. "My character is without reproach, I am willing to work under orders, I happily dispose of hoops, jewelry, ribbons, and bows. I confess I do not understand what the problem is."

"I see." Miss Dix squinted at Charlotte and Alice. "How old are you young ladies?"

"Old enough," said Charlotte.

Miss Dix sniffed. "Your insolent tongue proves your youth. How dare you speak to an elder in this manner."

"I had rather hoped that my credentials and determination would be more important to you than the number of birthdays I have celebrated."

"And how many is that, pray tell?"

"If you please, ma'am," Alice said, "I am twenty-six years old, and married. Charlotte is a very old twenty-eight."

Miss Dix smirked. "Miss Waverly, you are single. Another direct contradiction to my wishes of married women only. You are not old enough, anyway."

"Pardon me, but if we're going to discuss age, let me point out that Dr. Elizabeth Blackwell was just twenty-eight years old when she became the first woman to receive a medical degree in the United States," said Charlotte. "And she is unmarried."

"Her practice aids women and children, not men. There is a difference."

"What about Florence Nightingale? Would you turn her away based on her age, if she had come to you requesting to be a nurse?"

"Miss Nightingale is forty-one years old by now. She was thirty-four when the Crimean War broke out."

"But she was twenty-four when she first explored opportunities for women to nurse."

"Miss Waverly, bravo. You have done your research. I commend you. But age isn't your only barrier. You may be proud to hear that you are far too attractive for nursing, as well."

Charlotte, shocked, let out a laugh. "You'll forgive me for saying so, Miss Dix, but 'ugly' was never on the list of desired characteristics the W.C.A.R. put out in the papers."

"But it was on mine. We simply can't stir up the suppressed desires of the men under our care, now can we? Our endeavor would never be taken seriously if the patients and nurses mixed inappropriately. 'Modest, homely, married or widowed, between thirty and forty-five years of age.' I was very specific, for very specific reasons."

Charlotte balked, and Alice reddened.

Miss Dix smiled.

"Miss Dix, I have been well trained. I can do this work, and to be frank, you need nurses who know what they're doing. You can't deny that."

"What I need, Miss Waverly, is for my orders to be obeyed. If I let you in, if I sanction you as a nurse and you do not live up to the standards I have set forth for all female nurses, you will dilute the credibility of my project, and I will be a laughingstock for all of Washington. But I will have no one to blame but myself. So you see, I cannot give you an assignment."

Charlotte stood then, and Alice jumped up a moment later.

"You're thinking of your own reputation, Miss Dix." Charlotte's spine was straight, her chin lifted. "I had thought a reformer such as yourself would think more of those in need, the soldiers, the wounded and ill. It's what you're known for.

Standing up for what's right. What you did for the mentally ill in the insane asylums—you couldn't have done that for your own gain. You did it for the people who could not help themselves."

Miss Dix nodded, clearly suspicious of this line of logic, but nonetheless hypnotized by words of admiration for her thankless work.

Charlotte continued, her breath coming faster now, her words tumbling over themselves as she plowed ahead. "If you send me away, let it be on your own conscience that you'll be doing so to protect yourself. Not the men you swore to serve, the very men who are protecting our country."

Silence.

Charlotte clasped her hands together as she clamped her mouth shut. She had said enough. She could almost feel Alice shuddering next to her, her baby sister who had always wanted to please people, smooth things over, make peace. Sometimes you had to call up a little conflict in order to get to a peace worth having.

At length, Miss Dix spoke. "Miss Waverly, why are you here?"

"I'm here to serve my country."

"You could have stayed in New York and rolled bandages to do that, and gone to much less trouble. I will ask you again. Why are you here?"

"I'm here to make a difference. To do something valuable—"

"To prove to yourself and to the world that

even though you're a woman you can do more than look pretty, you can make the world a better place. Am I right?"

Hesitantly, Charlotte nodded. Where was this leading?

"I understand you completely, to be honest. You and I share this drive in common." The idea of being like Miss Dix may have appealed to Charlotte before she had met her—when all she knew of her was her great strides in reform against all odds. But now, standing in front of this small woman with concern lining her forehead and framing her mouth, with no hint of joy or warmth in her small black eyes, Charlotte bristled at the idea of being like her in any way.

Miss Dix went on. "But your reason for being here is selfish—you may want to help the 'dear boys,' but only as a means of proving to the world—and to yourself—what a good person you are. You're using their weakness to display your strength. Isn't that right?"

Charlotte could feel her face on fire.

"My dear, you are running from something, and you're running so hard and fast, you're so obviously desperate about it that you're willing to make a fool out of yourself in my presence. But hear me: This is war. Not an escape hatch. I will not let you use me as an avenue for whatever runaway scheme has hatched in that pretty little head of yours."

Charlotte felt as though she had been slapped. "Miss Dix, no one is sorrier than I am that you do not approve of me in person as you did on paper when Dr. Blackwell wrote to you. But you had an agreement with her, and with the Sanitary Commission, did you not? I would hate to think of what the Medical Department would say if they found out you were turning away the trained nurse they expected you to supply."

"Good day, Miss Waverly, Mrs. Carlisle."

And they were ushered out the door without knowing for certain if Charlotte's final words had hit their mark.

When Alice tearfully said, "I can't leave Jacob, I just got here!" as though there was even a possibility of being cast out, Charlotte snapped, "We're not leaving. We're not going anywhere."

"But Miss Dix said—"

Charlotte linked her arm through Alice's elbow. "Is there not a war on?" She waved toward the sound of marching, and of drums, and of cheering crowds. "It all sounds like a holiday parade at the moment, but can you imagine what will happen after the first major battle? The streets will be full, clogged even, but not with orderly rows of clean blue uniforms with shiny polished brass buttons. They'll be overflowing with casualties that have no place to go. Look around, Alice; this city is not ready for what is about to be required of her. We can help. We can still help."

"But how?"

"We will find sick troops, and nurse them. With or without Dragon Dix's consent. And you will avail yourself of the Sanitary Commission's needs."

Charlotte led the way back to Maurice and Mr. Olmsted's carriage. Her stride was certain, but the unwelcome words of Miss Dix still rattled around in her mind, their sharp edges chafing against her confidence.

Washington City
Wednesday, July 3, 1861

Charlotte's nerves buzzed like flies as she stepped inside the Georgetown Seminary Hospital. Though no one had sent her here, and no one had invited her, still she had come, wearing her washable petticoats, a grey cross-grained dress, and white apron with large pockets. Alice and Maurice had dropped her off to go scout out some other hospitals, and would pick her up again at two o'clock.

Inside the building, the air was almost as soggy as it was outside. Charlotte went to raise the few windows in sight, but found the sashes to be hopelessly stuck. Perspiration beaded on her forehead, and she could tell even without a mirror that her hair was curling beneath its pins.

With no doctor in sight, she began her rounds of the patients, distributing newspapers and Bibles to those who were awake and wanted something to read.

"Thank you kindly, ma'am!" said a measled soldier who accepted *Frank Leslie's Illustrated Newspaper.* "You've no idea what it's like having nothing to do but stare at the ceiling all day. I even asked Doctor Judson if he would move me to a different spot, seeing as I have all the cracks and such memorized from this point, but he wouldn't do it."

"And where is the good doctor, if I may ask?" said Charlotte.

"What time is it?"

"Ten o'clock in the morning."

"He'll be sleeping off his hangover about now, I'll wager."

"Surely not!"

"Right as rain. Stick around and see if he don't come in all haggard and such."

"Well," said Charlotte, straightening. "I'm more interested in you boys than I am in doctors anyway."

"Take a look at him, yonder, then." The soldier pointed to a bed a few yards away. "He'll have more need of you than the rest of us. He's not long for this world, that one."

Charlotte quickly passed out the rest of her reading materials, and then, stepping lightly among the beds so as not to disturb the resting patients, came to the yellow-tinged soldier whose sheets were fever-soaked. His tattered wool uniform still encased him, though his body radiated heat. Flies buzzed about him, landed in his beard, on his gaunt face and fingers, but he made no effort to wave them away.

Charlotte snatched up a nearby chair and stationed herself at his side, pulled out a fan from her apron pocket and began fanning.

"Mother?" he said. "Is that you?"

"There he goes again," muttered a crusty soldier beside him. "Been asking for his mother for three days."

His eyes fluttered open and tried to focus on Charlotte. "Mother, I'm so glad you're here. I've wanted to see you." His eyes closed again.

"Yes, it's me," Charlotte whispered. *God, if this is a sin, forgive me.* "I'm right here."

"Oh that air feels so good, it's like baking in an oven in here."

Charlotte could feel her own dress darkening with perspiration beneath her arms, her petticoats sticking to her legs. She licked the salty sweat off her upper lip. Still she fanned, switching arms when one became tired, until the sun was directly overhead outside. No ballroom dance, no theater performance, had ever given her more satisfaction than easing the passing of this soldier, whose name she did not even know. She gazed at his face as she fanned him, and thought of his mother. Did she even know he was ill?

Rapid footfalls broke her trance, and her head snapped up to see a short little man with a shiny dome of a head quickly coming toward her. He wore a stethoscope around his neck and a frown on his face.

"Just who are you, and what are you doing with that preposterous fan?" The eyes behind the spectacles were bloodshot.

"Nurse Charlotte Waverly." She kept fanning. "I'm a nurse trained at New York Hospital under the direction of Dr. Blackwell and the Women's Central Association of Relief. "

"You have no business being here. Nurses are commissioned by the Surgeon General, not the New York Hospital. By whose authority are *you* here?"

"Dr.—Judson, is it? The crucial question here is why this young man, clearly riddled with fever, is still in his wool uniform instead of a cooler cotton dressing gown? Do you lack the supplies necessary? Because if you do, the Sanitary Commission can outfit you immediately."

The frown deepened on Dr. Judson's forehead until his eyebrows nearly overshadowed his eyes. Having no response but anger just then, he turned on his heel and walked away, moments later returning with a reinforcement. Miss Dorothea Dix herself.

"Miss Waverly." She tilted her head. "How very curious that I should find you here when I

163

distinctly remember *not* telling you to come. And, as we all know, *I* have the final say in these matters. These patients are not your concern. Not only must you leave at once. You must never return."

Charlotte's gaze swept the room, rested on the fever patient for a moment, then returned to Miss Dix and Dr. Judson. "I have ordered my conveyance to return for me at two o'clock. The sun is hot, and I have no intention whatever of walking out into it. I will remain here and fan this poor man. He deserves no less."

Calmly turning her attention back to her patient, she continued to fan him.

"Say there, ma'am," one of the soldiers said to Miss Dix. "I mean no disrespect, but it does seem to me like this here soldier wants this Miss Waverly to stay, seeing as she's keeping the flies off him in his dying moments and all. Sure would be a shame to take away that last comfort for him, now wouldn't it? Seems like it wouldn't hurt anybody for this lady to just help him die."

Silence hung thickly in the air until it was broken by the sound of retreating footsteps.

Charlotte exhaled the breath she hadn't realized she was holding and focused on the patient beside her. "There, there," she whispered. "Everything's going to be all right."

But with doctors like Judson and Dragon Dix in charge, she herself didn't believe it.

Chapter Thirteen

Five Points, New York City
Wednesday, July 3, 1861

As Ruby walked up Baxter Street, rollicking voices spilled out of taverns and houses on either side of her. Just ahead, marching around in front of a saloon, women holding signs and Bibles from the American Female Reform Society chanted, "Repent of your sin! Turn to Jesus!"

What is my sin? Her heart cried out as she tucked her chin to her chest and walked past them. *What am I being punished for?*

A clear voice rang out above the rest of the women as a plump woman in a dark blue bonnet read from the small New Testament in her hand: "And Jesus said unto her, Neither do I condemn thee: go, and sin no more." Ruby lifted her head and listened.

The voice went on. "Then spake Jesus again unto them, saying, I am the light of the world: he that followeth me shall not walk in darkness, but shall have the light of life."

At this, Ruby did an about-face and marched right up to the woman who had been reading.

"Did I hear that right, missus?" Her voice sounded sharper than she intended it to. "Would you read it again?"

"It's the gospel of John, chapter eight," said the woman. "Do you know the story?"

Ruby shook her head.

"Some men brought to Jesus a woman who had been caught in the act of adultery, expecting Jesus to condemn her to death. But instead, He told her accusers that whoever was without sin should be the first to cast a stone at her. No one did, because everyone sins. Jesus asked her then, if any of her accusers remained. That's where I began reading, at verse eleven." The woman pointed to her Bible at this point and began reading from it. "No man, Lord. And Jesus said unto her, Neither do I condemn thee: go, and sin no more. Then spake Jesus again unto them, saying, I am the light of the world: he that followeth me shall not walk in darkness, but shall have the light of life."

Ruby chewed on her lip for a moment before raising her green eyes again. "I'm not perfect, missus, but neither have I been an adulterer or a prostitute. I'm a clean and decent woman, sure, but I can't make ends meet as hard as I yank on 'em and coax 'em together. I've pawned everything I own but the clothes on my back. I don't want to sell anything else. I don't want to walk in darkness."

"I'm glad to hear of it."

"You and these other ladies here are telling us to not walk in darkness, but where is the way out? Maybe you think I'm some sort of base woman just because you have found me on Baxter Street in Five Points. I'm not here because I want to be, but because all other doors have slammed shut in my face. I'll say it again: I don't want to walk in darkness. But show me the way out of here."

The reformer woman's gaze raked over Ruby's body, but not unkindly. "Where do you live?" she asked.

"Today? Mrs. Sullivan's Lodging House on Baxter Street. But at the end of the week I'm out on the street, in a flophouse, or in a brothel." Ruby wondered how often the woman had heard this story before.

The woman nodded. "You want to get away from here?"

"More than anything, if I can do it without selling my soul," said Ruby. "Problem is, I don't know that I can stay without selling my soul, either."

"Do you have any skills?"

"I can sew. But I can't make a living at it. I keep falling behind in my rent payments. And I already tried the House of Industry—they have no need of me."

"Have you any family responsibilities that require your time?"

Fleeting images of Meghan and Fiona passed in front of her eyes, followed by Matthew. He should be home by now. Or he should have at least tried to find her. But if he came home now, he wouldn't even know where to look. Maybe that's the way he wanted it.

"Miss?"

Ruby blinked and shook her head. "No, no family responsibilities."

The woman pressed her lips together. "I know of an opening for a domestic servant in a smart brownstone on West Twenty-first Street. The help just left, and the mistress wants a replacement right away. Can't seem to keep up with this one— but first I need to know about your character. Have you references?"

Ruby sighed. "None that will help you. But I swear on my father's grave, I am as upright and moral as I can be. I never have a drop of liquor, I don't make sport with my body. I work hard, and I'd never give you a reason to regret placing me. I swear it."

Another reforming woman sidled over and whispered loudly, "But Bertha, is she 'the worthy poor'? How do we know she is worth our charity?"

Bertha took a deep breath. "Ethel, we've been over this before. Charity and justice are two different things. If we are about the work of charity, it's not our place to mete out just conse-quences for the destitute's choices. And look at this one." She gestured to Ruby. "No bloodshot eyes from liquor, her clothing is not that of a prostitute, her posture tells us she has spent years bent over her needlework. She's asking about the

Bible, Ethel, for heaven's sake. What else do you want from her?"

"References."

"Please missus, I can't give you that, but I have to get away from here. Would I have approached you on my own if I weren't serious?"

Bertha sighed. "I hope you're right. I prefer to trust the good in people, although that has landed me in trouble on more than one occasion."

"Get me out of here," Ruby pleaded. "I have no pride. I'm an honest woman, I am. Just give me honest work and I'll do it." *Dear God, if You care at all . . .*

Bertha and Ethel looked at each other then, unblinking.

Finally, it was Bertha who spoke. "All right. Let's get you cleaned up and into some decent clothes before the stink of this place soaks into you any more than it already has. If Jesus gave the adulterous woman another chance, we should be able to give you one, too."

New York City
Sunday, July 7, 1861

The letter in Phineas Hastings's hand was nearly damp with perspiration by the time he dropped it into a post office box. He had tried to forget Charlotte after she had rejected his proposal that humiliating day in Central Park, but it was

169

no use. He had never met anyone else nearly as beautiful and refined. The war would be over by Christmas, this nursing nonsense would come to an end, and they could begin their new life together. Phineas hoped his letter's deep apology and romantic overtures would hit their mark in Charlotte's heart.

Now under the shade of an elm tree on West Twenty-first Street, he ran a finger around his neck, separating it from the stiff white collar constantly sticking to it. The high-pitched hum of cicadas throbbed in his ears as he scanned the street in both directions. No one was coming.

He crossed quickly in long strides before letting himself in the door at number 301 with his key. The strong smells of perfume and silver polish assaulted his senses as he hung his grey bowler hat on the hall stand and combed his black hair in front of the mirror.

"Mother?" he called out, now straightening the red cravat at his neck.

"Parlor!" Fanny Hatch's New York accent dropped the *r*'s from her words, irritating Phineas's sensitivity for proper diction, but he held his tongue and put on a smile as he walked toward her voice and the sound of clicking knitting needles.

"How are you feeling today, Mother?" He kissed her cheek and pulled up a low armless chair, upholstered in red velvet, to sit at her arthritic feet. The joints in her legs had become so painful she rarely moved from her chosen sitting position all day.

"Ah, Pottsy—"

"It's Phineas, Mother," he said, wincing at the sound of the name from another class and another life. "It's been Phineas for quite some time now."

"I don't care what you call yourself, your name is Potter. Always has been, always will be, and you'll always be my Pottsy. So. I was saying? Oh. My health, thank you for asking. It's not good, not good at all. My head aches so constantly, my nerves are so frayed. This city heat is not good for me. And did I tell you the help left?"

"Oh? Which one this time?"

"Bridget. No, Barbara. No, Bridget. Fidgety Bridget."

"I see. And what was the cause?"

"I fired her."

"Ah. For good reason, I am sure."

"Any reason is a good reason, am I right, Potts?" She chortled and slapped a veiny hand upon a darkly draped knee. Not that she was a widow. Or maybe she was, but no one knew. Regardless, it was much easier to play the role of widow rather than that of the abandoned woman. Phineas pinched the bridge of his nose. Any hint of guilt he ever felt for telling people his parents were dead was swept away every time he visited his mother. If anyone learned the truth about his background, his social standing would plummet. His chances as Charlotte's suitor would certainly be over.

"I was saying? Oh yes. Bridget. What a sack of lazy bones, between you and me, Potts, and good riddance. Absolutely no gratitude whatsoever, that one. Kept wanting time off. Lazybones."

Phineas grimaced. She knew how he hated that name, and she still insisted on using it. Without thinking, he reached into the pocket of his suit, pulled out the gold watch, and felt the reassuring weight of it in his palm.

"Well, you must have a replacement, Mother. Have you found anyone yet?"

"As a matter of fact, they sent me some fresh blood already."

"Who's they, pray tell?"

"Well I'll *pray tell* you." She snorted at her joke. "The Female Reform Society. You know, the group of uppity women who say they're trying to prevent the worthy poor from falling into the pit of prostitution. They find girls who are willing to work for very little, as long as room and board are paid for. Usually Irish."

"So tell me about your new girl." He certainly had nothing else in mind to discuss.

"Not nearly so fat as Bridget, a real slip of a thing."

"Starving?"

She shrugged. "Maybe. Didn't ask. And I don't eat with the servants, so I couldn't tell how fast she gobbles her food."

"What are her tasks?"

"Oh, the usual: dusting, polishing the brass and silver, brushing out the carpets, serving and cleaning up after meals. I still have Rose as cook, so I need no help on that account."

"Hmmm, splendid."

"You and your ten-dollar words," said Fanny. Phineas rolled his eyes. *Why do I even bother coming here?*

"I was saying? Oh. The girl is older than most I've had but says she has no family, all's the better for me. Reddish hair, green eyes, very white skin—but not fancy society white, more like sickly white. But she'll brighten up after she's been here a while. Who knows what kind of dark tenement living she's been used to."

"Sounds . . . lovely."

"Gah! Don't matter what she looks like—"

"Doesn't matter," Phineas corrected under his breath.

"What doesn't matter? Oh!" She swatted at a fly in front of her. "As long as she can work. Got a real funny name for a poor Irish girl, too; something fancy and rich-like. What was it?" Fanny gazed absently at the white marble fireplace across the room and pinched her chin until a coarse black hair stuck out between her thumb and the second knuckle of her forefinger. Disgusting habit. "Pearl. No, Emerald. No, Opal. No. Was it Emerald? Like 'the Emerald Isle'?

That's Ireland, right? Ah! Teatime! Good, I'm starved!"

Phineas sighed and rubbed his aching forehead with his meticulously cared for fingers. No wonder his mother's head hurt. She brought it upon herself with all that jabbering away. He could put her in fine clothes, in a fine house, on a fine street, but it was no use. Fanny Hatch didn't have a refined bone in her squat little body—and worse, she didn't care. Not like Phineas did. He had *made* something of himself. And even though he had changed his name—for who had ever heard of a gentleman named Potter Hatch?—he had remained loyal to her. When his father left him the "man" in charge when he rushed after gold in '49, Phineas had taken the charge seriously. He still did. As much as his mother's blunt and uncouth ways grated on his nerves, he would take care of her. She was the only family he had, and he was responsible for her. He just didn't want anyone else to know it.

"There you are, Emerald!" Fanny called out loudly now.

Phineas looked up to see the new girl, hunched over a silver tray laden with teapot, cups and saucers, and a mound of gingerbread cookies. Why was she staring at him that way?

"Come now, Emerald, put the tray down now, we don't have all day." Fanny flapped her arms. "Oh. This is my son, whose name is Potter, but who calls himself Phineas. Phineas Huckleberry. No, Hepzibah. No—"

"That will do, Mother," Phineas interrupted. "Here, let me help you with that." He took the tray from the new servant, but her arms remained bent at the elbows even after the weight had been lifted. Phineas studied her hands, still uplifted, the calloused pinpricked fingertips, before raising his eyes to meet hers once again. He knew this woman. He had seen her before on Broadway. That prostitute Emma's friend. An alarm rang in his mind. *Just how much did she overhear that day? Would she remember it? What was her name again?*

"It's Emerald, isn't it?" Fanny said again. "For your green eyes or your homeland or something?"

"No, missus," she said. " 'Tis Ruby. For my hair."

Chapter Fourteen

Ebbitt House,
Washington City
Monday, July 8, 1861

Charlotte stood by the window in their rooms at the Ebbitt House, watching the endless parade of regiments marching toward Virginia, while Alice paced in circles in their room. Jacob's regiment was scheduled to join them within days.

"Alice, you'll wear a track right through that carpet if you don't stop," said Charlotte without turning her face from the window. Tanned faces and trim bodies eager for battle kept filing by. She waved a little flag out the window for them, which was met by a manly cheer so loud it made Alice jump. Bright eyes and white teeth shone under their forage caps as they smiled at her from their ordered rows, and she boldly smiled back. These were her boys, and they were fighting for her country. For her. *Who could help but love them?*

"Why do you keep doing that?" Alice asked. "You are enjoying all of this far too much."

"Oh come now." She waved a hand in the window again, and roused another hurrah from a new set of faces. "Although you must admit, it *is* rather exciting to be part of history this way, isn't it?"

Alice shook her head. "Being part of history is far less appealing when that history is war, and your husband is leading a charge into battle. Speaking of men, did I see you receive a letter today from a certain man pining away for you from home?"

Charlotte chuckled. "It seems silly, doesn't it? Shouldn't it be the other way around—the love-sick sweetheart on the home front writing to her soldier on the battlefield?"

"We're not all fighters. What did he say?"

"He apologized for being 'rude' to me the last time we were together." *But he was worse than rude. He was frightening.* "And, oh yes, he wants me to marry him."

"What? Where is it?"

Charlotte held up the letter and Alice snatched it from her at once, scanning the slanted lines. "Why, he's quite romantic, isn't he? You know, Jacob never quite warmed to him—but it's not *Jacob* Phineas wants to marry. What will you tell him?" Her eyes were round, and although Charlotte was glad Alice's mind was diverted from Jacob going into battle, she wished her attention was not fixed so firmly on her love life.

"I haven't decided."

"Do you forgive him for his rudeness?"

"I suppose I ought to. He had never done

anything like that before, and he seems apologetic enough. But he has never really liked the idea of my being here, and that bothers me a great deal."

"But now he says he can understand it, and he'll wait for you to be together by—" she glanced at the letter again. "By Christmas. Yes, everyone says the war will be over by then, and there will be no more nursing to do anyway. So will you agree to his proposal then?"

Charlotte looked at her sister and tilted her head to one side, debating in her mind. She could think of no good reason not to marry him as long as she could nurse first. But then, she had trouble coming up with a compelling reason to marry him, as well. She had always thought when the right man found her, she would know beyond a shadow of a doubt. Maybe that's why Dr. Blackwell never married. Maybe that's why Dorothea Dix was still single. Neither had husbands, and both of them had accomplished so much. Did she really have to choose between love and duty?

"Charlotte," Alice said again. "Will you marry him? Women don't get marriage proposals every day, you know. Especially not at your age. You ought to think twice before letting it pass you by."

Charlotte gazed out the window at the soldiers marching by until the last one had vanished from sight. Not one of them had looked back.

Sanitary Commission Headquarters,
Treasury Building, Washington City
Tuesday, July 9, 1861

Frederick Law Olmsted could feel a headache coming on. He was a naturalist at heart, a lover of green spaces and fresh air. Sitting at a desk all day behind towers of papers, in a city that smelled and felt like the swamp it was built upon, did not naturally appeal to him. But it was necessary.

In the last ten days, he had inspected twenty of the volunteer camps around Washington, and he needed to make a report to the rest of the Sanitary Commission. The camps varied on several points, but he could make some generalities, at least.

At the forefront of his mind was the most disagreeable: the sinks. His nose wrinkled at the unwelcome memory of the stench of human waste. Grasping the pen firmly in his hand, he began to write:

> In most cases, the sink or latrine, is merely a straight trench, some thirty feet long, unprovided with a pole or rail. The edges are filthy and the stench exceedingly offensive; the easy expedient of daily turning fresh earth into the trench being often neglected. In one case, men with diarrhea complained that they had been made sick to vomiting by the incomplete

arrangement and the filthy condition of the sink. Often the sink is too near the camp. In many regiments the discipline is so lax that men avoid the use of the sinks, and the whole region is filthy and pestilential. From the ammoniacal odor frequently perceptible in the camps, it is obvious that the men are allowed to void their urine, during the night, at least, wherever convenient.

Mr. Olmsted paused to press his fingers against his temple. How those men could endure to live like that was beyond him. But, he realized, most of them had been plowing fields only a few months ago, and relieving themselves wherever they needed to had become a habit that until now, had hurt no one. Others were city dwellers, but didn't have indoor plumbing or properly functioning sewage systems there, either.

He kept writing.

Personal Cleanliness

In but few cases are the soldiers obliged to regard any rules of personal cleanliness. Their clothing is shamefully dirty, and they are often lousy. Although access is easily had to running water, but few instances are known where any part of the force is daily marched, as a part of camp routine, to bathe. The clothing of the men, from top to toe, is almost daily saturated with sweat and packed with dust, and to all appearance, no attempt is generally made to remove this, even superficially.

Clothing

The dress of the majority is inappropriate, unbecoming, uncomfortable, and not easily kept in a condition consonant with health. It is generally much inferior in every desirable respect, to the clothing of the regulars, while it has cost more than theirs. A New York soldier has been seen going on duty in his drawers and overcoat, his body coat and pantaloons being quite worn to shreds.

The Commission Secretary laid down his pen and gazed at the cufflinks at his wrists. How would he feel, both physically and psychologically, if he wore nothing but rags, and was still expected to march and drill and prepare for battle?

"Mr. Olmsted?"

He jerked his head up to see Charlotte Waverly smiling in front of him. "Miss Waverly, forgive me." He rose and remained standing until she sat on a hard wooden chair opposite him.

"I'm sorry, did I wake you?"

"No, no. I was just thinking about the uniforms

of our volunteer regiments. Most are of fine quality, but some of our New York regiments' uniforms are falling apart, even though they were sewn for them expressly for military use not three months ago."

"Homemade ventilation?" Charlotte fanned herself.

"Shoddy workmanship. Shameful. The men I talked to had to pay $19.50 of their own money for their uniforms, and they were the worst fitting garments I'd ever seen. Poorly cut, poorly sewn. I counted several different shades of blue and grey among them. Some of them didn't have buttons, and some didn't have buttonholes!"

"How is that possible? Weren't they ever inspected before they were delivered?"

"They were, all the more shame. It's a filthy rotten business deal, as rank as any camp latrine I've seen, you'll pardon me for saying so. A trial is going on right now in New York City—apparently Brooks Brothers is to blame."

Charlotte's eyes widened. "Brooks Brothers?"

"Indeed. According to the testimony of a lieutenant colonel in the Twenty-Sixth, the garments were made of this." He plucked a small scrap of material from the corner of the table, dropped it into his glass, and watched as it crumbled to pieces, turning the water a murky blue. "Shoddy. A phony fabric of glued-together sweepings, scraps of cloth, and lint. Looks like the real thing, and then it gets wet—either sweat or rain would do it—and it drops away in clumps. One fellow I met told me his uniform lasted all of a single week. Another said it ripped open upon putting it on for the first time. Scandalous!"

Charlotte gasped and fairly leapt off her chair. "I tried to get that uniform contract for the House of Industry in Five Points, but the State Treasurer refused. Twelve thousand uniforms in three weeks, he demanded, and thought Brooks Brothers could do it! I knew it was impossible!"

"Quite right." Olmsted nodded.

"Now here we are in this cramped little box of a room, trying to do good for our men and our country, without a dime of funding from the government." Her voice grew louder. "And then there are people who are taking in money hand over fist by doing a disservice to those who are already sacrificing their lives for us?" She was fuming now.

"Oh, people are getting rich in New York City, Miss Waverly, you can bet on it. They call themselves loyal Unionists, but all they care about is lining their pockets. Not much we can do about that, aside from calling attention to it." He drummed his fingers on the report in front of him. "That's all we can do about any of it. Identify the problems, make recommendations, and hope somebody in power will take it to heart and make some changes. The problems facing the army are much, much bigger than they care to realize. I fear that we ourselves are only seeing a small sliver of what needs to be reformed. But we can be sure of this much: if the army continues along like this for much longer, the Union will indeed dissolve like shoddy."

Act Three

WORKING HEARTILY

I HAVE SEEN SMALL white hands scrubbing floors, washing windows, and performing all menial offices. I have known women, delicately cared for at home, half fed in hospitals, hard worked day and night, and given, when sleep must be had, a wretched closet just large enough for a camp bed to stand in. I have known surgeons who purposely and ingeniously arranged these inconveniences with the avowed intention of driving away all women from the hospitals.

These annoyances could not have been endured by the nurses but for the knowledge that they were pioneers, who were, if possible, to gain standing ground for others,—who must create the position they wished to occupy. This, and the infinite satisfaction of seeing from day to day sick and dying men comforted in their weary and dark hour, comforted as they never would have been but for these brave women, was enough to carry them through all and even more than they endured.

—GEORGEANNA WOOLSEY, written in 1864

Chapter Fifteen

Washington City
Sunday, July 21, 1861

St. John's Church was emptier than usual today, and the conspicuous gaps in the high-backed pews distracted Charlotte from the sermon. Outside, the steady sound of carriages, gigs, hacks, and wagons rolling by was like one continuous low roll of thunder, punctuated by riders' laughter and song, and by champagne bottles clinking at their feet.

The first great battle of the war appeared to be imminent at Manassas, Virginia, about twenty-five miles west of the capital, and Congressmen, thrill-seekers, and sightseers did not mind breaking the Sabbath to picnic on the scene.

"Some trust in chariots, and some in horses: but we will remember the name of the Lord our God," the pastor was saying, quoting from Psalm 20:7, and bobbing heads agreed. God was on their side, the Union boys would surely win the day. Alice let out a deep breath.

Charlotte couldn't keep her mind from wandering to the fate of both her brother-in-law, Jacob, and dear Caleb. But they were in God's hands, not hers, just like the outcome of the battle. And everyone expected the Union army to cinch around the Rebels and close in tight, until Richmond, the new capital of the Confederacy, was in the noose.

After the service, stepping out into the blazing sun, General Winfield Scott, in his full dress uniform, shook hands of those faithful few who had not crossed the Potomac. "We shall have good news by morning," he told them. "We are sure to beat the enemy." And he left to take his afternoon nap.

Ebbitt House,
Washington City
Monday, July 22, 1861

The sun rose on July 22, but it did not shine. The morning dawned sullenly in a drizzle of rain, and with it came a knock on the door waking Charlotte from her slumber. A sharp rapping, incessant, urgent, demanding. Throwing her long flannel wrapper about her, she opened it just enough to see Mr. Knapp's face, etched with news she did not want to hear.

"Come quickly, you and your sister." He was nearly breathless. "We have been defeated at Bull Run and the soldiers are coming back to us—twenty miles of marching, through the night, after two days of battle, and nothing to eat, nowhere to go." His words spilled out all at once with no breath in between. "You must come immediately; the Commision is setting up tables on Pennsylvania Avenue and Fourteenth Street, for they are coming over the Long Bridge and the Chain Bridge and Aqueduct. They must have food; they are falling down in the streets. We are only seeing the first of them now, but who knows how many more are yet to come."

Shock numbed all physical sensation in Charlotte, but she managed to nod at Mr. Knapp's retreating back as he hurried away. She did not feel the door under her hand as she closed it, or the cold brass knob of the kerosene lamp as she lit it, or the soft round shoulder of her sister as she shook it.

"Alice, come," she heard herself say. "Get dressed. The men are flying back to us. Hurry."

Picking up Maurice on their way out the door, they fled the hotel as if death itself was on their heels, when in reality death—or the possibility of it—was what they were running toward. This was not happening. They were supposed to defeat the Rebels at Bull Run and crush the Confederacy altogether. It was supposed to end the war. How could they have been defeated? The hope of a short war disintegrated just as the uniforms fell apart in the downpour.

At a hastily assembled station on Pennsylvania Avenue, Olmsted and two white-haired women were already handing out chunks of soft bread.

In the rain they stood, tears and rain mingling together on their faces, and Charlotte and Alice joined them. Nearby residents, hardly believing what their eyes were telling them, told their hands to work, and so provided a steady supply of food to the tables.

"Water!" was all one soldier said as he lunged at the table. Charlotte brought a cup to his lips and he drank it as if his mouth were on fire. "We've walked forty-five miles in thirty-six hours," he said weakly. "There was no water after the battle in Centreville, for the army drained its wells dry on the way to Bull Run. You're going to have some very thirsty soldiers here, ma'am!"

By six o'clock, the slow stomp and splash of soldiers' retreating feet rose above the drumming of the rain. First at a trickle, then in a swelling stream, by noon the tide of returning soldiers was flooding the dark avenues of the Federal City. Smoldering fires glowed in the streets, made from boards the men wrenched from citizens fences to warm them.

"Look at them," Mr. Olmsted said to Charlotte. "Would you think them soldiers by looking at them now?" Muddy, smoke-stained, and unshaven, no two of them dressed exactly alike, some without caps, some without shoes, some without coats. Charlotte scanned the faces—some of them with black grins of cartridge powder sketched on them—for a glimpse of Jacob or Caleb. She

190

wasn't sure she would recognize either of them anymore.

Occasionally an army ambulance would clatter by, either driven by a terrified hired civilian, or commandeered by a terrified fleeing soldier, but not one of them carried a single wounded man.

Rumors rushed at anyone who would listen, crushing around them like an overpowering current.

Seventeen thousand Union killed!

They killed our wounded for sport!

Entire regiments were cut to pieces!

The Rebels will take the city by tomorrow morning!

"Stay calm," Mr. Olmsted said to Charlotte and Alice. They did not look up from their tasks, their vision blurred with tears and rain. They handed out bread and water as if their bodies were separate from their minds. *Here is bread, here is water,* said Charlotte's mouth, but her heart was screaming, *Where is Jacob? Where is Caleb? Where are the officers, where are the wounded, and where is the Grand Army of the Republic?*

"There must be some wounded finding their way into the hospitals." Mr. Olmsted scanned the street up and down. "Go, take whatever you need from our stores. Take my carriage."

Slowly, the wheels turned through the crowded, muddy streets, until Charlotte, Alice, and Maurice could pick up boxes of hospital gowns, splints, bandages, and lint and carry them to the village of Georgetown, clinging to the outskirts of Washington like a smudge of axle grease on a hem.

"This is a hospital?" Maurice asked as they lumbered up in front of the Union Hotel. "*C'est une blague!*"

"Only in a manner of speaking," said Charlotte. "Not every building should be made into a hospital."

If their arms weren't full of boxes as they entered the ramshackle building, all three of them would have instinctively shielded their noses against the foul odors assaulting them.

A small man in wire-rimmed glasses approached them. "More women?" he growled.

A woman with her grey hair in a bun swept into the room. "Never mind Dr. Wiggins. I'm Anna Moore, matron of this hospital. What have you got for us?"

"Hospital clothes," said Charlotte over the top of her box. "Bandages, lint, and splints."

"Wonderful, we could certainly use those." Anna clasped her hands.

"Put them there," said Dr. Wiggins, still scowling. "What else?"

"What do you need?"

"Delphinium, for killing vermin. These men are crawling with lice, and we have nothing for it.

And solution of persulphate of iron, to restrain bleeding."

"Did the Medical Department not provide you with medicines?" Charlotte frowned.

"Some. Not these. Can you help us or not?"

"Maurice, would you please find Mr. Olmsted again and ask him for these?" Alice fished out a scrap of paper and pencil from her apron pocket and wrote the names down, then sent him on his way in the carriage.

"How can we help?" asked Charlotte.

"Go to the kitchen for hot water and rags, wash the men—one of you upstairs, one of you here—and pass out whatever clean hospital clothes you brought, for we have none here. We have one hundred eight patients at present, and I fully expect more to come in."

Many of the battered soldiers looked as if they hadn't had a change of clothing in days or weeks, which would have been bad enough from camp life, but evidence of battle now crusted their uniforms—or what was left of them—to their bodies in places. Charlotte, whose white, slender hands had never touched a man's naked body before, hesitated for the slightest moment before following her orders. She had been assured during her training that there would be male stewards for this task. If her mother found out, if the gossip circles learned of this . . .

A snatch of Caleb's letter came back to her,

then. *And whatsoever ye do, do it heartily, as to the Lord, and not unto men . . .*

Armed with washbowl, soap and rag in hand, she came to her first dirty specimen and dabbed delicately his withered old face, careful of the dirty bandage that encompassed his head.

"Aaaaaah," he sighed with a checkered grin. "The honor of a lady to be washin' me! Bless ye, darlin'!" The old Irishman's pleasure took her by such surprise that they laughed together. Trousers, socks, shoes, and legs were one big mass of mud, and if he hadn't already taken off his shoes in front of her, she would have thought he was still wearing tall muddy boots.

"Where are you from, soldier?" she asked, scrubbing away at the layers of filth.

"New York City, lass, the Sixty-Ninth Regiment. A fine lot of lads we have, too, but our Colonel Corcoran didn't make it back with us. Captured, more's the pity. I'll bet he's givin' the Rebels a heap o' trouble now!"

Finding they shared a hometown in common, they found much to talk about. When she finished washing him, his wrinkled face beamed.

"Here now," she said, handing him fresh white hospital clothes. "Do you think you can manage to get your uniform off and put these clean clothes on yourself? Do you need any help?"

"Well, bedad! Look at that! I can manage, darlin'."

Charlotte went on to the next patient, and the next, going back to the kitchen every two or three patients for fresh water. Some took the washing like sleepy children, leaning their heads on her shoulder as she worked, while others looked silently scandalized. Several of the roughest colored like bashful girls when she tenderly touched their neglected bodies.

"May I try to make you more comfortable?" Charlotte asked the next patient. He turned to face her then, revealing a gunshot wound in his swollen cheek; only one eye remained.

"Might I have a looking glass?" he asked her.

It wasn't the wound itself that caused Charlotte's stomach to revolt. It was the juxtaposition of the disfigured half of his face next to the other half, still perfect, with its clear brown eye and bristly black lashes, high cheekbone and strong jawline. He had been handsome, indeed, and if one only looked at his left profile, he would have the appearance of all the bright strength of a wholesome youth.

Stuffing down her own emotion, Charlotte found a looking glass and brought it to him, praying he would see himself as a hero.

After a long gaze, he turned away from his reflection, and a tear welled up in his remaining eye. "What on earth will Sarah Brown say?" His voice cracked.

Charlotte took the glass gently from his hand,

and knelt down to his level. Placing a hand gently on his left cheek, she said, "If Sarah Brown has any sense at all, she will admire you all the more. You have faced the enemy, full on. You did not turn away, did you? No, you met him. This is your lasting mark of courage and honor."

"Do you think so?"

Charlotte nodded, willing herself to keep her tears in check. "Women consider a wound to be the noblest decoration a brave soldier could possibly wear. You are honorably distinguished."

He closed his eye and smiled faintly then as she washed his face as gently as she could before handing him his clean clothes.

When every man in the hotel-turned-hospital had been washed, there was a heap of muddy, soiled, blood-encrusted uniforms to be dealt with.

Dr. Wiggins was now making his rounds, inspecting wounds in the lobby. "Doctor, what shall we do with the dirty clothes?"

"Burn them," he muttered.

"And send them back to their regiments in hospital gowns? Surely not. Come now, you must have a laundry facility nearby. How do you wash the bed linens?"

He peered over the top of his spectacles at her then. "Do I look like a maid? Since when has laundry been the business of the surgeon in charge?"

"Well it must be somebody's business—"

"Then make it yours and let me do my job."

Swallowing the retort on her tongue, Charlotte turned and made her way up the dark, narrow stairway.

"Mrs. Moore?" she called, looking in the small rooms for the matron. "Mrs. Moore, I'm glad I found you. We have mounds of dirty laundry from uniforms the soldiers arrived in. What provision has been made for them?"

"Well, they need to be washed, don't they? And the bed linens, too; we're almost out. These fever patients soak them with sweat, and the dysentery patients, well—the poor dears, they can't help it."

"I agree. Where are your laundrywomen?"

Anna straightened and placed her hands on the small of her back. "Well, the position is currently open. Do you want a job?"

"What? No laundresses?"

"Oh, we've hired plenty of people, but we can't keep them here. You said you wanted to help, didn't you? Well, I'm afraid this is the help we need."

Charlotte's memory reeled back to the clean wards of New York Hospital, where she was in training, so she supposed, to be a head nurse. To supervise, to give directions. *All the most disagreeable hospital tasks will be handled by others,* they had said. *We would never dare ask the respected, refined ladies of society to work like slaves or immigrant day workers.*

"I'm not—I'm not trained for that," she stammered.

"You want training? I'll train you. Make a fire. Heat the water in the copper cauldrons. Shave soap into the water, stir it with a broom handle until it foams. Add the clothes, stir them up. Scrub any stains by hand on a washboard. Transfer to rinse water, hang to dry. If you see any piles of clean linens from yesterday, heat some irons and press the stiffness out. Fold. Repeat."

"You're serious."

"It's not a punishment, dear, though I know it may feel like one to your soft white hands. It's just a job that needs to be done. Think of the soldiers. Do it for them. OK?"

"She'll do it," said a small figure in a black crepe dress and a cameo brooch at her throat. "You did say you wanted to nurse, didn't you?"

"Doing laundry is not nursing, Miss Dix. I'm a little overqualified for that task, I'm afraid."

"I told you weeks ago. You are not a nurse here, for I did not accept you. If you want to stay, you will do as Mrs. Moore says and administer the linen room or I'll send notice to the Medical Department at once that you are not to be allowed in any hospitals in Washington or the surrounding vicinity."

"You know as well as I do that you are using your position to an unfair advantage," said Charlotte.

Miss Dix smirked. "No, I'm making a point."

"And that is?"

"That single young women have no business in an army hospital. That my policies were devised for good reason, because what is required of you now will prove to be too much for your gentle sensitivities. That my guidelines must be enforced." Her voice quavered. "To the letter."

Charlotte straightened her spine, lifted her chin and turned once more to the wide-eyed Mrs. Moore. "If you'll please be so kind as to direct me."

"All the way to the basement. You'll smell it before you see it."

Nodding, she turned and headed down the rickety staircase.

The smell of wet, rotting wood grew ever stronger as Charlotte descended into the pit of the hotel. She found the linen room abandoned, heaped high with soiled sheets so rank with filth and human waste she would have vomited if she had eaten any food that day. She tied a couple of her handkerchiefs together, end to end, and wrapped it around her face to shield her nose from the stench. It didn't help, and only made her feel as though she were suffocating.

Mrs. Moore's instructions had taken no more than a moment to communicate. Carrying them out, however, took hours. For as much as she hated to admit it, Miss Dix was right about one thing: Charlotte Waverly had never done laundry in her life. She could have just as easily said she was under qualified for the job as she was overqualified. Precious time ticked away on failed attempts to light a fire, only to have the flame snuffed out when she opened the door to the alley to fill pails with water from the pump. Shaving the soap into the water should have been the easiest part of the job, but she soon learned she needed to soak it in water to soften it; the bar of soap was as hard as a block of wood. The razor skidded across its surface, slicing into a fingertip. She wished she could be washing people again instead of their sheets and clothes.

Her back already aching from lugging the pails of water inside, she picked up piece by stiffened piece of laundry with the end of a broom handle and plunged it into the foaming, boiling water, stirring and agitating it until she thought the lice had died and most of the soil had dissolved out of the fibers. The water turned a yellow-brown. She scrubbed the stubborn stains on a washboard until her knuckles, already raw from the water and caustic soap, cracked and bled.

When her first loads had been washed, they needed to be rinsed, which meant more pails of water to be hauled in from the pump outside in the mud to the wooden tubs inside.

Since it was raining, Charlotte tied lines of twine upon which to hang the sheets until the low-ceilinged room looked like a maze of almost-white linen.

By the end of the afternoon, she had managed to wash three baskets of sheets, while nine more dirty piles waited, reeking even worse now from the humidity of the boiling water in the room. The uniforms hadn't even been touched yet—these soldiers wouldn't be needing them for a little while anyway.

She longed for nothing more than to take off her shoes, but her feet had swollen from standing on them all day and she wasn't sure she'd be able to put them back on.

"Mademoiselle?" It was Maurice, holding his handkerchief over his pinched nose.

"Did you get the medicines Dr. Wiggins asked for?"

"*Oui*, and at Mr. Olmsted's request, I brought supplies to five other hospitals in the city as well."

Charlotte nodded her approval, too tired to say anything she didn't have to.

"Mademoiselle, you must eat. Come up, the cooks have provided buttered rolls, soup, coffee. We are serving the men, and you must eat, too."

"What's happening out there?" she asked as she trudged up the narrow stairs in front of him.

"All day long, the army staggers into Washington like sleepwalkers," he said. "Some residents shout to taunt us, rejoicing in the Confederate victory."

"Any word from Jacob?"

"*Non.* I checked the Sanitary Commission office and the Ebbitt House. Nothing."

By evening, the stream of soldiers had slowed, and Charlotte, Alice, and Maurice finally took their leave of the Union Hotel Hospital, promising to come back tomorrow.

After tying Mr. Olmsted's carriage to a post behind Willard's Hotel, where he had a room, Charlotte and Alice dragged themselves back to the Ebbitt House, their sodden, mud-splattered petticoats and skirts pulling at their legs; Maurice, just as dirty and wet, beside them. Willard's was swarming with officers who appeared free of shame and dejection, as would be expected after such a defeat. Newspaper Row was twitching with news that would recant their earlier tales of victory, shocking the North with the ugly truth of retreat, collapse, defeat, as the capital city sat mired in mud, awaiting imminent capture.

Inside the Ebbitt House lobby, a single soldier stood waiting, covered in mud and soot, looking as though he were about to fall over.

"Alice, give that man some bread, if you have any left in your pockets." Charlotte headed to the front desk to send a telegram home.

A muffled cry behind her caused her to turn around again.

"Jacob!" Alice was sobbing into his filthy shoulder now, but no one begrudged them the display.

Charlotte stood back for a few moments while her sister and brother-in-law reunited. Tears mixed with rainwater on her cheeks once again, bitter and sweet together, just as the joy of the moment was tainted by her growing anxiety for Caleb.

Chapter Sixteen

New York City
Saturday, July 27, 1861

I should never have let her go. Phineas crumpled Charlotte's latest letter and jammed it into his pocket, nearly popping the stitches with the force. *I should never have let her out of this city, out of my sight.* The evening's chorus of chirping crickets seemed to be laughing at him incessantly. His breath came faster, his legs propelled him farther down Twenty-first Street in a blind fury. He kept his head down so no one would see his eyes under the brim of his black bowler.

He had written to Charlotte begging her to come home now that disaster had befallen so near to her. He had been kind. Romantic, even. At least he had thought so. But firm. And she had written back—but not for days—and said no.

She said no to me.

She had defied him, like his mother had always defied his father. The thought made him sick.

He should have known this would happen. There hadn't been a male influence in the Waverly household for twelve years, and oh how that void had taken its toll. Charlotte was used to thinking for herself, making her own decisions, without any sort of leadership over her to protect her from her own poor choices. She was acting like an overindulged child who thought she knew best. *Were her hands even soft anymore, or were they rough and cracked? Was her skin still lily white, or had she thrown off her bonnet and let herself get tough and brown? Was she gallivanting about town in a dull dress stained with another man's blood and vomit?* His stomach roiled at the thought.

She can't do this to me, she just can't.

She was a lady, proper, refined, beautiful. Everyone knew it. But now, her "adventuresome tales" from Washington were circulating in society circles like wildfire, as if they were Dickens's latest installment of *Great Expectations*. She was becoming less known as the beautiful, talented daughter of the widow Waverly, and more as the bold, brave, hardworking girl who willingly put herself on the level with low-class servants! She had thrown herself off of her own pedestal to rabble about with the ordinary people. It was bound to stain her. When you mixed clean water with dirty, it always came out dirty. And that was a fact.

The rattle of a horse and carriage grew louder, and Phineas began walking again with measured strides, as if no fire burned within him at all. The carriage trundled by, and he was alone with his thoughts—and those blasted crickets—once more. His eyelid twitched.

He couldn't stand it. She was moving away from him, and he had no control over it whatsoever. She was doing it to make him angry, the cunning little thing. Oh those eyes, they look innocent enough, but there's more to Charlotte Waverly than sweetness and light. He knew it. She knew what his wishes were, and she was rebelling against them.

Like his mother had rebelled against his father. Maybe, just maybe, his father never came back from the gold rush because he had given up on his wife ever obeying him, ever following his wishes. His father's disappearance had always been a mystery, but this now . . . this made sense. The constant harping, the willful disobedience . . . Who could live with that? If his father abandoned them because of his mother, he could understand it.

But it was cowardly. A man shouldn't be subject to the weaker sex. God made man to rule the woman and woman to be ruled by man. His father should have stayed and made sure he had the upper hand. If his mother didn't listen, he could have been more—persuasive. He should have been the man of the house. Instead, he had run away.

The coward.

But Phineas Hastings was no coward.

A quick sweep of the street in both directions confirmed he was still alone. Thundering up the steps of 301 West Twenty-first Street, he thrust his key into the lock and cranked it counterclockwise before shoving it open and slamming it shut behind him. He threw his hat on the stand in the hall and strode into the parlor to find that his mother, Fanny, had fallen asleep on the armchair. Her head tipped back, her jaw slack, knitting needles sticking idly out of her round, chubby fist like pins stuck in a pincushion. A gurgling sound rattled in her throat.

He shook his head in disgust and felt his temperature rising. He had given her all the trappings of a lady, but it was no use. She was a cheap imitation of the real thing. He hated her for it. If anyone found out that she was his mother and connected him with her, he would be labeled part of "the shoddy aristocracy," a class of people with just enough money to pretend to be rich. Some clever little newsman for the *Herald* had brought the phenomenon to the forefront of society's attention after the Brooks Brothers scandal over the uniforms made of shoddy hit the papers. The columnist just couldn't resist coining the term, and it had taken off. Now everyone was talking about it, how Fifth Avenue was filling up with Mr. and Mrs. Shoddy, with pianos that were all case and no music, gold that was all glitter and no carat, art that was all frame and no original masterpiece. Now every time someone mentioned the word "shoddy," whether in connection to Brooks Brothers or people, he suspected they were trying to make a point about him. *Enough!*

Fanny snorted loudly then, waking herself up. Her body jerked, the knitting needles clattering to the ground, and she saw him standing over her.

"Pottsy!" she said, and inside he seethed. "Come give us a kiss." Flabby arms reached up to embrace him.

"Afraid I don't feel up to it today, Mother," he said icily.

She retracted her arms to her sides. "Foul weather brewing?"

"I should say so, yes, as a matter of fact."

"Should you really? Oh my! As a matter of *fact* even? Heavens no! Whatever could the trouble be?" She was mocking him now, openly, brazenly, the way she had mocked his father until she had driven him away. He clenched his teeth until his jaw ached.

"Did you really expect father to come back?" His voice was low, steady, strangely calm. He slipped his hand into his pocket and wrapped his fingers around his watch.

Her watery eyes narrowed under droopy lids. "What kind of a question is that?"

"When he left for the gold rush. Did you know he was leaving us then?"

"Of course! He left to find gold. For a better life for us."

"Silly me—yes. He left to find gold, that much I'll wager is correct. But for a better life for *us?* Are you sure?"

Fanny gawked. "I can't understand you."

"My bet—and I'm very good at betting—is that he went off for a better life for himself. A life that did not include us, and one that was indeed, decidedly better."

"Why in tarnation would you figger that? What's gotten into you, boy?"

Phineas cossed his arms over his waistcoat. "It was you. Gold might have been the reason he left, but you were the reason he stayed away. Your constant bickering, pestering, heckling. You never respected him, did you?"

"Respect? I loved him. Didn't need to respect him, too."

"Ridiculous woman! You can't love a man *without* respecting him. But if you didn't respect him—and we know you didn't—all he felt was derision from you."

"De-what?"

"Oh yes. I forgot. Let me make it simple for you and your childlike vocabulary. You made him feel unloved and stupid and worthless. Do you understand? No man can live like that forever. It was only a matter of time before he did something."

"You can't blame me for him abandoning us!"

"No, it wasn't all your fault. He could have chosen to stay and do a little housekeeping in his family. He should have put you under his thumb and never let up."

"How dare you speak to your mother that way!"

He whipped around to face her. "How dare you pretend for *years* that you were the victim of a circumstance out of your control! You preyed on my sense of responsibility toward you, the same way you preyed on father's weakness."

"You give me too much credit. I have no control over you."

"I didn't have to provide for you the way I did."

"Oh yes you did. For your own sake, though, not mine. And that's why you'll never stop, either." She tapped her temple. "I'm not so dumb as you think I am, boy. You been trying to get away from your roots ever since you been waist-high. Couldn't have a poor momma, then, could you?" Another tap at her temple to prove her point. "You always do only exactly what you want to do. You live for yourself alone."

He opened his mouth to speak, but she held up a hand to stop him. "Gah! No use denying it, boy. You and I are cut from the same cloth, and it sure as heck ain't silk." She smiled then, knowingly, with the devil's gleam in her eyes. "Shoddy."

"What did you say?" All the frustration and

anger and disappointment boiled into a foaming rage.

Fanny threw back her head and cackled with diabolical glee. "Oh, don't think I don't know your little part in that sleazy business with the uniforms. I've got eyes, haven't I? Ears too."

Phineas crossed the room in two long strides and hovered over her like a thundercloud charged with electricity. "Talk."

"I don't know how you managed to make a little mint from it without your name getting dragged through the mud now with everyone else's. I don't know what you did to keep them from coming back for you and pulling you down with 'em. But you made off with a sum, didn't you? And no one suspects a thing." She shook her head in reluctant admiration.

"I should throw you out on the doorstep right now—"

"Doubt it! You do and I'll blab to the mayor and all your precious law professor colleagues about the dirty way you padded your income. Now understand, I don't mind so much, but I think they might. Something about a law professor not doing something that's strickly, you know, legal. Could be I'd have a mind to tell 'em all about the real Potter Hatch, and I'm just not sure they'd like to know you weren't completely honest about that rich and fancy blood you pretend like you've got runnin' in your veins."

Phineas ran a hand over his goatee and stared at his mother's smirking face. Technically, what he had done wasn't illegal. As a longtime patron of Brooks Brothers, he had simply helped them arrange a lucrative business deal—considered beneficial to both parties at the time—and accepted a "commission" on the contract. It was all off the books, of course. He knew how to be careful. But if anyone found out about his role in the matter, the investigation alone would ruin his reputation.

And my own mother is blackmailing me. Dark spots of rage dotted his vision.

"See what I mean? You and me, Pottsy, we're both the same. Shoddy. Only I don't mind so much. Facts is facts. But you—it's eatin' you alive."

"Cup of tea?" Ruby rounded the corner with her silver tray.

"Starving! Pottsy, join me for tea, won't you?"

"I regret to decline," he said through clenched teeth and stormed out the front door.

New York City
Sunday, July 28, 1861

Tiny beads of sweat formed on the back of Ruby's neck under her straw bonnet as she scanned Broadway up and down for any sign of more returning regiments. *Would I even recognize him? Would he recognize me?*

212

Up until last week, finding Matthew had been the recurrent thought nagging at her like a young puppy nips its owner's heels. But when news of the battle at Bull Run reached her, an ache had filled her chest until she was sure it had completely replaced her heart. She had no idea if he was dead or alive. More troops had come home yesterday, in defeat, their three-months' tour of duty complete, but as far as she could tell Matthew was not among them. *Where is he? Does he lie bleeding under the sun somewhere?* Perhaps he was on his way home to her even now. If he returned to her without a limb, it would mean any construction or labor job would never be his again. She hated that she even thought about that when his body could be already heaped up and forgotten in a dead-house somewhere.

Ruby wandered in and among the noisy throng listlessly until she came to an abrupt stop on some stranger's heels. He wheeled around to face her. A chill swept over her body.

"Aha, good day to you, Ruby." Her mistress's son doffed his cap and bowed to her. "Just the little lady I wanted to see. Let's take a walk, shall we?" He offered his arm, and she hesitantly placed a hand on it, wary of doing anything that might jeopardize her current employment.

Phineas clapped a large hand over her small one and held it firmly beneath his palm. She walked alongside him, silently, as he steered her through the teeming mass of people. Soon they turned a corner into a side street, and the din of the swarming shoppers on Broadway gradually fell away.

"Better, yes? Now we can actually hear each other," he said, still walking. "Let's just have a little chat now, shall we?" He grinned down at her. "You are looking quite well Ruby, much better than when you first started working for my mother."

"I s'pose it's so, sir."

"You're getting enough to eat? Sleeping well?"

"Oh aye, sir, perfectly well."

"Good. You don't look nearly so gaunt as you once did. Skin looking healthier, back a little straighter. And this is a new dress, isn't it? Charming. The green really brings out the color of your eyes."

Ruby nodded. It wasn't fancy like most of the other ladies on Broadway, but it was the nicest calico dress she'd ever owned, no holes anywhere. When she had seen it in the pawnshop, the tiny pink roses on a light green background seemed to nod to her on their dainty stems. She couldn't help but wonder, when she had bought it, if the previous owner of the dress would be coming back for it later, hoping to buy it back once she'd received her proper pay. But for Ruby, the dress had been a promise, fresh as spring, of a brighter tomorrow. One in which rags were replaced by black dresses and stiff white aprons during the week, and pretty, clean dresses on the weekends. No more hunger. No more being too cold or too hot. For Ruby, the dress was a symbol of hope.

"Lovely. Listen, I don't know how much you heard last night when Mother and I were having our—discussion. But it was a private affair, and I can't have you telling anyone else about it."

He tightened his grip on her hand. Still they walked, farther away from Broadway, away from the noise, away from the people. Did he know where they were going?

"Fine, sir, I didn't hear a thing anyway, I didn't." They had crossed Lafayette Street, and were still walking toward Centre Street. Her eyes widened and her pulse quickened. Soon they would be on the edge of Five Points.

"See that's the thing. I'm not sure you're telling the truth."

"Please sir, I'd rather not go any farther if it's all the same to you."

"You told me once that you were a needle-woman, and then I found you serving tea in my mother's house. You told me you weren't a prostitute, and yet here you are, on your Sunday afternoon off, walking the streets along with the rest of them. You do see my dilemma now, don't you, Ruby? I'm afraid I just can't trust you."

"Please sir, I'm a clean and decent woman, sure."

He steered her into a dark doorway then, and propelled her up a narrow staircase until he unlocked a room and shoved her inside. "There now. Now we can have some more privacy."

Only a bed and chair shared the small space. From beyond the thin walls she could hear the unmistakable sounds of people coupling in other rooms, as if they were in their own homes in the middle of the night and not in a public house a few blocks from New York's busiest street, while the light of day still shone. On a Sunday.

"Where—?"

"My own little room in this fine House of Assignation," he explained. "Oh well, it's not very fine after all, but who can tell in the dark?"

Her skin crawled. She rubbed her hand where he had been gripping it and stepped away from him.

"The problem is, you've become a liability to me, Ruby. What does any good businessman do to protect against liabilities?"

She shook her head, her mouth suddenly gone dry.

"He takes out insurance, of course. That's all I'm going to do, Ruby." He tossed his hat onto the bed and stepped toward her trembling body. Twirled the ribbon of her bonnet around his finger. "I just need a little insurance."

He yanked on the ribbon, untying it in a single jerk, pushed the bonnet off her hair and let it fall with a clap to the floor behind her.

She looked sideways at the door.

"Locked. Afraid you're stuck with me for now, Ruby. But don't worry, they all tell me I'm really quite good." His breath smelled slightly of whiskey, but this man was not intoxicated. He was calm, calculating. A lock of his jet-black hair curled onto his forehead as he leaned in.

His hands groped her hair, pulling the pins out until it tumbled loose around her shoulders. Lifting a handful to his nose, he smelled it. "Mmmmm. I'm glad you've been using the water closet since coming to my mother's house. This would be far less pleasant if you still smelled like a dirty immigrant living with the pigs."

Trapped like an animal in a cage with its predator, her chest heaved with shallow panting.

"Trouble breathing?" he said with a smile. "I can fix that too."

As he reached for the buttons at her collar, she struggled to knock his hand away, but he caught her wrist and twisted her arm back until needles of pain shot up to her shoulder.

"Listen Ruby, there's no use fighting it. I've simply got to have my insurance, and you're the only one who can give it to me. You hit me, I'll hit you harder. You kick me, I'll kick you until you walk with a limp and call it an accident. Don't think I won't. So just relax, you might even enjoy yourself."

"I thought a gentleman was supposed to protect a lady, not beat her!"

"Quite right. But you're not a *lady,* are you?"

"I *am* a lady, I am. I'm not a prostitute!" Her

voice sounded hoarse, as if the screaming she had been doing in her mind had already taken its toll on her throat. Her heart beat wildly against its cage.

"You are now. But here's the nice thing. You and I have an understanding. You keep my secret, and I'll keep yours. We wouldn't want Mother finding out her domestic is a prostitute, would we? You'd be out on the street in no time. And if the American Moral Reform Society finds out, why, I'm afraid they simply wouldn't be able to place you anywhere else, now that you're—well, reprobate. Whoops, big word, pardon me—hopelessly immoral?"

One by one, he unfastened the buttons of her bodice, slowly, tauntingly. Her eyes squeezed shut. With each open inch of her blouse, her body became stiffer. She imagined the roses of her dress being crushed beneath Phineas's feet. Tears flowing out from beneath her lashes and streaming down her face, she concentrated with all her might on the words of a prayer, not at all certain any prayer could be heard in the midst of a cardinal sin.

Holy Mary, Mother of God, pray for us sinners. Pray for us sinners. Pray for us sinners. Holy Mary Mother of God, Oh God please no Jesus Mary and Joseph please dear God Mary Mother of God please pray, please pray, dear God don't cast me away please Holy God don't leave me here dear God sweet Mary this is not my sin, it's not my sin, it's not mine it's not . . .

Chapter Seventeen

Washington City
Wednesday, July 31, 1861

Frederick Law Olmsted puffed on his pipe, the sweet, tangy smoke swirling, dividing, curling above his head in perfect chaos. Much like Bull Run, according to the report in front of him.

No pattern, no system. Absolute chaos. Disaster, and not just for the army, but for the government's Medical Department, as well. No commission member had been able to learn of a single ambulance that had carried a wounded soldier from the battlefield. Not one. The military drivers took their orders from the Quartermaster Corps and would not take orders from doctors on the field. Other vehicles, driven by civilians, had whipped their horses and fled the field at the first sound of firing. As a result, the worst cases of wounded soldiers had been simply left to their fate on the field. Some doctors stayed and were captured even as they tended the wounded.

The stampede of soldiers coming back that had begun July 22 and lasted for another three days had been only the least severely wounded, with a few exceptions. One boy who had his arm amputated on the field walked twenty miles to

Washington, only to die of gangrene within a few days of landing at the Union Hotel Hospital. All but five hundred wounded had been left on the field, their wounds undressed, exposed to the elements for days.

Those who had made it back to Washington City had only six hospitals to receive them, most of them improvised from former uses: an old hotel, a seminary, a college. Olmsted had sent a committee to inspect them on July 29, and had just received the report.

The Union Hotel Hospital Georgetown, was occupied as its name implies until recently hired for its present use. The building is old . . . with windows too small and few in number to afford good ventilation. Its halls and passages are narrow, and in many instances with carpets still unremoved from their floors and walls covered with paper. There are no provisions for bathing, the water closets and sinks are insufficient and defective, and there is no dead-house. The wards are many of them over crowded and destitute of arrangements for artificial ventilation. The cellars and area are damp and undrained and much of the wood work is actively decaying.

The Seminary Hospital, in the immediate

vicinity of the last is much better adapted to Hospital purposes, though it also is defective in water closets and baths and many of its wards are small and imperfectly ventilated. The absence of facilities for artificial ventilation will be productive of serious disease.

Olmsted scanned the next few paragraphs describing the Infirmary, C Street, and The Columbian College Hospital and The Alexandria Hospital, both formerly used for academic purposes, and found the same phrases throughout. *Narrow and tortuous passages. Poor ventilation. Totally unfit. Overcrowded. No deadhouse. Total want of water closets. No running water.*

Olmsted scanned down further to read of the treatment the patients received.

In the opinion of your Committee the medical and surgical treatment extended to the sick and wounded in the Hospitals is in the main excellent, and the supply of surgeons ample. The medical students supplied for the emergency from New York, as surgical dressers, with a few exceptions, proved very useful to the surgeons and were doing excellent service. The female nurses, also, as far as your

Committee could ascertain, were of great comfort to the sick. They were tolerated without complaint, and in several instances their services were even highly spoken of by the medical officers in charge. In regard to male nurses, on the contrary, there was much complaint as to their inefficiency and want of aptitude and disposition for their duties. This was especially remarked of the volunteers.

Well, thought Mr. Olmsted, *hurrah for Dr. Blackwell and her female nurses.* It was little wonder that the male nurses were complained of. All of them were convalescent soldiers. None of them had an interest in nursing anyway. Many of them tired quickly, and as soon as they began to master the duties required of a nurse, they recovered enough to return to their regiments, leaving a new batch of convalescents to be trained. *If I had signed up to be a soldier and found myself spoon-feeding other grown men and emptying their chamber pots instead, I'm sure my disposition would be lacking, too.*

The next few paragraphs were no surprise to Olmsted since hearing the account of Miss Waverly and Mrs. Carlisle: no hospital clothing, and no means to wash the dirty uniforms. The Sanitary Commission had made sure every patient had fresh hospital gowns within three days of the battle, and had employed laundresses to wash the soiled uniforms.

The services of a barber were also authorized to be procured for the sick, and your Committee can bear witness that he contributed not a little to their cleanliness and comfort. Wire frames for the protection of wounded limbs from the pressure of bedclothes were found to be wanted and they were supplied. Water beds of India rubber; drinking cups with spouts for administering food and medicine; splints, bandages, and lint have also been furnished. Bed tables with writing paper and franked envelopes have also been obtained and it is proposed to add easy chairs, games, and other articles for the comfort and amusement of convalescents, as they seem to be desirable.

A fifth wheel to the coach, indeed! Olmsted shook his head at Lincoln's ludicrous label for the Sanitary Commission. The aftermath of the first major battle proved the Commission's work was absolutely critical for the soldiers. A sense of vindication swelled in his chest. The last paragraph of the report before the list of recommendations, however, deflated him.

... if a larger proportion of our wounded had been consequently brought by ambulances to the Hospitals together with the wounded of the enemy, the Hospital accommodations and supplies would not have been sufficiently ample to have met their wants and the expectations of the nation. We would suggest that Government cannot err in making the most liberal provision for the sick and wounded and in the promptest manner by the accumulation of large stores of bedding and hospital supplies at safe and available localities near the main body of the army. It is a just estimate to assume the necessity of providing for ten percent at least of sick for an army in the field; and this would bring the number nearer 15,000 than 1,500, whilst with hard-fought battles in prospect, and the sickness of the autumn months, the percentage to be provided for will probably be much higher than this estimate.

Suggestions for improvement followed, as always: New pavilion-style hospitals, fully provided with water for bathing, washing, and water closets, with no more than thirty to sixty patients in a building, and ample space between so as not to poison each other. More trained nurses. A military hospital in the harbor of New York for overflow sick. Fix the problems in the current hospitals . . .

Mr. Olmsted signed his name and date to the end of the report, indicating it had been accepted and adopted by the Commission, and hoped it would not fall upon deaf ears. Surgeon General Finley had made no secret of the fact that he despised the Commission for all its criticism and "nosing around." Cooperation thus impossible, the only leverage the Commission had to move the government toward reform was that of public opinion.

Well, this should give the public plenty to form an opinion about.

Columbian College Hospital,
Washington City
Thursday, August 1, 1861

Charlotte dabbed a violet-scented handkerchief against her damp forehead and neck and stepped out of the scorching sun into the shade of the Columbian College Hospital—still hot inside, but at least it wasn't as bright. After she had spent a full week laboring over the laundry at the Union Hotel Hospital, Mrs. Moore had hired some Negroes to do the job, and Miss Dix had sent Charlotte here to nurse instead. It was about time.

"And you are?" A stout man with red hair and beard looked down at her.

"Charlotte Waverly, sir. Miss Dix sent me. I am at your service, trained in New York Hospital."

"Is that so?" His bushy eyebrows raised, looking more amused than impressed. "I'm Dr. Murray, and I don't need your help."

"Oh no, no, I'm sure you are very capable, Dr. Murray. I don't mean that you personally need help, but what about the patients? In a hospital of this size, couldn't you use another set of hands for dressing wounds, changing bandages, washing the men, feeding them, that sort of thing?"

Dr. Murray was walking away now. "Not interested, lady. Go knit some socks."

"If it's socks you need, then socks you shall have, along with anything else you request from the Sanitary Commission stores." Charlotte trotted alongside him to keep up.

"Splendid. We'll take three hundred pairs of socks, then, as much morphia powder as you can give us and—one other thing, what was it now? Coffins. Yes, we would like five dozen coffins as soon as possible, if you please."

"Coffins?"

"Or did you expect me to put the bodies in the ground in blankets? India rubber would probably be best. Waterproof, you know. Yes, if you have no coffins, send me blankets. You can help roll up the bodies."

"Dr. Murray, I don't understand you."

"Of course you don't." He stopped and turned to face her. "Here's the thing—the army does not give me what I really need. Like coffins. Like a dead-house. Like running water and water closets. But what I emphatically do *not* need, that it sends me." He looked at her pointedly, and she felt her cheeks grow warm.

"Perhaps you didn't ask for me, Dr. Murray, but I am willing to prove my usefulness to you."

"I told you already, I'm not interested. I don't need a woman to take care of when I've got two hundred fifty-eight patients to look after."

"I can take care of myself."

Dr. Murray shook his head.

"I'll do anything you need." Charlotte stood her ground.

Dr. Murray looked her over from head to toe, while Charlotte hid her broken nails and red, chafed hands behind her back. Finally, light sparked in his eyes and he nodded.

"All right, I've got a job for you then. As I mentioned, we have two hundred fifty-eight patients in the hospital presently, which includes the wards inside as well as the tents outside—for patients with typhoid fever, dysentery, erysipelas. Nasty stuff. As I also mentioned, we have no water closets. Zero. Which means, these men are continually filling up the chamber pots in their close stools. It's becoming a real problem for us, as you can imagine. Contagious disease emanating into the air from the vapors and all of that. You want to help? Empty the chamber pots. There's a trench in the rear. Just don't fall in."

"You're trying to force me out, aren't you?"

"Not at all!" He smiled. "The army has decided for me—without even asking my opinion—that I should have women nurses. I can't do anything about that. If you should decide to leave on your own, however, that would be entirely up to you."

"I have been assigned here, and I'm not leaving."

"Well, that's a relief." Charlotte ignored his sarcasm. The doctor pointed to the staircase. "You can start up there. The third and fourth floors haven't been emptied in a while. Too many stairs for the convalescent nurses, you know." He sighed. "It's going to be so nice having you here, Miss Waverly, especially with your *New York education*. We'll put it to good use."

As she turned to go, he called out after her. "But don't trip! It would be such a shame to get your snowy white apron dirty."

Up the stairs she marched, with a fistful of skirts in one hand and her handkerchief pressed to her nose with the other. When she reached the top and entered the first room she came to, she almost gagged on the stench. The rooms were barely large enough to hold a bed and a single chair. The patient, a large, dark bearded man with his leg in a fracture box, colored in shame when he saw her. "Don't come in here, miss, the air ain't fit for a lady such as yerself," he said.

"Well, let's see if we can take care of that, shall we?" Charlotte bent down to the close stool to slide the pewter chamber pot from beneath it.

"Lord a'mighty, why on earth are you doing that awful job?" He looked so mortified on her behalf that her heart ached with a desire to restore this man to some sense of dignity. But there she was, standing in front of him holding in her bare hands a bowl nearly brimming with his own urine and feces. The fact that the situation was no fault of his own made it no less humiliating.

A feeble, "Let's just get this out of here and I'm sure you'll breathe much easier," was all she could manage before slowly, carefully, making her way down the hall and down the staircase. All her concentration was required to keep the bowl steady as she climbed down the stairs. She held her breath for as long as she could before gasping for another supply of air. Her nose tingled and her eyes watered. *And I thought laundry duty was bad.* She carried in her hands a perfect cesspool of contamination, its wretched vapors spreading in the air with every step.

"Whoosh!" A woman stepped into the stairwell and waved a hand frantically in front of her face. "What on earth are you doing?" she asked Charlotte.

"Somebody needed to empty these chamber pots." She barely looked up. "I'm Charlotte Waverly, a new nurse here. And you are?"

"Cora Carter." She pinch her nose closed. Ruffles and bows on her fuchsia-colored dress flapped with every step she took downstairs.

"Not a nurse, I take it," Charlotte said slowly, still concentrating on her bowl. "What's your business at the hospital?"

"Why, I'm a *nurse,* same as you!"

But Cora didn't look like any nurse Miss Dix would have approved. Maybe she was attending a brother or sweetheart herself. "You have a loved one among our patients?"

"Oh yes." Cora giggled. "Heaps of them." And with a flash of gleaming white teeth under unusually pink cheeks, she glided down the rest of the stairs, leaving Charlotte alone with the foul-smelling chamber pot and her own suspicions.

At the bottom of the stairs, another voice startled her from behind.

"Goodness me, dearie! Bless you for doing that!"

Turning, slowly, Charlotte saw a pleasantly plump woman with greying brown hair, black dress, and white apron. The only adornment was her warm smile and bright eyes. Now this was a Dix nurse if she had ever seen one.

"I'm Hannah Stevenson, of Boston. Just got here a few weeks ago, myself."

Charlotte nodded. "Charlotte Waverly, pleased to meet you. Today's my first day."

Hannah bobbed her head up and down, her double chin quivering with each nod. "I can see that. Dr. Murray doesn't quite appreciate what we do here but the men are unspeakably grateful."

"Are there many? Nurses?"

"If you stay, you'll make five. There are three other physicians besides Dr. Murray, each of them younger-looking than you, no offense."

"I haven't met anyone besides Dr. Murray and Cora."

"Cora. Cora Carter? Did she tell you she's a nurse?"

Charlotte nodded.

Hannah pursed her lips. "Well dearie, I wouldn't swear on a Bible on that one. She goes in and out of the rooms all right, but never carries a roll of bandages in her hand or any hint of grief for their suffering on her face. That one's trouble, that's what. Whew! I'll let you be now."

Charlotte nodded and smiled, grateful for at least one friend in this place, and carefully conveyed her stinking cargo out the rear of the hospital. Outside, the earth beneath her feet had hardened into sun-baked ruts and ridges, threatening to throw off her balance. Her poise and posture training came back to her from her old refining school in Philadelphia, and she deftly navigated the terrain without spilling a drop of the waste. *Wouldn't my teachers go into apoplexy if they knew how I put their training into use today?* She chuckled to herself in spite of the appalling work.

Charlotte found a water pump, rinsed the bowl, threw the rinse water back into the trench, and climbed the four stories to return the bowl to its rightful owner. From start to finish, it had taken her almost ten minutes to empty one chamber pot. How many patients left to go? Two hundred fifty-seven? It would take her all day and she still wouldn't be done!

Fine. She lifted her chin. She would manage somehow, just as she had managed the laundry. At least the patients were grateful. It really was too much to ask anyone to be in the same room with those pots day after day. At least she could do her duty and be done with it.

After twelve hours of the same tedious, stinking labor, Charlotte had emptied most of the chamber pots in the four-story building, but none in the tents. Tomorrow would be easier, since the tents were already outside and on the same level as the trench.

"So you've decided to leave us after all." Dr. Murray stopped her just before she could walk out the door.

"I'll be back in the morning to do the rest." Charlotte stifled a yawn.

"I don't think you will."

232

"Pardon me?"

"If you walk out that door, you're clearly not committed to nursing. What nurse leaves her patients?" His eyes were as cold as his voice.

"I'm leaving the chamber pots, that's all. And I told you I'll be back."

"A deal is a deal. I can't force you out, but if you leave on your own accord, I must allow it. You just won't ever come back, that's all."

"Fine. I'll sleep here."

"Admirable. But I'm afraid we don't have suitable accommodations for a woman of your station."

Her eyes narrowed. "Then what sort of accommodations do you have?"

"The army sort. You're working for the army, you should live like the army."

"Speak plainly, Dr. Murray. I'm tired."

"Then why don't I just use pictures instead. Follow me."

Charlotte followed him outside, around to the rear of the building. Between the tents of patients with communicable diseases and the trench, itself full of communicable disease, he pointed to a patch of earth and said, "There."

She looked down at the ground. "There what?"

"You really are exceedingly simple, aren't you? This is your army-style accommodation for the night."

"You can't be serious."

"I assure you I am."

"I understand a bed would be far too much to ask for, but even those men have cots." She pointed to the tents. "Are you saying there is not one extra cot to be had?"

Dr. Murray shrugged. "Moot point. You're not sick, are you, that you should need a cot? No, perfectly healthy. As such, you will sleep like a soldier who is perfectly healthy."

"Even soldiers have blankets to lie upon."

"The lucky ones. You're not so lucky tonight, it seems. Oh, and, if you need to relieve yourself, help yourself to the trench like the rest of us."

The two stood facing each other, opposing each other, neither of them willing to give in.

"Well then." It was Charlotte who broke the silence. "I'll just need to send my sister a message so she doesn't wonder where I am."

"Sorry. Soldiers don't have access to telegraphs, messengers, or even to a very good post system either, for that matter. Hard to find stamps and a postman when you're in camp, you know. So no, soldier, I'm afraid a message would be impossible."

Though the night dew cast a chill upon her, the heat of anger kept her body warm long after Dr. Murray locked himself inside the small house on campus where the physicians slept. No one had ever treated her this way. Men had always fallen over themselves trying to flatter her. But that was a lifetime ago, and she had surely been a different person then. These army doctors did not see her beauty and charm—if she had any left. What they saw was a threat to order and male superiority. Dr. Blackwell had tried to warn her that their path would be thorny, but Charlotte didn't think even Dr. Blackwell realized what the women nurses would be up against. Charlotte seethed. Before today, if anyone told her this would happen to her, she would not have believed it.

But neither could she believe that she had lasted this long. She could last another night, and another day, and then do it again. And again.

The steady rhythm of the crickets' song pulsed in her ears to the faint beat of martial music. Columbian College Hospital was surrounded by encampments. The orange glow of their campfires dotting the horizon as the stars above the pine trees studded the black velvet sky. Had she really been in a feather bed in New York City only one month ago?

As dark grey clouds swirled in front of a sliver of moon, she untied her apron, turned it inside out and folded it into the shape of a crude pillow. *What do soldiers do in camp when they have no blanket or pillow?* Charlotte laid her weary body down on the cool, hard earth as a breeze of damp night air swept over her, bringing the eye-watering stench of the trench with it. She pulled the apron string out from her new pillow and covered her nose with it. *If I were ever to contract a contagious disease, this would be a remarkably opportune time.*

Washington City
Friday, August 2, 1861

When the first red streaks of dawn warmed the grey sky in the east, Charlotte pushed herself off the dewy ground with a groan. Her thighs were stiff from yesterday's climbing, her back ached, and her shoulders were sore from being hunched up to her ears during the night, trying to keep warm. If she hadn't been so completely exhausted, she wouldn't have been able to sleep a wink.

She needed to find a water closet, and quickly. She could endure many things in the name of nursing the dear soldiers, but relieving herself over a filthy trench in plain sight was not one of them. She hurried—as much as her sore muscles would allow—to the hospital entrance and breathed a sigh of relief when she found it unlocked.

But now where? If this had been a normal hospital, there would be a water closet in the lobby. But this was completely abnormal, and there wasn't a single water closet on the property. She'd have to use a close stool. And fast. She had been holding out all night, plus several hours before that. The need was becoming urgent.

She walked down the hallway, looking for a vacant room, but they had filled the ground level first. Footsteps sounded behind her—she ducked into a room and found the patient sleeping.

Please Lord, let him stay asleep!

She pushed the door closed, lifted her skirts and squatted over the stool. A faint trickling sound registered in her ears.

Oh no. This was one of the pots I hadn't had time to empty yesterday. Now it was overflowing the bowl, seeping into the wood floor beneath it.

Charlotte glanced at the still form on the bed next to her. Mercifully, he still slept. She held her breath as she bent down to dislodge the pot from the stool. She watched it carefully as she worked—the last thing she needed was to get this waste all over her dress.

Noiselessly she opened the door with her foot and began her slow journey out to the trench.

Dr. Murray stood in the hall talking with another surgeon, judging by the gold medical insignia on his armband. Charlotte kept her chin tucked to her chest and focused her eyes on the rim of the bowl she carried, wishing she could go faster, praying she would go unnoticed.

"I'd watch over his care myself, but I've got to get back to New Haven to muster out by the seventh," the surgeon was saying. "Please keep an eye on him. His wife has already passed and he has three small children waiting for him at home with an uncle."

"I keep an eye on all my patients, despite what few resources I have to work with," she heard Dr. Murray say. "Oh *nurse!*" She had passed them by a few paces, but he came trotting up to her. "Pardon me a moment, doctor," he called over his shoulder.

"So how did you enjoy camp life last night?"

"That's neither here nor there, doctor. The point is I remained here, and I have returned to my duty." Out of the corner of her eye, she noticed the other surgeon approaching them. She must look a fright, her hair wild with humidity, slipping out of its pins. Her dress was rumpled, wet and soiled.

"You don't mean you made her sleep outside last night, Dr. Murray?"

Charlotte kept her back to him, unwilling for him to see her cheeks blooming with heat.

"Says she wants to be a nurse, like a man. I don't suppose you have to deal with these strong-minded women as a regimental surgeon, do you? No, they're just in the general hospitals. They're swarming around Washington, like flies. Don't know when to leave. This one is the most stubborn girl I've seen yet."

Charlotte smiled without thinking.

It was the wrong decision.

Before she even realized what had happened, the front of her dress was dripping with urine and blood-tinged liquid feces, the rancid fluid soaking through her dress and into her corset.

"Are you mad, man? What do you think you're doing?" The visiting surgeon stepped between them, took the bowl from Charlotte's shaking hands and set it on the floor on the side of the hallway. He gave her his own embroidered handkerchief, and though she took it, wordlessly, she could not tear her eyes away from the dark filth spreading its misshapen stain like gangrene on her chest.

"She's clumsy." Dr. Murray shrugged. "You should be more careful, Miss Waverly."

"Charlotte?"

She looked up into grey eyes, framed by lines of worry. She rubbed a thumb over the initials on the handkerchief in her hands: CTL.

Oh no. Not like this. After all these months, she did not want Caleb Lansing to see her like this! But at the same, she could think of no other face she would rather see at this particular moment.

In the corner of her vision, she could see Dr. Murray watching her, waiting for her reaction, just willing her to shriek or cry or show any hint of alarm that might be construed as an emotional outburst. Female hysteria would disqualify her from nursing on the spot.

She would not give him the satisfaction. Though the fibers of her dress were soaked with contagion that may never come out, and a cry of indignation, disgust, and self-pity was already swelling in her chest, she pushed it down with all her strength, fighting for control.

"Why Dr. Lansing." She lifted her chin and took a deep breath. "You should have told me you were coming, I would have put on something more—presentable." The sound of her laughter surprised even herself, and apparently stunned Dr. Murray.

"You—you know each other?" His gaze flitted between Charlotte's dirty face and Caleb's stony expression.

"This woman belongs to one of the finest families in New York City," began Caleb.

"That has no bearing in an army hospital."

"She is a lady, and you are treating her like a slave."

"No, Dr. Lansing, she wants to do a man's job, and I'm trying to show her she doesn't have what it takes."

Caleb looked at Charlotte then. Hair coming down from its pins in damp wisps about her face and neck, dress and apron drenched with dew and diarrhea—and yet still standing tall.

"Doesn't she?" A corner of Caleb's mouth turned up under his mustache. "But that's not the only issue here, is it? Even if you don't get along with Miss Waverly on a personal level, I would think your sense of professionalism would keep you in line. Do you realize that this bowl contains discharge from chronic diarrhea? It's bad enough to order her to carry it through the halls this way, but to intentionally agitate the contents reveals an alarming recklessness."

Dr. Murray crossed his arms and cocked his head. "Finished?"

"Well, gentlemen," Charlotte interrupted, almost unable to swallow her gag reflex any longer. "I'm sure you've realized by now, I stink. Very badly, I'm afraid. If you'll simply allow me to change my dress, I shall return to take—"

"You leave, you don't come back."

"Nonsense." Caleb offered Charlotte his arm as an escort. "You'd be a fool to dismiss the bravest nurse you have. If she wants to come back, you'll accept her, or I'll report your behavior—and I do mean all of it," he tilted his head toward the chamber pot on the floor, "—to the Medical Department. You're a contract surgeon, aren't you? Not enlisted in the military yourself? Well, there are plenty of other doctors who would like to have your job right now, and believe me, that can easily be arranged. Now I strongly suggest *you* empty that pot of its contents and return it to the patient before he has to relieve himself on the floor."

With Charlotte's hand looped through his

arm, they walked out the front door, leaving a glowering Dr. Murray behind them. As grateful as she was to be leaving, something told her this little episode would not make her way easy when she returned.

A dozen thoughts tumbled over each other in Charlotte's mind, each one clamoring to be on top. *Where had Caleb been during Bull Run? Why didn't he send word he was safe? What was he going to do now?* But none of them could compete with the odor reeking from her body.

A low moan escaped her lips. "I am so disgusting," she said as Caleb helped her up into the army ambulance wagon on which he had brought his patient.

A smile softened his tanned face. "You know, this isn't the first time I've seen you like this." He tucked a strand of her hair behind her ear and her heart beat faster. "It didn't bother me then, and it certainly doesn't bother me now." His skin looked harder, weathered by sun and wind.

"You must admit, I reek," she said, as the wagon lurched forward.

"You are still the loveliest thing I've seen in a very long time."

Charlotte peered up at him, studied his face. He wasn't just tired. He was unwell. "What have you seen, Caleb?"

His eyes turned to steel and he looked straight ahead, then down at his hands.

"Nothing I would wish to tell you about."

"Caleb, I was here after Bull Run, at one of the hospitals. I saw the men who came back after the battle. You can tell me."

He shook his head. "You didn't see what my eyes have seen. The worst never made it off the field."

"But you helped those you could. You must find some comfort in that," she offered.

"I'm afraid I can find no comfort while my men are cut up and dying. I am their doctor. I am supposed to heal them. But these hands—" He held them up, his rough fingers spread wide apart, and shook his head, as though they had betrayed him. "These hands are no match for the weapons of war."

"But I'm sure you tried . . ."

"Of course I tried!" he snapped at her then, anger flashing in his eyes, before letting out a ragged breath. "Day and night, without food or water or shelter . . . the endless screaming of shells . . ." Caleb wasn't seeing her, she knew; he was back on the field in his mind. "My eyes were stinging from the sweat. Gun smoke in my throat tasted like sulfur. We were supposed to have ambulances, but the drivers fled without taking even a single patient for help. Hundreds left to bleed in the cornfields. I tried. God! I tried." It was a confession, not blasphemy. He put his head in his hands, gripping a thatch of his hair until cords of veins raised themselves on the back of his hand.

"I know you did," she said quietly. "You were the one who reminded me to work heartily, as unto the Lord. I know you did."

They sat together unspeaking, the only sound the wagon wheels turning on the ground beneath them.

"Everything I learned in medical school is useless," Caleb began again. "I have to relearn everything, practicing on living, breathing, human beings." He raised his head and looked at her with fire in his eyes. "Blast the French captain who invented the minié bullet! It flattens against human flesh on contact—" He clapped his hands together loudly, and Charlotte jumped. "And it does not pass directly through like the round ball does. Oh, no. This little devil of a deformed ball tumbles into the body, tearing through muscle and getting tangled in tissues; bones splinter and shatter into hundreds—and I mean hundreds—of spicules, which are driven through muscle and skin." He shook his head and cursed. "Tiemann's bullet forceps are as useful in getting a bullet out as a butter knife is in eating soup. No, I'm afraid the minié ball doesn't leave much debate about the necessity of amputation."

"Do you remember what else you said in your letter? You told me that God is the Alpha and the Omega, the Beginning and the End. That if He calls us to take part in the work He is doing somewhere in the middle, then we are to be faithful and do it and leave the outcome to Him."

He looked at her then, with sorrow in his red-rimmed eyes. "That was a lifetime ago."

"It was still sound wisdom."

"I'm supposed to be a healer, not a fighter. I want to mend bodies, not break them apart. They will call us butchers. There will be outrage." He looked at his hands again. "I am outraged myself."

Charlotte nodded mutely. The truth was outrageous, indeed.

"Did you know that we can only use chloroform within the first twenty-four hours of the wound? After that, we have to amputate without any kind of anesthesia or the patient would die from the dose. Do you know how many soldiers lay under the scorching sun for days after the battle, their open wounds crawling with maggots, buzzing with flies, turning septic and poisoning their bodies?"

She shook her head. She did not want to know.

"One would have been too many," was all he said.

Charlotte said nothing. Her words felt as powerless to comfort as Caleb's hands had felt powerless to heal the mangled wreck of the battlefield. Later, she would try again. But for now, the doctor needed some time to grieve his losses.

She watched him slip away from her once again, lost in memories that would no doubt haunt his dreams, even as the birds overhead still sang as if all was right with the world. She slipped her calloused hand into his, and he held on to it as though it were a lifeline, though his eyes remained closed. Words were inadequate. They were also unnecessary.

Finally Charlotte spoke again.

"I heard you say you're mustering out soon. The seventh, did you say? In New Haven? I'm sure your patients will be glad to have their doctor back."

"Then they're bound to be disappointed. I'm mustering right back in as soon as I can."

"But I thought you—"

"I'm going to try again. I have to. You, of all people," he waved a hand at her soiled dress, "should understand."

She nodded her disheveled head, and another strand of hair slipped out of its pin, falling over her forehead. "Emphatically," she said, and tucked the unruly hair firmly behind her ear.

Chapter Eighteen

New York City
Saturday, August 3, 1861

Ruby couldn't sleep.

The same mattress that had once cradled her body in softness now felt like a bed of nails, the sheets like weights pressing the air out of her lungs.

Like a body. Hot and heavy.

Ruby threw off the covers and jumped out of bed, gasping for air. Her racing pulse sounded loudly in her ears as she knelt down on the cool hardwood floor for the seventh night in a row, unshed tears swelling thickly in her throat. Would she ever be able to sleep in a bed again without being haunted by an unforgiving memory?

She had closed her eyes during the rape, wedding darkness to the deed. Now, when each night's blackness rendered her blind on a bed again, her mind reeled her back to the very moments she wanted most to forget. *What have I done to deserve that?*

If Matthew found out, he would kill her.

If Mrs. Hatch found out, she would turn her out on the street.

If the American Moral Reform Society found

out, they would refuse to place her in any other homes.

God already knew, and could never forgive her. He had turned His back on her already.

She was on her own now more than she had ever been before.

New York City
Saturday, August 3, 1861

Whatever pricks of conscience had needled at Phineas Hastings for engaging the services of a prostitute had died long ago. *Ruby hadn't even put up much of a fight. She probably wanted it, the hussy.*

Charlotte was still out of reach and his mother knew too much about the Brooks Brothers scandal for him to provoke her wrath, but now at least he had one woman under his control. Phineas Hastings slept easy that night.

By the time he sauntered up West Twenty-first Street the next day for his Sunday evening visit to his mother, he felt almost magnanimous.

"How are things, Mother?" He kissed her on her forehead.

"Gah! Can't stand this heat, I tell you!" Fanny squawked, fanning herself violently. "I'm like a pig without mud." Her knees were spread widely apart and she flapped her black skirts in front of them.

Disgusting. A pig indeed. Phineas turned from the sight and shook his head ever so slightly as if to erase the image from his mind.

"How's the help working out?" He tried to sound only marginally interested.

"Funny girl, that one, but she's trying my patience." Fanny flapped her skirts again. "Can't seem to get things right."

"Oh? How so?"

"Make some switchel, I says, and she uses too much vinegar, not enough ginger. Dust it, I says, and she leaves rims of the fuzzy grey filth on the edge of the mantelpiece." She threw up her hands in a state of helplessness, and Phineas murmured his sympathies.

"It's trying to not get the results you're entitled to, isn't it?" he said.

Fanny gulped at her lemonade before wiping her mouth with the back of her hand. "The girl seems so distracted lately. Don't know what's gotten into her. Used to be she was taking to the place and the work real well, usually not real keen on getting out for time off like Bridget and the rest. Started to get some color back into her skin."

Phineas nodded. He remembered her skin.

"She walks around like a sleepwalker, all dazed and such. Even found her falling asleep with her feather duster still in her hand a couple of times."

"Hmmm . . . does she have—how shall I put

this—nocturnal . . . activities? That might prevent her from sleeping?"

Fanny's chubby hand stopped fanning. Her eyes went wide.

"That little thing? Nah. She's meek as a mouse. She wouldn't fancy that sort of a life. She doesn't have a bit of flash or glamour about her either." Her fan started waving again as she shook her head. "Can't imagine that a man would look to the likes of her to warm his bed."

"Well, just a thought. You wouldn't want the rumors to spread that you're providing room and board for a common prostitute, now would you?"

"Oh that's right, Pottsy, always considerate of what other folks think of our own business, aren't you?" She chuckled. "Learn to relax." Turning her head to the doorway, she called, "Ruby! Tea for two!"

Shoulders hunched more than usual, hands trembling, face flaming red, Ruby shuffled into the parlor, set the tray on the side table and turned to go.

"Wait a minute, Ruby," called Fanny. "That's no way to treat comp'ny. You'll come back here and pour the tea for us."

Ruby stopped midstride, turned around and poured one cup.

"Two cups, Ruby. I said tea for *two*."

Her entire body was quivering now. Phineas watched her in fascination. Would she serve him, the man who had raped her? Or would she tell Fanny what happened, which would only succeed in getting herself fired? She would have to make the decision every week, for he wouldn't stay away.

A smile spread over his face as he watched her frail, bumbling hands tip the scalding amber liquid into his porcelain cup. So he had won. Again. But she had made him wonder if she would make a scene, and the uncertainty had disagreed with him.

Ruby turned to Fanny. "I've a headache, missus, something awful I do," she said. "I'll collect the teacups in the morning if it's all right with you. I'd like to put my head to bed straight away."

"Well Ruby, if it were real comp'ny—no offense, Potts—I would scold you for such impertinence and expect you to carry on with your duties." She paused. "But you do look right sickly, and frankly, I don't want to catch anything from you. So go on. And get better so's you can be a good help around here. It's not like you're stayin' for free, you know."

In a sudden swish of skirts, Ruby fled the room in a blur of black and white.

"I see what you mean about that one," said Phineas. "Not at all appealing."

But later that night, after the moon was high in the sky and Fanny was snoring snugly under her covers, Phineas came back to number 301 and let himself in the rear door. Up the stairs he climbed, two at a time, noiselessly, like a shadow.

He slipped into her bedroom, shut the door behind him, and tripped.

"Ow!" Ruby cried out.

He clapped a hand over her mouth. "What were you doing on the floor?" he whispered. "Trying to hide?"

She shook her head no. The shining whites of her eyes reminded him of a terrified horse that would be much better off with its blinders on.

Straddling her body on the floor, he leaned in so close to her face she could smell the pomade in his slicked-back hair. "Were you thinking of giving yourself away back there, Ruby? That little stunt you pulled. Not serving me tea. If you upset the applecart, you're the one who's going to be hurt, not me. Just remember that." He held up a key, glinting in the moonlight seeping in through the window. "I can get to you any time I want to, Ruby. I can take you any time I please, and I can make it hurt. When you least expect it, I'll be the creak on the stairs leading to your bedroom. I'll be the shadow in the corner. I'll be the nightmare in your sleep.

"But you're not going to give me any trouble, are you? My little insurance policy." He stroked her hair with his hand. She jerked away from his touch like a skittish horse that needed to be broken.

He slapped her across the face, hard, but not so hard the welts wouldn't recede by morning.

He'd tame her. He would break her, the way all wild horses needed to be broken.

It wouldn't take long.

Five Points, New York City
Tuesday, August 6, 1861

The hem of Ruby's calico dress slogged through the street-wide gutter behind her trudging steps. Filth, manure, and decaying food sloshed over the tops of her boots and soaked into the fibers of her dress, obscuring the color of the fabric, until it was difficult to discern where the ground ended and her dress began. A broad band of filth clinging to her skirt marked her, even from a distance, as a Five Pointer. The roses on her calico dress, Ruby realized, were not nodding in a gentle breeze as she had once thought. They were wilting. Fading. Dying.

But what choice did she have? If she had stayed with Mrs. Hatch, she would have been easy prey for Phineas, never knowing when he would take her again, unable to escape. No, she would take her chances somewhere else, somehow, rather than staying under his thumb. She never wanted to see his roguish face again.

"Get your nice hot corn, smoking hot, smoking hot, just from the pot!" The mournful cadence of young girls with dirty shawls the color of rusted iron filled Ruby's ears. Calling out from every street corner, at all hours of the day and night, their voices marked the change of seasons in Five Points, from the peak of summer to its dried out, burned up end.

Autumn was coming. And after that, winter. Ruby shuddered. Stretched out in front of her lay months of never getting warm, of constant runny nose and cough, of wind so cold and sharp as it came through the broken windows it would scrape her face like a razor. Her hands would become stiff and clumsy. She would make mistakes with her uncooperative needle, if she were so lucky as to find more work to do. Yesterday, she had asked the tailor Simon Levitz for some and he had said he didn't have any for her. That her position had been taken.

Work would be nice, but today her most pressing goal was finding a place to sleep. She had spent last night in a flophouse among drunks reeking of whiskey. She had tried a cellar room before that, but left when she was told that "boarders" were to remove their dirty clothes before sleeping in the tiers of canvas stretched between wood poles. *Don't want yer filthy rags soiling the beds,* the owner had said, preferring instead the soiled naked bodies, and yet providing no bedclothes at all.

Five Points was a nightmare from which she

couldn't wake herself. Living in Seneca Village—that had only been a dream. The slums were her reality. She was so tired. Too tired, anymore, to fight the crushing current that kept sweeping her back to this place.

"Repent of your sin! Turn to Jesus!" The ladies from the American Moral Reform Society still marched about in front of the taverns and saloons on Baxter Street, drawing Ruby like a beggar to bread.

"Is Bertha here today?" she asked.

"No she isn't. Is there something I can do for you?"

"She placed me as a domestic in a home, and it didn't work. I was wondering if she might have another spot for me somewhere."

"Well that depends, of course. Why didn't it work?"

"The mistress's son was treating me ill. Using me something fierce, he was."

"Who was this? Which family?"

Ruby sighed. Telling her secret couldn't make life much worse for her at this point. "It was Fanny Hatch's residence."

The woman's eyes sparked. "Fanny Hatch you said? Why, she doesn't have a son, as far as we know. But she did take the time to get a message to our office yesterday. She said you may come by."

This can't be good. Ruby shifted her weight

from one soggy foot to the other, waiting for more.

"Matter of fact, she told us you quit without notice before she even awoke Monday morning, after complaining of a headache the night before. That you'd been distracted lately and didn't follow directions."

Ruby listened silently. It was all true.

"She also said she suspected you of being a woman of the town. Not sleeping at night, falling asleep on the job . . . With a blemish like that against your character, we can't possibly place you in another home."

"What about what Bertha read from the Bible— about that lass caught in adultery, and Jesus telling her to go and sin no more? What about forgiveness and grace? Not that I'm an adulterer. I'm a decent woman, I am."

The woman shook her head. "Jesus forgives all sin, but this society has a responsibility to put only the most upright girls in the homes of our constituents. If we knowingly put a woman of questionable character in someone's home, we break our moral obligation." Ruby started walking away, but the woman kept talking after her. "People stop trusting us, and we can no longer give jobs to clean and decent women. Everyone loses. You see? We can't help you."

The words thudded in her ears like blocks of wood.

And then she heard a different voice. The voice of the only friend she had ever had this side of the ocean. *The only help we'll get is the help we give ourselves,* she had said. *Imagine . . . You never have to wear those rags again, or lack for a meal. . . . You could get out of here. Let me buy you a bonnie new dress. Clean you up, fix your hair. You could start a better life. 'Tisn't so bad if you don't think about it much.*

That wouldn't be very hard. Ruby was done thinking. All her plans had failed her. She had already been defiled by a man not her husband, and she could never erase that. Was it a sin if it wasn't her fault? Would it be her fault if the sin was the only way to survive? Everyone else had turned their backs on her. It was time for her to help herself.

It was time to find Emma.

Chapter Nineteen

Washington City
Wednesday, August 7, 1861

"Charlotte," Alice called down the narrow corridor of Columbian College Hospital. "Charlotte, may I have a moment, please?" She looked immaculate, as ever, her honey-blonde hair smoothly in place under her snood as she glided toward her sister.

Charlotte paused, eager to get back to her patients. She had finished mixing charcoal, quicklime, and sand together, thrown it into the trench to disinfect it, and was now writing letters for the boys. So far, Dr. Murray still insisted he didn't need her help with any actual nursing.

"You know I've been going around to the hospitals in Washington and Alexandria with Maurice to deliver supplies and let Dr. Blackwell know how the nurses are getting on."

"Did you go to Alexandria today?" Charlotte interrupted. "Did you get a chance to see Jacob while you were there?"

"Yes, thank heavens, and he sends his love. I was so disappointed he was out drilling last time I went. But back to my point—I've noticed something in all of the hospitals. I mean, I *haven't* noticed something."

Charlotte arched an eyebrow.

"Clergy. I've not seen a chaplain assigned to hospital duty. Wouldn't it be wise to have someone on hand to read to the patients, write letters, perform funerals, counsel the grieving family members? What do you think?"

Charlotte tapped a finger on her chin. "Well, that would certainly be invaluable at this hospital. Are there no chaplains assigned to any of the hospitals?"

"None."

"Right." Charlotte nodded. "Write to Professor Smith straight away. Surely he knows of a graduate of the Union Theological Seminary who would be glad of such an appointment and who has qualifications for such special missionary work. We can work on getting a government commission later, but let's get it started anyway."

Dr. Murray walked up to them. "Scheming again," he declared, more than asked. Caleb's visit had proven not to be the cure for Dr. Murray's malignant attitude toward Charlotte, but at least he was allowing her to sleep on a cot inside the building now.

"Chaplains for the hospitals," said Charlotte. "Surely you must agree we have need of one. He could pray with the men, comfort the dying, read to them from the Bible, perform funeral rites."

"Prayer won't save these men. Science will. Religion is a crutch for the weak."

"You'll pardon me for saying so," Charlotte said, "but in case you haven't noticed, science doesn't seem to be saving these boys either." She thought of Caleb, who had sent two dozen roses to her before he left Washington, and a pang of disloyalty shot through her.

"So then why don't we just close down the hospitals? Since we're not doing any good anyway, we can all go home! Just pray for the soldiers and leave them to God's keeping. It's all up to Him anyway, isn't that right, Miss Waverly?"

Alice glanced at Charlotte expectantly.

"That's not what I meant." Charlotte sighed. "God is sovereign, yes, but He wants to use us in the process. And we need to be concerned about both the body and the spirit. That's all I'm saying. We need doctors and chaplains both. Sometimes chaplains can provide hope when the doctor says there is none."

"Soldiers die, Miss Waverly. It's what they do. The sooner you can get that through your pretty little head, the better. Come with me."

"Go write to Professor Smith," Charlotte whispered to Alice as she followed on Dr. Murray's heels.

Hot wind whipped up dust devils between and around the tents behind Columbian College Hospital, either stirring up the miasma of contagious diseases, or blowing them away. At the third row, Dr. Murray climbed the two steps up to the wooden platform that served as a floor to the tent and lifted a heavy flap of dirty canvas. "Are you coming?" he called over his shoulder to Charlotte, his face flushed with heat. He had been as unbearable as this scorching weather. Unrelenting and blistering.

At the bedside of the patient in the corner of the dark tent, he stopped. "This is Private Mitchell Nelson, of the Second Connecticut Volunteers." He was drenched in sweat and delirious. If he had been well, he would be mustering out of military service at this very moment.

"Dr. Lansing's patient," said Charlotte.

"Used to be," said Dr. Murray. "Now he's yours."

"Mine?"

"You said you wanted to nurse, and Dr. Lansing told me to take special care of this man. You're perfect for each other."

A thrill of excitement shuddered through Charlotte. Finally, a chance to put her nursing skills into practice!

"What ails him? Typical fever?"

Dr. Murray shook his head. "Bullet passed through him. Entered at the left abdomen, exited out the right buttock. Watch this." He lifted Nelson's hospital gown to chest level, revealing a severely distended abdomen. After removing the blackened dressings from the abdomen wound, he pressed gently near the navel. Gas and feces exuded from the open wound.

Charlotte covered her mouth and nose with her hand, but the odor lodged stubbornly in the back of her throat.

"Same thing happened through the exit wound, too. The rifle ball cut through the bowel and the bladder. When he tries to urinate, feces and gas escape through the urethra."

"What can we do for him?"

"It's a mortal wound. Lucky for you, he'll die soon enough. But in the meantime, change the dressings often. They are continuously dirtied by fecal matter. After last week, you should be used to that."

"Is there nothing else to be done?"

"Cut away the dead material from the edges of the wounds."

"Cutting away skin—isn't that a surgeon's job?"

"I don't have time to waste on lost causes. If you think you do, then be my guest. As long as you mix and throw the disinfectant into the trench every day, he's all yours. Irrigate the wounds frequently with green tea. Boil it, then cool it to lukewarm so you don't scald him."

"Will it help?"

He shrugged. "It will relieve some pain, but it won't heal him. Nothing can. Not me. Not you." He squinted up into the cloudless sky, his fists on his hips. "Not even God."

Dr. Murray slipped out the tent flap and

disappeared. The thud of his retreating footsteps on the parched earth faded as she looked down at Private Nelson. Caleb's patient. Her patient.

She knelt down on the rough wooden floor beside his head. "Private Nelson," she said, not knowing whether he could hear her, "I hope the fact that I'm a woman doesn't bother you, but I'm going to be your nurse, and I'm going to try to make you as comfortable as possible." She laid a gentle hand lightly on his shoulder. "Allow me a moment to go and fetch some fresh bandages for you. You won't even know I'm gone."

On her way to the storeroom, a woman's laughter floated down the stairwell. Surely a nurse would have no reason to cackle like that on duty. A polite laugh or restrained chuckle, perhaps—the patients enjoyed sharing jokes—but not that sort of squeal.

Charlotte lifted her skirts and quietly climbed the stairs toward the sound. Perhaps the poor soul needed comforting.

"Hello?" Charlotte called at the fourth floor. "Everything all right?"

Whispers hissed, then fell quiet all together.

Down the hall Charlotte walked, peeking in every room she passed along the way.

"Shhh! Quiet! Someone's coming," came a masculine voice.

Charlotte stopped, frozen. Whoever was down there was decidedly not a poor soul, and not in need of *her* comfort. She waited in the hall to see who would emerge.

She didn't need to wait long.

Out tumbled the hospital steward, John Fitzburg, his normally slicked-back brown hair rumpled and falling down over his forehead.

"Why, if it isn't Miss Waverly! Standing in line, are we? I must say I'm flattered."

Charlotte was already hot from the August heat, but felt her temperature rise even higher at the insinuation. Before she had time to formulate a retort, Cora Carter appeared, smoothing her hair into place. Her skirt was crooked at the waist.

"Oh her." Cora sneered. "What are you doing here, anyway, Miss Chamber Pots?"

Charlotte lifted her chin. "I should ask the same of you, Miss Carter. Another day, another conquest? Don't you have some patients that need tending to?"

Cora shrugged, smiling, while she straightened her skirt. "They ain't going anywhere."

Charlotte turned to Mr. Fitzburg, then. "As much as I hate to admit it, I have need of your assistance. I need to get into the storeroom for bandages, if you please."

He raised his eyebrows and made a quick bow to Cora behind him. "Been a pleasure, my dear, and now if you'll excuse me, this fine lady has *need* of me." He jiggled his eyebrows up and down.

"Ha! Don't bother with the likes of her, Johnny, she's not as—accommodating of your needs as I am."

Mr. Fitzburg threw up a hand to silence Cora without turning around and walked briskly down the hallway, Charlotte following close behind.

"Who ordered the bandages?" he asked as they made their way down the stairs.

"Dr. Murray."

"Really? Doesn't sound like him. I had pretty much given up on him ever wanting to put you to work as a real nurse."

"Well, he's making an exception this time." Charlotte should have guessed this wouldn't be an easy process.

"Did you fill out a form? Requesting the bandages?"

"Oh—and some scissors."

"You'll definitely need to fill out a form for those."

"How long does it take to get the supplies after filling out a form?"

"That depends on how bad you want it." He flashed a toothy grin and raked over her body with a half-lidded gaze.

Charlotte didn't understand this game he was playing. There certainly had been no lectures at New York Hospital on how to manage lecherous hospital stewards. Maybe there should be.

Arriving at the storeroom, Mr. Fitzburg pulled

out a jangle of keys and turned one in the lock. The door opened to a hot, moist, room lined with shelves sagging with supplies for the soldiers. In addition to bandages and scraped lint were jars of peaches, knit socks, extra hospital gowns, mosquito netting, lead pencils, woolen mufflers, blankets, pillows, toothbrushes, and more—all mixed and scattered with no rhyme or reason.

"Mr. Fitzburg!" Charlotte gasped. "This place is a shambles! You're bound to waste valuable supplies—not to mention time—if you just leave it all topsy-turvy like this."

She stepped inside and pointed to a corner. "For one thing, you could separate by season. Mosquito netting and woolen mufflers would not go together. Separate the edibles from the inedibles, and put the things that will spoil in front of things that will keep."

"If you're so good at it, why don't you do it yourself, genius?"

"I'm not a genius. But I can organize and manage a household, and a hospital is much like a home, however different the circumstances and occupants."

Mr. Fitzburg rubbed his chin and narrowed his eyes at her. "You know, you're right. I could use the help in here, and you're just the lady to give it to me." He shut the door behind him. "Now wouldn't you just fancy that. You and me, alone in an empty room." As he stepped toward her, she stepped back until her back was pressed up against a stack of pillowcases.

"Mr. Fitzburg, remember yourself!"

Ducking under his arm, Charlotte grabbed the bandages and a pair of scissors out of a wire basket near the door and dashed out of the room without looking back.

"You didn't fill out a requisition form!" he yelled out after her.

But Charlotte was already out of the building, on her way to Private Nelson. The tea for his wounds would have to wait.

Washington City
Monday, August 26, 1861

Edward Goodrich had never been in a more detestable place.

The air was thick with mosquitoes, and he couldn't even open his mouth without a fly buzzing right into it. His cologned handkerchief was simply no defense against the odors that now assaulted his nose. Vapors from animal dung, overly ripe fruit, and sweaty bodies mixed with the distinctive smell of the pestilent Washington canals running warm and dirty through the city. Though it was already evening, he could feel his clothing stick to his body and grow damp beneath his armpits and collar.

Just remember why you're here, he told himself

as he climbed into a rickety hack and gave the driver the address. It was an opportunity like no other, and he had been especially chosen by Professor Smith out of all the Union Theological Seminary alumni for the express purpose. He was to be a hospital chaplain, without rank, but with full access to all the hospitals by the authority of Brigadier General Henry Van Rensselaer. And all because a pair of sisters saw a need and wrote some letters. Remarkable. The position seemed to mollify even his father. At least, for now.

Thanking the sisters who set the wheels in motion was item number one on his agenda. He imagined them to be very much like his own grandmother—huge hearts, trembling hands, quivering iron-grey curls, warbling voices. They would probably pinch his smooth, moderately chubby cheeks. They would tell him how charming he was. His token of gratitude thus paid, he would then be on his way to ministering to the souls of the great Union army. The harvest was plentiful.

Cracking his knuckles, he looked out from the hack and tried to take in the confusion of the capital around him. Outside bars and pubs, ragtag rabbles of regiments lingered in uniforms varying according to the state that sent them. Free blacks stood in clumps, as if they were waiting for . . . for what? Jobs? Shelter? Clothing? Edward had read only a bit about this in the New York papers.

Contrabands, General Butler had called them at Fortress Monroe, property formerly of the Confederacy, now property of the North. Some contrabands were put to work for the Union army, but these—well, it didn't look like they had any work to do at all. He held his handkerchief to his nose once again. Apparently the city's latrines and sanitation systems were not keeping up with the swelling population. *Disgusting city.*

On Newspaper Row, small boys pranced out of low buildings belonging to the *Western Union*, *New York Times*, *The Evening Star*, and *New York Herald*, hauling bundles of papers in their arms and shrieking the headlines now crackling on telegraph wires to all corners of the nation. A lady spy, Rose O'Neal Greenhow, had been arrested in Washington for leaking intelligence of Yankee movements to the Confederacy just before Bull Run. Two days ago, the mayor of Washington was arrested for refusing to take the oath of loyalty to the Union and sent north for imprisonment. What kind of godless place had Edward just moved into?

Arriving at the Ebbitt House, he paid the driver the fifteen-cent fare and lugged his suitcase into the lobby.

"Miss Charlotte Waverly and Mrs. Alice Carlisle?" he inquired at the front desk.

The man behind the desk nodded in the direction of door 1B.

"Thank you kindly."

He rapped loudly on the door and waited, hands clasped behind his back, a benign smile on his pale face.

"Yes, may I help you?" A petite young woman with honey-blonde hair and bright blue eyes, about his age, he guessed, was now staring into his confused face.

"I'm sorry, I must have the wrong—" Edward looked around. "Perhaps you can point me in the right direction. I'm looking for a—" He fumbled with a crumpled slip of paper, moist from being squeezed in the palm of his hand. "Mrs. Alice Carlisle and Miss Charlotte Waverly. Do you know them?"

She smiled. "Quite well, in fact. And you are?"

"How rude of me," he muttered. "Edward Goodrich, New York City. Union Theological Seminary." He gave a slight bow.

A spark of recognition lit her eyes. "Oh Mr. Goodrich, come in! We've been expecting you! I'm Alice Carlisle."

He heard the words, but his feet would not obey. "I'm sorry, but you couldn't be—Mrs.? Alice Carlisle? The old woman who convinced the army they needed a hospital chaplain?"

"Well! I can't be much older than you, Mr. Goodrich, but the rest is true." She paused. "Just how old are you, Mr. Goodrich? I'm only curious."

"Twenty-six." He ran his hand over his smooth cheeks. *Maybe I should try growing that beard again.*

"Ah! Fine. So am I. The old guard is convinced that's much too young to be of service in the war, but we'll prove them wrong, won't we? My husband is under thirty and nobody seems to mind him serving as an officer in the regiment. How about that for inconsistency?"

"Yes, well. I'll just step in for a moment, then."

"My sister, Charlotte, and I are so grateful you've come." Alice closed the door behind him and showed him to a seat. In a sweep of her arms, she gathered up newspapers that had been spread on the floor. "The men so desperately have need of you. Have you much experience?"

"I—well, I graduated at the top of my class this year." Edward rolled the brim of his hat between his fingers.

"Oh, yes, of course you did. Silly question. Charlotte and I had never been nurses before this year either and yet here we are! Oh—actually, Charlotte is more of a nurse than I am. She's been fully trained. I came primarily to be close to my husband and as a chaperone for Charlotte, but I make myself useful by delivering supplies for the Sanitary Commission and helping out with light work at whichever hospital needs me. Writing letters, feeding the men, reading to them, that sort of thing. Maurice helps too."

Edward nodded as if he already knew all about hospital life. "Is Miss Waverly out at the moment?"

"She'll be right with us; she only stepped out to post a letter to our mother in New York." Alice sat primly on the edge of a chair, ankles crossed, as if she were in a fine New York parlor once again, and not surrounded by boxes and crates of one-armed shirts, bed ticking, soap, old magazines, red flannel drawers. "Charlotte doesn't always come back in the evenings from her work at the Columbian College Hospital—the journey is rather tiresome, and sometimes she simply cannot get an army ambulance to bring her back. Before you go thinking I'm a horrid sister for not fetching her myself, I'll have you know I've sent Maurice on many an occasion, only to be turned away again because she either could not be found, or she could not be spared. Between you and me, Mr. Goodrich, I'm not altogether certain that doctor she works for is as upstanding as he might be." She lowered her voice. "They're not all heroes."

A commotion beyond the picture window caught Edward's attention. A short, tanned man with a black kepi on his head and a reddish mustache drooping down over his mouth thundered on his horse toward Willard's Hotel across the street. Billows of dust rose well above the stirrups, shimmering in waves of late summer heat. Every head turned to watch him.

"Now who's *that* character?" Edward walked to the window for a closer look.

"Small man, smaller hat, big horse?" Alice asked without turning around to see for herself.

Edward nodded.

"That, my dear, *is* a hero. Major General George B. McClellan and his trusty horse, Dan Webster."

"So that's him!" Edward craned his neck to watch McClellan dismount. "He took over after General Scott's disaster at Bull Run, if I'm not mistaken."

"Precisely." She turned around now. "Take a good look, Mr. Goodrich. He's another Napoleon, a military genius. That little man commands more admiration from civilians and soldiers alike than the president himself."

"That stocky fellow?"

"Believe it. If they both happen to be on the street at the same time, which happens often, since Mr. Lincoln seems to call after McClellan like a dog after its master, no one will give a second glance to the gentleman in the stovepipe hat. All eyes are on 'Little Mac,' as the troops call him, wherever he goes. He's adored by all. Our troops were whipped once already—now he's whipping them into shape in true military fashion, my husband tells me. No more of this armed mob mentality." She nodded a head toward the crowd gathering around the major general now. "Mark my words. You're looking at the man who will end this war. The North and the right will prevail, and soon."

Edward raised his eyebrows. "Is that a fact?"

"Everyone says so."

"The Messiah of the North? Our anointed savior?"

Alice laughed. "I wouldn't put him quite in the Holy Trinity, Mr. Goodrich, but to the Union he's certainly the next best thing."

"I see. What is his plan, then?"

"He hasn't told the New York regiments yet, and rumor has it that he hasn't even told the president. He's only been here a month. Let's give him time."

"Yet everyone trusts him?"

"Implicitly. No questions—or very few, at least—asked."

"Heavens. Such power for just one man."

"He needs it. We need him to have it. We need a 'savior,' as it were."

Edward nodded. "Yes, of course we do. That's why I'm here."

Alice looked at him quizzically.

"No, I'm no George McClellan," he said. "I'm here to point people to the true Savior. Jesus."

Relaxing into a genuine smile, Alice said, "Indeed. I must have sounded like a heathen just then. Would you ever guess that Charlotte and I attended classes at Union, too? It's a wonder we didn't meet each other there!" Edward was dumbfounded. But before he could formulate some kind of response, the door opened and another surprise swept into the room.

"Charlotte, meet Mr. Edward Goodrich, our very own hospital chaplain!" Edward stood, bowing awkwardly before the perfect paradox before him. Charlotte's posture was erect, like the lady of the house, yet she was clothed in a dull grey dress a domestic would wear. No hoops, no bows, no ornament adorned her, but she was nonetheless stunning for their absence. If anything, her natural beauty was given greater opportunity to shine.

"How do you do?" he said, recovering himself.

"Charmed, I'm sure!" Charlotte said with a twinkle in her caramel-colored eyes. "Manners. How refreshing!" Her face was radiant and sun-kissed, casting doubt on "pure white" as the standard of beauty for ladies' complexions. Her chestnut hair was not smoothed into place like her sister's, but twisting in humidity, with unruly wisps clinging to her neck.

"Please. What did I miss?" she asked.

"I was just telling Mr. Goodrich about Little Mac, but I'm afraid I wasn't being a very good hostess. Do tell us more about yourself," said Alice.

Edward cleared his throat. "Well, like your-selves, I'm from New York City and a graduate of Union Theological Seminary. I have loved books, and most particularly the Good Book, for as long as I can remember."

"Did you happen to bring any new books with you, Mr. Goodrich?" Charlotte's eyes brightened. "I confess I haven't much time for reading for pleasure these days, but I'd so enjoy picking up a book for a few moments here and there."

"Charlotte, let him finish. Go on, Mr. Goodrich." Alice nodded at him.

"I'll come back to that, all right, Miss Waverly? Now where was I—oh yes. Books have always been my first love, and I'm delighted to find myself in such good company now with you ladies. My own mother loved to read, as well, but my father was a man of few words, and he believed even less in the power of the printed word. He's always been more of a man of action."

Charlotte's close attention almost tripped his tongue. *How is it possible that this beautiful woman is still a Miss and not a Mrs., tending her own hearth with her own children hanging on her skirts?*

"He fought in the Mexican War," he continued. "And he's made it abundantly clear that he wished I had chosen the soldier's life, as well. As much as I wanted to please him, I could not sacrifice my own calling in order to do that. But! 'Do I seek to please men?' "

Charlotte jumped in. " 'For if I yet pleased men, I should not be the servant of Christ.' "

"That's right! Galatians chapter one verse ten."

"You're not the only one in the room with a disapproving parent." Charlotte smiled wryly. "But go on."

"Well, obviously I chose the path of pastoral studies. But when this opportunity arose, thanks to you and your sister, it seemed like a gift from heaven itself. I can pursue ministry, but in the context of the military. I know my father wishes I would shoulder a rifle, but I'm much better suited to wield a sword." He pulled a small Bible from his jacket pocket. "I am eager to start."

"They are eager to have you," said Charlotte. "The staff are a rough lot at some of the hospitals, but you will be the balm of Gilead to the patients, I am sure of it. You'll have to assign your own schedule, dividing your time among the hospitals in this city."

"Which hospital is yours, did you say?" He tried to sound nonchalant.

"Columbian College Hospital, just north of the city."

"Excellent." Edward grinned. "I'll start there."

Washington might not be quite so hideous after all.

Chapter Twenty

New York City
Sunday, September 8, 1861

The cool brick wall felt good against Ruby's back
as she leaned against it. Finally, the soggy heat of
summer had been blown away by the same cool
winds that now pushed white-gold clouds across
the azure sky. Church bells resounded from St.
Patrick's Cathedral, calling worshippers together
for holy mass, but Ruby would remain outside the
fence, again. She was not worthy to set foot inside
the solid brick perimeter, the boundary between
lost souls and saved. But if she closed her eyes
while the bells drowned out the sounds of Mott
and Prince Streets, she could imagine the wind
on her face was the brush of angels' wings.

Oh how she needed an angel.

The bells stopped their singing, and the sounds
of a New York City street corner filled her ears
once more. The spell was broken, but she did not
open her eyes. Not yet. It was too soon.

If she could just absorb a shred of the holiness
and purity that resided beyond this brick wall,
she would stand here for hours and not complain.
The rough edges of the brick poked and prodded
at her shoulder blades, almost as if they were

nudging her away. A rueful smile played on Ruby's lips. Even the walls knew her sin.

Hail Mary, full of grace. The Lord is with thee. Blessed art thou among women and blessed is the fruit of thy womb, Jesus. Holy Mary, mother of God, pray for us sinners, now and at the hour of our death.

It was the only prayer she knew, the only one that came easily to mind. And it applied. How many times would she have to say it in order to be heard? She had already prayed it in her mind more times than she could count. And yet so far, heaven had remained silent toward her.

Hail Mary, full of grace . . .

Ruby jerked her head back, banging it into the unforgiving wall behind her. She must have nodded off again. A low murmur of voices began to grow louder. Mass had just let out. It was time for her to go.

Smoothing the deep mauve skirt over the hoops Emma insisted she get used to, she pushed her shoulders back and began walking down the street. She still wasn't comfortable wearing such finery, but hoped it didn't show.

By the time she got to Broadway, it was beginning to fill with an injection of fancy-dressed ladies and gents. Ruby pushed her straw and ribbon bonnet back on her head, revealing painted cheeks and signifying that she was open for business. With every step she took, she seemed to separate her soul from her body until her body was just an empty shell.

It didn't take long for a fat, mustached man with spats on his shoes and a top hat on his ridiculous head to catch her eye and make some crude gesture. As he came closer, the grin widened until his eyes were only slits in his chubby face.

"Ten dollars," he said to her, puffing a haze of blue cigar smoke in her face.

She nodded and forced a smile, leading the way now to a nearby House of Assignation. *This won't take long,* she told herself as she climbed the stairs. And the $10.00 would last her through the next three weeks of "unemployment" before she would need to go through this again for more cash. The stranger behind her huffed in exertion, large drops of perspiration rolling down his face into his collar.

"You better be worth it," she heard him mutter as she led him into the room and locked the door behind them both.

She held out her hand. "Payment first." She had provided her services without being paid one too many times.

After he stuffed a sweaty, crumpled up ten-dollar bill into her palm, she could think of no other delay and braced herself for what was to come next. *My body was violated that fated summer day with Phineas Hastings,* she told herself. There was no way of reclaiming her innocence. What had been lost once was now lost forever. She might as well get some money for it. But no matter how much she reasoned with herself, the haunting sense remained that, try as she might, she could not separate her soul from her body. Her spirit rebelled against the acts of her body, and in turn, her body rebelled as well. Nausea was becoming her closest companion.

Hail Mary, full of grace. The Lord is with thee. Blessed art thou among women and blessed is the fruit of thy womb, Jesus. Holy Mary, mother of God, pray for us sinners, now and at the hour of our death. Hail Mary, full of grace . . .

New York City
Monday, October 7, 1861

"Next," said a large woman with black hair pulled tightly into a bun. Ruby stood and followed her into a small white room with an anatomical poster on the wall and chrysanthemums in a vase on the windowsill. "The doctor will be with you shortly," the woman said, and closed the door behind her.

Ruby's restless fingers played in and out of the pleats darting out from the waist of her plain blue muslin dress. It was not showy in any way, but modest and humble, the way Ruby saw herself.

The door opened, and in walked a demure older woman in a black dress and white point lace collar. She was exactly the same as Ruby had remembered her that day in Five Points.

"Dr. Elizabeth Blackwell." Her British accent was crisp as she extended her hand to Ruby.

"Ruby O'Flannery. I don't expect you remember me, but I met you last summer in Five Points. You gave me your card, and here I am."

"Really! I don't believe I have seen you there since then. Where have you been hiding yourself?"

A wave of heat washed over Ruby's face. "Oh, I'm not in Five Points any longer and I'll never be going back. Took a domestic job straight away after I saw you, I did." She hoped no further explanation would be necessary.

"Well Ruby, tell me what the trouble is. How can I help you?"

"For the last week or so, I've been sick every day. Can't keep my breakfast where it belongs, if you get my meaning. I get so I'm afraid to eat anything at all. Utterly worn out, I am, and I don't understand it. I'm not working overly hard. I'm just tired."

"Mmm hmmmm." Dr. Blackwell pressed her stethoscope to Ruby's chest. "Breathe in please. And out. Again." She dropped the stethoscope around her neck and reached for a thin wooden stick. "Stick out your tongue and say 'ah.' That's a good girl." She withdrew the tongue depressor and folded her hands in her lap.

"Have you eaten anything unusual lately?"

Ruby shook her head.

"Are your breasts tender? When was your last menses?"

"My what?"

"Your monthly flow of blood? Your female cycle?"

Slowly, painfully, the haze of confusion lifted.

"I'm late." She clutched her middle.

"How late?"

Ruby leaned forward, arms crossed over her stomach, and began rocking back and forth.

"Too late," she groaned. "Too late, I'm too late, it's too late!"

Hard rain drummed against the window, blurring the view outside. Dr. Blackwell leaned back in her chair and sighed. "I take it a baby is not good news for you."

Ruby pressed her fingers to her eyelids. She had been a mother twice, and lost her babies twice. Motherhood was the sweetest sorrow she had ever known. For years, she had half hoped she would conceive another child, but at least her empty womb meant she would have no more mouths to feed and bodies to clothe and keep warm. She had considered herself a barren woman. To conceive now was the cruelest trick yet played on her.

"What about the father?" Dr. Blackwell asked. "Won't your husband be pleased?"

Ruby's laugh sounded faraway and crazy even to herself. She wasn't sure which question to dodge first. "It's a long story." She looked out the window. "You wouldn't understand."

"I bet I would. You're not the only woman with an unplanned pregnancy I've ever seen. Your husband isn't the father, is he?"

Ruby shook her head. "I don't even know where my husband is. He's been with the Sixty-Ninth Regiment, never sent a penny to me as he promised, left me here to support myself." Her gaze was fixed, unblinking, on the chrysanthemums on the windowsill past Dr. Blackwell's shoulder. "I did my best, Doctor, but surely you know how it is in Five Points. Impossible. It was impossible."

"So you turned to prostitution."

"I was driven to it."

"My dear Mrs. O'Flannery. Are you familiar with the name William Sanger? No, not likely. He was commissioned about six years ago to conduct a study on the surging prostitution industry in New York City, and has updated the findings since then. You must not think your position is rare. There were nearly eight thousand prostitutes in 1855, and I cannot think the number has changed much since that time. Almost three thousand of them Irish."

Ruby's fingers curled into claws and dug into her waist.

"I tell you this as your doctor. Most prostitutes are not long for this world. They die within four years either from venereal disease or alcoholism, which your race, for some reason, is particularly prone to."

The hackles raised on Ruby's neck, even though she could not deny the evidence of Irish drunkenness she had seen. Dr. Blackwell's accent gave her away. She was English—the race that dominated the Irish even worse than the way Southern plantation owners dominated their Negro slaves. "What do you know about *my race?*"

Dr. Blackwell's eyes softened. "Don't misunderstand me, Mrs. O'Flannery. I mean no insult. I harbor no ill will toward you or your race." She paused. "My daughter is Irish."

"What?"

"I adopted Kitty when she was seven, and I was in England. She's twelve now. She looks a bit like you—your hair." She smiled. "And I'm telling you what I would tell my own daughter. You must find another way to survive."

Cold raindrops pelted themselves against the window now. Ruby would be drenched as soon as she left the infirmary.

"And what should I do instead?" She searched Dr. Blackwell's eyes for an answer she knew was not there. "You're just like the rest of them, you are. Saying 'Be good and moral and don't sell your body, don't sell your soul,' but you don't understand. I used to be a clean and decent woman, and in my heart I still am. I hate the way I make my money. You see? Telling me to leave this sort of life is like telling a man with no legs to get up and walk. I have no legs. Do you see? I have no legs."

Dr. Blackwell nodded slowly, leaned back in her chair, and drummed her fingers on the papers in her lap. She leaned forward. "What would you say if I offered you a pair?"

"What?"

"A pair of legs. A way to get out, and far away from here—to Washington. Ruby, how would you like to get paid by the government for doing laundry? With a roof over your head, and food every day."

"I don't understand."

The older woman pulled a piece of paper from her pocket. A letter. "I just so happen to know of a military hospital in dire need of a laundress. It's a difficult job. The linens are soiled with blood and filth, and the stink would be enough to curl the hair on your head. But if you could handle Five Points, you could handle this. Here is your way out."

Ruby could not have been more surprised if Matthew himself had showed up in this room. *Matthew* . . . If he found out she was pregnant with another man's child, he would surely kill her. But if she could find him soon, and if they could have relations, it may not be too late. He was never very good at math. If Matthew was still with the Sixty-Ninth around Washington City, she just might be able to salvage the situation.

Ruby looked Dr. Blackwell in the eyes and took a deep breath. "When do I start?"

Chapter Twenty-One

New York City
Saturday, October 12, 1861

Charlotte Waverly dug her fingernails between the grooves of her cherry wood bedpost and braced herself for another sharp yank from behind. For Alice and Jacob, a weeklong furlough in New York meant resting at their estate in Fishkill. For Charlotte, it meant only performance.

"Tighter," said Caroline, straining with the corset. "Did I tell you even Jane has a beau now? You really must look your best for Mr. Hastings tonight. That he should call on you after you spent the entire courting season nursing strange men— well, it speaks volumes for his character. You really do know how to put a man's head into a lemon squeezer."

Charlotte couldn't argue the point. Caleb's face surged before her, and she wondered where and how he was. After he mustered out of Connecticut's Second Regiment, he had mustered right back in with the Seventh. In his last letter, sent from Annapolis, Maryland, he had told her they were about to embark to Port Royal, South Carolina. Before the ship left port, she had sent Maurice to him with a basket of food, extra medicines, and a volume of Tennyson. That was the last they knew of his whereabouts.

Another tug on her waist.

Charlotte sucked in her breath. She was right back where she had started. Caleb was not here. He had his own life to live. The freedom she had flexed as a nurse in Washington was clearly meant to stay there. This was the life she had left behind, and the life that would always be waiting for her.

She had forgotten how many layers a woman's wardrobe was supposed to have. Stockings, long-legged muslin drawers, a linen shift, the whalebone corset, two lace-trimmed petticoats, steel hoop skirt, and then, finally, a gown to top it all, measuring a fashionable fifteen inches in diameter at the waist, and six feet wide at the skirt.

Caroline inspected Charlotte's reflection in the three-way mirror in her dressing room. The layered flounces of golden silk and blonde lace trim shimmered in the kerosene lamp's amber glow.

"Well, it fits you better since you lost some weight." Caroline looked pleased.

"Odd. It still feels tight."

"Charlotte, what's that?" Caroline jabbed a finger toward a faint line on her neck, a demarcation between the white skin that had been hidden under the nursing uniform all summer, and the slightly darker shade of her neck and face, a souvenir of the scorching southern sun. The difference was barely discernible now, but it still smacked of outdoor labor. Caroline was horrified.

"The opera cloak will cover it." Charlotte reached for the orange-and-gold striped wrapper. The gold tassels on the hood and edging of silk fringe complemented the skirt peeking out from beneath.

"Make your lips into pretty shapes when you talk! Prunes and prisms!" Caroline instructed.

Her dressing and toilette complete, Charlotte stared out her bedroom window at a smoky autumn sunset, and waited. For the first time in months, the hands which had flown about making beds and beef tea, writing letters, dispensing medicine, and dressing wounds, were now idle. They looked listless in her lap. *Probably in need of stimulants,* she mused.

A knock sounded on the door below. For a moment, Charlotte listened to Jane greeting Phineas and Phineas greeting Caroline before she rose and swept down the stairs.

Her pulse quickened the moment her eyes met his. She had forgotten how handsome a man could be. He was perfectly whole, perfectly polished, and perfectly dressed, as always. Beneath his black wool frock coat, he wore a grey silk waistcoat with satin stripes, pleated shirt and bow-tied cravat, both of gleaming white. Doffing his top hat, he bowed low to her, and pressed her hand to his lips in a warm, lingering kiss that left her just the slightest off balance.

"At last," he said, still holding her hands. "My heart has come home to me." He held her in his gaze, and her breath caught in her throat. The scent of musk was both comforting and exhilarating. Good gracious! How long had it been since she'd been around a man who smelled not of beef tea or filth, but of cologne! She breathed it in again. Heavenly.

"Are you well?" His eyes swept from the russet leaves in her hair to the lace-trimmed petticoat peeking out beneath her flounces. "I've never seen a more beautiful sight. Please say you'll let me take care of you now."

Charlotte matched his smile with one of her own. "Yes, please," she whispered, overwhelmed at the height of her emotion. She had forgotten, utterly and completely, what it was like to be cherished. To be noticed and cared for, rather than always caring for the needs of others. And now here was a man who saw her beauty and did not try to soil it, like some of those she had met in the hospitals in Washington. He wanted to nurture her, and she could not help but warm to him, like a flower turns her face toward the sun.

Phineas held her hand in his as he helped her into his carriage, and she did not chafe. Before the war, such a gesture made her flighty hand feel like a bird trapped in a cage. But now, Phineas's hand around hers felt warm and solid. She enjoyed it.

Strange, how such fulfilling work as a nurse could drain her until she was so empty. She needed to be restored, to remember a world without moans, pain, and death. She needed Phineas.

The opera they attended that evening was like stepping into another world—one in which things made sense. The music was beautiful and orderly, all the instruments keeping time to the rhythm of a single conductor. Not a note was out of tune with the rest. Any pain portrayed in the characters was temporary, and served a greater purpose. By the conclusion, all problems had been resolved, and the audience was satisfied. It was the antithesis of the war.

When the doors opened, a heavily perfumed tide of fur, silk, and top hats washed around her, carrying her on its current as the crowd spilled out of the opera house. The sweeping crush of elegance around her seemed as unreal as the opera she had just watched.

It bothered her.

She wanted to enjoy herself, but wherever she looked, she saw faces of her patients—some of them surviving, some of them dying. Her mind's eye played tricks on her under the gas lights until the ravages of war mingled hideously within this mass of silk and jewels. A crimson rose in a gentleman's lapel was a bloody wound. A lady's fluttering fan chased buzzing flies off a gangrenous limb. A white-tipped cane in the hand of a gentleman was a walking stick for an amputee.

Corset pressing on her lungs, Charlotte's breath came in shallow sips. She squeezed Phineas's arm but kept silent about her hallucinations. She did not want to admit, even to herself, that images of war were lodged within her spirit like fragments of bone shattered by a minié ball—hidden, painful, and impossible to remove.

New York City
Monday, October 14, 1861

Phineas was running out of time.

In just two days, Alice and Jacob would be returning to Washington, and so far, Charlotte still planned to go with them.

Crackling logs glowed in the marble fireplace of the Waverly parlor as tongues of flame licked at the rising smoke. Charlotte's hair shone copper and gold in the firelight, her silk dress of rust-and-black stripes shimmered. The rosewater scent of her wasn't nearly as sensuous as the violet perfumes of other women he had been with, but it was feminine and refreshing. She could frustrate him beyond all measure, but she was still the most beautiful woman he had ever seen. Dazzling.

He had to win her.

"Darling," he began. "Don't you know that a man longs to protect the woman he loves?"

She looked at him from under black bristly lashes, a slow smile warming her face. "I admit, I didn't understand what there was to be protected from before I went to Washington, but now I do."

Heat rushed to his head. "Did someone hurt you? Did anyone touch you? Did—"

She held up her hands to stop him. "No, I'm fine." She chuckled. "Only one man—a boy, really—made any sort of attempt to steal a kiss."

"Why didn't you tell me?"

"It wasn't worth mentioning. He is a fool, not a threat. I wouldn't want you to worry."

"You never know which fool will turn into a threat," he said. "I wish you wouldn't go back."

Charlotte sighed and methodically stroked her cat, which was clearly enjoying the warmth of the fire. "We have been over this too many times to count. I wish you would not take this personally."

"How can I not? You are making a conscious decision to invest yourself into this cause instead of into me and our future together."

"This 'cause' is temporary. The war will come to an end. If you and I are meant for each other, that commitment will be forever. Am I not worth waiting for?"

A smile twitched under his black mustache. "Well played, my dear."

"This is not a game, Phineas. Or is it? These never-ending volleys of points and counter-points—I'd like to think that we both desire to come to a resolution. Not a winner and a loser."

The gold flecks in her hazel eyes began to glow brighter. She was getting angry.

"Of course, darling!" He took her hand in his. "We are on the same side!"

"Are we? Because I might as well tell you, I sometimes wonder about that."

"Skip the riddles. Speak plainly." He fought to suppress his impatience.

"You once said that we each fight for the Union in our own ways. At that time, you conceded that my way was by nursing. Your way was to inspire others to fight. Well, I think that stage is over now, Phineas. What else are you doing for our country? Or don't you care enough to make any personal sacrifices of your own?"

Phineas was stunned. She had never spoken so boldly to him before.

"Your months away have loosened your tongue, I see." His tone was as tight as the muscles in his face. "Perhaps Medical Director Tripler was right about the Sanitary Commission when he called you a bunch of 'sensation preachers, village doctors, and strong-minded women.' "

It was the wrong move. Phineas winced as Charlotte rose to her feet, sending the cat, yowling, to the floor.

"Charlotte, I'm sorry. It was too far. Forgive me."

"Phineas, we nurses have so many critics. I would hate to think that *you* are one of them." Her voice trembled then. "Besides, who cares what Charles Tripler thinks? Major General McClellan publicly praises the Commission and our work. I know you wish I was not a nurse. It is a revolutionary concept, I know. But have faith in my character! I am not strong-minded. I am just trying to do good where the door has been opened to me."

This rare glimmer of vulnerability filled him with a swelling desire to possess her, and with hope that it could be done. If he was careful.

"You're right." He stepped to her side and clasped her hands. Lotions and almost a week of ladylike idleness had made them soft once again. When she was finished with this nursing business, her spirit could become just as soft in his hands, as well. But he must not push her too hard, or she would fly. Women could be skittish that way.

She searched his eyes now, looking desperate for his approval. It was a good sign.

"I want you to know that I am your greatest admirer, darling," he said. "Obviously, I can't just take leave of the university, but allow me to help the Sanitary Commission in another way. What do you need?"

"Everything."

"What?"

"Our coffers are nearly dry. We've received more than sixty thousand donated items, but it's a drop in the bucket. Mr. Olmsted and I drafted a letter 'To the Loyal Women of America,' calling on them to give more. It was in all the papers—did you not see it?"

"I tend to skip over articles directed to women."

"Well, it was a desperate plea for contributions. Mother has been working unceasingly with the W.C.A.R. but you know the women of just one city can't possibly supply the entire Union army. We need blankets, quilts, woolen socks, bed gowns, wrappers, undershirts, drawers, slippers, small hair and feather pillows and cushions for wounded limbs, cornstarch, condensed milk." She looked at him pointedly. "And money. The Sanitary Commission receives not one dollar from the government. We need money. And lots of it."

"Then it's settled. I shall donate ten percent of my salary, every month, for as long as the Commission needs it."

Charlotte's eyes lit up with something even more alive and beautiful than the firelight they reflected. She threw her arms around his neck. Phineas breathed in deeply, inhaling her rose-water scent, and relished the warmth of her body in his arms. She lightly kissed his cheek before stepping out of the embrace.

"Thank you." Her cheeks flushed.

"Just remember," he said. "I am your greatest admirer."

Phineas went to bed that night realizing that Charlotte would soon leave him. Again. It was not how he had planned the evening to end, but he did not fear losing her anymore.

Some horses were kept in line with a whip. Others responded better to a carrot.

New York City
Tuesday, October 15, 1861

Charlotte had expected Dr. Blackwell and the W.C.A.R. would want to send back some supplies with her when they left for Washington again. She had not expected part of that cargo to be human.

"Her name is Ruby O'Flannery. She will be of help to the hospitals, I assure you, doing menial work that the elite nurses should not be required to perform," Dr. Blackwell explained to her now. "I have a ticket purchased for her already. I would just like you and the Carlisles to escort her down to the city and get her established in her work."

"What would you like her to do, exactly?" Charlotte asked.

"She's willing to be a washerwoman, and from what you and Alice shared in your letters, the hospitals could always use more of those."

Nodding, Charlotte wondered, *What's so special*

about this woman that Dr. Blackwell would pay her fare down to Washington, just so she can do the laundry?

"Just see that she is settled in. She is looking for her husband, who's with the Sixty-Ninth New York Regiment. Surely your sister understands how trying such a separation can be."

"Of course." Charlotte promised to do her best for Ruby O'Flannery. If Dr. Blackwell had an interest in her, she must be a respectable woman.

Act Four

EYES AND HANDS

IT SEEMS A STRANGE THING that the sight of such misery should be accepted by us all so quietly as it was. We were simply eyes and hands for those three days. Strong men were dying about us; in nearly every ward some one was going. . . . Last night Dr. Ware came to me to know how much floor-room we had. The immense saloon of the after-cabin was filled with mattresses so thickly placed that there was hardly any stepping room between them, and as I swung my lantern along the row of pale faces, it showed me another strong man dead. . . . We are changed by all this contact with terror, else how could I deliberately turn my lantern on his face and say to the Doctor behind me, "Is that man dead?" and stand coolly, while he listened and examined and pronounced him dead. I could not have quietly said, a year ago, "That will make one more bed, Doctor." Sick men were waiting on deck in the cold though, and every few feet of cabin floor were precious; so they took the dead man out and put him to sleep in his coffin on deck. We had to climb over another soldier lying up there, quiet as he, to get at the blankets to keep the living warm.

—GEORGEANNA WOOLSEY
in a letter to her mother while aboard the
Ocean Queen on the York River, May 1862

Chapter Twenty-Two

Washington City
Wednesday, October 16, 1861

The journey from New York had been long, but Ruby hadn't minded. She could think of no greater freedom than to be sped away from the three-mile radius in New York City that had been her home since she landed in this country more than a decade ago. Here in Washington, she could start over. Do things right. Put the past behind her, find her husband, and let life in the slums become no more than a faded memory.

Ruby closed her eyes and indulged in a rare, but genuine smile. Maybe she did have a guardian angel. Perhaps the baby growing inside of her was the only way she would have gone to Dr. Blackwell, which was the only way she could have gotten her ticket out of misery. If she found Matthew in time, and they could . . . and he'd believe the baby was his . . . could she dare to hope? Could she keep the baby and her husband both?

A bugle call sounded faintly, and Ruby opened her eyes. The carriage that held her, Miss Waverly, Mrs. Carlisle, and crates of supplies was going uphill, to a four-story brick building surrounded by trees almost as tall. Leaves of crimson, mustard, and gold danced and bowed in the crisp wind.

Once at the white-pillared entrance, the driver helped the women down from the carriage and left the horses snorting and swishing their tails against the flies as he showed them inside the building.

"Let's just let the hospital steward know about the supplies we've brought and we'll see about getting you settled in somewhere," Charlotte said to Ruby.

Before they had covered the length of the hall, a young woman in bright purple satin emerged from a room.

"Cora," said Charlotte, her tone suddenly thick with accusation. "If you please, I would like a word with you." She turned back to Ruby and Alice. "Pardon me, you must think I'm terribly rude, but this cannot wait another moment."

Alice gently nudged Ruby and whispered, "Watch this."

Cora straightened her French hat on her hair and smiled. "Is anything wrong?"

"Yes, Cora," replied Charlotte, lifting her chin. "I'm afraid you are."

"Me?"

"Indeed. I simply can no longer pretend that I do not know what you're doing."

"Why, whatever do you mean?"

"You know exactly what I mean, and I will not

have it in this hospital another minute. The women here all have the men's best interests at heart. All of us, that is, except for you. You, my dear, clearly have your own best interests at heart. It's plain as day."

"I never!" Cora gasped, but her cheeks did not redden with shame.

Ruby's eyes widened as the two women squared off. Cora flashy and defiant, Charlotte staunch and indignant.

"You are no nurse, Cora. I don't know if the men pay you or if your own base satisfaction is payment enough for you, but either way, your depravity has no business here. You must leave now. Your presence hurts all of us. Women like you make it so much more difficult for honest women like Mrs. Carlisle and me—and Mrs. O'Flannery here—to be granted positions and to be taken seriously as nurses. And who knows but that you are spreading venereal disease through-out the wards. You must leave."

The dim realization of what was happening in front of Ruby grew brighter until it almost blinded her.

"On whose authority?" Cora crossed her arms across her corseted waist and thrust a hard stare at Charlotte.

"Mine." It was a male voice, from behind them.

"Fine," Cora huffed, stirring up the thick violet scent she wore. "I was finished with all you old, used-up men anyway." She swept down the hall, turning back only once to say, "You know, there are a lot of other hospitals in need of my 'services' anyway. I'll have no trouble finding other *work*."

"Good riddance," said the man under his breath as they watched her flamboyant exit.

"Dr. Murray," said Charlotte. "What—?"

"Don't look so surprised, Miss Waverly. There are four hundred fifty brothels in Washington just crawling with Union soldiers, picking up venereal diseases as they go. Last thing I need is some prostitute prancing around right here under my nose, making house calls. Just hadn't had the opportunity to confront her about it yet. I'm trying to heal patients, and they're coming up with more work for me to do. Imbeciles." He walked off, still muttering under his breath about brazen prostitutes.

Ruby could feel her posture sagging, her shoulders hunching forward. She wanted to sink into the floor beneath her feet.

Charlotte turned to Ruby now. Her face, which had been so stony a moment ago, now softened into gentility once again. "Mrs. O'Flannery, I do apologize that you had to witness that exchange. A prostitute parading around as a nurse. Enough is enough. Some women are just born reprobate."

Ruby swallowed hard and looked down at her hands. Her heart was beating so fast against her bodice she was afraid it would betray her. "I'm a decent woman, I am." Her voice was weak, as if she herself had already been accused.

"Of course you are." Charlotte laid a hand on her arm.

"I'm Catholic."

"Is that so?" Charlotte's eyes lit up. "Then I think we have the perfect place for you to work, if Alice agrees."

"Yes?"

Charlotte looked at Alice. "Of course!" said the younger sister. "The Washington Infirmary at Judiciary Square, on E Street. It's attended by a number of nuns from the Sisters of Mercy. You'll feel right at home."

The Sisters of Mercy had quickly welcomed Ruby, a fellow Catholic, into the Washington Infirmary, and had just as quickly ushered her down into the linen room. She did not feel at home with the nuns at all, despite Charlotte's prediction. But the linen room, with its low ceiling, cracked window, and steam rising from soiled heaps of filth, reminded her very much of home. Her stomach roiled, as it did every day now, but whether from the pregnancy or the putrid vapors trapped in the room with her, she could not tell.

One other laundry worker, Sister Agnes Teresa, pinned up the sleeves of her habit and churned the sheets in cauldrons of boiling, foaming water

305

with a long stick until the filth loosened from the fibers. Linens with stubborn stains were given to Ruby to scrub on a washboard until they, too, were set free. When she was successful, she was elated to see the white sheet pure and pristine once again.

But not all stains would cooperate. Some of them would not budge.

All the dark blemishes of her past seemed lodged in those stains. Every sin, every sorrow, disappointment, betrayal, sin, every grief, every sin, every sin, every sin . . .

Ruby scrubbed and scraped until her knuckles bled, and yet the stains would not come out.

Ruby's nausea was getting worse, not better. Sister Agnes Teresa believed it was from the fumes of the linen room, and Ruby did not deny it. Was that a sin, too? Deceiving a nun? She swatted the thought aside. Ruby had given up praying anyway.

One morning, between rinsing one load of soiled sheets and boiling the next, Sister Agnes leaned on her broomstick and turned to Ruby. "We've got a new batch of patients upstairs. Can you tell from the sheets what kind they are?"

"What?"

The sister smiled sheepishly. "It's a little game I like to play to pass the time. See if you can guess. Go on, it isn't hard."

Ruby cast a brief glance at the pile by the door. The sheets were sodden, but thank goodness, not with dysentery or diarrhea this time. They were yellow.

"Fever," said Ruby flatly. All she cared about was keeping her hardtack down. The nuns were a stoic lot, subsisting on the bare minimum.

"Right. Several from the Sixty-Ninth have just been moved from their regimental hospital here."

Ruby nodded, unhearing. She was about to throw up again.

"Guess it's a big Irish regiment, from New York. Say, didn't you say you were from New York? I wonder if you know any of them."

Suddenly, Ruby's queasy stomach was forgotten. "What did you say?"

"The New York Sixty-Ninth Regiment. Some of them are here, upstairs."

Ruby looked up sharply at the low ceiling above her. "Here?"

"I just said so. Is something wrong, Mrs. O'Flannery?"

She dropped the sheet she had been scrubbing back into the dirty water and stood up. "My husband."

"What?"

"My husband, Matthew, he's in the Sixty-Ninth! I need to know if he's up there!"

"One way to find out! Go on!"

Ruby untied the wet apron from her waist and

307

spread trembling hands across her belly. It was still flat. No one would guess yet she carried a child within her.

Out of the dark, moist linen room Ruby climbed, breaking through at last onto the ward of fresh fever patients. She caught at the black robe of a passing nun.

"Matthew O'Flannery? Is he a patient here?" The slightest hesitation raked against Ruby's nerves. "I'm his wife! For God's sake, is he here?"

"Go and see for yourself." The nun yanked her robe out of Ruby's grip.

With blood rushing in her ears and heart pounding against her ribs, she picked her way between beds of men so gaunt, so yellow with fever she had to squint at some of the faces to make sure it wasn't her Matthew.

But when she came to his bed, she immediately knew him, even though he now resembled the skinny teenager she had fallen in love with in Ireland more than the brawny, calloused man he had become in New York.

She knelt down beside him and whispered his name.

Nothing.

"Matthew."

A flutter of the eyelids.

"Ruby?"

The floodgates opened, and all the unshed tears of the last six months suddenly came pouring out as she laid her head upon his concave chest. Her voice could utter no words, but her heart cried out a single refrain. *I found you.*

"How?" Matthew croaked out.

"Shhhh," said Ruby. "It's all right. I'm a laundress downstairs! Paid by the government, same as you." It wasn't the whole story, but it was enough.

Over the course of the next several days, Sister Agnes allowed Ruby ample time to visit Matthew, who grew stronger with each dose of quinia, opium, beef tea, and his wife's tender touch. Finally, when he had the strength to tell it, his own story came out.

Why didn't you send the money?

There was no money to send.

Why didn't you send me a letter?

There were no stamps to be had.

Why didn't you come home after Bull Run?

I did, and you weren't there. Nobody knew where you were.

So you came back?

I came back. Here I am. Here you are. You look like an angel, what happened?

I made some changes.

Will you stay?

I won't leave.

I missed you.

I need you.

These brief exchanges, while Matthew was still

quite weak, had been easy in their simplicity. But suspicion seemed to grow along with strength, and his questions became more pointed.

How did you survive?

I sewed.

That's not enough money, Ruby, and I know it. How did you make money?

I became a domestic.

How did you get here?

I met a kind doctor . . .

Did you do favors for someone?

She knew of this job . . .

A woman doctor? Don't you mean a man?

She sent me here herself, she did.

You're not telling me something. I know it.

But by the time Matthew was well enough to be sent back to his regiment, they still had not had time alone together, and still the baby grew inside of her.

The fear of losing Matthew had been replaced by the fear of him learning the truth. Matthew had never been bent on understanding another person's point of view. Even if she began to tell him the whole story, all he would hear would be the very thing he feared the most. His wife, pregnant with another man's child, conceived while he was at war.

She would not be able to complete a single sentence after that before his fists would pummel into her. If he was drunk, he wouldn't stop beating her until the strength drained out of his arms.

He'd never forgive her. He had beaten her before for as much as an unsatisfying meal. The punishment for carrying a bastard child? She'd be a scapegoat for his violence for the rest of her life.

She had heard she had a choice in the matter. She had heard, more than once, there was an answer to her growing problem. Madame Restell on Chambers Street in New York City was famous for providing these answers, for a fee. Back then, Ruby had condemned the idea. But back then, the problem wasn't hers.

Washington City
Tuesday, October 22, 1861

In the burnished edge of October, the wind chafed and bit, carrying with it the scent of wood smoke from the camps encircling Washington. Ruby tugged her shawl closer around the shoulders of her black-and-brown gingham dress. In the apothecary window, there were several bottles of pills, fluid extracts, and medicinal oils labeled in the "Women's Health" category. *Female Regulator, Periodical Drops, Uterine Regulator, Woman's Friend.* These vague names sounded vaguely familiar.

The bell clanged on the door as she stepped inside to take a closer look. Pulling a bottle marked *Graves Pills for Amenorrhea* off the shelf, she read, "These pills have been approved by the Ecole de Medecine, fully sanctioned by the M.R.C.S. of London, Edinburgh, Dublin, as a never-failing remedy for producing the catamenial or monthly flow. Though perfectly harmless to the most delicate, yet ladies are earnestly requested not to mistake their condition [if pregnant] as MISCARRIAGE WOULD CERTAINLY ENSUE." The ingredients were hellebore, ergot, iron, and solid extracts of tansy and rue. "Supplement the doses by drinking tansy tea twice daily until the obstruction is removed," the label instructed. The bottle might as well have read, "Abortion pills." Death in a bottle, for $5.00.

She weighed the bottle in her hand, and felt the heaviness of decision. Grief pressed down upon her, for two babies she had already watched die, for a baby she was ready to kill, and for the part of herself that was willing to do it.

With trembling hand, she rattled the bottle back on the glass shelf. She couldn't do it.

At least, not yet.

Chapter Twenty-Three

Washington City
Wednesday, October 23, 1861

"Good morning, soldier." Edward Goodrich smiled at a convalescent nurse in the Alexandria Hospital.

"No."

"Excuse me?"

"I said no. It isn't. Afraid it's not going to be a good morning for you, either, chappy." His eyes had the hollow look so common to men who had once been strong, men who had long since lost hope of ever recovering their former selves. It was the look of resignation to the grim and uncertain reality of war.

Edward motioned toward a pair of Boston rockers. "Let's have a talk," said Edward, and Private Simmons told what was ailing him.

Ball's Bluff. The battle, which had taken place two days ago, had been a massacre. Union troops stampeded over a cliff and were shot like fish in a barrel. Some of them drowned without the speedy death of a bullet.

"Did you notice that red color in the Potomac River yesterday?" Simmons asked.

Edward shifted his weight in the rocking chair. "I hadn't."

"That was their blood. Do you know what the soldiers around Washington have been doing since then? What I'd a been doing if it weren't for this gimpy leg of mine?"

Edward didn't know. Part of him didn't want to know.

"Fishing. For bodies. Bloated, soggy corpses. Some of them just boys, floated downstream to Washington and washed up on shore like trash. And now their comrades-in-arms are pulling 'em up, trying to pretend they're giant fish and not human beings fighting for the same cause as them."

The taste of bile climbed into Edward's mouth. "I didn't know . . ." he trailed off. He was a chaplain; he was supposed to have answers. But he didn't.

"Oh no, they're trying to keep it real quiet. But word will get out. How do you 'spect the parents and sweethearts and children of those dead men will feel when they hear the truth? There's no dignity in that kind of death. Every soldier wants to die a hero, if he must die, but it doesn't work that way, now, does it?"

Still, no answer came. Edward's mouth had gone dry, and Simmons nodded in agreement. No answer would suffice.

"Now I hate to break it to you, chappy, but the task falls to you to write some letters home to folks telling 'em the fate of their loved ones. Can't hardly recognize most of the corpses. Fish got to their faces before we did, if you know what I mean. It's a right sick business. I don't envy you." With that, Simmons rose, clapped Edward on the shoulder, and limped away.

Minutes passed by—perhaps longer—while the chaplain sat frozen in his rocking chair, composing in his head what he dreaded to scratch on paper.

Dear Mr. and Mrs. ____,
You may have heard by now from official sources that your son has given his life for the glorious cause—

That wouldn't work. War may be necessary, but it was not glorious. Edward tried again.

Dear Mr. and Mrs. ____,
You can be proud of your son, who has recently made the ultimate sacrifice for his country.

No. There was no pride in running off a cliff and being shot while trying to swim away. And was it really called a sacrifice if the death did not contribute to any sort of progress? No. In this case, it was just a waste.

He had to start over.

Dear Mrs. ___,
Your husband did not die in vain—

Maddening! Impossible task! Ball's Bluff was a complete defeat! Of course the men died in vain! Edward clenched the arms of the rocker with white-knuckled fists.

There was a reason he could not bring himself to follow in the footsteps of his father's military career. He hated war. He admired the soldiers and was grateful for their service, but the ugliness and brutality of it all—it was so far from the paradise of Eden and heaven. It was like hell on earth. Nothing in seminary training had prepared him for this. His own faith, which he had felt was so secure, was now in the crucible, where it would either burn up like chaff or be proven as gold.

Edward leaned forward and put his head in his hands. His only prayer was, *Show yourself.* For if he could not see God for the fog of war, how could he point others to Him?

Sanitary Commission Headquarters,
Washington City
Friday, November 1, 1861

A door slammed from somewhere down the hall, and Frederick Law Olmsted jolted awake. He had fallen asleep in his clothes at his desk, again, last night. It was becoming a habit he could do little to hide. *Get some sleep! Go home!* some told him. But those who knew what he and the Sanitary Commission were up against didn't bother.

Donations were down. Contributions were starting to trickle in, and if what Charlotte Waverly had told him about a New York benefactor was true, they would soon see a tide of generosity pouring in. But in the meantime, he waited. The hospitals waited, and so did the patients.

Dr. Blackwell had recently sent him a report of the women's band of nurses, the conclusion of which had been dismal, but not altogether shocking.

The association does not feel authorized to send on more from the same class of life from which these have come—certainly not until their position and relations are essentially improved. The society is deeply convinced of the wisdom of absolutely withholding all nurses not over thirty years of age, and of sending none but those of settled character with marked sobriety of manners and appearance.

The battle for better health care did not end there. Surgeon General Finley was a blockhead. After the ruin of Bull Run, he had been given the opportunity to ask Congress for whatever he needed to make sure nothing of the kind would ever happen again. And what had he asked for? Almost nothing! Forty more medical officers for the army, fifty young medical students to serve as wound dressers, and the right to employ some civilian nurses in the general hospitals. Idiot!

After that, the Sanitary Commission had asked for Finley's removal or resignation, and for remedial legislation. So far, neither had been accomplished, and still men were suffering for it.

At Ball's Bluff, a surgeon had been forced to fire at ambulance attendants to make them function. Why there was still no trained ambulance corps was absolutely beyond Olmsted. It was madness, and it had to stop.

But for some unknown reason—unknown even to God, Olmsted thought—even the press had turned against the Commission. *The New York Times* had published a spirited defense of the Medical Department. The imbecile reporter had the gall to charge the Sanitary Commission with "trying to supersede the established authorities, and thus robbing the soldiers of the boon of having their welfare watched over by men of long military experience." They had called the Commission a group of complaining busybodies sitting safely behind their desks, but not actually doing anything that would put themselves in harm's way.

The nerve. Of course they were complainers. That's what the Commission was designed to do—inspect, recommend, rattle some cages until the authorities decided for themselves to fix what was broken. That's all he wanted to do. Fix it.

Olmsted could feel his temperature rising, and pulled at the white linen collar of his rumpled shirt. Maybe he should have stuck with landscape design. Creating green spaces for public enjoyment, remedying the great social ill of urban crowding . . . that was his specialty. It was so much easier to work with grass and trees and lakes than it was to deal with people. Easier on his eyes, too, he mused, pressing the heels of his hands to his eyelids.

"Is this—sorry, I'm looking for Charlotte Waverly."

Olmsted looked up to find an attractive woman in a calico cotton dress tucking a strand of auburn hair behind her ear. Her accent told him she was Irish. Her eyes told him she was nervous.

"I'm Frederick Olmsted, Secretary of the Sanitary Commission. You wouldn't think it to look at me, though, would you?" *Bother these rumpled clothes.* "And you are?"

"Mrs. Ruby O'Flannery. I came down to work as a laundress a couple months ago. Dr. Blackwell sent me."

"Ah yes! I remember the name. Do sit down."

"That's all right, sir, I just—um . . ." She looked down at her hands, then slid her gaze over the mess of papers on his desk, his uncombed hair, and wrinkled suit. "Is everything all right sir?"

"Not perfect, no," he told her. "You see, my job is to report on what we—the Sanitary Commission—find wrong with the army, and then we tell them how to fix it. But they don't always listen, even though we're experts on the things we recom-

319

mend. Do you have children, Mrs. O'Flannery?"

Her cheeks turned pink as she shook her head, no.

"Well just imagine if you did. Imagine that you see your small child walking toward a fire, and you call out to him, 'Stop! That will burn you!' But he doesn't stop, and what's worse, you are paralyzed to stop him yourself. Or imagine he is poking himself with the end of a stick and wondering why he feels pain. You say, 'If you poke your leg, it will hurt. Stop doing that and you'll be just fine.' But again, he doesn't listen to you, and you are not allowed to remove the stick from his hand. No. You just stand by and watch your child get hurt by his own hand."

He paused, rubbing the back of the neck with his hand. "That, my dear woman, is what we have going on here. We see the Medical Department doing something—or not doing something— which will cause harm to the army. We say 'Stop that' or 'Do this instead,' and more often than not, they completely ignore us, and we are left powerless to do anything else about it."

The woman before him nodded, but clearly, her mind was elsewhere. He had gotten carried away again.

"Now then, Mrs. O'Flannery." Olmsted pushed the Medical Department to the back of his mind and focused on her instead. "Why don't you tell me why you're really here?"

She shifted her weight from one foot to the other. "I was hoping to—well, I need to find Miss Waverly. Do you know where she is?"

"I'm afraid she is across the river bringing a few things to the Alexandria hospitals today. May I help you with anything?"

Ruby shook her head. "Just need to find her, I do."

"Is there trouble at the hospital where you work? Perhaps I can be of service."

She looked down at her hands. At length, she said, "I need to borrow five dollars."

"That's not a trifling sum." Olmsted stroked his mustache. "May I ask what it is for? If you need to purchase for the hospital we might have the very thing you need right here, free of charge."

"It's not for the hospital," she said, still avoiding his gaze. Olmsted waited for more, but she held her tongue. Intriguing.

"Would you like a cup of tea, Mrs. O'Flannery? It's quite dreary out there today, let's at least get you warmed up as long as you're here." She watched as he put a small teakettle of water over a spirit lamp to boil. "You're from New York then? How do you know Dr. Blackwell?"

Ruby bit her lip. "I met her in Five Points." Humiliation threaded her voice.

"Five Points?" Astonishing. How could anyone from Five Points have escaped?

"I'm not a Five Pointer, understand," she quickly said.

"Aha. Then, where is home for you?"

"The Washington Infirmary."

"No, no, I mean in New York. I simply wanted to know if you'd ever been to Central Park."

She laughed. "Aye. Does living in it count?"

"I beg your pardon?"

"My husband and I lived in Seneca Village for several years." Olmsted was suddenly wide awake. He studied her face as she spoke. "Life was good there, it was. Better than what we knew in Ireland, to be sure. It was a small neighborhood, but good people. Immigrants and free blacks. All of us with something in common." She lowered her gaze. "We didn't fit in with the rest of New York. Outcasts, you know. But in our own neighborhood, everyone belonged."

Olmsted nodded. And waited.

"Then someone told us we had to leave. Where should we go? we asked them. They didn't know. They didn't care. They just said leave. They were going to build a park for the rich folks, and they wanted to do it right where we lived."

"Why, Central Park isn't just for rich people, though—it's for everyone, that's the beauty of it, the entire point!" He didn't want to sound defensive, but he certainly felt that way. "A place to come and enjoy fresh air, green grass, blue skies unobscured by the tall buildings now crowding the city. Rich or poor, white or black, native or immigrant, it doesn't matter. That park was made for you."

"No, sir, it was made in spite of me."

Olmsted cleared his throat. "What I mean to say is, all have equal rights to enjoy the nature and clean spaces of Central Park."

A sarcastic laugh escaped Ruby's lips. "We don't have equal rights to anything. Out of all of New York City, they needed—*needed,* mind you—our village. Funny, isn't it? We're the people who would have the hardest time getting back on our feet, and we're the ones they knocked down."

"Yes." Olmsted rubbed a hand over his face. "It is . . . unfortunate." It was an understatement and he knew it. He had long dreaded having a conversation like this one, ever since he learned that more than two hundred people had to be evicted from their homes to make way for the grandest park the city had. It wasn't exactly his fault, but he was not so guiltless that he wanted Ruby to know his part in the matter. "So what did you do?"

Ruby shrugged. "Found a place in the Fourteenth Ward."

"And then?"

"Then Matthew—my husband—left to fight, never sent a dime, and it was up to me to fend for myself."

"I'm sorry."

"Couldn't make rent, though I worked my fingers to the bone. Had to move again."

"To Five Points?"

"I tried. The place was a horror. Listen," she said, rising. "I'm not here to talk about myself. Trying to forget most of that and start again here, you know?"

"Quite." Olmsted stood as well. Either a pang of guilt for her past or a glimmer of hope for her future—he could not be sure which—compelled him to press a five-dollar note into her hand before she could turn to go. "I wish you all the very best life has to offer, Mrs. O'Flannery. I will tell Miss Waverly you were here."

With tears just beginning to veil her green eyes, she said, "Thank you. No need to tell Miss Waverly—I'll be on my way now. I won't be a bother to you anymore."

Mr. Olmsted watched her leave, then, wondering whether those were tears of joy or of sorrow he had seen in the Irishwoman's eyes. Suddenly, he wished he had found out more about why she needed that money.

The teakettle shrieked in his ears, but she was already gone.

Washington Infirmary,
Washington City
Monday, November 4, 1861

Everyone else was asleep when Ruby stole down to the linen room in the dark, a sputtering candle in one clammy hand, the burning bottle of Graves Pills for Amenorrhea in the other. "MISCARRIAGE WILL CERTAINLY ENSUE" read the label. It was exactly what she needed.

Wasn't it?

Beads of sweat formed on her forehead as she opened the bottle and held a small round pellet in her hand. Was it a pill or a bullet? Medicine or a murder weapon? She closed her fist around it, slid down to the floor, and tucked her knees under her chin. Eyes squeezed shut, she rocked back and forth in the agony of uncertainty.

She had been so sure before. It was the only logical thing to do. How could she possibly have a baby? Matthew would be enraged as soon as he found out. Besides, she would not be allowed to work and be seen in public as soon as she grew large, and then what would she do to survive? If the baby survived the pregnancy, how would she afford to feed it? If the baby survived infancy, would it be raised in Five Points to sell apples or hot corn on the streets? Or worse? How could she bring anyone into a world like that? It would be a mercy to the child to snuff it out now.

Death was a fate more merciful than life.

Wasn't it?

Wet sheets hung up to dry, hovered over and around her like white, silent ghosts of soldiers who had passed from life to death at this very infirmary. Had they thought death was the greater mercy? Some probably did. But she had seen how hard most of them fought for a chance at life, even life without limb, or eye, or jaw.

We do what we can for them, the nuns had said, *but God is the Author of Life. He gives, and He takes away. In the end, it is not up to us whether they live or die.*

The words were meant to give comfort, but they tormented Ruby now. *It's not up to us. God is the Author of Life.* A ragged groan tore its way up from somewhere deep within Ruby and filled the room. Life was not up to her. It was not her decision to make.

She had so much to regret already, so many stains she could not wash out. Part of her said one more would make no difference. It would be better, said the tempting voice in her head, to make her own life easier. She deserved a break. And yet, she could not bring herself to add the bright, angry red stain of murder to her heart.

At last, sleep overtook her, and she sank, exhausted, into it, helpless against the nightmares that ravaged her peace. The haunting wail of unborn life soared and swelled in her ears until she awoke, her face wet with tears, to hear her own voice weeping as well. She opened her fist to find the pill was still in her hand—and yet the wails from her nightmare did not disappear. They grew louder.

They were the clanging bells of a fire engine.

Through the small cracked window, she saw the Sisters flapping in the square outside, their shorn heads gleaming eerily as they screamed for help. Stooped figures of men in uniform—they must be the Metropolitan Police—were flooding in, asking where the patients were, how many could walk, how many would need to be dragged from their rooms.

The building was on fire. No one would think to look in the linen room. She had to get out.

Or did she?

This was her punishment, God's vengeance for even considering taking the life of an innocent baby. Ruby had thought the only way to keep her terrible secret was to kill it, so she would not be cast out into the streets upon being discovered as a prostitute. And now the building itself was casting her out. This place of healing, infused with the holy Catholic faith, could not bear to contain her sin any longer. She was being purged, as she had almost purged out her own baby, her own flesh and blood.

Thick cords of smoke writhed and curled around her now, snaking down her throat and choking her.

Maybe—just maybe—this was not punishment, but mercy. Taking the life of her baby would be unforgiveable sin. But to die by accident, to never have to wonder what will become of her child, or herself again, to just have it all end—no one could blame her for dying in a fire. They may never even find her at all.

She eyed the stairway across the room, where dense black smoke came pouring down. Her eyes burned, her mouth filled with the taste of ash. The clanging alarm was drowned by the roar of fire, the thunder of falling timber as the infirmary surrendered to its foe.

Was a just God punishing her? Or was a loving God ending her miserable life as a favor to her? *Either way,* Ruby thought, *the fire is here for me.*

Washington City
Tuesday, November 4, 1861

When the horses and fire trucks thundered by the Ebbitt House in the chilled, predawn hours of the morning, Charlotte was already awake, and glad for the distraction. Ever since she had learned of the hurricane that had damaged or sunk nearly a dozen of the seventy-seven Union ships bound for Port Royal in South Carolina, she could not shake the image of Caleb Lansing drowning at sea. Official reports said his ship had come through unscathed, but she longed to see the proof in his own familiar scrawl. Unreasonable fears always loomed larger in the dark.

The darkness of this night was gone, however. The sky glowed orange with fire, not very far away. From across the street, she spied Frederick

Law Olmsted's limping gait as he exited Willard's Hotel, and knew he was coming for her.

This time, she was dressed when she met him at the door.

"It's the Washington Infirmary." He was breathless. It didn't look like he had slept at all yet that night.

"Ruby!" said Charlotte, Olmsted nodding, and they were on their way out the door. If anything happened to her, it would be Charlotte's fault for placing her there.

By the time they got there, all one hundred four patients had been removed from the burning building, including the forty who could not walk. But when Charlotte asked if anyone had seen a woman with red hair, no one could help her.

"You must have the wrong hospital, lady," said a policeman. "Ain't no such thing as a redhead nun."

"No, she's not a nun. She's an Irish laundress. I know she's in there, she has no place else to go." Charlotte's voice rang with alarm. "Did you try the linen room? In the basement?"

"Lady, no one is doing laundry in the middle of the night. That building is about to collapse. I'm not sending anyone down there."

"For God's sake, check the linen room!" shouted Olmsted.

A fireman jogged over, so covered in soot his silhouette melted into the night. "Somebody still in there? The Sisters said we got all the patients out."

"If you haven't seen a red-haired woman, she might be in the basement in the linen room." Charlotte shouted to be heard. "Please."

"You go in there, son, you may not come out." The policeman shoved a finger at the fireman.

He ignored it. "Which way is it?"

"I'll show you!" Charlotte took off toward the wall of smoke, with the firefighter by her side.

"Stop." He thrust an arm in front of her. "Stay here." And he plunged through the wall of flames and smoke, while Charlotte prayed fervently that she had not just sent a young man to his death.

Please Lord, bring her out. Please let them both be OK. She must have prayed it a hundred times. No, a thousand. The fire brigade seemed helpless to control the blazes, and still Charlotte stood, with a handkerchief pressed to her face, eyes watering, lungs starving. Blasts of heat washed over her in waves. How could Ruby still be alive in there? Every second was a minute, every minute was an hour.

Olmsted was at her side now, his intense black eyes reflecting the flames before them. "She didn't deserve this," he was muttering. "She just needed to get back on her feet . . . She's got to be OK."

Suddenly, out of the smoke, the firefighter emerged, carrying what looked like a giant white cocoon. It was Ruby, wrapped in a wet sheet.

A miracle that he found her. A miracle he made it out alive. But she wasn't moving.

On the other side of the square, the fireman laid Ruby down on the cold pavement and stepped back while Olmsted and Charlotte crouched over her. "I found her under a pile of wet sheets," he said.

November wind swirled around them, and Charlotte gently unwrapped the soggy laundry from around Ruby's body. Was it a life-saver or a shroud?

Charlotte checked Ruby for a pulse and lifted her eyelids to see her pupils. "She's alive. But she's inhaled a lot of smoke into her lungs. I think she's in shock. Quickly, let's take her to the Ebbitt House." She turned to the young man still standing there. "Thank you. I can't thank you enough."

"Just doing my job," he said with a nod. "She going to be OK?"

"We'll do the very best we can for her. Help us lift her into Mr. Olmsted's carriage, won't you?" The firefighter scooped up Ruby as if she were a porcelain doll and laid her in the backseat of the carriage.

Back at the Ebbitt House, Mr. Olmsted helped take Ruby into Charlotte's room.

"Alice," said Charlotte, as Mr. Olmsted lit a fire in the hearth. "We've got company."

After a final look at Ruby, Olmsted limped out of the room, and the sisters went to work on their first female patient. They removed the soiled flannel nightgown, sponge-bathed her body, and dressed her in a clean hospital gown from the collection of supplies lining the walls.

The girl was a mystery. What *had* she been doing in the linen room at that hour of the night, anyway?

Hours later, when her eyes fluttered open for the first time, she had burst into tears. "I was supposed to die in that fire," she said in her delirium.

"No," Charlotte said, "you are supposed to live. God has spared you, miraculously, for a purpose."

Eyes closed again, Ruby shook her head. "No," she muttered. "Not me. God has no purpose for me."

Ebbitt House,
Washington City
Sunday, November 10, 1861

Ruby awoke to the sound of her own moaning. How many days had passed since the night of the fire? Snatches of memory came to her as she squinted at the ceiling from her cot. The bottle of pills. The fire, then blackness. Charlotte Waverly's face, wavy through Ruby's veil of tears. A sponge of cool water on her skin, the gentle tug of a brush through her hair. A soft quilt pulled up to her chin, the crackle and heat of the fire in a nearby hearth. Charlotte's voice, singing.

Ruby sat up and pushed her hair out of her face. Charlotte sat across the room in her rocking chair, knitting red wool socks in the amber glow of a kerosene lamp, singing that tune again.

Through many dangers, toils and snares,
I have already come;
'Tis grace hath brought me safe thus far,
And grace will lead me home.

"Pretty song." Ruby hugged her knees to her chest. "Only 'tisn't quite true, is it?"

Charlotte snapped her head up. "Good morning! Or rather, good evening!" She smiled as she put her knitting down and came to Ruby's side. "What were you saying?"

"That song you were singing. 'Grace has brought me safe thus far.' 'Tisn't true. Not for me, anyway. I've run out of grace."

Charlotte sat on the cot and laid a hand softly on her shoulder. "That's the thing about grace, Ruby. It's not about how much *we* have. It's about how much God has for us. And His supply knows no limits."

Ruby shook her head. "All I know is, I have not been brought 'safe thus far.' My life has been dirty and messy."

"But God has brought you safely to this point. Don't you see? It's no coincidence that you met Dr. Blackwell, that she sent you down here, that we placed you in the very hospital where you found your husband again."

"The very hospital that burned to the ground."

"But you didn't. You could have died in that fire, but you were saved—kept safe thus far—by God. Don't you see His hand guiding you?"

Ruby knew that Charlotte had no idea what she was talking about. Ruby had been on her own for quite some time, and she had made a mess of things. Maybe if God had truly been guiding her, she wouldn't be in this place.

"Listen," Charlotte started again. "I realize your life has been much different than mine. It isn't fair, and I know I can't fix everything for you. But Dr. Blackwell saw something in you that she thought was special, and she placed you in my care while you are here. You are a good, hard-working woman and I'm going to make sure you are taken care of while you're here."

Ebbitt House,
Washington City
December 15, 1861

Snow fell gently outside the Ebbitt House as Charlotte and Ruby knitted socks in the rocking chairs by the fire.

"Is Alice at the hospital?" Ruby asked.

"No, she's with Jacob in camp this evening." Her knitting needles paused midair. "Ruby, your husband is likely not very far away. Wouldn't you like to visit him, or have him come here, now that you're no longer sick?" It was only last week that Ruby's nausea and vomiting from exposure to the fire had stopped.

Ruby's eyes darted down to her waist and back up to Charlotte. "No, thank you. It's enough to know he is nearby. I don't want to bother him. I'm sure he's very busy."

Charlotte laughed. "You know what they say— 'All's quiet on the Potomac.' McClellan isn't doing anything but drilling the troops for the winter. I'm sure a visit could be arranged—"

"I said no! Thank you. It's too late."

Charlotte let her knitting fall to her lap as she eyed the small red-haired woman on the other side of the hearth.

"Too late for what?"

"I'm tired." Her tone was clipped. "I need a lot of sleep lately. I'd like to go to bed soon."

"Of course. I didn't mean we'd go out in the snow and look for him tonight. Another time. Soon."

But Ruby shook her head, tucked her knitting into the basket and stood. "I told you, I'm tired." And she went to bed.

It was half past eight.

Tybee Island, South Carolina
Tuesday, December 24, 1861

Outside Dr. Caleb Lansing's tent, the air was spiced with scents of evergreen and wood smoke. He watched a dozen soldiers decorate trees, their voices lifting Christmas carols in their native German tongue. *Stille Nacht, heilige Nacht, alles schläft; einsam wacht.*

The row of Christmas trees twinkled with the blinking light of crude candles and were adorned with strips of salt pork and beef, and with hard-tack cut into confectioner shapes.

With his hands wrapped around his tin cup of coffee, Caleb closed his eyes and sang the English version quietly to himself. *Silent night, holy night, all is calm, all is bright. Round yon virgin mother and child, holy infant so tender and mild. Sleep in heavenly peace. Sleep in heavenly peace.*

In a former lifetime, Charlotte had stood next to him in a poinsettia-filled church service, her clear alto voice harmonizing with his bass to these very words. Her face, framed softly by an ermine stole, was radiant in the candlelight, the gold flecks in her eyes shone brightly. The stained-glass angels looking down on them looked dull and plain in comparison. As a young man, Caleb had been awed by the glow of her innocence and beauty, then.

That was years ago, before her father's death,

before the war. He felt he had aged twenty years since then. He had been surprised last time he looked in the mirror, not by the patches of lightened hair at his temples, but by the fact that he had not gone completely grey yet.

Charlotte had grown, too, and he was still awed by her. The memory of her as he had stumbled upon her in the Columbian College Hospital last August—dress covered in diarrhea, eyes full of fire, head still held high—inspired a grin every time it crossed his mind. Which was often. She was even more like an angel as a nurse than she had been wearing the finest Parisian fashions.

Caleb shook his head to jar loose the growing affection taking root in his mind. It wouldn't be fair to nurture any feelings beyond friendship while the war kept them apart. He had no time for that, and neither did she. They both had work to do, and the last thing either of them needed was the distraction of love—or even heartbreak. All he could do was write to her, keeping up the familial friendship that stretched back over decades.

The music and flavor of Christmas followed him back into his moldy canvas tent, where he took out a sheet of paper, rubbed his hands together to warm his fingers, and began writing.

Dear Charlotte,
    It seems a very strange thing to be celebrating Christmas, the advent of peace

on earth, while far from home in a camp of war. I must confess that had it not been for my caroling neighbors, I may have forgotten the date all together. I have been so consumed with the work here that all my days run together in one unending sick call.

You speak of our hospital here as if we already have one—we do not. We are told we will, in due time, but when that happens it will be no thanks to the Medical Department. Dr. Cooper, the Medical Director of this expedition, urged the necessity of a hospital. General William Sherman so ordered one, but Surgeon General Finley—the old goat—countermanded the order. No need, said he. "In this fine mild Southern climate, tents will do very well for the men to have fevers in," said he. I'd like to see him brave three days of a Texas norther in scanty apparel and see what he thinks of the climate then! To keep our fever patients, with their lowered vitality, warm in the tents, we place warm thirty-two-pound cannonballs at their feet, and another glowing stack of them in the middle of the floor.

Neither do we have the medicines we need. There is one supply table of medicines for hospital use and another for field use. Some very important, almost essential, are not furnished for field service. When your patient needs them, he is to go to the hospital. Very good. But where is the hospital for us? That's right—we haven't got one. So before we came here, I made a special requisition for some things not found on the field supply table, such as serpentaria, and some of the salts of iron, and went in person to the purveyor's office to request it. No use. The fever itself is madness, and it is madness to not have the medicine.

Our tents, flimsy speculator's ware at best, are now in a most deplorable condition. I am distressed to think of the impending long rainy season with no other shelter.

With "Stille Nacht, heilige Nacht," ringing in my ears, I wish you a merry Christmas, dear Charlie. Sleep in heavenly peace, for Christ the Savior is born.

> Affectionately,
> Caleb

Chapter Twenty-Four

Ebbitt House,
Washington City
Wednesday, December 25, 1861

As far as Charlotte was concerned, Christmas had already been a success.

No patient in Washington was without at least one new pair of wool socks for the holiday, and the nurses of each hospital had decorated their wards festively with evergreen boughs, holly branches, and bright red-and-green tissue paper. All patients who could stomach food were indulged with true Christmas feasts of roast turkeys, loaf-cakes iced with filigree, pies, cream puffs, cranberry sauce, and puddings of all sorts.

Now it was time to prepare for a Christmas evening visit with Jacob in camp.

"Aye, such a bonnie dress," said Ruby as Charlotte finished buttoning her bodice. It was only a walking dress, made of wine-colored silk and trimmed with gold braid at the neckline, cuffs, and hem. All her formal gowns were waiting patiently in her dressing room in New York City. Still, she wore hoops under her dress for the first time in months—mainly because without them, the three-tiered skirt would drag

340

on the ground. "I really don't think I should come with you."

"And spend Christmas alone in a hotel room?" Charlotte looked up at her. "Nonsense! You're coming."

"I have nothing to wear!"

Charlotte flashed a smile and winked at Alice. "Oh yes, you do!" She held up a hand to stop Ruby's protest. "I know we said no gifts, but Alice and I decided to make one little exception." She walked over to the clothes rack and, with a flourish, she unveiled a new dress. "Merry Christmas, Ruby." She smiled.

Ruby's hands flew to her mouth. "No, no, it's too good for the likes of me. I won't be putting on airs. I know my place."

"Ruby." Alice's voice was firm, but her blue eyes glimmered. "This is a gift. It would be our pleasure for you to have it."

"Don't want to pretend to be something I'm not."

"And what's that?"

"A respectable lady, that's what."

Charlotte laughed. "Ruby, I have more respect for you than I have for a dozen shallow women who wear much finer things than these. You have a big heart. You work hard. You are selfless. The women in my set from home can boast none of those qualities. Come now, and take it. See how beautiful you can be."

Still shaking her head in doubt, Ruby stepped forward and took the green silk dress in her arms as if it were Cinderella's ball gown instead of just a walking dress, like Charlotte's. The bodice formed a fashionable jacket spreading over the top of the skirt, and Scottish plaid satin banded the cuffs and hem of the jacket and skirt.

Wordlessly, Ruby turned her back and stripped down to her chemise and petticoat.

"Here, let me help you." Charlotte held open a steel hoop-lined petticoat. "Step in, please."

"I can tie it myself." Ruby snatched the ties from Charlotte's hands. "I can manage it. Thank you."

The dress looked beautiful on Ruby, but didn't fit as perfectly as Charlotte had expected. It was a little snug in the bust and waist.

"Do you want me to tighten your corset, Ruby?" Alice asked. "We're pulling the fabric just a little tight here."

"No thank you, it's as tight as I can stand it." She stepped back.

Strange. Charlotte had had three working dresses made for Ruby after the fire, which had all fit fine, but this one, cut to the same measurements, was clearly too small. Then again, she had been eating more lately. And why shouldn't she? Only God knew how deprived she had been in Five Points. If her natural, healthy shape didn't fit the fifteen-inch waist standard, so be it. The size of her heart mattered far more than her figure.

"You look radiant." Charlotte turned Ruby by the shoulders so she could see herself in the mirror. She brushed Ruby's dark red hair until it shone in the kerosene-lamp light, braided it in sections and pinned them in coils behind her head. Sprigs of red-berried holly added the finishing touch.

Alice handed Ruby an unwaisted cape edged with red fox fur, along with a matching muff and hat. "The rest of your Christmas present."

With a timid smile, Ruby said, "Thank you, fairy godmothers."

Nodding, Charlotte pulled on her own fitted wine velvet cape bordered with white fur and ermine tails, grabbed the matching hat and muff, and held the door open. "After you, Cinderella."

Ruby was sure the spell would be broken at any moment.

With their hands warm in their muffs, and a fur blanket on their laps, the ride to Alexandria reminded her of the Courier & Ives lithograph she had seen hanging in the Ebbitt House. Fine white flakes fell from a black suede sky, the horses' bells jangled in rhythm with their snow-muffled hoofbeats. Though the brittle wind nipped at their noses, everyone in the carriage was smiling in the lantern light—especially Edward Goodrich, whom they had picked up at the Mansion House

Hospital on their way to Cameron Run, Jacob's camp west of the city.

Edward's eyes had lit up when he had seen Charlotte, and Ruby couldn't blame him. Charlotte was beautiful in a hoopless nursing uniform. Tonight, she was stunning. Maybe Charlotte didn't notice the way Edward took in the sight of her, as if he was taking a long cool drink of water after spending days in the desert. But Ruby did.

Once they were at Cameron Run, a pretty hillside dotted with tents like miniature glowing pyramids, Captain and Mrs. Carlisle behaved toward each other like no other married couple Ruby had ever known. He looked at her with such adoration, almost like the stained-glass disciples gazing up at the Virgin Mary in St. Patrick's Cathedral on Mott Street. They spoke softly, lightly, to each other. He guided her with his hand on the small of her back and stood until she sat—even if the seat was nothing better than an overturned barrel. A gentle word from her made his battle-hardened face soften into a smile. A wink from him brought pink into her cheeks. *Was there ever a time when Matthew and I acted that way with each other?* Ruby reached back into the sleeping depths of her memory. *When did our relationship go from love to simply a way to survive?*

The smell of fresh coffee filled Jacob's tent, competing with the heady aroma of a sticky, homemade pine needle wreath Alice had brought.

"Mrs. O'Flannery," Captain Carlisle said. "We have one more Christmas surprise for you." Ruby's gaze skittered between him and the rest of the group. All of them were beaming. *What on earth?*

"No, please no. I don't have gifts for anyone."

"I'm afraid we can't take this one back. At least, not until later tonight." Captain Carlisle pulled back the flap of his tent. A soldier ducked inside, brass buttons gleaming in the lantern's glow, sword gently swinging from its hilt at his side. He was almost too tall for his light blue trousers, but the dark blue jacket looked almost loose on his frame. A red cloverleaf topped the blue kepi he now held in his hands as his bright blue eyes scanned the little group.

"Matthew!" Ruby cried. The fairy-tale Christmas was complete.

He stared at her, as if unseeing. He had never seen her like this before, in an English hoop skirt, her hair braided and coiled on her head. Even her posture was much straighter, now that she wasn't hunched over her sewing fifteen hours every day. She took a step forward then, holding out trembling hands.

"It's me," she said. " 'Tis Ruby!"

"Bedad!" he said, and studied every inch of her. "You're so bonnie, lass! What happened?"

Nervous laughter rippled through the group.

"Come, let's leave these two alone for a while," said Alice, and the foursome quietly filed out of the tent toward the music of the regimental band. Suddenly, Ruby and Matthew were alone for the first time since before the war began.

Matthew reached out, tentatively, and took Ruby's hands in his. "Is it really you?"

"Aye," Ruby whispered, and tears pooled in her eyes. "You're looking better. How do feel? After that fever?"

Matthew shrugged. "I'm not the same as I was before it, but I'm not so bad as I was with it, either."

"You've lost some weight in this war, haven't you?" she said.

"Seems to me you've found the missing pounds."

Ruby jerked her hands out of his and stepped back, folding her arms across her waist. A shudder of fear rippled through her.

"You look—healthy," Matthew finally said. Ruby was stunned. "I never wanted you to go hungry, Ruby." It was as close to an apology as she would ever hear from him. For her, it was enough.

"I know you didn't."

"Was it very bad for you this year? When I went away, and they didn't pay us for months, and then I didn't know how to reach you when they did start. How did you survive?"

Ruby fixed her gaze downward, landing on the

brass button above his leather belt. *Not that question. Please don't ask me. Please.*

He lifted her chin with his finger so she could not avoid his probing gaze. "You thought I left you. For good. Didn't you?"

"I didn't know. I didn't even know if you were dead or alive."

Silence.

"How did you get here, with these rich friends of yours?"

Ruby explained it to him, again. She had told him this in the hospital, but she was not surprised he needed to hear it again.

"It still doesn't make sense to me."

"I think I make them feel guilty about the rich and easy lives they've had," Ruby said. "They are trying to make themselves feel better by being kind to me."

"So you're their pet project?"

"Aye. Like the House of Industry in Five Points."

"If it means you have a place to sleep, and food, and clothes, take it. You've got to get by, any way you can. Right?"

Ruby blinked. "Any way I can?"

Matthew narrowed his eyes at her. "Well, almost." He pierced her with a gaze as sharp as shards of glass. "What have you done, lass?"

"Survived."

He answered her with a slap.

"You're keeping something from me. You belong to me. Don't think I won't figure out your little secret."

Ruby covered her burning cheek with her hand as her stomach dropped to the floor.

The fairy-tale spell dissolved. Her dress might as well have been the threadbare calico she had worn in the slums, her hair stringy and greasy, her skin pin-pricked, her muscles cramped. Matthew knew who she really was. And soon enough, he would know what she had done. A squalling baby would tell him.

Outside Jacob's tent, it was impossible to forget the war, even on Christmas, surrounded as they were by uniformed soldiers warming themselves by smoky fires.

"We never thought we'd still be here at Christmas," said Jacob, looking out over the encampment.

"Well, I for one, am very glad you are!" Alice squeezed him around the waist just for a moment—a display only permitted in times of war, surely.

"Yes, darling. Of course I'm glad to be near you, too. But at some point, we're going to have to break camp and make a move. March somewhere, fight some Rebs. Drilling to perfection does not win a war."

"But isn't McClellan ill?" asked Charlotte.

"Terribly so, I'm afraid." Jacob sighed. "Fever. It's enough to make every soldier here take notice when the major general succumbs to it in the dead of winter. None of us are safe."

"Oh, don't say that." Alice linked her arm through his.

"It's true," said Charlotte. "You remember just two weeks ago, Prince Albert died of it, making poor Queen Victoria a widow! They say she is in such deep mourning she had all the finials in London painted black."

"Now that was an interesting marriage," said Alice, a hint of humor in her tone. "Can you imagine, Jacob, if I were queen, and you just a prince, and you had to obey me instead of the other way around?"

"No thank you." Jacob laughed. "I like things just the way they are."

"And yet their story is one of the most celebrated romances in history!" said Charlotte. "The hierarchy of power certainly seemed to work for them. Maybe Florence Nightingale isn't the only British woman from whom we could take a lesson."

"Charlotte!" Alice jabbed an elbow at her sister.

"I'm joking." Charlotte laughed.

"Only half. I know you."

Another chuckle escaped Charlotte, and she wondered what Mr. Goodrich must think of her now. By the look in his eyes, he was more amused than offended.

In the lull of conversation, the lively music of the regimental band curled around Charlotte and drew her toward it. "Come!" she said. "We're already stomping our feet to keep warm, we might as well stomp in time!"

Jacob and Alice gladly obliged, and Charlotte looked expectantly at Edward. She hoped he wasn't lonely. She certainly would be, if she didn't have Alice and Jacob here.

Smiling, Edward drew her to himself with a feather-light touch. His hand, holding hers, grew warm almost immediately.

"Are you thinking of a sweetheart back home tonight, Mr. Goodrich?"

"No," he said quickly. "No sweetheart at home. Home seems like such a faraway dream now, doesn't it?"

Charlotte nodded. "And one day, so will this."

One-two-three and one-two-three and one-two-three—

"You look lovely tonight, Miss Waverly."

"Thank you," she replied. "So do you."

He cocked his head and frowned. "Not exactly what I was eager to hear, I must say."

"I'm sorry, Mr. Goodrich. There must be a little brandy in that punch."

"Wouldn't doubt it."

"I meant you look handsome. You really do." The baby fat had melted off his face in the last few months since he had come to be a hospital chaplain. The flicker of eagerness in his eyes had mellowed into subdued thoughtfulness. "You look wiser," she went on. "You've walked alongside suffering. You were already an intelligent and devout man, Mr. Goodrich, but now you have been tried in a baptism of fire, haven't you? It shows in your eyes." *Like Caleb's,* she thought.

"Please. Call me Edward."

She smiled. "And you must call me Charlotte."

One-two-three and one-two-three and one-two-three—"It's been difficult, I'll be honest. It's a relief that you understand, without my having to explain anything to you, of the sights and sounds that accompany our work in the hospitals. Some days I have to remind myself I won't be here forever. The war, no matter how it seems right now, will not last forever. This is just a season."

" 'To everything there is a season, and a time to every purpose under heaven.' "

He gripped her hand a little tighter and smiled. " 'A time to kill, and a time to heal; a time to break down, and a time to build up.' "

" 'A time to weep, and a time to laugh; a time to mourn, and a time to dance!' " Charlotte smiled brightly. She had resolved that tonight, in celebration of her Savior's birth, was a time to be happy. "I understand how you feel," she went on. "But please, know you are making a difference, bringing hope and light where there is so little these days. Alice and I are so grateful you answered our call for a chaplain, and I often hope you don't regret the decision. I'd blame myself if the work didn't suit you."

The corner of his mouth tipped up. "It suits me. No regrets." His voice was husky.

"Good. We need you."

"And I—" Edward broke off and slowed his steps ever so slightly before picking back up again in time with the music. Bright pink blotches bloomed above Edward's collar on his neck, and his small frosty clouds of breath came quicker. His hand was sweating now.

He was uncomfortable. Perhaps he had not been to many dances during his years at seminary. *I shouldn't make him feel like we need to talk throughout the dance,* she thought. *Maybe he needs to concentrate on the steps to lead.*

Charlotte, on the other hand, could waltz in her sleep. Closing her eyes, she let the music—and Edward—carry her away, and couldn't help but remember the last time she had waltzed. She had been so upset about the war breaking out, and her helplessness to do anything to help, that she hadn't wanted to be at the ball at all. Her dancing was purely mechanical, and she had been sure she would make a misstep.

And then Caleb had shown up. *What if your stepping out of formation was actually a step in the right direction?* he had said. *What a shame it would be if you were always confined to a prescribed number and pattern of steps.*

Had he known then, that his words were the perfect prelude for her becoming a nurse? The man was a prophet. She hoped he was enjoying himself tonight, wherever he was. Caleb always knew the right thing to say.

The music ended, and Charlotte opened her eyes. She curtsied to Edward, but the smile lingering on her lips was for Caleb.

It was no longer Christmas by the time Charlotte, Alice, and Ruby returned to the warmth of the Ebbitt House. Ruby had been ready to leave hours earlier, and had fallen asleep in the carriage on the way home. All she wanted to do was curl up in her cot and forget about her expanding waistline and swelling bust. Her secret would be out in a matter of weeks, she guessed, and she had no idea what to do about it.

"Come on, sleepyhead." Charlotte linked her arm through Ruby's elbow. "Time to take off those glass slippers."

Don't worry, I've been walking around barefoot ever since I saw Matthew, she thought, but said nothing.

"I'm sorry you couldn't spend more time with your husband," Alice said. "I know it never feels like enough. But I do hope it was better than nothing."

"It was sweet of you to find him," Ruby forced out, though all she felt was bitterness.

"Speaking of which—" Alice said. "Charlotte, your Christmas present came a little late this year. So sorry. Merry December 26!"

Charlotte's heart leapt. *Caleb?* Her eyes searched the lobby until they settled on a gentleman in a black cutaway suit and gleaming white bow-tie cravat.

"Phineas!" Charlotte gasped and held out her hand to him. "Heavens, what a surprise! I thought you couldn't get away!"

"Better late than never, am I right?" He bowed low, and gallantly kissed her hand.

Alice leaned over to Ruby. "Charlotte's suitor, Mr. Phineas Hastings. Just arrived from New York tonight. Shame he couldn't have come to camp with us, but he's more suited to the finer things of life, anyway."

Ruby's heart stopped. Was she dreaming? Phineas Hastings was Charlotte's suitor? Had she even mentioned him before? She ducked her head, avoiding his eyes. *Dreadful. Impossible.*

"Pardon me," Charlotte said. "I've been rude. Allow me to introduce you. This is Mrs. O'Flannery, our roommate. This is the woman who survived the fire last month, remember, darling? I told you about her."

"Well, you certainly look fit as a fiddle now, thank God." He gave her a polite bow.

"I'm Phineas Hastings. Charmed, I'm sure."

Ruby could barely hear him over the blood rushing in her ears. She curtsied, but said nothing, unwilling for her Irish accent to betray her. Her heart beat frantically against her corset, her feet were ready to take flight.

She chanced a glance at his face again. No hint of disturbance had hardened his features. He chatted amiably with Charlotte and Alice, and she was once again on the outside, an unimportant accessory. He had looked Ruby in the face, but had seen only a stranger. *Was it possible? He didn't recognize her?* Suddenly she remembered that her new dress and fur-lined cape had not, in fact, disintegrated into the dirty calico she had worn in New York. Her hair was still arranged and adorned as if she were a genteel lady, and she wasn't nearly as skin-and-bones scrawny as she had once been. Right now, he only had eyes for Charlotte, anyway.

"All right, you two, I know you have some catching up to do, but I do believe I hear my bed calling my name," said Alice, and she whisked Ruby into the safety of their room.

Finally, it was time to take off her false identity, layer by layer. Hat, cape, dress, corset, hoops, petticoats, chemise, drawers, stockings, boots. Feeling stripped and exposed, Ruby donned her flannel wrapper in the dark and curled up on her cot under the covers. She placed a hand over the small mound of her belly and tried to plan a new escape. But even after she heard the soft click of the door and the rustle of sheets as Charlotte climbed into her own cot, she still had not thought of a way to leave.

Chapter Twenty-Five

Washington City
Sunday, January 19, 1862

The gaiety of Christmas seemed a world away now that January had arrived dreary and dismal in Washington City. Grey marble buildings rose up out of the sludge and blended in with the drab winter sky. The unpaved streets choked on ridges and puddles of red clay–tinged slush. *Oh for a good New York snowfall to cover this mess!* Charlotte thought.

Still drying out from the ride back to the Ebbitt House from church, clouds of steam floated up into Charlotte's face as she poured hot water into a tin canteen. She screwed the cork tightly in the top, wrapped it in flannel, and handed it to Alice.

"Ah, thank you," Alice said with a sigh. She cradled her cup of raspberry tea in one hand and hugged the hot water bottle against her middle with the other. "Be glad you don't have to experience this month after month like the rest of our sex. It's like somebody's in there, twisting fistfuls of my insides."

Charlotte cringed, and glanced at Ruby. "Tell the truth now, Ruby. Is my sister exaggerating? You've certainly never complained the way Alice does—" She stopped. *She's never complained at all.* Ruby had been living with them for a little more than two months now, and she had never made so much as a peep about any kind of menstrual pain.

"I do wish you weren't so stoic about it, Ruby, you make me look so weak!" Alice chided, laughing, but Ruby wasn't smiling. The color had drained from her face and her hands trembled, clumsily knocking her knitting needles together in front of her stomach. *She's trying to hide her belly. The appetite, the fatigue, the weight gain— why didn't I see it?*

"No, I don't believe you've suffered the monthly cramps yourself for quite some time, have you, Ruby?" Charlotte asked with a smile.

"What?" Alice frowned. She looked at Ruby until comprehension smoothed away the confusion written on her brow. "You're going to have a baby! How wonderful!"

"Don't bother denying it, Ruby," said Charlotte. "You can't hide behind knitting needles and bundles of laundry forever! Congratulations! You and Matthew must be so happy!"

"Oh," cried Ruby. "Please don't say anything to Matthew!"

"You haven't told him?" Surprise edged Charlotte's voice.

"He'd send you home, wouldn't he?" said Alice, nodding. "I know if I was in the family way, Jacob would not rest until I were safely back in New York instead of here on the edge of war."

"Is that why you kept your secret from us for so long?" Charlotte asked. "You didn't want to be sent away?"

"Aye," said Ruby. "I have no other place to go."

"I feel the same way about being near Jacob," said Alice. "I used to think a woman's place was in the home. Now I realize that home is where my husband is. My proper place is as close as I can be to Jacob. I understand. Your secret is safe with us, Ruby. When it gets too difficult for you to do laundry at the hospital, you just give it up. We'll take care of you."

Ruby's shoulders sagged with visible relief, but Charlotte couldn't help but think her husband should know. Wouldn't he be better off with the hope of a baby in the near future? Or would the added responsibility really be too much for him? *Either way, something just isn't right about this.*

The White House,
Washington City
Monday, February 24, 1862

The huge gilt mirrors in the East Room of the White House were draped in mourning, black fabric covering the frames, and white on the glass. Grief hung so thickly in the air Edward Goodrich felt as if he was choking on it. He had never been to a child's funeral before, and he'd never dreamed that his first one would be for President Lincoln's boy. But four days ago, in this very mansion, typhoid fever had claimed the life of eleven-year-old Willie. The entire nation mourned the loss, and Edward had a front-row seat to the gut-wrenching grief of a parent burying his child.

Torrential rain and howling wind rattled the windows of the White House with a vengeance, reflecting the violent storm of sorrow within the mansion itself. Mary Lincoln was so overcome with the loss of her favorite son that she did not come to his funeral, but stayed, weeping, in her room instead. Another Lincoln son lay ill in another bed, while the funeral proceeded downstairs.

President Lincoln was bent with emotion. His oldest son, Robert, was at his side, and congressmen, senators, foreign dignitaries, members of the cabinet, soldiers, and chaplains were all witnesses. Even General George B. McClellan was there, himself only recently recovered from the disease. Not one of them had dry eyes. For this one moment, Lincoln the great president was Abraham the grieving father, a poor soul to be pitied above all men.

Edward's head throbbed and his eyes burned in sympathy for the president's personal loss. No joy could be wrung out of the news of Union victories in the west when the president's son lay dead in a casket.

How would I comfort this family, if it were my responsibility? Edward wondered, and could come up with no magic words to ease the pain. *I'm a hospital chaplain and a man of God; I should be able to do this!* Angry tears gathered in his eyes. Had all of his faith, all of his seminary training been for nothing? *God, what good can come from a child's death? How does this bring You glory?*

Edward's emotions matched the pitch of the storm raging outside as Reverend Dr. Gurley, pastor of New York Avenue Presbyterian Church, rose to make some remarks.

"The eye of the Nation is moistened with tears, as it turns today to the Presidential Mansion." Dr. Gurley projected his voice over the booming thunder. "The heart of the Nation sympathizes with its Chief Magistrate, while to the unprecedented weight of civil care which presses upon him is added the burden of this great domestic sorrow; and the prayer of the Nation ascends to Heaven on his behalf, and on the behalf of his weeping family, that God's grace may be sufficient for them, and that in this hour of sore bereavement and trial, they may have the presence and succor of Him, who has said, 'Come unto me, all ye that labour and are heavy laden, and I will give you rest.'"

Yes, but is that rest here on this earth or do we have to wait until we die to get it in heaven? Edward thought.

"Oh, that they may all be enabled to lay their heads upon His infinite bosom, and find, as many other smitten ones have found, that He is their truest refuge and strength; a very present help in trouble."

If God were so helpful, He wouldn't have let the child die in the first place!

"It is well for us, and very comforting, on such an occasion as this, to get a clear and a scriptural view of the providence of God. His kingdom ruleth over all. All those events which in anywise affect our condition and happiness are in His hands, and at His disposal. Disease and death are His messengers; they go forth at His bidding, and their fearful work is limited or extended, according to the good pleasure of His will. Not a sparrow falls to the ground without His direction; much less any one of the human family, for we are of more value than many sparrows."

And yet the sparrows still fall, America is still torn asunder, the soldiers are still shot down and cut to pieces, and children still die in their beds. This is the direction of God? This is His will? My God, where is the comfort in that? How cruel that God sees and yet does nothing to stop it!

Brilliant lightning cracked open the sky. Dr. Gurley continued. "What we need in the hour of trial, and what we should seek by earnest prayer, is confidence in Him who sees the end from the beginning and doeth all things well. Only let us bow in His presence with an humble and teachable spirit; only let us be still and know that He is God; only let us acknowledge His hand, and hear His voice, and inquire after His will, and seek His Holy Spirit as our counselor and guide, and all, in the end, will be well."

The wind moaned and wailed in protest. All was not well today.

"In His light shall we see light; by His grace our sorrows will be sanctified—they will be made a blessing to our souls—and by and by we shall have occasion to say, with blended gratitude and rejoicing, 'It is good for us that we have been afflicted.'"

A glance at President Lincoln's face told Edward that he was far, very far, from being able to count his afflictions as good. From somewhere in the rooms above them, Mary Lincoln wept, and outside the heavens wept with her.

For the first time since Edward was a small child in Sunday school, he was beginning to doubt the goodness of God. All of his studies, all of his Scripture memorization, could not keep up with the deluge of human misery flooding his spirit here in Washington. His heart beat wildly in his chest. *What business does a chaplain have doubting God?* His palms perspired into his tear-soaked handkerchief. *What business does a doubter have pretending to be a chaplain?*

Chapter Twenty-Six

Ebbitt House,
Washington City
Monday, March 17, 1862

Dear Phineas,

Finally, at long, long last, McClellan is making a move. The great Army of the Potomac, still thawing from its winter in camp, is now bound for the Virginia Peninsula.

Alice is beside herself because they say we cannot possibly accompany the army now, and she has been spoiled, I fear, from being able to visit Jacob on an almost daily basis. But it's too dangerous for us to go any further, they say. Since we cannot be near Jacob, who is now the colonel of his regiment, Mother is pressing us to come home. But we continue to work on Jacob, and with a great deal of luck, he will come around and make a way for us to go with them.

Fondly,
Charlotte

New York City
Tuesday, March 25, 1862

My dear Charlotte,

It is one thing for you to nurse while staying the night at a fine hotel. But to follow the army into the battlefields, beyond enemy lines, this is too much. Your brother-in-law will do right if he refuses you. Don't be upset with me, darling, for you know it is only from a loving heart I speak these things.

Yours, as ever,
Phineas

Washington City
Tuesday, April 15, 1862

Dear Phineas,

You need not attempt to limit the scope of my usefulness. Jacob is already doing that, for he is proving to be more stubborn than I had imagined he could ever be. To our dismay, so far, we have no hope of following the army. But I have not given up yet.

Ruby, the laundress who nearly burned at the Washington Infirmary last November—remember, you met her over Christmas—would like to come, too, to follow her own husband and I am inclined to take her with us, assuming we secure permissions. I confess I still feel slightly responsible for her more than for any of the elite nurses Dr. Blackwell sent down to us.

Affectionately,
Charlotte

New York City
Tuesday, April 22, 1862

Ruby? Could it possibly be the same? Phineas reread the letter, his eyelid twitching. *I met her over Christmas?* He vaguely, vaguely remembered meeting a very quiet but beautiful Mrs. O'Something-or-other. *What was it?* O'Sullivan? O'Brian? O'Flaherty? Phineas slapped a hand to his forehead. *Now I'm starting to sound just like Mother.*

Meeting that woman had been just a blip, an all together forgettable incident right after he had seen Charlotte again for the first time in months. It would be strange if he did remember the name. And then he hadn't seen that woman again during his entire visit.

It couldn't have been her. The Ruby he knew wasn't married. She had told his mother that she had no family. She could have been lying, of course. She had lied about other things. Or she could have meant that she had no family in town

366

to care for, which would still allow for a husband fighting the war . . .

It would be preposterous to believe that the woman he most wanted out of his life somehow ending up as the pet of the woman he most wanted to win. Irish immigrants didn't travel. They stayed stuck. It couldn't be her.

Or could it?

Phineas rubbed a hand wearily over his goatee and groaned. He had truly turned a corner in his life since Charlotte had come to visit in October. Her gratitude for his regular donations to the Sanitary Commission had pleased him. Charlotte believed in him, and he believed in himself. But if this Ruby was the same Ruby he knew, she had the power to unravel the life he had knit together with Charlotte.

He was walking now, as if his legs knew what to do even before his mind had thought of it. He picked up his wide-brimmed hat and brown wool frock coat as he clamored down the steps to hook his horse to his carriage.

On his way to lower Manhattan, Phineas reached into the pocket of his brown silk brocaded waistcoat, and held firmly to his gold pocket watch.

"I'm sorry, you just missed her," said the lady behind the desk at the New York Infirmary for Women and Children. "Dr. Blackwell leaves at four o'clock on Tuesdays."

Phineas put on his most charming smile. "Then perhaps you can help me. I need to know about a friend of mine who came to visit Dr. Blackwell last fall."

"I'm sorry, our patient records are strictly confidential."

"This is important. My friend—Ruby—she was looking for her husband, with the army. I've just heard from him myself, and he wants to know where she is. She has moved, you see, but left no forwarding address. Surely you wouldn't want to keep this couple apart, after so many months of war came between them, now would you?"

The lady narrowed her eyes at him, tilted her head to the side. "Just what kind of information are you looking for?"

"I need to know where to find her, if I can. And if she is well. After all, if she came to the infirmary, should I now be looking for her in a morgue? Please. I know you can help me."

"I could be dismissed for this."

"I'm prepared to make it worth the risk you're taking." He pulled out a wad of bills and pressed them into her palm. "Please. Just help me."

After a momentary hesitation, the woman slipped the money into the pocket of her apron and went to the file cabinet. Turning around, she said, "What's the last name?"

"Try O'Connor. Or O'Neil . . ."

"You don't know her last name?"

"I know her first name is Ruby. That should be enough to go on. I think she . . . recently changed her name anyway."

"Well, when did we see her?"

"I'm sorry, I don't know the exact date. It would have been sometime between August and October."

"For being her 'friend,' you sure don't know much about her."

"I paid you, didn't I?" He was losing his patience.

"No last name, no date of appointment. It's going to take me awhile to go through all these records."

"I'll wait."

"I can't do it right now, I have other duties. You'll have to come back later."

"When?"

"Tomorrow. No—Thursday. Come back Thursday at five thirty. If there's something on your friend, I'll have found it by then."

"And if there isn't, I'll take a refund."

"Minus a fee for my time."

"Of course." Phineas smiled stiffly, and walked out.

Two days of waiting seemed like two weeks, but finally the time passed. If this information was reliable, it was worth every minute and every cent Phineas had spent to get it. The receptionist slid a folded piece of paper across the counter to him, and he took it with a sweaty hand. He opened it slowly, as though the information might fly away if startled.

Ruby O'Flannery. 5'4", 110 pounds, red hair, green eyes. Irish. Seen October 14, 1861. Diagnosis: Pregnant.

O'Flannery. That was it. "Are you sure this is accurate?" Phineas said.

"Why wouldn't it be? I've got better things to do than sit around making up stories about strangers, you know."

"Where is she? Where has she gone?"

"I have no idea. She left the address line blank on our form."

"I need to find her!"

Her eyelids thinned to a glare. "What's the urgency? Two days ago you couldn't even tell me her last name. Sorry. Can't help."

A muscle twitched next to Phineas's eye as he turned to go.

New York City
Friday, April 25, 1862

"Here we are, mum, a nice cup of tea and your favorite—cherry tarts." Jane spoiled Caroline, plain and simple. She had been a blessing since she started working in the Waverly home two years ago, but in the last few weeks, she seemed even more eager to please.

"You've been looking rather radiant lately, Jane," Caroline said as she cut into a steaming pastry. "Things going well with your beau, I take it?" She glanced at the daisy Jane had tucked into her braid and at the roses now blooming in her cheeks.

"Indeed mum. Now that you mention it, I—I need to share some good news with you."

How good can it be with her face that color already? thought Caroline. "Oh?" was all she said.

"William and I are—well, he asked me to marry him. I'll be moving with him to a farm out west— in Iowa." She clasped her hands in front of her apron and waited.

The cherries turned sour in Caroline's mouth. "Congratulations, Jane!" She dabbed the corner of her mouth with a linen napkin. *So she'll be leaving me, too—it will feel like a tomb in this house!* "When is the happy day?"

"July fifth, mum."

Caroline's sigh betrayed her. "I'm so pleased for you, Jane, and I hope you'll be very happy together. But I shall miss you around here!"

A knock at the door sounded.

Jane bobbed in a curtsy and swished out of the room. When she returned with the guest, Caroline almost choked on her tea.

"Josephine?" Caroline Waverly barely recognized the apparition in black mourning attire standing before her. "My dear, I—" Dread replaced the words in her mouth. Jane quietly left them alone.

Josephine Lightfoot was a widow, like Caroline, but her husband had passed years ago. Now she grieved for someone else. She had no sons. She had a daughter. A daughter who had gone to the Washington hospitals. Like Caroline's daughters.

"Louisa?" The word croaked out.

"I am undone, Caroline." Her face was chalk white, her eyes rimmed with red. Her face had aged twenty years since Caroline last saw her, a month ago.

Caroline felt sick as she led Josephine to the settee. She braced herself for a story she was sure she didn't want to hear.

"It was bound to happen, you know. I should have known." Josephine folded and unfolded a lace-trimmed handkerchief, over and over, as she spoke. "When one exposes oneself to contagious disease, one cannot stay healthy forever." Fold, unfold. Fold, unfold. "It must have come on suddenly, she didn't even tell me she was sick. She just stopped writing. I didn't know she was sick, Caroline. I tell you I didn't know!"

Caroline's face was wet with tears, her heart galloping like a runaway horse.

"She died alone." Despair strangled Josephine's voice. "I didn't know. She died without her mother—" Josephine covered her face with her crumpled handkerchief and wept. "Do you know what it's like to have your very heart die— without you even there?"

Goosebumps covered Caroline's skin in a wave from head to toe. She knew.

"I should never have let her go, Caroline. We were wrong to let our daughters go to war." Josephine gripped Caroline's hands in a white-knuckled grasp. "Even if you have to drag her home yourself, if she hates you for the rest of your life, *go!* Get your daughter back. I can never get mine."

After Josephine took her leave, Caroline stood nearly paralyzed in the parlor.

No. No. No. No. The word pounded in her mind with every frantic beat of her heart. She wrung her hands. *Lord! Don't take my girls!*

Dickens emerged from behind the draperies and began grooming himself on the French rug right in front of her. How she had always hated that cat. It reminded her of how Charles had always indulged Charlotte's every whim, even against Caroline's wishes. Charlotte had always been her daddy's girl. He adored her.

Far more than he adored his wife. And Caroline resented it. She almost resented Charlotte.

Charlotte had been the one at Charles's side when he died. It should have been his wife. The fact that she had not been there to say good-bye haunted her every day of her life. It was why she still wore black.

She would not wear black for a daughter, too.

Dickens paused and stared up at Caroline with yellow-green eyes, as if he could read her mind.

"Well, Dickens," she said, heart still in her throat. "How would you like your mistress back?"

Alice would never return to New York as long as Jacob was in Washington, but Charlotte— Charlotte had to come home. She had to go and get her.

"Jane," she called weakly, walking down the hall toward the kitchen.

"Why mum!" Jane's eyes widened at the sight of Caroline's tear-stained face. "Whatever is the matter?"

"I need to go to Washington, right away," she said. "Please pack my things."

Jane blinked. "By yourself?"

"Don't be silly, child, of course not. Please send word to Phineas Hastings that I'll need him to escort me. Tell him I need him to get us two tickets on the next train out. It's time to bring Charlotte home."

Chapter Twenty-Seven

Washington City
Friday, April 25, 1862

"Alice." Charlotte nudged her sister, barely visible in the blue shade of night. "You awake?"

"I guess so. Now. What is it?"

"You remember that Miss Dix once accused me of wanting to nurse because I was running away from something?"

"Mmm hmmm."

"She was right. I was running from idleness. Maybe from being stifled by Mother. Nursing was just a convenient opportunity that fit the bill. It seemed like a good way to prove that I could be useful."

"OK. You're certainly proving that much," Alice mumbled. "What will you do when the war is over?"

"That's what I've been thinking about. Mother and Phineas are hoping this is just a stage I'm going through. That I'll give it up after I've tried it on for size, the way I gave up clarinet lessons when I was a child."

"That doesn't answer my question."

"I'm getting there." Charlotte sat up on her cot. "I won't want to stop nursing when the war is over."

"What?" Fully awake now, Alice turned over and looked at her sister's silhouette. "How would you even be able to nurse anymore when the need is gone?"

"No more war may mean no more sick and wounded soldiers by the tens of thousands. It may mean no more national emergency. But there will always be sick people in need of care, no matter the cause."

"They'll never let women keep nursing after the war, Charlotte. This is a sharply peculiar situation."

"We never thought they'd let us nurse here either."

"If you haven't noticed, it hasn't been going very well."

"But it's getting better." Charlotte tucked her knees under her chin and gazed out the window at the empty street in front of Willard's. Gas lights spilled pools of yellow on the ground. "Just because something is difficult doesn't mean it isn't worth doing. I want to be a nurse. And not just for the war."

"You can't be serious." Now Alice was sitting ramrod straight up on her cot, as well.

"Nursing can be a science, not a hobby. It can be a real profession, as doctoring is a profession. It doesn't have to be just charity work. You know how so many people still believe women are limited in our intellect?"

"Yes, of course, I know. Idiotic."

"Of course it's completely false. But what have women done to prove it wrong?"

"Charlotte, you can't change how the world views women all by yourself."

"This isn't just about proving those old beliefs wrong. I must admit I have a purely selfish motive, as well."

"Such as?"

"I like myself better when I'm helping patients. When my world revolves around myself, it is very small indeed. Nursing is fulfilling to me, the way taking care of Jacob is fulfilling for you."

"Aha! Then nursing is just a substitute until you marry and have your own husband and household to care for," said Alice with a yawn, sliding back under her covers.

"I don't think so," Charlotte whispered into the darkness. "Must I really choose to either be married and limit my world to the realm of the home, or to be useful beyond it and remain alone?"

But Alice had already fallen back to sleep. No matter. She would not be able to answer these questions anyway.

Ebbitt House,
Washington City
Saturday, April 26, 1862

Alice's knitting needles clicked together in steady rhythm while Charlotte tried to focus on the letter she was composing to her mother. It was the same argument as ever. *We haven't yet given up hope. We may still be able to follow the Army of the Potomac. I'm sure Jacob will see the sense in having us within an hour's ride of any battlefield, where we can do some good . . .*

A knock on the door. Merciful distraction.

Charlotte opened the door to find Frederick Knapp, Mr. Olmsted's right-hand man with the Sanitary Commission, looking jittery and pre-occupied, as usual.

"Mr. Knapp! What brings you here so early on a Saturday morning?" she said, welcoming him in the room.

"Precisely! Big news, ladies. We're on the move."

"Pardon me? We who?"

"The Sanitary Commission. With the Army of the Potomac. The Peninsula Campaign."

"Have a seat, Mr. Knapp. Start over, if you please."

"What has our Sanitary Commission been about, if not for making up for the inefficiency of the government in caring for its soldiers? At least this time, the new Surgeon General is in agreement. That William Hammond, he's going to make a name for himself, I predict. I also predict he'll have a battle with the government on his hands for every change he wants to make, regardless of how right he is."

"Yes, I'm afraid the Commission was born at odds with the government and will remain at odds for as long as they refuse to admit they need our help," said Charlotte.

"Forgive me," Alice cut in, "but what does this have to do, specifically, with your current errand?"

"Right." Mr. Knapp wiped a handkerchief over his shiny bald head and dipped his brown beard to his chest as he collected his thoughts. "For all these months we have had to plan for this Peninsula Campaign—you've heard of it?"

"Not much," said Alice.

"Right. Briefly then. Richmond, the Confederate capital, is one hundred miles south of us, but instead of invading from the north, over easy terrain, McClellan's plan is to send troops down to Fort Monroe, which is—" He squinted at the ceiling. "It's about eighty miles southeast of Richmond in Hampton, Virginia, but still under Union control. It's at the tip of the Virginia Peninsula. From there, he plans to send troops up the James and York Rivers that border the peninsula until they can attack Richmond. 'Peninsula Campaign.' OK? Supposedly they won't expect it. But can you guess the problem?"

He barely paused for breath before plunging ahead. "Those big rivers become small, winding creeks through dense swampland the closer they get to Richmond. The government has made no thought or provision for how to evacuate the sick and wounded from these marshes. None whatsoever," he explained with disbelief. "Medical Director Tripler says he has only received one hundred seventy-seven of the two hundred fifty ambulances he asked for, and most of those are the bone-rattling two-wheeled contraptions that will half-kill a man by the time he reaches his destination . . . *if* he ever does. That mud is like nothing I've ever seen. Horses sink up to their shoulders in it. If they want to cross it, they have to first lay down lumber. No small task."

"What do you propose to do about it?" Alice's needles were silent now in her lap.

"Olmsted not only proposed a plan, he got it accepted, too. We are fitting up old steamships, given to us by the Quartermaster Department, to be used as hospital transport ships. If we can't get the men to us, we're taking the hospital to the men, at least as far as we can go by water. We've just today been given the first ship—the *Daniel Webster*—for the purpose."

Charlotte glanced at Alice, then back at Mr. Knapp. "You'll need nurses."

"Precisely. A few. Perhaps. That is, there is the possibility, so Mr. Olmsted thought I should see how you feel about the matter. If we can make the arrangements suitable for ladies to be on board, how should you view it? Would you like to come aboard?"

"Yes!" the sisters said in unison. Looking at Ruby, Charlotte added, "You'll need a laundress."

"Can't do laundry on the ship. Besides, we have contrabands for menial jobs like that," Knapp said.

"What's a contraband?" asked Ruby.

"A contraband is a slave who ran away from his or her previous owner, came to the North, and is now considered contraband of war. Our property." He cringed as he said it. "Meaning, we are under no obligation to return them, and they can work for the Union cause if they so desire. Many of them do."

"I'm used to menial work," said Ruby. "Been doing it all my life, I have."

"Let's not get ahead of ourselves just yet." Knapp wiped his head again. "This project is in utter confusion at the moment, the ship is filthy, and we aim to leave tomorrow. Battle is on the horizon, you see, and lives depend upon us being there when it breaks out. If I have only succeeded in getting your hopes up for nothing, I do apologize. If I discover that you can be useful, I'll send for you." Knapp touched his hat and took his leave.

Charlotte had never been very good at waiting. Today, she was an utter failure at it. *The opportunity to nurse aboard a hospital transport ship was the perfect solution and a total surprise!* God Himself must have arranged this for them. It would be too cruel if, now that the offer had been half-extended, it should be taken away just as quickly. Charlotte had planned to get out and enjoy the spring weather today, but refused to leave her room for fear of missing any message from Olmsted or Knapp.

Three hours later, the sun was high in the sky, and Mr. Olmsted himself appeared at the door, rumpled as usual, but eyes bright with a plan.

"Mr. Olmsted! Should we pack our things?" Charlotte fairly pounced on the small man as soon as she opened the door to him.

"Not just yet, Miss Waverly. I've just been to the ship and it is remarkably dirty. I can't let you on it."

"Dirty? Mr. Olmsted, I've emptied chamber pots. I've scrubbed blood and feces out of linens. I've mixed and thrown disinfectants into trenches whose stench would make your eyes water. And now you're telling me I can't board a ship because it's dirty? Fiddlesticks!"

"I shoulder the responsibility for the ladies working for the Sanitary Commission, you know."

"And the Commission has a responsibility to the army of sons, brothers, husbands, and fathers the public has sent to war," Charlotte shot back.

"I have a band of male nurses, doctors, medical students, and contrabands all lined up to go. I'm not convinced I need you ladies, too."

"We wouldn't just be there to offer the tender

female touch, you understand. If there's one thing Alice and I know how to do, it's how to manage a household, including servants—or in this case, your band of men. I've been trained to superintend, and I fully intend to do so."

Olmsted rubbed the back of his neck and shook his head. "Your families never agreed to this. They only agreed to let you nurse at the general hospitals here in Washington, safely within the encircling camps of our own troops. Down in the peninsula, it's a different story all together. We'd be behind enemy lines. I can't ensure your safety. If anything should happen to you . . ."

"Do you believe in God, Mr. Olmsted?" asked Charlotte.

He looked up, confused. "Are we changing the subject here?"

"I believe He is sovereign, even in war. If he means us to be safe, we will be safe here, on the peninsula, or in our homes. If our days are to end, then they will end, no matter where we happen to be. He is ultimately in control of our well-being. Not the government, not the Sanitary Commission, not you. So please. Let us come, and leave our safekeeping in God's hands. We have work to do."

Mr. Olmsted paused before giving his measured reply. "We must be prudent, Miss Waverly. Just because we can do something, doesn't mean we should."

"And just because it's never been done before doesn't mean we shouldn't try."

Mr. Olmsted smiled ruefully, and Charlotte bit her tongue in regret. She had gotten carried away again. Olmsted, though he seemed quiet and tame, had been pushing for things that had never been done before ever since he was named General Secretary of the Sanitary Commission. She had overspoken. Again.

"Forgive me," she said. "I said too much."

"I am a reformer at heart, the same as you," he said. "But we must both remember that some precedents have been set for good reason. We would be foolish to change everything just for the sake of change." With that, he bade them good day, and walked away.

Charlotte's shoulders sank as she watched his limping form retreat, and with it sank her heart. Had her outspokenness cost them their chance?

New York City
Saturday, April 26, 1862

At five o'clock, the train screeched and hissed at its platform before chugging into motion. With Mrs. Waverly sitting quietly beside him, he closed his eyes and imagined the moment of their arrival at the Ebbitt House. Charlotte would answer the door, surprised. Would she be happy for his presence or immediately rebellious against both him and her mother? In October, she had seemed like soft candle wax in his hands, easily shaped and molded. He could only hope that the intervening months had not hardened her to his touch. He did not want her to think of him as a kidnapper. He wanted to be the knight in shining armor, coming to rescue his princess from impending danger. The problem, however, was that Charlotte had never been convinced she needed rescuing in the first place.

And then, of course, there was Ruby. He had to get them away from each other somehow, and now.

The locomotive picked up speed, and Phineas felt the tension ease out of his shoulders and neck. The city whizzed by in a blur of cobblestones, bricks, and glass until the view gave way to fresh green countryside lined with split-rail fences and dotted with farms and silos.

Phineas breathed in deeply, then exhaled. The gentle rocking rhythm of the moving train comforted his frayed nerves. He was on his way, at last.

Washington City
Saturday, April 26, 1862

At five o'clock, the sun pierced through the thick wool blanket of clouds that had hovered over the city all day, and Mr. Olmsted came scurrying back to Charlotte and Alice's room once more.

"I've just come from the *Daniel Webster*," he said from the doorway, not bothering to remove his hat. "The boat isn't nearly as dirty as I thought it would be. Be ready tomorrow morning at seven to ride to Alexandria. The *Daniel Webster* will sail south as soon as we have the provisions aboard. Your duties, if you should accept them, will be strictly managerial. You will organize the supply rooms, make the beds ready for patients, oversee the kitchen, and manage the special diets for the patients."

Turning to Ruby, he added, "Mrs. O'Flannery, are you up for a change of scenery?"

"Aye, sir," she replied quietly.

"Then it's settled. Bring only two dresses each with you, including the one on your back. There will be no room for anything more. See you at the wharf. I'll be on board by the time you get there, no doubt. Just climb aboard and be ready to roll up your sleeves."

With a quick nod and bend at the waist, he departed, leaving a wake of gleeful women behind him.

Charlotte grabbed the letter she had written to her mother that afternoon and crumpled it into a ball. Pulling out a clean sheet of stationery, she once again put the pen to paper.

Dear Mother,

Providence Himself has opened the door to us to follow the great Army of the Potomac on its Peninsula Campaign. Mr. Olmsted has just informed us that we are to be nurses/superintendents aboard the hospital transport ship the *Daniel Webster*. We set sail in the morning!

Alice is beside herself with joy to be following Jacob, of course. She even sent Maurice home to Fishkill, confident she can take care of herself. Can you imagine?

Pardon haste. We will write more after we embark, I am sure.

Love,
Charlotte

Chapter Twenty-Eight

Washington City
Sunday, April 27, 1862

Caroline's stomach growled, and her eyes burned with exhaustion. What had been a stiff neck before the train ride was now a cramped mass of knots spreading their way into her shoulders and back. At the front desk of the Ebbitt House lobby, Phineas rang a bell and drummed his fingers on the counter until a slender, balding man appeared.

"Charlotte Waverly, please," said Phineas.

"Sorry, just missed her."

"She's at church already, then?" Caroline should have known. "When do you expect her back?"

"I don't." The small man crossed his needle-thin arms across his chest.

"Pardon me?"

"She's canceled her room. Packed most everything up last night and asked me to mail them tomorrow morning for her."

"Mail them where?" Phineas's voice rose.

"New York City, most of them. Some to Cooper Union, some to Sixteenth Street."

"And the other boxes?" Caroline asked quietly, as if to compensate for Mr. Hastings.

"Some are marked for the Sanitary Commission headquarters at the Treasury Building. Sure looks like she and her sister won't be coming back any time soon, parceling out all their things that way. Shame. They were good customers."

Phineas leaned in and a vein throbbed in his temple. "They didn't say where they were going? Or why?"

The man rubbed his chin. "I don't suppose it's any of my business," he said. "Is it yours?"

"Did you see which way she went?"

"I'm sorry, sir, but stalking women is not included in my duties. If there is nothing else, you will kindly leave the premises."

Caroline tugged on his arm. "It's all right, Mr. Hastings. Jacob must have talked them into coming home when the army marched south. He would never have allowed . . ." her voice trailed off. So far, Charlotte and Alice had been the ones to talk Jacob into their ideas, not the other way around.

Mr. Hastings shook her hand off his arm and stared at her wild-eyed, almost twitching in anger. "Are you really so blind?"

Caroline inhaled sharply. "No, Mr. Hastings," she said cooly. "I am not."

Suddenly, Charlotte's intentions weren't the only ones in question.

Daniel Webster,
Potomac River, Virginia
Sunday, April 27, 1862

It did not feel like a Sunday.

Neither did it feel like a war, thought Charlotte. Cool breezes stirred the water and pulled strands of hair from the knot at her neck, twirling them until they curled gaily to her shoulders. Closing her eyes to the sun's blinding, rippling reflection, Charlotte lifted her face to the brilliance and let the golden warmth radiate through her, infusing her like honey. *This is a holiday,* Charlotte told herself, and almost believed it, for she had never felt so free, so single-minded.

The gutted, filthy old steamer *Daniel Webster* was being transformed into a hospital transport even as it sped down the river. Contrabands were scrubbing and sanding the floors and whitewashing the walls. Carpenters built bunks under Olmsted's direction. Olmsted, Knapp, and a few other gentlemen unpacked quantities of stores while the women sewed a large hospital flag to identify the ship. They sang hymns and recited psalms as they stitched in an attempt to remember that it was the Lord's Day, after all, even if they were not in church.

Soon the *Daniel Webster* would be full of living, pulsing cargo, men needing beef tea and brandy, milk toast and gruel. Charlotte wouldn't get a moment's sleep until they were all washed, bedded, fed, and cared for. She would snatch back to life men teetering on the brink of death. Fever patients would rage in their madness, and she would not rest until they were consoled.

Charlotte couldn't wait.

New York City
Monday, April 28, 1862

A hard rain pelted the windows of the Waverly parlor as Caroline and Phineas stood, dripping, just inside the front door.

"You mean they aren't here?" Caroline's voice rang with alarm.

"Well, no, mum. Did you expect them to arrive before you?" Jane's cheeks flamed red.

"I knew it," said Phineas. "I knew she's gone off with the army."

Caroline leaned on Jane for support as her knees buckled beneath her.

Thunder growled and fine china rattled in its cabinet in protest like delicate women tittering nervously.

"She will write," said Jane. "She would have sent a letter before leaving, to you, mum, or to Mr. Hastings. A letter will come soon, and then you'll know. You must be patient."

But Phineas had been patient for more than a year. He was running out of patience.

Daniel Webster,
Ship Point, Virginia
Sunday, May 4, 1862

Night fell over Cheeseman's Creek like a heavy curtain, but sleep was far off yet. Rocked by the rippling creek below, Charlotte carefully tipped a dipper of water down a sun-baked soldier's throat, while humming mosquitoes swarmed them both in the yellow gleam of lantern light.

The first batch of patients had just arrived on the hospital transport, plucked from the spongy shore at Ship Point by the tugboat *Wilson Small*, and slung on stretchers through the hatches of the *Daniel Webster.* They were found covered in vermin, sweltering in their wool uniforms, and ripe with typhoid fever.

It was not a surprise. It was why the *Daniel Webster* had come.

"Won't you have a little more?" Charlotte coaxed. "If you can handle this, we have oranges for you to suck on, too. How long has it been since you've had an orange, soldier?"

The soldier mumbled, staring straight ahead with glassy, unseeing eyes, and the water dribbled down his chin in an unsteady track through his stubble.

"Come now, we can do better than this." She tried another spoonful, but he clumsily bumped her arm away and picked at his uniform with feeble fingers. "We'll get you into some clean clothes in no time," said Charlotte. "Just as soon as everyone is settled in and has a little something in their bellies, all right?"

He shook his head. "Tell, tell . . ." he muttered, still scratching at his collar. Charlotte loosened his collar then, and her fingers caught on a small leather pouch hanging around his neck against his clammy skin.

"Is this what you want?" Charlotte opened it and pulled out a curled, cracked photograph of a beautiful woman and five small children. "Your family?" She swallowed. "They are beautiful, soldier; you must be proud of them. And I'm sure they are proud of you."

He nodded listlessly, and said again, "Tell them." Then he was gone—not yet dead, but no longer responsive.

Footsteps grew louder in Charlotte's ears until Dr. Robert Ware was standing beside her. As he listened to the soldier's heartbeat with the stethoscope, Charlotte asked, "Will he live?"

"No, not likely."

"Is there no hope?"

"Without a miracle, I'm afraid not."

Charlotte stared into the solemn faces of the woman and children in the photo cupped in her hand. Tears slipped from her eyes and traced a clean path through the film of sweat on her face.

"No, my dear girl, you must not do that." Dr.

Ware's voice was quiet, but edged with warning. "You cannot cry."

Charlotte wiped her cheeks with the backs of her hands, embarrassed. She knew better than to let emotion show. In fact, she had gotten quite good at suppressing her natural sympathies in order to get her tasks done. But for some reason, this picture of the family now without its leader tugged at her heartstrings.

"It's impossible not to care at all." Another tear slipped down her face.

Dr. Ware handed her his handkerchief. "Care by doing, not by feeling. There will be time for emotion later—we will be feeling these days for the rest of our lives, perhaps—but right now is our one moment to do. To act. To save all we can without allowing any sentiment to slow us down."

"My mind knows all of that, but right now my heart just isn't listening."

"Then kill it. You must."

"Pardon me?" Charlotte looked up sharply.

"It is the only way. Deny your heart, if that's what slows you down, and let your mind, your eyes, your hands take over."

Kill my heart? Sorrow gave way to indignation. It was one thing to maintain self-control on duty—that she could agree with. But deny her heart completely was simply too extreme.

"I disagree." Her face now dry, she handed the handkerchief back. "Compassion—a function of my *heart*—makes me a *better* nurse. Compassion motivates me to give my all for these men. It makes me tune in more to their needs, and the moment I stop feeling for them, I'm sure I would not have the energy to work hard as I do."

Dr. Ware sighed wearily as he tucked the handkerchief back in his pocket. "This is why nurses have always been men. Women aren't made to handle the casualties of war." His voice was not unkind. "It's too hard on you. If you would like to disembark, you have only to say the word, and it shall be arranged."

Dr. Ware studied her face, and she returned the even gaze. He was a young man, younger even than she was by a few years. Short brown hair curled at his temples and a trim beard and mustache covered a lean, almost gaunt face. But his eyes were troubled waters, framed by lines of unspoken anxiety. Like Caleb's, the last time she had seen him.

"It is not too hard on me." Charlotte lifted her chin. "I will stay."

"All right. But consider that right now we have just thirty-five patients on board. You want to weep over one of them. What will you do when we have hundreds? You will never see them recover, you realize. We catch them at their worst, care for them only for a matter of days, and send them on to other hospitals for their convalescence. We will be surrounded by pain and suffering without the satisfaction of seeing them healed. You'll not be able to escape it on this ship. This is what you want?"

It would be difficult, Charlotte knew, but that was not reason enough to avoid it. "I want to help." Her tone was steeled with resolve.

Dr. Ware rubbed the back of his neck. "Then follow this advice: think of these soldiers not as men, but as patients only. You will go mad if you do otherwise." He waved over half a dozen medical students. "Stay if you like, and learn something."

As the students approached, Dr. Ware told them to change the patient out of his uniform and into a clean hospital gown while Charlotte turned her back. As they did so, they peppered the doctor with questions—not about the soldier's name, or his family, but about the disease he had succumbed to.

"He is near the end." Dr. Ware timed his pulse for a moment. "One hundred forty beats per minute. The cerebral disturbances have just given way into a stupor or coma. Look at this." Charlotte held her lantern closer as Dr. Ware lifted the soldier's lips with a tongue depressor, revealing dark crusts on the gums and teeth. "Sordes," Dr. Ware called them, then lowered the patient's jaw with his thumb and extracted his tongue. It was brown and dry, cracked with deep gashes.

"Does every typhoid fever patient's tongue look like that?" one student asked.

"No, this is an advanced stage," replied Dr. Ware. "In the early stage, it looks quite different. In many cases, the tongue is large, indented on the edges by the teeth, flabby and pale. The surface is smooth, the papillae hardly noticeable, and covered with a white fur thickest on the edges. This is especially true for scorbutic cases."

Dr. Ware's entourage followed him to the bedside of another patient, who obligingly showed them his furry tongue.

"Is it the first sign of fever?" asked a student.

Dr. Ware shook his head. "No. Ironically, the first sign is a chill. A headache. Then comes the hot skin, the loss of appetite. Notice the icteroid hue—that yellow tint of the skin, almost like he has jaundice. It's often accompanied by nausea, vomiting, gastric tenderness, delirium, or at least cerebral confusion."

"Madness?"

"Yes, eventually. You see those fellows muttering over there. One wants to know where his Sunday clothes are. Another has been screaming out 'Johnny Miller,' but we don't know whether that is his name, or if he is calling for a friend. That one—" he pointed to a man being fed by Alice, "that one wants to find his wedding ring, which he is convinced is on the bottom of the river. We've got to keep an eye on him. The mental haze can clear away if the patient recovers. It's only temporary, unless . . ." He turned to the patient again, who appeared to be listening. "Well. It can get better. Now my good fellow, would you be so good as to lie back for me? That's a good man." He pressed gently near the right hipbone, and a distinctive gurgling sound escaped. "Hear that?"

The students nodded, scribbling in their notebooks again, and Charlotte fished in the pocket of her apron for pencil and paper to do the same.

"What's that?" cried the patient. "Blasted rebel shells, get down! Under the water!" Lunging forward, he gripped Charlotte by the arm and yelled, "What are you doing here?" and knocked her off her feet, sending her tumbling into a bulkhead before she hit the deck. "Stay down!" he shouted at her. "This ain't no place for a lady!"

Dr. Ware dropped his notebook and pressed the patient back into his bed, but arms and legs thrashed wildly, kicking and punching Dr. Ware.

"You're not in the swamp anymore, soldier," she said, pushing herself back to her feet.

"You're hit, you're hit!" he cried frantically. Charlotte touched her fingers to the side of her face, and they came away slick with blood.

"You must have snagged a nail head." Dr. Ware examined the wound. "It's not deep—head wounds just bleed a lot. Go ahead and get yourself cleaned up."

The soldier huffed. "I told you this ain't no place for a lady."

Chapter Twenty-Nine

Hospital transports,
York River, Virginia
Monday, May 5, 1862

Heavy rain drummed fiercely upon the tugboat *Wilson Small* as it threaded its way through the York River, bobbing in the wakes of three hundred army fleet steamboats. Moonlight wrinkled on the water. Ruby was resting in a cramped cabin, but Charlotte watched from the bow of the *Wilson Small* in wonder as heavy steamers swept past her, each with a tow a quarter mile long, on their way to Fort Monroe. Alice watched with her as the floating lights from the rigging grew dark in the distance, and the bands and bugle calls faded away.

Mr. Olmsted had sent the *Daniel Webster* north when its human cargo reached nearly two hundred patients at Ship Point, Virginia, and the Sanitary Commission had been given an empty boat at Yorktown that they would soon transform into another much-needed hospital transport.

"There it is." Mr. Olmsted pointed through the rain at a dirty boat labeled *Ocean Queen* in cracked and peeling paint. He leaned forward and squinted at two small sternwheel steamboats alongside the *Ocean Queen*, one on each side. "No, no, no," he muttered. "This isn't good."

As soon as they were next to the sternwheel boats, Mr. Olmsted boarded them in the downpour, Charlotte and Alice close on his heels.

"What's this all about?" he asked an officer in charge.

"What does it look like?" was the response. "I've got two boats full of sick men I've been ordered to deliver to the *Ocean Queen*."

"You can't be serious," said Olmsted. "We aren't ready! The boat is a mere hulk. We have no beds or bedding, no food even for the crew, not a surgeon on board—we haven't even begun to prepare for its use! Give us a few hours, at the very least."

"Orders are orders. Look, little man, these men were left behind when their regiments were ordered forward last night." The roar of artillery rose above the beating of the rain. "Do you hear that? That's their regiments, at this very moment engaged in the battle of Williamsburg. I've got to unload my charges and get over there to do my part," the officer told them.

Mr. Olmsted held his lantern high and peered at the men in tattered uniforms covering the floor all around him. Hollow eyes set deep in yellow faces stared vacantly back at him. They were soaked with storm and fever sweat.

"These men have been for twenty-four hours

without nourishment of any kind," the officer in charge went on. "The racking of the ambulances over eighteen miles of corduroy roads—log bridges over the swamps—has sent many into a delirium that will claim their lives if they do not receive stimulants, warmth, medical care."

"None of which can be had on the *Ocean Queen!*" Mr. Olmsted's voice was sharp. "I tell you we have nothing for them."

"I tell you they will die."

Charlotte had watched Mr. Olmsted work long enough to imagine the invisible battle taking place in his mind. Of course he wanted to help. This was why the Sanitary Commission had invented hospital transports in the first place. But without proper preparation, chaos would reign, and nothing would be accomplished.

Olmsted rubbed a hand wearily over his rain-washed face. "Let me go back to shore and find a doctor," he said at last. "Place an officer at each gangway, and let no one board the *Ocean Queen*, except these ladies—Miss Waverly, Mrs. Carlisle, would you go aboard and begin unpacking whatever you find?" The women nodded, instantly alert despite an already full day of work. "No one goes aboard until we are ready!" Mr. Olmsted threw over his shoulder as he limped away. "Use force if necessary, gentlemen. Lives are saved by order and system, not by a mad rush of panic." And he disappeared into the rain once more.

No sooner had Charlotte and Alice reached the belly of the rusty ship in search of anything useful than they heard footsteps above them, and the low drone of men on board. The officers had, in fact, given way, and now a tide of sick and starving men crashed down upon the two women, before a single nail had been removed from a single box of supplies.

Lord, help us feed them! It was the only prayer Charlotte had time to utter in her heart, but it was enough. Within minutes, she had found a barrel of Indian meal from a dark corner of a bilge, and Alice had found two large spoons.

"It will do!" said Charlotte. "The disciples fed the five thousand with their two fish and five loaves of bread. We can feed a few hundred with ten pounds of gruel."

"The disciples had Jesus with them," Alice reminded her.

"And so do we."

By the time Mr. Olmsted arrived with a civilian surgeon, Charlotte and Alice were ladling hot gruel out of the ship's deck buckets and into the tin dippers of the pale, emaciated, shivering wretches covering the cabin floors. Trembling voices cried, "God bless you, miss! God bless you!"

Within two hours, Frederick Knapp and Dr. Robert Ware came from Cheeseman's Creek on the *Elizabeth*, the Sanitary Commission's supply boat. Soon bed sacks were filled with straw, and hoisted, along with bales of blankets and stores of medicines, into the *Ocean Queen*. Mr. Knapp went on shore, found and shot a rebel cow at pasture, and quickly brought the beef along with another surgeon.

By ten o'clock that night, every sick man—nearly six hundred in number—was in a warm bed, and had received medical treatment. Beef tea and milk punch had been served to all who required it. All but three of them survived the night.

Ruby had come because she had known no other option. But now that she was here, she could not imagine a better situation for her. It was impractical and nearly impossible to do laundry on the ship, so they nailed it up and sent it north to be washed, for now. Ruby was put to use making beef tea in the kitchen with some other women, mostly contrabands. Every day, for every hundred patients on board, they were to make two and a half gallons of beef tea, four gallons of gruel, and half a gallon of milk porridge. Every day was the same, and though the work was not difficult, it did require attention—a mercy to have less energy to dwell on her past and wonder about her future.

The haggard countryside of Ireland, the slums of New York City, the pestilential steam of the Washington hospitals—all that had happened there, seemed irretrievably far away now. Until one day, Charlotte came to find her.

"A letter for you, Ruby," she had said, with a question in her eyes.

The envelope was stamped in New York City and addressed to Ruby O'Flannery in care of the Sanitary Commission, Hospital Transports, Cheeseman's Creek, Virginia. She opened it slowly, pulled out a single sheet of paper, and gasped.

Ruby,

You hold your fate in your own hands. Tell Charlotte about me, and you'll be out on the streets again when I tell her your dirty secrets. I'll bet your husband would be quite interested to know what his little wife has been up to while he has been fighting for her, too. Keep your mouth shut, and all will be well.

Phineas

He had figured it out. She was not free. She would never escape her past, not ever.

Wilson Small,
York River, Virginia
Tuesday, May 13, 1862

Rain dimpled the river as a butter yellow sun tucked itself into folds of grey flannel clouds.

Charlotte wanted nothing more than to sink right down with it, but a stack of neglected correspondence called out pitifully to her from her carpetbag.

Mother wanted her to come home. So did Phineas. Edward Goodrich wrote from Fortress Monroe to tell her he had a military commission now and was close enough for a visit if time permitted. Caleb wrote with more tales of the hurdles in the medical care in South Carolina, and with more snippets of poetry, as always.

Her eyelids were heavy, and she longed more for sleep than anything else. But Mother's letters, at least, would have to be answered.

Dear Mother, she began. *Time escapes me. I am told it is Tuesday, but I certainly thought it was Thursday. Alice and I keep well.* She stopped. It was such a subjective statement. She was fine, actually, satisfied and fulfilled, but her mother would never call it "well." Charlotte and the rest of the women never knew where they would lay their heads at night, or when, or for how long.

The hospital transport system had grown since that first day in April. The tugboat *Wilson Small* was the headquarters boat, where Olmsted kept his office. Several smaller coast-steamers had been acquired to deliver patients to Fortress Monroe, Washington, and Baltimore, but could not make the trip beyond Philadelphia. As for large transports capable of sailing to New York City and back, the *Daniel Webster* was joined by the *S. R. Spaulding*, whose stable odor still lingered from the cargo of horses it formerly carried. On any given night, Charlotte never knew until the moment for sleep arrived on which ship she would lay her head. She had no bed, but curled up wherever a corner presented itself. The only thing she could be sure of was that she and Alice stayed on the peninsula while other doctors and nurses traveled north to the hospitals with the patients. They were too valuable at the front for Mr. Olmsted to part with them, he said.

The women's time was divided into three- and six-hour shifts, but emergencies sprang up requiring all hands on a regular basis. After all the patients had been fed and cleaned, wounds packed with lint, bandages soaked or changed, order enforced in the pantry and kitchen, she may get a bite to eat. Pieces of bread served as plates and her fingers as forks and knives. The top of an old stove was the dinner table, lumpy carpetbags the chairs. No, these were not details she could share with her mother.

I am happy in my work, she wrote, and paused. This much was true. But as soon as her hands stopped working and she had any moments off duty, the sounds of fever patients moaning, amputation patients screaming, was almost too much for her.

We do not order our days according to the sun and moon anymore, she continued. *Instead, we sleep between shiploads of sick coming up to us. The idea you suggest of the possibility of infection here is perfectly ridiculous. The ships are well ventilated and we each take our daily quinine dose religiously—*

"Miss Waverly." Mr. Knapp stood before her now, lit up by flashes of lightning cutting jagged holes in the sky behind him. "A telegram. A hundred men left on the ground at Bigelow's Landing. Ambulance train just left them there. No food or drink all day. 'Dying in the rain,' it says. One other nurse is coming but I need more help. Will you come?"

Before he had finished speaking, Charlotte had swept her letter back into the carpetbag and was now pulling a shawl around her shoulders, her feet carrying her toward the door. What was a letter, when there were lives to be saved? Who needed sleep, when the rush of emergency propelled her?

Chapter Thirty

S. R. Spaulding,
Pamunkey River, Virginia
Saturday, May 17, 1862

In a rare moment of calm, Ruby rubbed her aching back and eased herself into a chair on deck as the last hour of daylight washed over her. The baby in her belly was almost out of room, and Ruby felt every stretch and somersault as tiny hands and heels pressed her from the inside out. She knew she was running out of time, but for now, just for this moment, she pushed the thought aside and relished the enchanting scenery and the song of the whippoorwill instead.

The shore was so close to the steamer the trees leaned over and brushed its smokestacks with their branches. Trees and shrubs of every shade of green lined the river, broken up every now and then by creeks, running up through meadowlands into the distance. The river was narrow, and it doubled back on itself so many times Ruby felt as though she were floating in a watery maze.

Like her life. So many twists and turns, some of them taking her backward, some propelling her forward into an unknown wilderness. Was she really getting farther away from the life she once knew, or was she truly just in a tangle of unnavigable, rock-bottomed creeks and streams that would only dump her on the same barren shoal from which she had begun?

The sun set as the *S. R. Spaulding* rounded another bend, and the sky and water gleamed golden alike in the sunset, dazzling Ruby's eyes until all the trees suddenly looked black.

Suddenly, sharp pain clutched Ruby's belly and tightened like a vise. She held her breath until it released its grip.

Night was hastening on.

White House Landing,
Pamunkey River, Virginia
Monday, May 19, 1862

Army tents and wagons dotted the sloping fields at White House Landing, the Army of the Potomac's new supply depot on the Pamunkey River. The White House plantation overlooking the water had once belonged to Martha Washington and was named for the manor house they called "White House." The original house was no longer there, however, and the home that replaced it was much darker, and not nearly as big as its name implied. The current owners had fled before the Yankees arrived. *How shocked they would be to see the place now,* Charlotte thought.

Grass that was lush and green just days ago had

been trampled to dust by horses, caissons, and soldiers. Pie peddlers threaded their way through the men waiting for action, selling six pies to a man. *Eat while you can,* they cried, *you won't find these on the battlefield!* The Pamunkey River was crowded with schooners, gunboats, and steamboats, including the *S. R. Spaulding,* where the women waited, as directed, for Mr. Olmsted to return from his meeting with the Medical Director, Charles Tripler.

By the time Mr. Olmsted appeared on the gangway, Charlotte could tell he was angry.

"God forbid," he muttered, "that there should be a battle tomorrow." He forcefully wiped the sweat from his forehead with a damp, balled-up handkerchief.

"What happened?" Charlotte ventured, almost afraid to hear the answer.

"What *didn't* happen, is the more suitable question, Miss Waverly. It's what *didn't* happen that boggles the mind."

Not again, thought Charlotte. She glanced at Alice to see if she were listening. She was.

"For the life of me, I can't understand why the government insists on keeping that Tripler fellow as the army's Medical Director! No—" He paused to correct himself. "I know why—he's of the old guard. He's been in the service longer than most, so they let him have the position. Thank heavens the Sanitary Commission doesn't get a dime from the government. At least our independence from the bureaucracy means we can do things our own way. A far better way than the path they're taking, that's for sure."

"But Tripler," Charlotte interrupted. "What has he done—or not done—this time?"

Olmsted shook his head and paced the deck. "That fool. He is up to his ears in disarray. The sick are already collecting at White House, with no system yet conceived as to how to dispose of them. I should not be surprised if we have thousands upon our hands within days." He rubbed the back of his mosquito-bitten neck. "The *Daniel Webster* and the *Elm City* should be here tomorrow and can take six hundred off, and Knapp has gone to Yorktown for the rest of our boats. But would you believe, that in the course of my brief meeting with Tripler, we were interrupted no fewer than *four* times by separate messengers telling us of more sick arriving, and no accommodations to be had for them?"

"What about the house?" asked Alice. "White House?"

He shook his head. "You mean the brown cottage. No, no, federal guards have been placed around it as a building of historic importance that shall not be desecrated. It belonged to Martha Washington, and her granddaughter, Mary Anna Custis Lee—you'll remember she's General Robert E. Lee's wife—has left a note requesting that we honor the memory of our first president by leaving it alone. McClellan has agreed."

"So then, has the army no tents?" Charlotte asked.

"Tents, yes! Tents they have! But no detail on hand to pitch the blasted things. And if they were pitched, there would be no beds to put in them! And as for medicines in any adequate quantity—" He shook his head and laughed darkly.

"Dare I ask what provision has been made?" Charlotte asked.

"Tripler says he has sent numerous telegrams to various authorities, since March fifteenth, requesting supplies for the army of one hundred forty thousand men. He asked for thirty contract surgeons and one hundred forty-four four-wheeled ambulances—the two-wheeled are good for nothing. He asked for medical supplies for five thousand men."

"And?"

"Just today he has received some cooking utensils and a little liquor and furniture, and one hundred ounces of quinine. That is all."

"Just one hundred ounces?"

"He requested two thousand last week. There are five surgeons and assistants, one steward, no apothecary, and no nurses. Two wells have been dug but the water from neither has been found fit for use."

Mr. Olmsted's words hung in the air, heavy and

dark, like the four black gunboats sitting in the river next to the *S. R. Spaulding.*

"How much time do we have?" whispered Charlotte.

"The army marches tomorrow." He looked at the shore now teeming with life. "A battle may occur at any time. We are not prepared for it."

Mr. Olmsted gripped the railing of the deck until his knuckles turned white. "Hang it all!" he shouted into the wind. "We are supposed to *support* the Medical Department, not do everything for it!"

Sweat beading on his pale, pinched face, he ripped the tie from around his neck and cursed under his breath. Turning to Charlotte and Alice, he said, "I cannot ask you to go ashore and help in the field hospitals. You are each under my responsibility, and your duties, as we have outlined them and told your families, were to be confined to housekeeping and cooking on the ships themselves."

"We can do more than that," said Charlotte. "I'm a trained nurse. I have worked as such in Washington City, and by now Alice could do it on her own, too, she has spent so much time in hospitals."

"No," he said quietly. Then louder, "No, it is not the same, you cannot pretend that what you have done was in any way similar to the devastation you are about to witness. I cannot, I will not, ask

413

you to descend into the misery that is a field hospital after a battle."

"And what will we do? Stay on the ship twiddling our thumbs until patients arrive?" said Alice. "Unthinkable. My husband is out there."

"We are all well aware of that fact, Mrs. Carlisle," he said. "So is Mrs. O'Flannery's. But you have no idea what you are about to do." A heavy sigh slumped his shoulders. "I wash my hands of this stain that will forever mark you."

Charlotte's heart thudded in her chest. But she would not be swayed.

Mr. Olmsted sighed. "As I said, I cannot ask this of you. You are ladies. You were meant to be protected." He looked them in the eyes now with eyes like burning coal. "But if you desire of your own accord to go ask the surgeons if they would be agreeable to your services, I will not stop you."

White House Landing,
Pamunkey River, Virginia
Tuesday, June 3, 1862

Trains of wounded and sick men had begun arriving from the Battle of Fair Oaks two days before, and still they did not stop. A thousand men, two thousand, three, four . . . Charlotte could avert her gaze from the ghastliest sights, but she could not get away from the constant sound of moaning and crying, even screams.

414

Or from the smell. It wasn't just the sickly sweet, metallic scent of blood she remembered from her father's sick room. It wasn't just the sour smell of fever and body odor, or the eye-watering stench of dysentery. No, it was more. It was worse. The horrible odor of rotting flesh crawled up into Charlotte's nostrils and lodged there, filling her mouth with the taste of spoiled meat.

The Sanitary Commission had set up a large tent that housed the kitchen, storeroom, and bakery, along with twenty Sibley tents along the railroad. But it was not enough.

The war-trampled plain surrounding the White House was littered with bodies stretched out and exposed beneath the merciless, glaring sun. Whippoorwills were replaced by circling vultures and buzzing flies.

The Sanitary Commission and the government had been reinforced by more civilian volunteers. The Sisters of Charity were there, as well as men and women from the Christian Commission. Since the government had made no plan for stretcher bearers, Mr. Olmsted had rounded up a work crew of Negro contrabands for the job. Four Negroes from the Lee estate helped in the kitchen tent, and nine of them did the hospital washing in their cabins.

Civilian doctors picked their ways through row upon row of ill and wounded patients, refusing to help. They were only interested in *surgical cases,* they insisted. *Looking to get some experience with the amputation knife and the bow saw.*

Butchers! Charlotte thought, shuddering at the screams that filled her ears. They did not come from the patients themselves, for with a little chloroform, they were unconscious during the five-minute procedure. No, the shrieking came from those waiting in line, watching man after man go to the table with four limbs, and come off of it with three. Or two.

So this is what Caleb had to do, she thought darkly, and watched with morbid curiosity as a surgeon some distance from her tent wiped his knife on his blood-covered apron between patients. As he brought the metal down to meet body, she quickly looked away. But the loud rasping of the saw on human bone would stay in her memory forever, she was sure, followed by the dull thud of the limb falling to the ground. Bile rose in her mouth, but she swallowed the bitterness back down until her stomach roiled with churning acid. *Mr. Olmsted was right,* she thought. *These moments will mark me forever, yet I cannot turn my back on these men.*

The only way to stop the noise was to drown it out with something else.

"Mine eyes have seen the glory of the coming of the Lord," she began singing, softly at first, voice quavering with emotion. "He is trampling out the vintage where the grapes of wrath are stored." Alice joined her voice to Charlotte's. "He hath loosed the fateful lightning of His terrible swift sword: His truth is marching on."

One by one, other women raised their voices while their hands remained busy at their tasks: baking bread, simmering beef tea, pouring brandy and water down the soldiers' throats, washing fever-blistered faces, sponging over crusty bandages. *Glory, glory, hallelujah! Glory, glory, hallelujah! Glory, glory, hallelujah! His truth is marching on.*

The a capella chorus floated above the mewling of the sick and wounded. Those men who could find the strength and voice joined in, too.

He has sounded forth the trumpet that
    shall never call retreat;
He is sifting out the hearts of men before
    His judgment-seat:
Oh, be swift, my soul, to answer Him! be
    jubilant, my feet!
      Our God is marching on.

In the beauty of the lilies Christ was born
    across the sea,
With a glory in His bosom that
    transfigures you and me:
As He died to make men holy, let us die
    to make men free,
      While God is marching on.

In the middle of the next stanza, a gentle touch on Charlotte's elbow made her jump.

It was a surgeon, haggard and bloodstained. The few strands of hair that had once been pomaded over his bald head now blew wildly in the wind.

"I need to take an arm off a patient on the government ship just over yonder, and, well—he hasn't eaten all day. As it turns out, we—we have no food—on board, you see. Would you bring over some beef tea and eggnog for him?" He did not meet her eyes, and for good reason. When Mr. Olmsted had asked this very doctor if his ship had everything it needed some time ago, the response had been *Yes, we are all ready,* spoken with burning condescension.

So, you're not ready at all, then are you? Charlotte thought. But "Yes, of course," was all she said.

With flasks of the beef tea and eggnog tied to her waist Charlotte packed soft bread in her pockets and crossed the coal barges to the government ship. After she fed the soldier about to undergo amputation, she fed two others with what she had left. The ship was packed with patients, but as far as Charlotte could tell, there were no provisions for them, and they were about to set sail on a three-day voyage North. *Criminal!* she fumed.

Her pockets and flasks now empty, Charlotte

marched up to the officer in charge and introduced herself.

"I understand you're about to carry your cargo north, sir; is that correct?" she began.

"Yes, just as soon as I get the all-clear from my superior."

"And how will you feed them once you are at sea?" Charlotte asked.

"Excuse me?"

"Well, they are human beings, aren't they? Not your regular shipment of cargo. They will need to eat, you understand. Do you have any beef?"

The officer cleared his throat. "No."

"I see. Lemons?"

He shook his head.

"What food do you have then?"

"Hardtack."

"No nutrition whatsoever, most of it either moldy or rock hard . . . I'd hardly call that food. You *do* have clean water then, for drinking and bathing?"

He tugged at the collar of his uniform and looked around. *He wants someone else to blame,* thought Charlotte. But she would not let him go so easily.

"No water? Really? For three days' time? Well, that's an interesting choice, isn't it? Have you any cups?"

Silence.

"No, of course not. What use is a cup without

any water? How very right you are. Maybe this lot just isn't hungry. Or thirsty. But it's very obvious they do have wounds. You do have lint and bandages for fresh dressings, don't you? Or do you prefer to smell the festering wounds all the way to New York and have a deck covered in blood from their saturated bandages?"

The officer's face darkened into a deep red. "Do you have some military rank or authority I don't know about? Has McClellan himself sent you? Just who do you think you are, anyway, addressing me in this manner?"

Charlotte stood her ground. "I'm a member of the United States Sanitary Commission, and it is my right and my responsibility to make sure these men are cared for in the absence of their own mothers and wives. As the officer in charge of this ship, I would think you would feel the same responsibility, but as you clearly do not, I am stepping in."

"No, you are stepping off. Get off my ship. Now."

Charlotte lifted her chin, leveled a steely gaze at the man, and said, "I'm sending supplies to this ship immediately. If you are not here to receive them, our Commissioners will stock your ship without your signature."

She whirled around and marched off, seething inside at the officer and all others like him. *Stupid! Imbeciles! I could run that ship better myself, but just because I'm a woman, I have to argue my way onto one just to hand out tea! Hateful, wasteful, shameful, criminal behavior. Idiot! Doesn't he know there are lives in the balance?*

Back on shore, Charlotte spotted Mr. Knapp's bald, sunburned head. He was absent-minded enough to forget his own hat, but when it came to supplying the soldiers, he held all details firmly in his mind. At once, he set the wheels in motion to supply the "all ready" government ship from the Sanitary Commission stores. If it weren't for Mr. Knapp, Mr. Olmsted, Dr. Ware, and Caleb, Charlotte would have been ready to condemn the entire lot of men in authority.

Her errand complete, she shielded her eyes against the sun's relentless rays and looked out over the masses of those who still needed help. It was overwhelming. Each soldier represented a family back home, a wife about to be widowed, a mother about to be childless, a little boy or girl about to be fatherless. The dull ache of helplessness encircled her heart and squeezed until she had to shut her eyes to the scene.

Lord, there are too many! Her heart cried, and she stood, paralyzed, like a piling driven deep down into the mud of a dark Virginia swamp.

Deny your heart, if that's what slows you down, and let your mind, your eyes, your hands take over. Dr. Ware's firm voice filled her mind now from that first batch of patients on the *Daniel Webster. Think of these soldiers not as men, but as patients only. You will go mad if you do otherwise.*

He was right. To indulge in her own emotions now would be an utter waste of time when there was so much work to be done, so many lives depending upon it. Upon her. *Eyes and hands,* she told herself. *Eyes and hands.*

And so, she saw with her eyes that the bodies beaten down by the sun needed water, and told her hands to fetch it. Bucket after bucket of water she hauled for the men, crouching down beside them and bringing the dipper to their parched lips. Some of them had not had water or food in three days, and had slept just under the dew until they had been transported by railroad to the White House plantation.

Next, she and Alice and a score of other women volunteers brought porridge and gruel, with a little stimulating wine mixed in, to put something in their bellies. When a soldier was in obvious pain, the women gave them a little brandy from their flasks to dull it.

"No, thank you," said one smooth-faced boy, through gritted teeth. Thousands of men here hadn't shaved in days or weeks—this one was either very tidy or very young. "No brandy for me."

"Are you sure, soldier?" Charlotte asked. His

light-blue trousers were now dark red from blood.

"I want to keep my wits about me."

"I daresay you're the only one—most of your comrades here just want to forget as much as they can. But your leg—won't you let me fetch a doctor for you? You need some attention."

The soldier groaned, eyes squeezed shut. "The very thing I want the least!"

"Pardon me?" Charlotte was truly puzzled. Whoever heard of a wounded soldier wanting to be ignored?

"I need your help," said the soldier.

"Of course! But you need a doctor, not just me."

"I need you," he said again, his voice low. "Woman to woman."

Charlotte gasped. "What! You're—you're—"

"Shhhh! Yes, I'm an ugly, tall woman dressed as a man. You can call me 'Marty.' Only thing I ever wanted to do since the war broke out was to fight for my country. Wasn't my fault I wasn't born a man, but I'm a right good shot. I served the Union well. But if you let a doctor look at my leg, go pokin' around, he'll learn I'm not a man, that's sure. And then he'll send me home in disgrace, with no chance to come back and fight again."

And I thought I was brave to be a woman nurse! Remarkable!

"My dear, we can't just ignore your wound! You must have it attended to. Be reasonable." Charlotte sat on her heels, a film of dust and sweat

423

on her face and the grit of sand between her teeth.

"I've got it all planned. Just put me on one of them big ships and send me back to New York. I'll recover in a hospital there, and then come on back to my regiment. But if my secret is discovered here, I'm done for. Just put me on a ship. Send me home."

It might just work. This woman had given up far more than Charlotte had to be here, serving her country. *How can I take away her unconventional dream when I am following my own?* A doubt niggled at her, but she ignored it. *She deserves a chance. Far be it from me to be the one to take that away from her.*

"You're sure about this?" Charlotte asked.

Marty nodded slightly. The color had all but drained from her face. She would be in shock soon.

"Well then, if it's neglect you want, the government ship is the place for you. Our doctors on the Sanitary Commission transports would discover your secret before the first night away from shore, but no fear of that on a government ship. Come on, let's go."

Charlotte signaled two contraband stretcher-bearers to come over and helped hoist Marty onto it. Through the field, across the coal barges, up the gangway, and into the overcrowded ship they went. *Clearly there's no system for keeping track of who is here, and where,* thought

Charlotte. *No one to write down names and regiments.* She directed the stretcher-bearers to lower Marty down in a far corner of the deck.

"Ready for some brandy now?" Charlotte asked, kneeling again by her side. She held Marty's head on her lap and urged her to sip from the flask. When Charlotte left the ship, Marty was picking at the soft bread Charlotte had pressed into her hand.

Marty would be fine. She'd be back on the peninsula—unless she changed her mind—in a couple of weeks.

Chapter Thirty-One

White House Landing,
Pamunkey River, Virginia
Wednesday, June 4, 1862

Ruby had been relieved when she had been ordered to stay on the ship. She had not been trained as a nurse; her belly was so large that even stirring a kettle of gruel was a challenge.

But even though she was removed, Ruby was still tied to what was happening on shore, as much as the boat that was tethered to the dock.

Brisk footsteps on the gangway grew louder.

"Ruby." Charlotte walked toward her, her skirts wind-whipped against her legs. Her hair fought against its pins, curling strands plastered to her damp neck. Her dress was dark with perspiration, her apron oily with beef tea and stained with other men's blood.

"Ruby," she said again, gold flecks glinting in her caramel eyes. Something was wrong.

"Matthew?"

A nod from Charlotte, nothing more. It was enough.

Charlotte linked her arm through Ruby's and supported her lopsided weight down to the dock, onto the shore, past the railroad cars, to the field of mowed-down men, to the side of the husband she had once loved instead of feared.

His eyes were glassy, his skin a hue of dirty yellow. His hair was matted down with sweat.

"Matthew . . ." Ruby touched his hand—it radiated heat.

"Tell him," Charlotte whispered.

Ruby looked at her, pleading with her eyes.

"Hurry!" said Charlotte, more firmly now.

Ruby turned to Matthew. "Matthew, I'm—going to have a—baby."

His eyelids fluttered open and he cast a fleeting glance at her large belly, almost reaching her knees as she knelt beside him. "A baby?" he said in a hoarse voice. "Bedad!" His blistered lips cracked into a hint of a smile. "A new baby. We will call her Fiona, and she will be safe with us now."

Ruby sucked in her breath. A rash of heat radiated up her neck. *Did he think this was their second child? The one who had died of consumption in the tenements before her fourth birthday?*

"Has he gone mad?" she whispered to Charlotte.

"It's—quite possible." Charlotte bit her lip and looked down.

"Ruby," Matthew squeezed her hand in his burning palm. "The cradle won't be empty anymore. It's a new start for us. We will keep her safe. She will be well. She will survive." His

427

words came slowly, with effort. "We will survive. It's a new start."

His eyes closed and his mouth grew slack. She looked down at his hand, amazed at the intensity of heat seeping into her from it. This hand had once tenderly stroked her hair, cupped her face, wiped the tears from her cheeks, held their tiny babies.

This hand had also slapped her. *When had that started? Was it the alcohol? Was it the bad company in the slums?* Tears fell freely from Ruby's eyes. How the years had changed them both.

If only this were truly a new start for them. If only she could go back to the days when the hope of a baby had filled them both with joy. Flesh of their flesh, proof of their unity as husband and wife. Yes, their love had been imperfect. It had foundered like a ship at sea, battered by churning waves of poverty, discrimination, suspicion, fear, and grief. Still—they had been a family once.

The fire in Matthew's hand began to ebb away, and Ruby looked up, hopeful.

"The fever is breaking," she whispered to herself, half-believing it. *I should pray a Hail Mary over him.* But Ruby knew Mary was not listening.

Charlotte put her arm around Ruby's shoulders. "Do you believe in heaven? Do you trust in the Lord?"

Ruby shook her head. "The Lord wants nothing to do with me. There is no 'Amazing Grace' in my life. I am still lost, and will never be found. I am still blind, and will never see."

Matthew's bony fingers, curled around on Ruby's, grew cold and stiff, like talons.

Now Ruby had no one. Even the baby inside her wasn't fully hers.

This was not a new start. This was the end.

The baby kicked her from the inside, and Ruby's shoulders heaved with sobs.

"What am I going to do now?" Ruby wailed. "Mercy, mercy, God have mercy! I can't go back to Five Points, I'd rather die! Surely even hell can't be worse than what I've already been through!"

Charlotte hugged Ruby awkwardly, the baby a wedge between them. "Ruby, you are going to be OK."

"No, I'm not! I have never been OK! I don't want to marry again but I can't survive without a man!"

"Yes, you can," Charlotte said firmly. "'A father of the fatherless, and a judge of the widows, is God in his holy habitation.' He will take care of you. I will take care of you."

Ruby fixed her with a confused stare. "How?"

"You're a good person, Ruby. Honest and upright. I'll make sure you have what you need from now on."

Honest and upright. Ruby groaned inwardly. *If these are the qualifications, I fall miserably short.*

"I want you to have this." Charlotte fished a small Bible out of her apron pocket and thrust it into Ruby's hands. "The Christian Commission is handing them out, and I thought you could use one. I've underlined some verses in there I thought would be good for you, and I wrote the page numbers inside the front cover. See?"

Ruby opened the cover and nodded.

"I only had time to do a few. I will mark more passages when there's more time—" She waved a hand toward the masses of men still needing attention. "These verses really comforted me when I lost my father . . . You don't already have a Bible, do you?"

Ruby shook her head as she wiped sweat and tears from her cheeks. No, she didn't have a Bible already. She didn't have anything.

Suddenly, Ruby's breath caught in her throat as her belly constricted itself into a compact ball, pain radiating into her back. She grabbed Charlotte's hand, placed it on the rock-hard mound and watched the color drain from her face.

Of all the times to have a baby, of all the places!

Charlotte hiked her soiled skirts a few inches higher and laced her way past men faded from thirst, dull with shock, famished for nourishment, writing with maggots feeding on their open wounds.

"Just a little longer," she heard herself saying to them as they passed. "Help is on the way."

Upon finally reaching the kitchen tent, she headed straight to Alice, who was pulling fresh loaves of bread out of the oven.

"Ruby's having her baby!" she blurted out.

Alice nearly dropped the pans. "Now?"

"Soon enough! Is there a doctor—" She stopped herself from completing the ridiculous question. Yes, there were doctors. But only a few dozen, spread over four thousand men who desperately needed their attention. Not one of them would come for a birth. And Charlotte could not bring herself to suggest such a thing.

"I'm not a midwife," Charlotte said instead.

"You have to try!" said Alice. "Charlotte, you've never failed at anything you've set your mind to. You've been trained as a nurse—I haven't. Ruby will do all the work, anyway."

"And if there are complications? If the baby is turned, or if Ruby bleeds too much? It's not that I don't want to help, Alice; I'm just not a midwife!"

The rest of the women in the tent turned and stared. It was so strange, Charlotte knew, to speak of babies—new life—in this environment.

A nun in a billowing black habit walked quietly over, her white wimple flapping like wings on either side of her head.

"Is there to be a baby born somewhere?" she asked.

"Yes, Sister," Charlotte replied impatiently. What would she know about it anyway?

"I haven't always been a nun, you understand."

"I'm sorry, but I don't." *This is not the time for small talk,* thought Charlotte.

"I was once a midwife. Allow me to help. But let us make haste. Old sheets, scissors, water—can any of these be spared?"

"Hurry," Ruby panted between contractions. "This is my third baby—it will come fast."

Charlotte's eyes brightened with unspoken questions, but now was not the time to ask. The baby was coming, and unless they wanted to have it on the field in the middle of thousands of men, they needed to move. Now.

But where?

Going back across the coal barges to the *S. R. Spaulding* was not an option for Ruby. Staying here was out of the question. All of the tents were already packed over full with the worst cases of the soldier patients.

"There." Charlotte pointed to the White House, usually guarded by sentinels, now guarded only by tall, stately oak trees. It would work.

By the time the three women reached the house, Ruby's legs were about to give way. Rose bushes in full, fragrant bloom hugged the outside of the house. The note Mr. Olmsted had mentioned was still there, nailed to the door: *Northern soldiers, who profess to reverence the name of Washington, forbear to desecrate the home of his early married life, the property of his wife, and now the home of his descendants.* It was signed, *A Granddaughter of Mrs. Washington.*

Beneath it, someone had written in pencil his reply: *Lady, a northern officer has protected this property within sight of the enemy and at the request of your overseer.*

"My apologies, dear lady," Charlotte muttered under her breath. "At least we're not soldiers. We'll try to be the best houseguests we can be. Under the circumstances."

The home had been stripped until it was almost bare, leaving only some quaint pieces of furniture and a pair of brass firedogs. Charlotte immediately went to work lighting a fire and hauling water from the well as Sister Agnes helped ease Ruby down onto a sheet on the hard wood floor. That she had given birth in worse places went through Ruby's mind.

"It would be better if you took off your skirts now," said the nun.

Never thought I'd hear that coming from a Sister, Ruby mused. *And I never thought a nun would be delivering my very own bastard child.*

Pain clutched her middle in breath-stopping waves, now, closer and closer together.

"You've got to breathe, child," Sister Agnes was saying. "Don't hold your breath when the pain comes. Breathe through it. In through the nose, out through the mouth. In—that's right—and out. It will lessen your sense of pain."

"I've done this before," Ruby said through gritted teeth. *And neither time did I have any help.* "I can deal with the pain." *I would hardly recognize my life without it.*

Finally, as though someone had popped a balloon inside of her, she felt the distinctive release of water rushing out of her womb, soaking the sheets and rags Sister Agnes had piled up to staunch the flow. The sour smell of amniotic fluid filled the room, and Ruby's mind took her back to the births of Meghan and Fiona, the image of Matthew cradling their tiny bodies in his strong hands, and wept with fresh grief over the loss of her entire family. This baby clawing its way out of her now—this was an imposter, a fraud, a cheap counterfeit of the family she had once had. It was not worth all this fuss.

The patches of light warming the floor grew dim until nightfall closed in around White House like a satin-lined cloak. Charlotte lit the kerosene lamp and looked back at Ruby, her face twisted into worry.

From the slave quarters just above the bank, a low chorus rose above the cacophony of crickets, cicadas, and bullfrogs. The Negroes of the Lee estate had gathered outside their houses and were singing a condensed version of the creation of the world, one singing out a line and then the others joining in. Then they sang a confession of sin, and a pledge to do better, until, suddenly, their humility seemed to strike them as uncalled for, and they sang out at the top of their voices:

Go tell all de holy angels
I done, done all I kin.

Ruby repeated the words in her head. *I done, done all I can!* Her heart was torn between guilt and the confidence that she could have done no differently. Still, there had been consequences to her choices.

Maybe the baby will be born dead, with the cord wrapped around its neck. Maybe I will bleed to death. How merciful.

But the labor proceeded, and finally, Ruby's womb expelled the living, writhing proof of her guilt. Conceived in shame, delivered in darkness. Sister Agnes scooped the tiny mouth and swiped the nose with her finger, then wiped off the blood and fluid before handing the mottled infant to Ruby.

It was a boy.

Of course it was.

Ruby looked up from the squalling creature and stared at Sister Agnes and Charlotte. Their eyes gleamed in the lantern light, as if this baby had been wanted. As if he were an answer to prayer instead of confirmation that God had not been listening at all.

Ruby barely felt the afterbirth slither out, and watched mutely as Sister Agnes tied off the umbilical cord and snipped it above the knot.

"He's beautiful," the nun said, her hands still sticky with birth matter.

Ruby cringed in pain as he suckled at her breast, draining her from the inside out.

"What will you name him?" said Charlotte, washing the sweat from Ruby's brow.

"Aiden," replied Ruby, for he was indeed a "little fire" in her soul.

Act Five
HOME AT LAST

THE MEDICAL DEPARTMENT IS greatly improved, and the Sanitary Commission, who were chiefly instrumental in putting in the new Surgeon-General (Hammond), who in his turn has put in all the good new men, finds its work here at an end, and might as well retire gracefully. Four thousand sick have been sent north from Harrison's Landing. . . .

The army is quiet and resting, and the surgeons of the regiments have been coming in constantly to the Sanitary Commission supply boat with requisitions for the hospitals. We are giving out barrels of vegetables. The *Small* will run up the river and be ready to fill a gap in bringing off our wounded prisoners, and it will be a comfort to do something before going home ignominiously.

—GEORGEANNA WOOLSEY in a journal entry written while aboard the *Wilson Small* off Harrison's Landing, July 12, 1862

Chapter Thirty-Two

White House Landing,
Pamunkey River, Virginia
Monday, June 16, 1862

Alone on the *Wilson Small* at last, Ruby's body longed for sleep, but her anxious spirit needled her relentlessly. What was she supposed to do now? Nearly two weeks had passed since Aiden was born, and she still had no answers. She was living on borrowed time as long as she remained a tagalong to the Sanitary Commission, and she knew it. It wouldn't last forever. She would end up back in New York, right where she started—only this time, without even the hope of a husband to provide for her, and with another mouth to feed.

Sweat beaded on Ruby's forehead as she ticked off her options in her mind. *The charity societies won't have anything to do with me, not after Phineas ruined my reputation. Outworker sewing: no, I'd never have enough time to finish the work with Aiden to care for. Domestic service: no, not with a baby. That's work for single girls. Laundry: it wouldn't be enough. I'd have to pair it with some other form of income, and that would leave no time for Aiden. Factory work? Who would watch Aiden during the twelve-hour shifts? I would still need to nurse him* . . . Ruby closed her eyes and groaned. Who would watch Aiden, indeed. How could she forget there were more basic questions to be answered first? Where would they live, where the filth and foul air wouldn't kill Aiden like they had killed Fiona? What would she eat, that would be wholesome enough for a nursing mother?

Every thought she chased circled back to one solution—the undeniable convenience of prostitution. Just an hour or two of work every few weeks, and she could spend the rest of the time with Aiden. It would pay the bills. She could keep her baby. She had done it before . . .

And I hated it! Nausea filled her stomach at the thought of selling her body for the rest of her life. What kind of a life would she be setting her son up for? But what else was there? She had no education. No family. No references.

No hope.

Ruby reached for the Bible Charlotte had given her and read again the passage in John 8 she had first heard from the women of the American Female Reform Society. Jesus had not condemned the adulterous woman who had come to Him. It was almost unbelievable. But He *had* told her to go and sin no more. *But how on earth am I going to manage unless I go back to that? I'm trapped. I can't get out.*

She kept reading, and though she struggled at

first to understand some of the language of the Bible, a glimmer of comprehension began to glow in her heart. *If ye continue in my word, then are ye my disciples indeed; and ye shall know the truth, and the truth shall make you free. . . . If the Son therefore shall make you free, ye shall be free indeed.*

Freedom. Wasn't that what this war between North and South was all about? But the words of Jesus pointed to a greater truth. True freedom was freedom of the soul, something no man or country could give or take away. Ruby's heart was so heavy it pulled her to the floor until she was kneeling, head in her hands, rocking to the rhythm of the bobbing ship. *I'm in bondage, chained down by guilt, condemnation, grief, shame.* Even as she waged war in her mind against going back to prostitution, she felt herself becoming entangled once again in that dreadful lifestyle.

"Lord Jesus, free me!" she pleaded aloud through her tears. And though she did not know exactly what that meant, she prayed that, as the verse said, she would soon know the truth, and that the truth would set her free.

In the shade of a shore tent, with whippoorwills providing the lullabies and soft, pillowy clouds floating across the sky, Aiden slept peacefully in the crook of Charlotte's arm as she rocked him back and forth, waving a hand over his body almost constantly to keep the mosquitoes at bay. Since there was a lull between trainloads of patients, she joyfully volunteered to watch him for a spell while Ruby slept.

He was perfect. Peach fuzz hair, clear blue eyes, and smooth, creamy skin. Ruby was rapidly losing weight, but he was packing it on in delightful little rolls. His knuckles were mere dimples in his chubby little hands, and his mouth was a tiny rosebud set between his full cheeks. He was the darling of the Sanitary Commission women, even the contraband women who had been hired to help in the kitchen.

And yet, Charlotte could tell Ruby was depressed. And why shouldn't she be? It was quite common, after delivering a baby, to experience severe emotional fluctuations, even despair. But to have watched her husband die only hours before giving birth to his son—of course, this was too much for any woman to take with dry eyes and a stiff upper lip.

"Hush-a-bye-baby, on the tree top," Charlotte murmured, "When the wind blows the cradle will rock . . ." *What would it be like to have a son of my own?* She chided herself for allowing the dead-end thought to form in her mind. It was useless to wish for what was not meant to be.

"You look good with a baby," said Mollie, one of the former slaves of the Lee estate. She had no idea she was driving a stake into Charlotte's heart.

When the mail came, and a letter from New York was brought to Charlotte, she ripped into it, thankful for the distraction. This one was from Phineas.

My dear Charlotte,

When we heard the *Daniel Webster* was steaming into New York, your mother and I were there to meet it at the dock at the appointed time, expecting to see you walk off it, even if for only a few hours' visit. Imagine our distress when we realized you were not on it, but still halfway down the country laboring under the summer sun in the malarial swamps of Rebel Virginia.

We were all heartbroken. Your mother is much altered since you have seen her last. The strain of worry has aged her a great deal, and I fear her health is breaking down from it. As for me, you know how I feel about you. My heart needs yours like my lungs need air. You may be doing what is most fulfilling for you right now, but consider the toll your adventure is taking on those you say you love.

One of the soldiers on the government ship that pulled in to the harbor about the same time died during the voyage, from a leg wound that had turned septic. Turns out it really should have been taken off, the doctors here said. Now listen to this: the soldier was a woman! Disguised as a man to deliberately put herself in mortal danger. Sometimes *you* astound me Charlotte, but I thank God you are not so foolhardy as this woman was—

Charlotte clutched Aiden to her as she struggled to breathe. It was Marty, the girl who had asked her for help. Now she was dead and it was Charlotte's fault.

Back and forth Charlotte rocked Aiden. She squeezed her eyes shut, but hot, stinging tears escaped anyway, spilling down her cheeks and landing on the baby. *What have I done? What have I done?* But the answer was right there on paper. She had killed a woman. No, she had not shot her in the thigh with a minié ball, but she had the means to save her life, and instead of doing that, she followed her heart and made a mistake that had cost a life. *If only I had followed Dr. Ware's advice! "Deny your heart." I didn't realize following my heart would hurt other people, too.* Charlotte watched her teardrops darken Aiden's cotton blanket in a random pattern of small polka dots.

Lord, her heart cried out in desperation. *Forgive me! If my own selfish ambitions have been my driving force, humble me and help me submit to whatever it is You want me to do, even if it takes me away from nursing. Have I pushed my plan when it wasn't Yours? I don't trust myself. Please God, show me the way!*

Charlotte lifted the letter again and wiped the blur of tears from her eyes.

My dear, have you ever considered that the people that most need your help are the ones who are closest to you already? Please don't think me harsh and mean-spirited but I must point out that you are not the only nurse the Union army has. You are not indispensable to the North. If you quit your "duties," another will fill your place. But no one can fill your place in my heart, or in your mother's. We have suffered your absence long enough. You are breaking our hearts. Come home. Come home.

Alice touched Charlotte gently on the shoulder then.

"Are you all right?" she asked.

Charlotte nodded, waving the letter. "Phineas has written again, pleading with me that I come home."

Alice was quiet for a moment before asking, "Will you? Have you given enough of yourself here yet?"

Charlotte grazed a palm over Aiden's fuzzy hair.

"If you had asked me that last week, I would have said no. But now . . ." A lump lodged in her throat. She could *not* believe she was considering anything but staying here, where she was needed.

"Sister, you have such a good heart. Impetuous, but good." Alice chuckled. "You want to be where you are most needed, don't you?"

"More than anything."

"Well . . ." Alice took a deep breath and plunged ahead. "It just might be that, after more than a year away from home, the people who need you most are your family. And Phineas."

Charlotte stared at her younger sister. "Do you really believe that?"

"With all my heart. I am here, not out of my great love for my country—although rest assured, I am as patriotic as anyone. But my main purpose in leaving my home in Fishkill was to be as near as possible to my husband. I am happy to serve patients while I'm here, but if Jacob weren't here, I would be wherever he is. After serving God, my top priority is serving my husband."

Charlotte sighed, but this was not a surprise to her. Only Charlotte was here to prove that women could be useful outside the home. Alice was here, ironically, only to be a good wife.

"You know, Charlotte," Alice continued, "I want to give you the benefit of the doubt because we've all been under such tremendous strain.

But I might do you more harm than good if I don't say what's been on my mind lately."

Charlotte eyed her warily, and hugged Aiden to herself. "Go on," she said. She had just asked God to humble her. *Here it comes!*

"You seem to be developing a strong disrespect for the male race."

"Well Alice, you have to admit, most of the men we've had contact with are wholly disrespectable! They are idiots!"

"There—you see? What about Jacob, Mr. Olmsted, Mr. Knapp, Dr. Ware? What about the soldiers? You care for them with the most tenderness and efficiency. Surely you don't think they are idiots, too, fighting for their country."

"Of course not, don't be ridiculous."

"So is it only men in authority over you that you chafe against? This doesn't bode well for you, Charlotte. A woman is under the leadership of her husband. Everyone has to obey authority, even women who never marry, even men themselves. It's called order."

"No, it's called being ordered around," Charlotte shot back. "You're quite good at it, aren't you?"

Alice's eyes narrowed into ice-blue slits as she studied her sister's face. "What is that supposed to mean?"

Charlotte briskly swatted mosquitoes away from Aiden's soft head. "You do what you're told, like a good, culturally acceptable woman should."

"You make it sound like an insult."

"If the shoe fits!"

Alice's eyes blazed with light. "What on earth is this all about?"

Charlotte looked down at Aiden now, amazed and thankful he was still asleep despite the arguing going on just over his tiny head.

"I'm just saying," said Charlotte, "sometimes those above you are not well-intentioned. And sometimes you just need to make choices on your own." She paused. "If I had obeyed Mother like you did when Father was sick, he would have died alone."

Charlotte sighed, deflated from the unfairness of her own statement. Alice had only been fourteen years old at the time. She was right to go with Mother.

"You were right to stay with Father," said Alice quietly. "And you would be right to go back home now, too. Don't you see? Your presence was irreplaceable to Father. No other nurse could have brought him the comfort you did. And your presence is irreplaceable to Mother and Phineas, too. Sometimes the people who most need our help are the ones God has already placed in our lives. If you go back to New York, no one here will fault you. Many soldiers volunteered only for three months. You have served four times that length."

"But you will not be coming home."

"I am home when I am near my husband. You are home when you're with family."

Charlotte leaned her head back against the rocking chair and sighed in resignation.

"Read this." She held out Phineas's letter.

After a few moments, Alice looked up at her sister again, a soft smile on her face. "It appears, dear sister, that Mr. Hastings and I are on the same page on this matter. But the question remains— where are you?"

"Mrs. Carlisle." It was Dr. Ware.

"Good morning, Dr.—" Alice stopped, and Charlotte watched her fair skin lose all its color. "Not Jacob," she said.

The doctor looked down. "I'm afraid so."

Alice and Charlotte were on their feet in an instant, their eyes immediately drawn to the gleaming white rows of tents next to the railroad tracks.

"Wounded?" Fear tinged Alice's voice.

"Chickahominy fever. Typhoid-malaria. Utterly broken down with it, I'm afraid."

"Did he just arrive?" Charlotte looked around. "I didn't hear any train."

"No, no. He's been here since yesterday but only now is conscious enough to tell me his name. I'm sorry."

Charlotte's heart caught in her throat. She reached out to lay a hand on her sister's arm, but Alice was already slipping away toward her husband. She could not imagine what her sister

449

was going through right now—or what she had endured up until this moment. *How selfish I've been!* With every patient, Alice must have imagined that it could be her own Jacob, but for the grace of God. *Grueling!* And now the moment had finally come. It was Jacob's turn, at last.

"Dr. Ware!" Charlotte called after the doctor's retreating back.

He turned and looked at her. How old he had grown in a few short weeks, how tired and careworn!

"Is it really so very serious?" she asked.

"The *Daniel Webster* sets sail for New York tonight," he said. "The Carlisles must be on it. Will you be joining them?"

Aiden awoke with a start and began crying in Charlotte's arms, clamoring for his mother's milk.

The gentle rocking of the Pamunkey River beneath the *Wilson Small* failed to put Charlotte to sleep. Somewhere out on the Atlantic Ocean, Alice was no doubt still awake on the *Daniel Webster*, as well.

They had not parted on the best of terms.

"Mother will never forgive me if we come home without you," Alice had said.

"Just a little longer," Charlotte had countered. "Ruby needs to rest a little more before making the journey. Besides, the Commission can't lose its two best nurses at once."

But Alice had just shaken her head and said, "I have enough to deal with as it is. I am not my sister's keeper." She boarded the ship, as they had done together hundreds of times, and set sail for home without Charlotte.

Now in the stillness of the night, Phineas's letter came back to haunt her, and her mind landed on Marty's death once again. The weight of her guilt was crushing. Maybe she should have left on the *Daniel Webster* tonight after all, and sailed away from any possibility of doing more harm.

In the yellow glow of the lantern light, Charlotte pulled out the small Bible that had once belonged to her father and held it to her chest, wishing she could somehow hear what he would say to her now if he were still alive.

Hear what your heavenly Father has to say to you, her heart told her. *He is still alive.*

She turned to the psalms first, finding comfort in King David's expressions of anguish followed by words of praise. Hadn't he sinned greatly by deliberately taking another man's wife and then having her husband killed? And yet he had been restored to God, and had been called a man after God's own heart.

She flipped to the Gospels, where her father's hand had underlined so many of the words of Christ. When she came to Luke 6, she stopped, and her vision clouded with tears once again. *Be ye therefore merciful, as your Father also is merciful.* The verse that inspired her to have mercy on the sick and wounded Union soldiers in the same way her father had had mercy on the cholera patients in Five Points. Five Points . . . Ruby and Aiden. She had promised Ruby she would take care of her. Could she really do that best by keeping her amid the sick and wounded? What if either one of them caught the fever? Maybe showing mercy now meant leaving this place and returning to New York.

But there were so many here who needed her help, and so few to give it.

She was more confused than she had ever been.

Scrounging up a pencil and using the top of the sugar box for paper, Charlotte knelt on the deck and poured out her heart to Caleb as she wrote her letter on top of a cask of water. She held nothing back, using her letter as if it were a personal journal entry. She told him about Dr. Ware's advice to deny her heart and she confessed her fatal mistake with Marty. She told him about Ruby and Aiden, the letter from Phineas, and Alice's similar advice. *What do I do?* she asked him, as if she were sixteen again, and he was the only one who could see clearly the path ahead.

Her letter finished, she crept back to her cabin and slept only fitfully as the tug *Wilson Small* bobbed in the water, up and down, back and forth, as if the boat itself could not decide which direction to go.

Chapter Thirty-Three

New York City
Tuesday, June 17, 1862

Phineas Hastings felt as if he had been kicked in the stomach. The shock, the pain, the disorientation. The anger.

Alice and Jacob had returned home, and Charlotte had stayed behind. What was the girl thinking? How long would this nonsense continue? After all the money he had poured into the Sanitary Commission since October, as if he had money to burn. He was running out, truth be told. He had considered the donations a worthwhile investment if the return on it would mean Charlotte's hand securely in his, and her wealth securely his, too.

He had never dreamed her ambition would drag out for so long. *Who could have imagined such a thing?*

Phineas reached into his pocket and clamped down on his gold pocket watch until it became slick with his sweat.

He was done waiting for her to come home. If she refused to come of her own accord, it was time to act like a man and make her obey. His father may not have been able to force his own wife into submission, but Phineas certainly would.

Tybee Island, South Carolina
Monday, June 23, 1862

By the time Caleb Lansing had finished reading the letter from Charlotte, his shoulders sagged. So she knew now what it was like to make a mistake that would cost a human life, when your only mission was to save it. His heart ached for her. That kind of guilt could drive a strong man mad. But she must not be paralyzed by it . . .

And this Phineas fellow was still in the picture? Caleb was shocked. *How could Charlotte— sweet, smart Charlie—possibly be still entangled with that dolt?* Disappointment in her judgment and guilt that he had not tried to win her love himself played tug-of-war with his heart.

He had to write to her. He had to tell her how he felt about her.

But he was so tired. He hadn't shaved in days, neither had he made the effort to bathe. It was too exhausting, and what was the point? He'd be sweating in this southern climate until almost winter, anyway.

Suddenly, winter itself seemed to settle on his skin. He was so cold. Though the sun shone bright and hot in the Carolina blue sky, Caleb's body was seized with violent shaking. He curled up on his cot and shivered under a single blanket for the better part of an hour. Then, as quickly as it had come, the chill had vanished into the hot, wet air of his tent.

He reached for his looking glass, vaguely noting his rapid pulse as he did so. His heart beat as if he had just done a double-time march of five miles, carrying his fifty pounds of gear. A look in the mirror proved what he had suspected. His skin had turned opaque, the color of light red clay.

And no serpentaria for miles around, was his last thought before succumbing to the overpowering pull of sleep.

Fortress Monroe,
Old Point Comfort, Virginia
Wednesday, June 25, 1862

Edward Goodrich strolled the circular walkway in front of the Chesapeake Hospital on the banks of Hampton Roads. He tried to imagine what his father would think of him now, in a true military uniform, with a genuine military commission, in the only Union fort in the Upper South. Just last month, a bill had been signed officially authorizing a chaplain for each permanent hospital. Edward had requested Fortress Monroe, the Army of the Potomac's base for the Peninsula Campaign. Now that he was here, he daily—if not hourly—relished the fact that he was within a single boat ride of Charlotte Waverly at the Sanitary Commission's headquarters at White House. If he was honest with himself, Charlotte's approval was even more important to him than his father's.

And so was her proximity. The memory of their Christmas dance together was still fresh, and powerful enough to make his heart pound. When Charlotte had told him she would be following the movements of the Peninsula Campaign on the floating hospitals, he all but despaired to think of being in Washington City without her. She understood him so well. She knew just what to say to encourage him. It didn't hurt that she was so lovely to gaze upon, either. He was a chaplain, not a priest. He was a man, after all.

Seagulls squawked and the sea breeze misted his face as Edward climbed the front steps to the entrance of the female seminary-turned-hospital. He slowly paced the wards, looking for someone coherent enough to talk to, or write a letter for. When a thin, yellow hand reached out for Edward, he stopped.

"Well, hello there, Charlie!" Edward pulled a chair next to the cot and sat down, genuinely glad to see this patient looking stronger today.

"Charlie?" he said, one eyebrow cocked. His voice sounded thin and distant.

"That's what you said when I first saw you, soldier. I assumed that was your name—was I mistaken?"

"I did? Oh. Well. Yes. No, my name is Dr. Caleb Lansing."

"Pleased to meet you, Dr. Lansing. Can I do anything for you today?"

"Yes, actually. I wonder if you would be so kind as to help me write a letter, if I dictate it to you."

"My pleasure, Doctor," Edward said, pulling out his paper. "Ready when you are."

Dr. Lansing took a deep breath. "Dear Charlie," he began.

Aha, thought Edward as he wrote the words. *A friend. Of course.*

"Don't be alarmed at the unfamiliar handwriting. I am only sick with fever, and am now close to convalescence, and the chaplain—I'm sorry, Chaplain, what's your name?"

"Edward Goodrich."

"Right. Edward Goodrich is writing this on my behalf. I received your letter just before I fell ill. Please don't think my silence meant judgment or disapproval." He paused to breathe. "The few conscious moments I have had since I read your letter have been filled with thoughts of you." He stopped then, clearly searching for the right words, and Edward realized that this friend was a woman.

When he began again, the thoughts came out only in halting phrases, leaving Edward to fill in the blanks to form complete sentences. *I understand how you feel . . . responsible for Marty's death . . . must let that go. Do your best . . . Pray for guidance . . .*

Dr. Lansing broke off again and closed his eyes,

and for a moment Edward thought he had fallen asleep.

"I can't think straight," Dr. Lansing finally said. "Is any of this making sense?" He was almost out of breath with so much talking already.

"If I may be so bold, sir, you seem to be beating around the bush," said Edward. "But war is no time for hedging. Come right out with it and say plainly what you feel. Take your time."

Nodding, he slowly dictated:

> It is no wonder that this surgeon, Dr. Ware, advised you to deny your heart, for it is the only way we can survive what is required of us. I've been so busy and focused on saving other people's lives, that I have denied my own heart in many ways. I am not boasting here, but confessing. For I have denied you.

The effort cost him, and he fell asleep. Edward tucked the letter away and came back for three more sessions of dictation before Dr. Lansing had finally poured his heart into the letter and confessed his love to this woman.

"How was that?" he whispered, and Edward assured him the message was convincing. He pitied the poor man, so thin and jaundiced-looking, blisters still on his skin from the relentless fever. He looked to be a poor candidate to win anything more than a woman's sympathy and motherly ministrations.

Love could be so painful. Dr. Lansing seemed like a good man, though, and Edward truly hoped it would work out for them. Caleb signed the letter with his own weak hand, then fell back on his pillow from the exhaustion of such an effort.

"Where shall I address it, Doctor?"

Dr. Lansing's breath came rapidly, his beating heart could be seen pumping beneath the thin wall of his chest. He closed his eyes and whispered, "Charlotte Waverly, Sanitary Commission Floating Hospitals, White House Landing, Virginia."

Edward may as well have been struck from behind, so shocked was he as he watched his hand obediently address the envelope. Dr. Lansing now asleep, Edward rose in a daze, and his feet carried him across the ward, out the hospital, and down to the walkway by the water.

Though the sun hid her face behind a veil of steel-grey clouds, a wet blanket of heat pressed down oppressively on Fortress Monroe. Thick, sticky wind whipped up Hampton Roads just over the bank. A layer of sea mist combined with the beads of sweat on Edward's face until it all ran down together in salty rivulets, soaking the collar of his wool uniform. *Suffocating.*

The letter felt like it was burning a hole in Edward's pocket as he walked laps around the circular sidewalk in front of Chesapeake Hospital, but he would not take it out to mail it. He would not touch it at all until he decided what to do. At the outer rim of the walkway, he was within just a few yards of the water, lapping hungrily at the bank, and Edward had to fight the temptation to feed it with Dr. Lansing's letter.

Just mail it, Goodrich! He had always sought to do the right thing before. If he was nothing else, he was an honest man. He was even honest with God about the holes this war had poked in his faith. *Why is it so hard to be honest now, and just mail the blasted letter? Do I trust God for the affairs of my life without trying to manipulate what happens?*

She is not engaged yet, his heart cried out. *It is not manipulative to simply make your own case. There is still a chance. Seize the day and write your own letter! Do it now, just do it, just write her a letter and pour out your heart!*

The Union flag snapped in the wind above him, and seagulls screamed overhead, like sirens. But all Edward Goodrich could hear were the words now forming in his head. *Dear Charlotte, you may think me very bold, but I cannot deny my heart . . .*

Chapter Thirty-Four

White House Landing,
Pamunkey River, Virginia
Wednesday, June 25, 1862

Charlotte should have known it would come to this, eventually. But it was still a shock to see Phineas Hastings stride down the rickety gangway of the *Daniel Webster* at White House Landing, looking wholly out of place. Smooth fair skin, perfectly groomed hair, mustache, and goatee, immaculately trimmed fingernails—it was as if Prince Charming had been plucked out of his fairy-tale world and dropped into the swamps. The contrast was jarring.

Mosquitoes droned in Charlotte's ears, echoing the alarm sounding in her head as he made his way to her.

"Charlotte." His tone held accusation rather than a greeting.

"You're here," said Charlotte, but her voice did not hold much surprise.

"So are you." The charge, leveled. There was no denying the statement.

She looked down at her dress, acutely aware that if he had ever considered her his princess, the spell must surely be broken now. From chin to belt, she was sticky with sugar, yellow with lemon juice, greasy with beef tea, and pasted with milk porridge. Her apron and skirts were stiff with blood and human filth. *And I am a member of the Sanitary Commission? Oh, that I could whitewash myself!*

Phineas flicked a finger under the hem of the shirt she wore over her dress. "What do you call this?"

"Dr. Agnew left some flannel shirts behind when he returned to New York. He didn't need them anymore, and our shirtwaists were positively filthy—we were only allowed to bring two uniforms, and getting any laundry done is quite an ordeal." She bit her lip. She sounded nervous, even to her own ears.

"You mean to tell me, you are wearing men's clothing now over your hoopless skirt? What's next, Charlotte, trousers? Like the female soldier I told you about?"

Charlotte stiffened.

"We're going home."

Had Charlotte been found guilty in court, she would feel no less condemned and sentenced than she did right now. Phineas's gaze held hers firmly, almost daring her to contest the decision as she had done a thousand times before, with passion, confidence, and self-righteousness.

But this time was different. She made no appeal. She had killed a soldier—maybe more, who really knew? Caleb had never written her back with the reassurances she so desperately craved from him. And Ruby—well, this was no place to raise a baby. If Aiden caught swamp fever, his death would be upon Charlotte's stubborn head, too. If Ruby's turn for fever came, Aiden would surely follow. Charlotte could not take that risk.

Lowering her chin, Charlotte whispered, "I am not indispensable." It felt like confession.

Phineas's shoulders relaxed. "When can we leave?"

"When one of the ships bound for New York fills up with enough men." Charlotte replied like one in a trance. "We're bringing Ruby and the baby."

"Pardon me?" His face paled slightly. Maybe he was still recovering from the choppy voyage.

"I told you about her. She had a baby, and we can't leave them here. They're coming back to New York with us."

"And then what will you do with them, pray tell?"

Charlotte paused. "Phineas, her husband has recently died. She has a newborn baby. Let's just get her back to New York. There is nothing for her here, not now."

She studied his face then, and wondered why his eyelid was twitching.

The sound of footsteps on the gangway grew louder in Ruby's ears until there was no question they were headed toward her.

Charlotte entered first. "Ruby," she began, "are you ready to go home?"

And where might that be? she wondered.

"I'm sorry?"

"Phineas has come down for me. It's time to go back to New York, away from these marshes. Much better for the baby . . ." Charlotte kept talking, but the sound of her voice trailed away in Ruby's mind almost as soon as she heard Phineas's name. Her gaze darted furtively around the cabin, and she instinctively clutched Aiden to her a little closer.

"He's here?" She interrupted Charlotte without thinking.

"Yes, you might remember you met him after our little camp Christmas party—but you were so tired then . . . Ruby, are you all right, dear?"

She was not all right. Heat bloomed at her collar and climbed up her throat until she felt like her skin was on fire. Phineas had just stepped inside, filling the small doorway with his frame, hand outstretched toward her. Woodenly, she returned the gesture and allowed him to kiss her hand. Her skin burned where his mustache had grazed it. But one glance at Charlotte told her she still didn't know their history.

"We'll be getting married soon," Charlotte was saying, extending her hand to show off a sparkling diamond and sapphire ring.

Ruby gasped. "When was this decided?"

Charlotte fixed her eyes on the ring. "He just put the ring on my finger a few moments ago."

Aiden stirred, and Ruby tucked his cotton blanket about him. *Married? No, no, why would she do that? She's too good for him! She'll be in for a lifetime of sorrow and regret with his wanderin' eye and heavy fists.* She could hardly stand the thought. *But if I say anything to her, she'll ask how I know. If I tell her the truth, I'm sure she'll cut me off like she cast out that prostitute at the Columbian College Hospital when I first arrived . . .*

"That's quite a good-looking little baby you've got there," Phineas said, reaching out to touch his cheek. "I'll bet his father is mighty proud, isn't he?"

Goosebumps broke out over Ruby's body, covering her with a chill.

"Phineas," Charlotte hissed, pulling him aside. "I already told you! His father died not long ago."

"Is that so? My, my, for a loyal, devoted wife, you seem to be holding up well without him around. Or had you already been used to that?"

Ruby's heart leapt into her throat, and her mouth went dry. Where on earth was this going?

Charlotte tugged hard on Phineas's arm, clearly a sign to make him watch his tongue.

"It's different when there's a child involved, though, isn't it?" Phineas plowed ahead. "A child needs a father. Especially a son. It wouldn't be right to deprive your boy of a man in the house. Do you plan to marry again?" His bristly black mustache twisted in a smirk.

How cruel! Of course no one would marry me, and you know it.

"It's too soon to speak of such things," said Charlotte, backing out toward the doorway now.

"Never too early to plan your future, I always say." His eyes gleamed. "You know, the Five Points House of Industry back in New York has teamed up the Children's Aid Society to take unwanted children into their care until they are adopted by respectable families."

"Who said anything about Aiden being unwanted?" Charlotte interrupted. "His mother is right here!"

"Ah yes, my dear, but can the mother sustain both him and herself back in New York, without the shelter of a hospital ship, nor the provisions of the Sanitary Commission? It's something to consider. Many of these children who stay at the House of Industry are mail-ordered to families out west—Illinois, Iowa—as far away as you could get from the slums, I'd say. They'd give him a real wholesome upbringing on a farm, most likely. Doesn't that sound like a better life than you could give him?"

Ruby recognized the glint in his eyes. This was not a helpful suggestion, but a threat. What he was really saying did not escape her: *Keep your mouth shut or I'll have your son sent out west.*

Aiden cried for milk, and Charlotte and Phineas left mother and baby in privacy. Invisible pins and needles pricked Ruby's breasts from the inside as her milk let down, but it was no less painful than the pricking of her conscience by the choice she must make. Should she try to protect Charlotte by telling her the truth? Or try to protect herself—and, more importantly, Aiden—by keeping quiet? She knew what Phineas was capable of when he felt threatened. For Aiden's sake, she would do her best not to provoke him. She stroked the top of the baby's velvety head. *Her* baby. Half hers, anyway. She may not have wanted him at first, but he was all she had left. He was not the one to blame. She had to do right by him, whatever it took.

Fortress Monroe, Virginia
Thursday, June 26, 1862

Edward was keenly aware of every bony vertebrae as the hard pine pew pressed against his spine. The irrational thought that the pew itself was repulsing him crossed his mind as he leaned forward to prop his head in his hands.

Should I send Caleb's letter or mine? The same question had been rattling around in his brain for days, but it was no use. Even here, in the Chapel of the Centurion, he felt no closer to having an answer.

As he trudged out of the chapel, he scanned the small village of white tents that housed the contrabands in the neighboring yard. Fortress Monroe had been dubbed Freedom's Fortress, for all the runaway slaves it put to work. But Edward had never felt more in bondage than he did right now. His thoughts were as stuck as the horses that sank up to their harnesses in the Virginia swamps.

"Something wrong, Preacher?" It was Willie, an older contraband who had taken a special interest in Edward from his first day at the fortress.

"Hello, Willie." Edward raised a hand in greeting. "I've just got a decision to make and can't bring myself to go either way on it."

Willie nodded, his dark face shining with perspiration beneath his tightly coiled grey hair. From the looks of it, he had been hard at work in his garden recently, cultivating onions and potatoes to sell to the soldiers.

"Well, Preach, the way I look at things, most choices ain't that tricky. You can't serve two masters, and don't we know it, sure enough." He threw an arm back to point at the tents behind him. "You can work for the wrong or work for the right. Like us here. Once we'se working for the Confederacy under our Southern masters until we up and came here, and now we'se serving the Union. See that?"

Edward nodded. "We're grateful for all you do for the cause, too."

Willie waved the comment away and swatted at mosquitoes on his arm. "But do you get it? You can serve the Enemy or you can serve God. Don't matter what the decision is, usually. I'se not talking about whether you want to eat a banana or a peach with your grits. I'se talkin' about bigger stuff. Make sense to you? If you lie, cheat, steal, kill, you'se serving evil. Satan. But if you'se honest, unselfish, keeping others in mind ahead of yourself, you'se doing the right thing and serving God."

Edward suddenly had the uncomfortable sensation that he was being preached to—even more surprising, he needed a good sermon right about now. "After all you've been through, do you still believe in a good and loving God?" Edward asked Willie.

A smile spread wide over Willie's face, revealing yellowed and missing teeth. "Course I do, sure enough."

"But the slavery . . ." Edward trailed off. Willie's thin cotton tunic, wet with sweat and clinging to his back, was raised with scar tissue where whips had once raked through his flesh on his back. It had reminded Edward of a relief map of a dozen roads and rivers. *How could his faith remain so strong after that?*

"Nah," said Willie. "Wasn't God who whup me

and rode me harder'n a driving horse. People did. You can't get the two confused. God is still good. It's people who ain't."

Against his will, tears filled Edward's eyes. "But God is sovereign!" he said.

Willie shrugged. "True enough. But all people get choices, too, right? Like the one you gotta make. Some people, they choose right, and some people, they choose wrong. I ain't got the book learnin' like you, son. I don't know how it all works together. But God does, that's for sure, and that's good enough for me." He paused, and Edward had the feeling Willie could read his soul just by looking at his face. "Now make up your mind and do the right thing, even if it hurts. If you know what God says about it, well, obey that. And don't try to figure your way out of it to please yourself."

All these moments of agonizing indecision— was it really so simple to come to a conclusion? *If I were more concerned with God's approval rather than Charlotte's, I would not have had any question about what to do at all!*

He sighed, clapped Willie on the back in thanks, and made his way over to the post office. This nonsense had gone on long enough. *If I really love her, I will give her the freedom to make her own decisions without manipulating the situation.* Edward looked heavenward, Willie's words still echoing in his mind. *You give us the freedom to make decisions without manipulating them—and that's how we ended up in this ugly, awful war.* A flicker of insight flared within Edward. God was still sovereign. But He would not force humans to make the right decisions.

Edward picked up his stride with confidence now, and mailed Dr. Lansing's letter to White House Landing. Charlotte's choices were not for Edward to steer.

Off White House Landing,
Pamunkey River, Virginia
Friday, June 27, 1862

All of it, up in flames.

Charlotte watched the sky grow thick with smoke above White House from the deck of the *Wilson Small,* along with everyone else. Fire flashes illumined the night sky with an eerie orange glow.

McClellan and Lee had been at each other's throats for three days, getting closer to White House Landing all the time. If Lee's army had reached the White House before the hospital transports had gotten away, they would have stolen or burned all the Sanitary Commission supplies. The sick and wounded would have been killed or captured. Now the hospital transports were running away from Stonewall Jackson, back down the Pamunkey and into Fortress

Monroe to await further instructions. Which side was winning, no one could tell. *How many casualties will there be?* Charlotte had wondered. *Where will they congregate? What will we do with them once we find them? We have nothing left!*

And then she remembered. It was no longer her concern. At least, it shouldn't be. As soon as the smoke cleared and the *Daniel Webster* was filled with soldiers, she, Phineas, Ruby, and Aiden would be on it, steaming back up to New York.

"This is why I didn't want you here in the first place," Phineas was saying. "Can you see that now, Charlotte? Do you understand I've been trying to protect you all this time?"

She pretended not to hear him as the boom of unseen cannons shook her, body and soul. It seemed she had no answers anymore, only questions. What was McClellan doing? The battle had begun on Wednesday, with the Union just a few miles southeast of Richmond, But since then, the army had been falling farther and farther back. They could all hear the scream of battle inching its way closer to them. Was it a long, protracted defeat? How many lives would it cost this time? For the first time, Charlotte dared to entertain the idea that the North could lose. It had seemed absolutely impossible before, but now she had lost that comforting assurance that victory would be theirs. *But God!* her heart cried. *The North is right! We cannot lose! All those lives, lost for nothing! Sacrificed for defeat! May it never be!*

Her eyes burned. She was dizzy from lack of sleep. It all seemed like a nightmare to her. Nothing made sense, there was no purpose, no context. Only terrifying images and a sense of inescapable danger.

Phineas wrapped his arm around her, and she buried her face on his shoulder. She was finally ready to go home.

Off Harrison's Landing,
James River, Virginia
Tuesday, July 1, 1862

Seven days of steady fighting. Seven.

Already the ground at Harrison's Landing was littered with McClellan's haggard, retreating army, their faces nearly black, their hair stiffened with dust and dirt, their bodies molded to their waists in Virginia clay.

A few wounded had straggled in today. But where were the rest? Part of Frederick Law Olmsted hoped they would be delivered to them at Harrison's Landing at any moment, for if they were not here, they were surely dying alone in the swamps. On the other hand, what could be done for them? There were no hospital tents at all, and only three walled tents to shelter the wounded. The only building in the area—the Harrison Home—had been appointed for hospital use by the new medical director, Jonathan Letterman, who had just arrived to take over for Tripler last week. *Nothing like jumping right in with both feet,* he thought, and trusted that Letterman would be more effective than Tripler had been.

Olmsted rubbed the back of his neck with his hand and picked up a pencil.

To the Reverend H. W. Bellows, D.D.
President, Sanitary Commission.

I am at a loss as to what I can do. The armies have been at hard battle for a full week now. You may know better than I, from the papers, which side claims the victory, for I daresay the losses on both sides have been tremendous. The North is farther away from Richmond and victory than ever.

For the wounded there is no provision: no beef—none at all. They have scarcely begun to be collected yet. The largest depot will be four or five miles above here. . . . There are a few hundred ashore here, nothing yet for them to eat. They will begin loading them tonight.

<u>Anything and everything that you can send is wanted in the largest possible quantities. Buy all the beef stock and canned meats you can, and ship by earliest opportunity.</u> We shall have the

Elizabeth here tonight, and land her supplies at once, probably.

Very respectfully yours,
FRED LAW OLMSTED

The next day, the trickle of wounded became a steady stream flowing into Harrison's Landing. From morning until night, and all through the following day as well, the cold pewter sky hurled heavy rain down upon them in sheets, turning the dirt on their bodies into mud, matting their dusty hair to their heads. And still the hospital tents did not come, and thousands of sick lay down in the mud, again, racked by dysentery, fever, malaria, and scurvy.

Eventually, cauldrons and beef stock came, and medical officers and cooks worked by relay day and night. Six thousand were sent away on transports, and nearly thirteen hundred sick remained. By Letterman's estimate at least 20 percent of the army was sick.

If McClellan himself couldn't see it, Olmsted could, plain as day. The Army of the Potomac was spent. Sending fresh reinforcements during the hottest part of the summer would only mean more sick on their hands. The Peninsula Campaign was finished, and so were the Commission's hospital transport ships. It was only a matter of time before they retreated back to Washington in defeat.

McClellan, the savior of the North indeed.

Chapter Thirty-Five

New York City
Friday, July 11, 1862

If she had been the mother of the prodigal son of the New Testament, Caroline was sure she couldn't have been any more relieved to have her child back home.

"Have some lemonade, dear." Caroline brought Charlotte a glass and smiled at the amused look on her daughter's face. It may have been the first time Caroline had ever been the one to serve refreshments. But Jane was gone now, and she just hadn't been able to muster the energy required to search for new candidates for the position. *Advertising the job, requesting applications, speaking with references, conducting interviews . . .* Caroline sighed. *Exhausting process! Right now I just want to focus on Charlotte, and Alice and Jacob when I can.*

"Mother, I'd like to talk to you about something." Charlotte ran a fingertip around the rim of her glass before looking up. Her eyes were sincere, hopeful. *When was the last time she looked at me that way? As if I had something she wanted and she thought I might actually give it to her?*

"Yes?"

"It's about Ruby and Aiden. I'd—like them to stay. You have more than enough room for them, you know you do."

Caroline's lips pressed into a thin line. If only Charlotte had asked for something more reasonable! "My help just left, Charlotte," she began. "I understand you're concerned about them, but I can barely keep this household going as it is without adding guests to it. I simply can't take care of them all properly."

"Please." Charlotte grasped her hand. "They have no place else to go. They won't be a bother, I promise. She's used to living on little anyway, and she's a very hard worker."

"You ask for too much, daughter! You want them to be permanent guests? Or for me to adopt them as members of the family? I'm afraid it's quite out of the question." *Lord, I don't want to always be at odds with her, but this is too much!*

A muffled bang from the kitchen turned their heads.

"I thought you said the cook was ill today, Mother."

"She is. She hasn't been able to work since Wednesday." *Then what on earth?*

"Oh no—have you seen Dickens lately?" Charlotte asked, a tinge of apology in her tone. Caroline shook her head.

Charlotte was the first to reach the kitchen, and

almost as soon as she poked her head in the door, she came right back out. "Look at this, Mother."

Caroline pushed the swinging door open just enough to see Ruby standing at the sink, elbow deep in dishwater, scrubbing away at the stack of dishes left on the counter. Hearing the hinges squeak, Ruby tossed a glance over her shoulder.

"Oh, pardon me, missus. I hope you don't mind. Aiden is sleeping and I've nothing else to do, at that. I'm happy to help."

"Not at all," Caroline answered, and stepped back into the hallway. Her mind whirred. She looked at Charlotte, whose eyes were suddenly bright again, and knew the same idea had just occurred to her.

"Would it work?" she whispered to Charlotte.

"Perfectly." She gave Caroline a smile that she thought had only been reserved for her father.

"What about references? Is she of a high moral character?"

Charlotte laid a hand on her mother's shoulder. "Come now. Isn't my word enough for you? I have lived with her since last fall. I tell you she is above reproach."

"But what about before you met her? Just how much do you know about this woman?"

"Enough. Please trust me, Mother. It would mean so much to me." A shadow of doubt crossed Charlotte's face as she waited for Caroline's decision.

A few moments passed as Caroline stood in the doorway appraising Ruby before joining her at the sink. "My daughter here tells me you're a hard worker."

Ruby nodded, still scrubbing.

"Have you had any experience in a household? As a servant, I mean?"

"Aye, I have. And I can sew, too."

Caroline nodded and looked over her shoulder at Charlotte once more. "Well, then." She turned back to Rudy. "If you're genuinely happy to help, how would you like to *be* the help?"

Ruby's hands froze and she looked up, green eyes wide. "I beg your pardon, missus?"

"My help left and I've not even begun searching for a replacement. I need a new domestic. I have a cook, a gardener, and a coachman, but I desperately need a maid. Room and board included, with reasonable wages besides. What do you say?"

"But my baby—"

"Yes, I know. He stays with you, of course. It's been awhile since we've had a baby around the house. A welcome distraction to the news of war. I wouldn't exactly mind helping to watch him while you do your work, you know." *Alice is in Fishkill, Charlotte is barren—I never thought there would be another baby in this house again. But oh! how wonderful it would be!* Caroline's face brightened with a hopeful smile.

Caroline glanced at Charlotte while they waited for Ruby's response.

"Aye." A smile warmed Ruby's face. "I'd love to."

New Haven, Connecticut
Friday, August 1, 1862

Caleb Lansing lay on his bed and stared at the ceiling. After virtually a year of sleeping on moldy cots or on the ground, the softness of his own bed still surprised him. He still couldn't quite believe he had been sent home to recover when they needed his bed at Fortress Monroe.

Fortress Monroe. He groaned and squeezed his eyes shut, but he could still see himself lying there in the Chesapeake Hospital, waiting every day for mail call only to be sorely disappointed. It just wasn't like Charlotte to not write back at all. *I poured out my heart to her! I said too much. Or too late. Wherever she is right now, her heart belongs to Phineas.*

In the end, it was the only explanation that made sense, and he went about the painful work of removing her, piece by piece, from both his memory and his hoped-for future. She was so far embedded into the fiber of his being, he could never pull her out. Instead, he decided, he'd just bury her. Very, very soon, he would be well enough to work again. But it had to be all-consuming. The simple ailments of peaceful New Haven wouldn't require enough of him. It was time to return to war.

New York City
Wednesday, August 6, 1862

Charlotte took a deep breath as she stepped out of her dressing room wearing her wedding gown for the first time. In just two more months, she would be Mrs. Phineas Hastings.

Caleb had never responded to her letter, and his name had not appeared on any casualty list in the papers. He had been appalled at her role in Marty's death and wanted nothing to do with her anymore, or he was far too engrossed in his medical duties to respond to a letter. Neither possibility should surprise her.

"What do you think?" Charlotte asked, turning to give her audience the full effect. The off-the-shoulder dress was made of white silk and overlaid with Brussells lace trimmed with satin ribbon and silk flowers. Her veil, held in place by a circlet of white silk roses and orange blossoms, almost reached the floor.

Caroline and Alice, who was visiting with Jacob from Fishkill this week, gushed with approval. Ruby was there, too, dusting the bedroom furniture, but said nothing.

"Ruby?" Charlotte tried to draw her out.

"You're a seamstress—how do you think they've done?"

Ruby just shook her head, her attention focused on Aiden playing with a rattle on a blanket on the floor. She tickled his feet as if she were indifferent to Charlotte's question but pink blotches on her neck betrayed her. Her lips began to tremble.

"Why, Ruby, what's wrong?" Charlotte asked, worry threading her tone.

"Lord have mercy," Ruby blurted out as she threw a glance up to the ceiling. "But you can't marry him, miss. You just can't."

Stunned silence.

"What is it, Ruby?"

"He's not who you think he is." Her gaze flitted to each woman in the room. "He's not a good man."

"What do you mean?" Caroline asked, her eyes intent on Ruby. Charlotte's heart seemed to stop while she waited for the response.

"He isn't honest," Ruby choked out. "He—he—finds *pleasure* in female company. He uses prostitutes."

The sound of Alice and Caroline gasping sounded strangely far away to Charlotte. The room spun. She looked down at her pristine white wedding gown and steadied herself with one hand on the bedpost.

"I wish it weren't true, miss, I didn't want to

have to say it, but you can't marry him. He'll not be faithful to you. You deserve better than him. He's an awful man, he is!"

"Are you sure?" Alice put an arm around her sister's shoulders. "How would you know?"

Ruby dropped her face into her hands, her feather duster now forgotten on the floor at her feet.

"You might as well—hear it—from me," she sobbed.

Caroline's face drained of all color. "Out with it then," she said quietly.

Charlotte sat down on her bed, wrinkling her gown and not caring a bit about it.

" 'Tis better if I start from the beginning," Ruby said, taking deep, shuddering breaths. Then the floodgates of her history opened to the spellbound circle of women. Pain seeped through the cracks in her voice as she told them about the potato famine, Meghan and Matthew, coming to America. The hope and eviction from Seneca Village, the tenements, Fiona, her crippling outworker sewing, Matthew's enlistment, Five Points. And finally, Brooks Brothers, Mrs. Hatch, and Phineas.

Charlotte felt sick. She wanted to say it couldn't be true, but what reason would Ruby have to lie about such a thing?

"Wait a minute." Charlotte looked at the cooing baby on the floor. "Aiden. Matthew couldn't have been the father! Are you telling us Phineas is Aiden's father?" Her composure was beginning to crumble.

Ruby shook her head.

A wave of relief was quickly replaced by a new shock. "Then who is his father?"

Ruby bit her trembling lip. "I don't know," she finally said.

"What are you telling us, Ruby? That you were a working prostitute before you went down to Washington? Before I vouched for your character throughout our work for the Sanitary Commission?"

Tears streamed down Ruby's face. "I didn't want to do it! I hated every minute of it! But after Phineas had his way with me, I was already sullied. I had to do it just to survive, just once every few weeks, you understand."

Charlotte was shaking her head and pacing the room now. She put a hand over her thudding heart. Her mind reeled in confusion and hurt swelled in her chest until she thought it would burst out of her.

Charlotte did not want to believe Phineas capable of such vice. Neither did she want to remember that he'd grabbed her in Central Park last year, or that last week he'd taken her mouth with such force she thought her lips would be bruised, or that yesterday in his carriage his hands had roamed too far . . .

Ruby's story rang true.

She let out a shaky breath. "Ruby, why didn't you tell us before?"

"Phineas said if I told you about his—activities—he would tell you about me. You would believe him, not me, and I would be back in Five Points. He as much as said he would take Aiden away from me if I told you the truth."

"What?" Disbelief creased Alice's brow.

"He said people out west are sending for unwanted children to adopt," Ruby responded. "Aiden's all I have. But I couldn't stand it anymore. I can't just stand by and let you marry that . . . that monster while you have done so much for me."

Alice nodded. "I believe you, Ruby." She turned to Charlotte and Caroline then. "Haven't either of you read Victor Hugo's *Les Miserables*? It just came out in June—I read it after Jacob and I returned home. It's a similar story—Fantine, the poor factory girl is taken advantage of and has a baby, Cosette. To provide for her, she does everything she can before resorting to becoming a 'lady of the night.' Sometimes, there really is no other way out—at least, that these poor women know about."

Wringing her hands, Caroline shook her head. "This is no novel, my dear, this is my life! A prostitute, living and working in my house . . . and her bastard son!"

Charlotte groaned inwardly. *If Mother couldn't stand the thought of Father going to Five Points, how will she ever allow Ruby to stay?* "Mother, plea—"

"No, Charlotte. I'm still the mistress here. I won't have you filling my head with any more of your revolutionary ideas."

Ruby took Aiden from Alice's arms and held him close. "I s'pose you'll no longer be needing me here, then."

All eyes were on Caroline for her verdict, but moments passed in silence.

"What about 'Amazing Grace'?" It was Alice who finally spoke—Alice, who had never disagreed with her elders in her life.

"I beg your pardon?" Caroline's head snapped up.

"Father's favorite hymn. 'How sweet the sound that saved a wretch like me.' You and Father taught us that God's grace has no limits. Does yours? Maybe it just doesn't cover a woman like Ruby. But you know what, Mother? Father's would have."

Caroline gasped. "Why, Alice! You've never crossed me before!"

Alice bowed her head for a moment before looking up at Ruby and the baby, then back at Caroline. "Forgive me, Mother, but sometimes the stakes are too high to keep silent." Alice winked at Charlotte, who was stunned beyond words.

"Be merciful," whispered Ruby, and Charlotte's head snapped up.

"What did you say?" Charlotte asked.

"Be merciful, as your Father is merciful."

"Was," corrected Caroline. "Her father is dead, remember."

Ruby shook her head. "No. Her Father is alive. He is merciful. And He is my Father, too." Her voice was steady once again.

"Excuse me?" said Caroline. Caroline's tone bordered on indignation. But Charlotte understood perfectly.

"My old life is behind me now," Ruby continued. "I won't go back to it, I won't, even if it means we starve instead. 'If any man be in Christ, he is a new creature: old things are passed away; behold, all things are become new.'" She paused, allowing the words to penetrate. "I'm a new creature, Mrs. Waverly. In Christ."

A slow smile lifted the corners of Charlotte's mouth. Compared to the wisp of a woman Ruby had been last fall, she was a new woman now indeed. Though Charlotte's mind still reeled from the revelation of Phineas's character, her heart warmed as she looked at Ruby, standing tall now, in front of her. If what she said was true, how could her mother possibly turn her out now?

Moments of agonizing suspense ticked by before Caroline dabbed her eyes with her handkerchief and crossed the room to Ruby.

"Forgive me, Ruby," she said, taking her hands in her own. "You are all right—you, my daughters, and my late husband. We all need mercy, and grace. I need it, too. If it were up to us to earn it, all of us would fall short. God gives it freely, and so should we if we are His children."

Her gaze fell to the black skirts draping her knees, a symbol of mourning for a husband who had proven to be far more merciful than she.

"Mr. Waverly, bless his soul, would have wanted you to stay," she said, smiling sadly through her tears. "He would have said we should love our neighbors, and I'm sure he would have thought of you as such. Surely I can do more than wear mourning attire to honor his legacy. Please stay."

Charlotte breathed a prayer of thanks, then caught her sister's eye. "Thank you," she mouthed.

Ruby closed her eyes and sighed. "And the truth shall make you free," she whispered with a smile. Then she jerked her head toward Charlotte. "But will you marry Phineas?"

Charlotte felt three pairs of eyes on her.

All of her arguments with Phineas came rushing back to Charlotte. Caleb's face surged before her. *Don't you think that instead of yanking you back into place, the right partner would step out with you? Daring to believe that another dance, a different dance, could be just as elegant—or even more so?* Phineas had never been the right partner. It had always been Caleb, but he had rejected her by his silence.

"I will marry no one," she said, and unfastened the veil from her hair.

New York City
Thursday, August 7, 1862

"There is nothing more to say, Mr. Hastings." Charlotte's tone was the only cool thing in the stifling parlor. The cicadas outside the open window grew to a deafening pitch in the lull of their conversation. He should have known there would be trouble this evening when it was Ruby who had opened the door.

Phineas squeezed his fist around the sapphire and diamond engagement ring Charlotte had pressed into his hand, his nails slicing into his palm. He set his jaw and held his breath to keep the rage from boiling out of him.

She sat there so calmly on the settee behind her fluttering fan, as if this were simply a business deal she was reneging on. The corner of his mouth twitched with the irony. It was a business deal, after all. But he had never imagined he wouldn't actually close the deal.

"Tell me again," he said, careful to keep his voice even. "Why the sudden change of heart?"

Her fan stilled for only a moment before stirring up the thick air again. "We're not the best

489

match." She shifted her position, fluffing the skirts over her hoops. "Even if you loved me before the war, you cannot love me now. I have changed too much, grown too independent for you. I'm afraid I've been ruined for any hope of being marriageable."

He stared at her. The weight she had lost during the war only made her more beautiful. Her cheekbones were more prominent, her jawline sharper. Her body looked frail, as a woman's should. But her eyes sparkled with rebellion.

"Go on," he said. "I'm just waiting for one speck of anything that makes sense."

"I could not be subject to you, Mr. Hastings. I don't respect you. I can never marry you."

The words might as well have been a slap to his face. *She doesn't respect me?* Blood pulsed loudly in his ears. *Just like my mother,* he thought, his heart racing. *Just like my mother. Just like my mother.*

He reached into his pocket and fumbled for the gold pocket watch. He pulled it out and stared at it as he ran this thumb over the inscription of his father's initials. Of his own initials. *Am I just like my father?* The thought sent a jolt of electricity through his being. *Weak, unable to take control of his woman, a doormat. A coward.*

Phineas narrowed his gaze at Charlotte once again and saw genuine fear register in her eyes. Good. A woman should fear her man.

"This was Ruby's doing." A muscle near his eye twitched, then one in his cheek, until his face felt like it was going into spasms. "Wasn't it?"

Charlotte held his gaze but said nothing.

"She's nothing. She's lower than nothing; don't you know by now what kind of a *lady* she is? Don't you listen to her!"

Charlotte slapped her fan closed in her palm and curled her fingers around it. "And how would you know anything about her, Mr. Hastings? You only met her at Christmas for the first time, right?"

"Well, she's from Five Points—that says it all, doesn't it?"

A grim smile lifted Charlotte's lips as Dickens bounded into her lap and nudged his head under her palm. "I never told you that." She set her fan on the table next to her. "I fear there is something you aren't telling me. But I really don't want to hear the details. My mind is made up. Please do not call again." She stood, clasping her hands. Dickens sauntered over and rubbed against Phineas's trousers. "Good day," she said coolly. "You know where the door is."

How dare she! Fury swelled and writhed within his chest until it could be kept inside no longer. With a swing of his leg, he sent the bundle of fur, yowling, aross the parlor. His hand flew up and struck Charlotte in the face with such a force that she fell back on the settee.

"I do not retreat!" he shouted shrilly, incensed that she had not remained cowering on the settee, but was now standing upright again, chin lifted high though a bright red welt had already formed on her cheek.

"You will take your leave, *sir!*"

Phineas looked up, chest heaving with anger, to find a man in uniform standing before him.

With a hand still pressed to her burning cheek, Charlotte watched in fascination as the two men sparred.

"You will not lay another finger on her." The calmness in her brother-in-law's tone belied the glint of warning in his eyes. His were hands raised, palms out, as if he were approaching a wild animal. Charlotte's skin crawled at the resemblance.

"And who do you think you are?" A feral smile curved Phineas's lips, but he backed away.

"I am Colonel Jacob Carlisle," Alice's husband announced, "and I am this woman's protector. You will leave now."

When Phineas hesitated, Jacob took another step forward, sending her former suitor scurrying toward the door.

"And you will not come back. If you appear on this street again, I'll have you arrested." His tone was even, and his face composed. Yet he commanded more respect from his carriage and character than Phineas could ever hope to force with his demands and fits of fury.

As Phineas stormed out of the brownstone, Charlotte breathed a prayer of thanks that she had escaped a life with him. She didn't need to be bound to such a lowlife. She needed a real man, like Jacob.

No, she corrected herself. *Like Caleb.*

Chapter Thirty-Six

New York City
Saturday, August 30, 1862

The long summer day finally tucked itself away, and Charlotte climbed into a bed that smelled of lilac water. Not brandy or lemon juice or beef tea. Lilac water.

Almost two months had passed since Charlotte had come home on the *Daniel Webster. Or rather, since I came back to New York.* For her spirit had yet to come home. Though she relished being with her family again, the easy, gentle life she had been raised in and bred for no longer fit her as it once had. It chafed against her skin and pulled tightly in all the wrong places. *Like the shoddy uniforms from Brooks Brothers. Sure to fall to pieces in the rain.*

Charlotte felt as though she were a guest here—but she hadn't even been able to play that role very well. She couldn't stand to let Ruby serve her afternoon tea or lemonade when she was used to serving beef tea to thousands of soldiers. The soft bed that she had once craved now gave her nightmares, visions of what she had left behind. She wore the hoop skirts again out of modesty and deference to her mother's sense of propriety, but she desperately missed the freedom of movement she had enjoyed without them for more than a year. She had dutifully attended ladies teas, brunches, and knitting circles for the soldiers, but she loathed their idle chatter.

Lord, I don't fit in anywhere anymore, she prayed. *What am I good for now?*

Slumber finally quieted her questions, but didn't last long.

The shriek of newsboys invaded Charlotte's dreams, taking her back to the Ebbitt House on the end of Newspaper Row. "The Battle of Bull Run" was on their lips as they hawked the *Evening Star.* It had been such a terrible battle. Charlotte willed herself to wake up before the nightmare became vivid and haunting like all the others.

But with her eyes wide open, and her bare feet on the cool hardwood floor, the shrieking did not stop. She flung open the window and listened carefully.

"Second Battle of Bull Run!" a small boy shouted below her window.

Charlotte gasped. *Not again!* No, no, she had lived this reality once before. She had woken up from the nightmare; this wasn't happening. "The Bulk of the Rebel Army Engaged! The Great Struggle Still Proceeding!"

By the time she heard, "Arrangements for the Care of the Wounded!" she had already tied a flannel wrapper around herself and was running down the stairs, flying out the front door, still barefoot. She wanted to snatch the words out of the newsboy's mouth and shake him. She wanted to tell him he was wrong, he had to be wrong.

Instead, she pressed a coin into his hand and snatched only the paper.

Ruby was waiting for her just inside the house, her hair in a braid down her back, her face illuminated by the kerosene lamp in her hand.

"Well?" she said, gently bouncing Aiden in her arms.

Charlotte unfolded the paper on the dining room table and read it out loud. The first line:

The Battle of Bull Run substantially began the war—has been the common remark on the streets this afternoon—and the new Battle of Bull Run is now ending it.

"They thought the war would be over after the First Bull Run, too," Charlotte muttered. She scanned quickly, hungrily, until she came to the call for volunteers to care for the wounded. It was madness. The War Department "made request for volunteer nurses to proceed immediately to the battlefield."

"What!" Charlotte's voice rose. "Just anyone? They must be desperate. If there are so many wounded that they are asking for civilian volunteers, we are definitely not winning the war with this battle!"

Her heart pumped warning through her veins as

she read the official request. *Each volunteer will provide himself with a bucket and tin cup, to supply water, and also a bottle of brandy.*

"And just how many soldiers do they think one bottle of brandy will serve?" Ruby said, patting Aiden's back.

. . . Transportation will be furnished for all as rapidly as possible at the rendezvous by Capt. DANAS, corner of Twenty-second and G streets. Those who can, should provide their own transportation.

"Their own transportation?" Charlotte laughed. "The wounded will need coffins, not nurses, by the time wagons can make their way on those torn-up Virginia roads." She continued reading.

Shortly after these regulations were issued, the government began impressing the hacks and all other means of conveyance. The Street Railroad Company tendered their omnibuses, recently bought from the late omnibus line, and a large number were accepted. Large numbers of citizens began preparing to go down. Many of them have gone already, and many more start out at daybreak.

Trains are running out to Manassas again, and telegraph communication is restored.

Charlotte closed her eyes and groaned. "How shameful! The army needs its own working ambulance system. This, my dear Ruby, is what goes wrong when an army doesn't prepare to take their wounded from the field."

"Won't the volunteers do any good?" Ruby asked.

"No! They will bring chaos, not help. They will be terrified and run, causing more confusion, taking up precious time, not to mention space on the railroad cars that should be used to evacuate the wounded."

The newspaper between them, the women read each other's faces.

"You're going, aren't you?" asked Ruby.

Charlotte smiled even as urgency consumed her. "They asked for volunteers, didn't they?"

Washington City
Tuesday, September 2, 1862

If Frederick Law Olmsted had been surprised to see Charlotte suddenly before him again in her nursing uniform, he did not take the time to show it.

"You must be on your way." His first words to her. "Forty-three wagonloads of supplies were sent forward by the Surgeon General and they were all captured by the enemy when Pope's men retreated. They have nothing but what we supply."

He cupped her elbow and escorted her out of the Treasury Building. "We've sent fourteen wagons with supplies already, and the last two are on their way out to Centreville right now. You can ride on one of them."

The streets were eerily vacant since the army had commandeered nearly every vehicle on wheels to act as ambulances already. Energy coursed through Charlotte as Olmsted helped her into the last supply wagon on its way out of the city.

"I'm sorry, Miss Waverly," he said, still holding her hand.

"Whatever for?" She was afraid to hear the answer.

"You'll understand when you arrive. I'm sorry. I wish I could protect you from what you are about to experience—"

"I do not wish to be protected." She hoped she sounded brave.

"We need you more than we ever have before."

"I'm just a nurse, not a surgeon. But I will do what I can."

"I'm afraid you will do more than that." The intensity in his eyes almost frightened her. "The inspectors I sent with the supplies, and the relief agents, including Frederick Knapp, they haven't come back yet. They've been dressing wounds."

Charlotte stifled the urge to call them unqualified for the task. Hadn't the War Department invited the general public to come help? At least the Commission men wouldn't be drinking all the brandy on the way to the battlefield.

"It's quite bad, then, isn't it?" A sick apprehension settled over her.

"The worst of the war, so far."

The driver cracked the reins on the horses' backs, and the wagon began its twenty-five-mile journey to Centreville.

Night had already descended by the time their wagon arrived at the train station, and the thin coating of sweat on Charlotte's body now chilled her in the night wind. With her flasks already filled and pots of jelly in her apron pockets, she left the driver to unload the boxes and set off for the perimeter of darkness surrounding the railroad platform.

Wind rushed through the pine trees above her with the roar of an ocean tide. She lit her candle and held it high. A sea of broken bodies stretched out before her as far as she could see. She felt a tugging on her skirt, and imagined she was being pulled beneath the surface of this gruesome ocean, that she would surely drown in its current before she escaped.

"Water?"

"Better," she said, gathering her training about her. "Have some brandy." She knelt and held the flask to his lips, scanning his body with the candlelight as he choked down the liquid. His legs were broken, bones thrust up through his trousers like jagged branches of driftwood rising up out of the beach. She focused again on his face, on relieving his thirst with stimulants. It was all she was asked to do. She would not be in a position to make the same mistake she had with Marty.

She moved to the next man, and the next, dribbling brandy into their mouths until her flasks ran dry, and scooping jelly into their mouths with her fingers. She had not moved ten feet beyond the platform before she returned to the station for more. Over and over, she repeated the process until her thighs burned from squatting near the soldiers, her back ached from hunching over their forms. Her own throat grew parched and scratchy in the night air, but she barely noticed. Sobs of relief broke from the men and boys at her feet. Some called her an angel, but she was all too aware that she was only human.

Slowly, dawn chased the darkness away, exposing miles of broken bodies. Emaciated, blackened with gunpowder, shattered, suffering.

"We will die here on this field before we ever reach a hospital," one man told her. "Our ambulances and wagons—we left them on the Peninsula."

"It's not so bad." She tried to smile. "You'll be on the train soon."

But the trains were doing nothing. Maybe one, maybe two, had come and gone, while the bodies multiplied on the steaming ground as the sun rose higher in the sky.

Charlotte swatted at the flies now nestling in the edges of the wounds. Standing, she straightened her back and squinted into the distance, but she could find no end to this mass of human suffering.

Some distance away, another man crouched low and spoke calmly to a soldier as he wrapped a tourniquet about his leg. He was thin, but moved with determination from soldier to soldier, his voice a comforting wordless drone to her ears. A gold medical insignia brightened his armband. This was no drunk civilian nurse.

He stood stiffly to stretch, and spotted her. He waved her over to him, his hand bloody from another man's wound, and she picked her way between the bodies, watching every footstep carefully until she was close enough to speak to him.

"I need you—" they had both begun at once.

The hint of a smile lifted her lips, and she raised her face to his for the first time.

It was Caleb.

For a single moment, their eyes locked in recognition. Unasked questions stuck in Charlotte's throat. But this was not the place for personal pain, when the country lay bleeding at their feet.

"I need you." It was Caleb who broke the spell.

"I've been trying," she said. "But there are so

many. I can't get to them all, and brandy and jellies are not enough!"

"We'll never save them all," he said. It was not the answer she wanted. "So we must save the ones we can."

"What? How?" Exhaustion clouded her brain. She could not understand what he was trying to say.

"There is limited room on the trains. We need to make sure the people we put on them don't die on the way to the hospitals. Do you understand?" He paused. "We can only send back people who have a good chance of living. The others—God have mercy on their souls—we will load onto the trains later."

The fog in her mind slowly cleared and panic began to settle in. "As cargo? You mean, not as passengers?"

"I need you to choose," he said, and she shook her head.

"You want me to choose who will live and who will die?" Dread filled her mouth like an unclean paste.

"No. Only God can do that. I need you to *think*. Look at the wounds around you. Who will have the best chance at a hospital? Get them out first. Even the slightly wounded will die of starvation if left here long enough. Save the ones we can. Organize them into groups. I need your help, Charlie!"

"I can't do it!" She took a step backward and thunder rolled in the distance. "I can't! You don't understand—you didn't get my letter—"

Caleb grabbed her by the shoulders. "I got your letter," he said, pinning her down with his eyes. "Right now, I need you to obey my order, as a doctor to a nurse. Help me. I know you can do it. I order you to do it."

Charlotte was paralyzed. *I can't. I'll make mistakes. I don't want this responsibility.*

"Hang it all, Charlie!" He shouted at her, chest heaving, as if he could read her mind. The voice she'd always remembered as warm and comforting was now white-hot with conviction. "This isn't about us, about how we feel, about the nightmares it will give us! It's about them. *Them!*" He spread his arms wide above the fallen soldiers. "There are people here we can actually help, but they are mixed in with the lost causes. Find the ones we can help! Sort them out from the rest so they have a chance at a hospital! You have a brain, and I want you to use it! Will you do that?"

Cool drops of rain splattered on their bodies like drops of water sizzling in frying pan. They faced off, both of them pulsing with emotion, both of them aware that as they argued, more men died. There was no time for this, and Charlotte knew it. *Lord, give me strength and courage!* she prayed desperately. *Give me discernment!*

Armory Square Hospital,
Washington City
Saturday, September 6, 1862

Charlotte's footsteps sounded distant to her as she trod the halls of Armory Square Hospital. It was an amazing place, constructed according to Sanitary Commission recommendations: one thousand beds in twelve pavilions. She had barely slept since arriving back in Washington.

After four days of loading the wounded onto the trains, they were finally all off the field, except for the ones now at rest in shallow graves within a stone's throw of the railroad station. *They would have died anyway,* Caleb had said. *We got all the rest home.* Anywhere not on the battlefield was home enough for the wounded, at least for now.

But of course, the work didn't stop here. Charlotte's hands hadn't stopped bathing and feeding patients, changing dressings, and soaking bandages since they arrived here with the last load of wounded. And Caleb's hands hadn't stopped cutting off arms and legs.

The pile of limbs outside the surgery window grew ever higher as it baked in the sun. The nauseating stench drew hordes of buzzing flies that scattered only to make room for another deposit dropped out the window.

On her way to replenish her tray of bandages,

Charlotte paused outside the surgery room to catch a glimpse of Caleb. His arms were stained with blood up to his elbows, his face haggard beneath a week's worth of stubble. He had been standing at that surgery table for almost forty-eight hours, refusing a break until his knees refused to support him anymore. She watched helplessly as he collapsed from exhaustion.

Charlotte stepped away from the door as two men hauled him out and lowered him onto a cot to sleep. When they had shut themselves back into the operating room, Charlotte studied Caleb's face in his near-catatonic sleep, wishing she could offer him some words of comfort and receive some in return.

Instead, she fetched a basin of water, a sponge, and a bristle brush, and sat by his side, washing his arms and hands. Every stroke of the sponge on his arms came away red—not from his own blood but from the carving away of men from their limbs. She scrubbed blood from his fingernails, just as he had once done for her after her father had died. Tears fell from her burning eyes, rippling the scarlet water in the basin, her heart aching for what this war required of Caleb. Of all of them. *Some wounds are invisible.*

No wonder he had not responded to her letter. He was married to his work, for the sake of the country. It was as it should be. She would not distract him from it.

· · ·

The setting was perfect.

They may be able to keep me from their house of snobs on Sixteenth Street, thought Phineas as he watched Charlotte from a safe distance, *but no one will look for me here.*

Learning her whereabouts had proven easy enough from the rumors circulating about Charlotte Waverly's latest exploits. Following the trail that led to her had been his driving force ever since that cretin, Jacob Carlisle, had driven him out of the Waverly brownstone. *Humiliating!* The idea that Phineas had played the coward had writhed in his belly ever since. It would not happen again. Next time he met any opposition, he'd be prepared.

Phineas felt the weight of his father's revolver on his hip and took a deep breath. He'd never be a coward again. He'd show Charlotte, too, when the time was right.

If anyone questioned his presence at Armory Square Hospital, he had planned to say he was a civilian volunteering at the request made by the War Department. But when he found a Union uniform that fit his frame in one of the linen rooms, he rejoiced at his good fortune, and grabbed a cane for good measure. No one would question a convalescent soldier limping about a hospital complex of this size.

Phineas's lips curled into a twisted smile

beneath his mustache as he observed the scene unfolding before him now. He had been watching Charlotte care for patients for hours, but this one was different, he could tell immediately. The way she bathed that man with such tenderness and intimacy—it just wasn't decent.

Phineas studied his face for a moment longer. He looked familiar . . . *It couldn't be!* Could it? The man who waltzed with Charlotte at the ball right after the war started. The only man not wearing the proper black tie formal attire, as if he'd come at the last minute. The only partner Charlotte had danced with that he hadn't already known. An "old family friend, that's all," she had said, but she hadn't introduced them to each other. *Why hadn't she?*

Suspicion bubbled into a boiling rage. *Had she harbored feelings for him the entire time?*

He turned his attention back to Charlotte. She was filthy herself, smudged with locomotive soot, dirty, sweaty. Her hair was a tangled mass at her neck. No hint of breeding or refinement was about her. He was sure he didn't love her anymore—but that was beside the point. She had humiliated him, and she would pay for it.

No, Phineas corrected himself. *That man— the doctor she was caring for with obvious familiarity—would pay for it.* If she loved him, any pain he felt would be felt just as much by her.

With one hand holding his father's pocket

watch, and the other on the gun at his hip, Phineas spun on his heel and limped away, chanting silently to himself. *Phineas Hastings is no coward. Phineas Hastings will not be duped. Potter Hatch is dead. Phineas Hastings is in control.*

Phineas scanned the rows of beds in the amputee ward until his eyes settled on the angry face of a young man whose legs had been amputated well above the knee. Both of them.

Just the man I'm looking for.

Striding up to his bedside, Phineas squatted on the floor beside him.

"What do you want?" said the boy.

"Hey now, I'm on your side, soldier," said Phineas. "What's your name?"

"Nathan."

"Well, Nathan, I see you've come upon some tough times, haven't you?"

Nathan glared at him.

"Have you got a girl back home?"

"Used to." He snorted.

"What happened?"

"Just wrote her a letter breaking things off."

"Oh, is that so? Did you tell her what happened?"

Nathan shook his head. "Nah. But I couldn't let her wait around for just half a man, see? She needs to give me up and move along."

"Such a shame." Phineas clucked his tongue.

"You're a real good-looking young man. I'm sorry this happened to you."

Nathan's face glowered. "The doctor said if he didn't take my legs, I would die. Something about the poisons from the wounds infecting my entire body until it killed me." He gave a brave shrug. "I figured at least my mom would still want me, even without my lower half."

"Yes, well. Do you remember the doctor who told you this? Can you tell me what he looks like?"

Nathan described the man Charlotte had been bathing. Phineas's heart beat faster. This was going better than he expected.

"Oh no," said Phineas. "Oh my heavens, oh no no no. It isn't right."

Nathan's eyelids thinned. "What?"

"That doctor is notorious, I'm afraid. A butcher. Just for the fun of it, he will take off a leg or an arm, or two—" he nodded at the empty space on the cot where Nathan's legs had once been. "I hate to say this, son, but I overheard another doctor say your legs could have been saved—both of them." Phineas shook his head in mock sympathy. Nathan's face looked as if it had been set in stone. He didn't move. "Such a needless tragedy. Absolutely senseless. Just think, you could have been a whole man yet, could have gone home to marry your girl, have children. And now you're destined to be carried around by your mother like a baby for the rest of your life. Quite hard to feel like a man that way, I daresa—"

"Enough!" Nathan exploded.

"You have every right to be upset, my dear boy, but not at me. I am only the messenger." Phineas leaned in and whispered. "Are you mad enough to do something about it? To make sure it never happens again to any other soldier?"

Nathan's chest heaved with rage, his eyes narrowed. A good sign.

Phineas reached into his jacket and grasped the cool barrel of a six-shot Walker revolver. "You'd be a hero, son," he said, and pressed the handle into Nathan's hand.

Chapter Thirty-Seven

Armory Square Hospital,
Washington City
Sunday, September 7, 1862

At six feet three inches tall, Surgeon General William Hammond cut an impressive figure walking down the halls of the Armory Square Hospital. Charlotte had seen him make his rounds before, checking on the casualties from Second Bull Run. Word had it he felt personally responsible for the men. *That's only right,* Charlotte had responded. *He is.*

Today, however, he came straight to her.

"Do I have the pleasure of addressing Miss Charlotte Waverly?" he asked, as if she were in hoops and silks and not matted down with grime.

"At your service." She smiled.

"At last," he said, exhaling. "I'll make this brief. We've just opened up a new hospital for the sick and wounded at Portsmouth Grove, Rhode Island. It's near Newport."

"Very good," said Charlotte, wondering what this had to do with her.

"The surgeon-in-charge there is in full favor of having ladies work there, even in positions of leadership."

"That's wonderful!" *Still waiting . . .*

"What do you say?"

Charlotte blinked. "Pardon me?"

"Please, Miss Waverly. Miss Katharine Wormeley was asked to be director, but she refuses unless she has a co-director. From what Mr. Olmsted tells us, you are the perfect fit for the position. Resourceful, determined, highly adaptable, and trained in our own Sanitary Commission methods of nursing and administration—a major benefit. You and Miss Wormeley will hire your own nurses, matrons, special diet cooks, arrange everything to your liking. The only caveat is that we would need you to come at once. There is much work to be done." She was speechless. A co-director of a hospital?

"You don't have a family, do you?" Hammond prodded bluntly.

Charlotte felt her cheeks grow warm as she shook her head. "I am unattached."

"Are you attached so firmly to Washington City that you would not leave it?" She cast a glance toward Caleb, who was now making his rounds with amputee patients.

"We need you in Rhode Island, Miss Waverly. Do you accept?"

In the span of just a moment, she calculated the factors. Washington City was now crawling with nurses, some approved by Miss Dix, but many just volunteering and learning on the job. She could be replaced, easily. She already had been, in fact. The training in New York City had prepared her to be a matron, an administrative head. She was not putting that to use here. And Caleb—well, she had already decided he was doing exactly what he should. She was better off not interfering.

"I accept your offer, sir," Charlotte said, the promise of a new opportunity, a fresh start, buoying her spirit.

As soon as Hammond pumped her arm once more and told her details would be forthcoming, she hurried over to Caleb and waited while he finished examining a patient.

"Hello, Nathan, I'd like to take a look at how you're healing up, if that's all right," he was saying.

The sullen patient said nothing, his arms folded tightly across his chest. He watched both Caleb and Charlotte with a sharp eye.

Charlotte edged in a little closer to watch as Caleb carefully snipped the gauze bandage and unwrapped the stump, layer by layer. A subtle movement in the corner of her vision drew her attention away from the hypnotic unwinding. She glanced at Nathan. He was sweating. *Poor boy,* she thought. *He must be in pain.*

"It looks good, Nathan," Caleb said, smiling. "You're doing very well." He glanced at Charlotte. "See that cherry red color of the skin on the edges of the stitching? And that. Laudable pus. Signs of healing. Right on schedule." He handed her a bandage roll and asked her to re-dress the wound while he unwrapped the second stump.

Edward Goodrich couldn't believe his eyes.

When he had been sent back to Washington after the Army of the Potomac left the Peninsula, the last people he expected to see were Charlotte Waverly and Caleb Lansing. Hadn't they both gone home? But here they were, right in front of him. Together.

His heart gave a faint throb at the sight, but at least he was absolved of the guilt of waiting for so long to mail Caleb's letter. She had gotten it, obviously, and all was well between them.

A glimmer of light caught his eye as the patient they had just been working on pulled a revolver from nowhere. Raised it, cocked it, steadied it.

"Look out!" Edward shouted. Though his legs felt mired in Virginia swamp mud, he lunged in front of Charlotte and Caleb, hurtling himself at the patient to knock away the gun. And heard the crack of gunfire, the thud of his own body staggering against the cot, falling to the floor. Blazing pain seeped out of his shoulder, dark red and slick. *So this is what it feels like . . .* Charlotte's scream bounced off the walls as she crumpled over him on the floor.

The boy cocked the gun a second time. The shot rang out, and Dr. Caleb Lansing buckled and fell beside Edward, with Charlotte bent, weeping, over them both.

Edward fought to retain consciousness. *God, save us,* he prayed. Almost as if on cue, the sickening sound of a muffled gunshot sounded. Charlotte's crying vaguely registered in his ears as he struggled up to his good knee to see. Through the haze of gun smoke he saw the boy had hit his final target. The gun clattered to the floor from the lifeless hand that had fired it.

Armory Square Hospital,
Washington City
Monday, September 8, 1862

Charlotte's voice floated toward him as if she were speaking underwater, and he struggled to open his eyes.

She was there at his side, saying something to him. He didn't know what, and he suspected it didn't matter. Her presence alone was enough to comfort. When the cool of her hand connected with his forehead, he jerked back to full consciousness, his eyes popping open.

"Edward," she said, her voice smooth as silk. "You were very brave. How are you feeling?"

Fire seared through his right shoulder, tracing the path of the bullet. "Fine," he told her.

"Thank God it went straight through." She laid a hand gently on his bare shoulder near the bandage and a shock of electricity surged through him. "I'm going to change the dressing now."

He caught her wrist with his left hand. "Please don't." His voice was raspy. "Can't I have another nurse?"

"Edward, I assure you I'm fully capable of this." Her tone was tinged with hurt.

"I know you are. But you're making it very hard on me, you see, not to . . . wish for more . . . of your time," he finished lamely. What good would a confession of love do now? "How is Dr. Lansing faring?"

Charlotte's face relaxed with relief. "He will do well. Another surgeon was able to pull the ball from his back, still intact. Thank goodness they were not minié balls!"

"I'm glad," he said. It was the truth.

"I just don't understand how Nathan had a gun in the first place. All patients' personal things are collected when they are admitted. Where did the revolver come from?"

"One of the patients saw a tall, dark-haired man slip him a gun on Saturday."

"Why didn't he say something sooner?"

"I don't know, but the gun was inscribed with some initials, so maybe that will give the police a clue about where it came from." He shook his head. "Such a shame. Such a shame. I need to write to Nathan's mother." *What an awful task that will be.*

"I'm so glad Caleb wasn't hurt more severely,"

Edward continued. "If Nathan had been a better shot—" he broke off. "You two make a perfect match, you know."

Charlotte blushed. "I don't know about that." The uncertainty in her voice stopped him. *Doesn't she?*

"You got his letter, didn't you? The one I wrote for him while he was sick with fever at Fortress Monroe?"

Her head jerked up, and the color drained from her face. "He was sick?" she whispered.

"You didn't get it? You didn't get it?" *Lord, I sent it! This is not my fault!*

"When did you send it?"

He told her.

"A week's worth of mail was lost when we moved from White House Landing to Harrison's Landing!" Hope filled her eyes. "What did he say? Tell me!" She clasped his hands in her own, and he closed his eyes to savor her touch.

"Have him tell you himself. And Charlotte, please. I need a different nurse." Warmth flooded his face. "Trust me."

Finally, understanding registered in her eyes, and her cheeks pinked.

"Thank you, Edward," she whispered, giving his hand one more squeeze. "You are a good man. And a *wonderful* chaplain." Smiling, she slipped away.

Edward sagged back into his pillow. *A wonderful chaplain? But Lord, I still don't have all the answers!*

The Word of God resounded in his mind. "The fear of the Lord is the beginning of wisdom."

Edward sighed. *Yes Lord,* he continued praying. *I fear You. But I don't understand.*

"Trust in the Lord with all thine heart and lean not on your own understanding. For my thoughts are not your thoughts, neither are your ways my ways."

God, I fear I'm stumbling along in the dark as I try to be a good chaplain. I'm afraid of falling, of failing You, and those You've called me to serve.

"Though a good man may fall, he shall not be utterly cast down: for the Lord upholdeth him with his right hand. And lo, I am with you always, even to the end of the world."

Edward scanned the rest of the ward now, his gaze resting on each bed's soldier in turn. Like a veil being lifted, he saw that having all the answers didn't matter to these men. What mattered to them was that he was there, reading the Scriptures to them, praying with them, and walking through the struggle of life and death together.

Yes, Edward still had questions. But he trusted that God had the answers.

Washington City
Monday, September 8, 1862

The wool uniform Phineas Hastings still wore chafed against his skin and his better judgment as he marched north on Second Avenue, away from Armory Square Hospital. *I shouldn't have stayed so long,* he chided himself. But he couldn't resist staying long enough to hear the shots fired from inside the seventh pavilion. Charlotte's screams had been music to his ears. But they'd also drawn attention—something Phineas wanted to avoid, for once. He hadn't taken the time to go back for his own clothes, but at least he had had the presence of mind to keep his watch and money with him at all times.

"Halt!" The voice rang out, but Phineas pressed on, covering his nose as he crossed the rickety wooden bridge over the sewage called Tiber Creek. His face darkened as he quickened his pace toward the Baltimore & Ohio Railroad Station. *If only there had been a way . . .* But it was impossible to get the gun back. He reached into his pocket and rubbed his thumb over the engraved initials on the back of his gold watch. Sweat beaded on his forehead. *The initials.* His heart raced. They were the same as those on the gun. *They'll never find it,* he told himself. In less than thirty minutes, he'd be on the train and chugging back to New York.

"I said stop right there!" A force out of nowhere knocked Phineas to the ground from behind. The heel of a boot dug into his spine as he writhed in the dirt on the unpaved road. Two large men in uniform stood over him, scowls slashed onto their faces.

Finally, breath returned to Phineas's lungs. "What the blazes do you think you're doing?" he shouted, and passersby paused to stare.

"We should be asking you that, you dirty scoundrel." A sharp kick in Phineas's side sent flaming darts across his back.

The gun? How did they know? How could they have found me so soon?

"Do you know what the penalty for desertion is, soldier?"

Phineas stared up at them, uncomprehending. "I have no idea *what* you are talking about!" Rage seethed between his words.

Sneering, they yanked him up by the armpits. "Sure you don't. Pretty bold move, seeing as we've had so many deserters, and seeing as we caught you in a uniform on your way to a train station. Oh, I can see why you'd run off. A little too dandy for the hard life of a soldier, ain't you?"

Phineas looked at his accusers and his mouth went dry. For the first time in his life, he had no words to speak. What could he say?

If he let them believe he was a soldier, they'd surely arrest him. If he told them he wasn't a soldier, they'd take him in anyway for questioning. Either way, they'd search him. *Hanged if I tell the truth, hanged if I don't.* The gold watch burned in his pocket, those condemning initails branding his thigh.

"Well? What do you have to say for yourself?"

The soldiers stared at him, eyes slitting, as if daring Phineas to oppose them. "How about your name, to start with?"

Like a cornered animal, Phineas's gaze skittered from one bulky soldier to the other, gauging his chances of escape. They weren't good.

"Ah well." The rancid breath was hot against Phineas's face. "Doesn't matter anyway. Billy Yank, you are under arrest for desertion."

Desperately, Phineas grabbed the watch from his pocket, spun on his heel, and hurled it back toward Tiber Creek, hoping against all odds that its golden arc would end in the open sewer, never to be found.

The last thing Phineas Hastings remembered before his world went black was one soldier running after the watch and the other ramming the butt of his rifle into Phineas's head, trapping the guttural groan in his throat.

He heard her coming before he even turned around.

"Edward—Chaplain Goodrich—said you wrote me a letter," Charlotte said in a rush when she found Caleb in his ward at Armory Square Hospital. Instantly, the pain in his back receded. All of his attention was now riveted on Charlotte.

"Of course I did. You didn't get it?"

Charlotte shook her head, holding her gaze with his. "Please," she whispered, pleading in her caramel-colored eyes. "Tell me what you said."

Caleb groaned inwardly. What did it matter now, anyway? But one glance at Charlotte's face told him she wouldn't let him off that easy. He glanced at the rows of patients, said, "Let's take a walk," and escorted her out into the sun.

Gravel crunched beneath their feet as they strolled through the massive hospital complex.

"I don't know if I can remember exactly what I said then," Caleb confessed, and raked his hand through his hair. "That was a long time ago, and I was still in and out of my right mind from fever. It might have been filled with gibberish." He laughed nervously, irritated with his rising heart rate.

"Well then, what would you say to me now?"

"Would it matter?" His tone was tired, his lips flat. "Aren't you promised to that Phineas Hastings fellow?"

She shook her head. "No, Caleb. As it turns out, you were quite right about him. He wasn't the best partner for me after all."

His pace slowed. "Do you mean you're—free?"

Charlotte laughed, nodding. "But I hope not for long."

Caleb stared.

She stood in front of him now, lifting her radiant face to his. "So let me ask you again. What would you say to me now?" Her voice was as smooth as a gentle melody.

Caleb's heart skipped a beat—no, two—before he could speak. "Charlie, forgive me," he said, emotion thick in his throat. He tucked a strand of her hair behind her ear. "This is long overdue. Once upon a time, there was a flickering flame between us, and I snuffed it out—at least, I tried. You must have hated me for it. I almost hated myself. But it had to be done, to protect you from making a choice just because it was easy."

Charlotte opened her mouth to speak, but Caleb held up his hand to stop her. "Please," he said. "Please let me finish. Hear me out." She nodded. "I was your good friend after your father died. I'm sure you knew I loved you then. But asking you to love me back when you were still so raw from your father's illness and passing would not have been right."

Charlotte started to reply, but once again he hushed her with a finger to her soft lips. *How many times have I dreamed of kissing them?* A rush of heat prickling his body made him forget that it was autumn. He swallowed the urge to kiss her right then, though it took all of his strength. "Neither of us would have been sure you were really loving me back or merely showing gratitude for getting you through your father's worst times. I had to leave. Don't you see, Charlie? Otherwise I would have always wondered if you had only fallen in love with me as one falls into a rut."

Tears glistened in Charlotte's eyes as Caleb continued.

"Over the last year, you've proven that you do not choose a path because it looks easy, but because you are following your heart. I had hoped that once the smoke of battle clears and the war is over, your heart would lead you back to me."

He reached for her hands and traced the lines of her palms with his thumbs. "Are your hands calloused from work?" He brought them to his lips and kissed each one. "I love them better than if they were smooth and soft. When your uniform is stained and dirty, don't be ashamed, for these are the marks of service. You are more beautiful now than you have ever been before. I loved you years ago, and I love you even more now. I love your desire to make a difference in the world. I love that you take risks and gave up a life of ease to help others."

He looked down into her eyes now, mining for gold. "But I want you to choose me, not settle for me."

Caleb wrapped his large hands around her waist, igniting a heat that spread through her body like wildfire. She reached up to smooth away the lines of worry from his brow and rested her hand on his cheek. "I choose you," she whispered, and he wrapped his arms around her, pulling her close.

Charlotte's hope surged, but it was gone in an instant. "I need to tell you something," she said, pulling away. "I have my own confession to make." She read a question in his eyes, but he held her hands firmly in his own.

"First of all, you probably know by now that when I told you I didn't care for you, I was lying. I just wanted to hurt you for hurting me. I'm so sorry." She fought against the rising lump in her throat. *So many years! Wasted!*

A sad smile tipped his lips. Moments passed before he found his voice again. "We were practically children then. I understand." But his eyes were filled with tears.

"I should have apologized. I meant to. I mean I did—" Her voice broke and she bit her lip. "But I didn't send it."

Caleb waited, allowing Charlotte to continue at her own pace.

"I learned something about myself that I wanted to keep from you. To protect you from a future that wouldn't be good for you. I must be far more selfish now, though, because I don't want to keep you away from me any longer." Tears spilled down her cheeks.

"Darling, you speak in riddles! What can possibly be so horrible?" He cupped her face in his hands. Oh heaven help her, those eyes were as warm as wool.

"I—apparently I can't—" She swallowed and turned away, her cheeks burning. "I can't have children."

She peeked back at his face. He looked surprised, but not crushed.

"Says who?"

"My body. Not made for it."

Caleb stroked his chin. "Ever hear of a thing called adoption? I hear they'll let just about anyone take in a child these days." He grinned, but his eyes were intense. "We'll figure that out later. For now, all I want is the promise of *you*."

She could barely take it in. The truth had come out, and yet he still wanted her! Her heart dilated with joy. Somehow, in the middle of a civil war, they had found peace and love in each other—at last.

Oh no—the war. Rhode Island! Charlotte's conversation with the Surgeon General resounded in her ears. She winced as the pang of disappointment pierced her. Surely she could not keep both Caleb and the new position. Yet how could she give one up?

She buried her face in her hands and groaned. *Oh, the agony of decision!*

"What's this?" Caleb lifted her chin. "This doesn't look like tears of joy to me." Worry etched his brow.

"I never had a chance to tell you." She willed her voice to be steady. "Dr. Hammond has asked me to co-direct a hospital in Rhode Island. He asked me on Sunday, you see . . . and I—" She grasped at words that did not come.

Laugh lines fanned at the sides of Caleb's eyes. "A general hospital? Women have never been allowed to work in them at all, and now you've been asked to co-direct one? That's brilliant! I hope you accepted." He squeezed her shoulders.

"What?"

"You would be wonderful. You *will* be wonderful. It's a great opportunity!"

"But what about—us?" She faltered. Was his love for her so shallow he wouldn't even try to persuade her to be with him?

"Charlie. You of all people should know that a woman need not give up her mind in order to follow her heart. But listen. I'm not going back to New England for a while. I'll be serving wherever the army is, and God forbid the war comes to our own doorstep. I want to be with you, Charlie, but we both have work to do, don't we? Am I—are *we*—worth waiting for?"

She threw her arms around him once again and relished the warmth of his body against hers. "Yes!" she whispered in his ear. As soon as his lips touched hers, she knew—in both her mind and her heart—that this was where she belonged. She tucked her head beneath his chin and felt his heart beating in rhythm with her own. This, finally, was where she fit. "You are home to me."

The History
behind the Story

One rainy October afternoon, in the archives of the Adams County Historical Society in Gettysburg, Pennsylvania, I met Georgeanna Woolsey. A wealthy, twenty-eight-year-old woman in New York City when the Civil War broke out, she left all her comforts to become a nurse with the United States Sanitary Commission, which would be the forerunner of the American Red Cross. Georgeanna's life and personality provided me with more than enough inspiration for Charlotte Waverly. (For everything you want to know about the Woolsey family, check out *The Woolsey Sisters of New York* by Anne L. Austin, and *My Heart Toward Home: Letters of a Family during the Civil War* by Georgeanna Woolsey Bacon and Eliza Woolsey Howland.) Georgeanna's sister Eliza and her husband, Joseph Howland, inspired the characters of Alice and Jacob Carlisle.

The fictional character of Dr. Caleb Lansing is based closely on Dr. Frank Bacon, a Yale-educated surgeon in the Union army who was a close family friend of the Woolseys and married Georgeanna one year after the Civil War ended. They remained childless for unknown reasons, but, among other achievements, together they established the Connecticut Training School for Nurses at the New Haven Hospital. They proved to be the perfect partners for each other.

Phineas, Ruby, and Matthew are purely fictional characters, but they reflect the attitudes and plights of their respective social classes. The scandal with the shoddy Brooks Brothers uniforms really happened, along with other war profiteering, and gentlemen of the Victorian era very commonly used prostitutes. Their reasoning was that "true women," their delicate and refined sweethearts or wives, were morally superior to men, and had no sexual appetite. It was often quite common for even churchgoing men to leave true "spirituality" to women, the official moral compasses of society. Five Points was a real place, then the most notorious slum in the world. Ruby's various attempts to provide for herself followed the typical immigrant's options at the time.

Edward Goodrich's character was based on Chaplain Harry Hopkins, who became the first hospital chaplain due to the requests of Georgeanna Woolsey and her two sisters, Eliza and Abby. (Edward's romantic feelings for Charlotte were purely fictional.)

Many characters in *Wedded to War* come straight out of the pages of history. Their legacies deserve to be mentioned here, at least briefly.

After the war, Dr. Elizabeth Blackwell returned to England where she and Florence Nightingale opened the Women's Medical College. Her adopted Irish daughter, Kitty, remained her life-long companion. Blackwell's New York Infirmary for Women and Children became what is now the New York Downtown Hospital, the only one in ethnically diverse lower Manhattan.

Frederick Law Olmsted, landscape architect of Central Park, remained the General Secretary of the Sanitary Commission until 1863. Later, he returned to Washington and designed the Capitol grounds. (His son, Frederick Olmsted Jr., would later design the National Mall, Jefferson Memorial, White House grounds, and Rock Creek Park, among other projects.)

When Jonathan Letterman replaced Charles Tripler as the medical director of the Army of the Potomac, he made drastic reforms for improved care of soldiers, the most memorable of which was his ambulance reforms. Before Letterman's system was in place, whole divisions were without ambulances. Near the end of the Peninsula Campaign, an army corps of thirty thousand soldiers was reported to have ambulances enough for only one hundred men. But by the Battle of Antietam in September 1862, Letterman had an ambulance for every 175 men, and trained drivers chosen by the Medical Department. By the Battle of Gettysburg in July 1863, Letterman commanded

650 medical officers at the battlefield, along with one thousand ambulances and three thousand trained ambulance drivers and stretcher men. His three-part evacuation system (a field dressing station, field hospital, and large hospital away from the field) was adopted for the U.S. Army by an Act of Congress in 1864 and continues as the model for military evacuations today.

For biographical sketches and photos of these and other historical characters who populated this novel, visit the website at heroinesbehindthe lines.com

The text in this novel from Sanitary Commission reports, newspaper articles, and Dr. Gurley's sermon at Willie Lincoln's funeral came straight from the original sources. These documents can be viewed in their entirety at heroinesbehindthelines.com as well.

Selected Bibliography

Adams, George Worthington. *Doctors in Blue: The Medical History of the Union Army in the Civil War.* Baton Rouge: Louisiana State University Press, 1952.

Anbinder, Tyler. *Five Points: The 19th-Century New York City Neighborhood that Invented Tap Dance, Stole Elections, and Became the World's Most Notorious Slum.* New York: Penguin Putnam, Inc., 2001.

Austin, Anne L. *The Woolsey Sisters of New York: A Family's Involvement in the Civil War and a New Profession (1860–1900).* Philadelphia: The American Philosophical Society, 1971.

Bacon, Georgeanna Woolsey and Eliza Woolsey Howland, edited by Daniel John Hoisington. *My Heart Toward Home: Letters of a Family during the Civil War.* Roseville, Minnesota: Edinborough Press, 2001.

Barnes, Joseph K. *The Medical and Surgical History of the War of the Rebellion* (Volume 2). Washington: Government Printing Office, 1870.

Behling, Laura L., editor. *Hospital Transports: A Memoir of the Embarkation of the Sick and Wounded from the Peninsula of Virginia in the*

Summer of 1862. Albany: State University of New York Press, 2005.

Burrows, Edwin G. and Mike Wallace. *Gotham: A History of New York City to 1898*. Oxford: Oxford University Press, 1999.

Freemon, Frank R. *Gangrene and Glory: Medical Care during the American Civil War*. Chicago: University of Illinois Press, 1998.

Garrison, Nancy Scripture. *With Courage and Delicacy: Civil War on the Peninsula, Women and the U.S. Sanitary Commission*. Cambridge, Massachusetts: Da Capo Press, 1999.

Giesberg, Judith Ann. *Civil War Sisterhood: The U.S. Sanitary Commission and Women's Politics in Transition*. Boston: Northeastern University Press, 2000.

Ginzberg, Lori D. *Women and the Work of Benevolence: Morality, Politics, and Class in the 19th-Century United States*. New Haven: Yale University Press, 1990.

Hamilton, Frank Hastings. *A Practical Treatise on Military Surgery*. New York: Bailliere Brothers, 1861.

Lee, Richard M. *Mr. Lincoln's City: An Illustrated Guide to the Civil War Sites of Washington*. McLean, Virginia: EPM Publications, Inc., 1981.

Leech, Margaret. *Reveille in Washington: 1860–1865*. New York: Time Incorporated, 1941.

Letterman, Jonathan. *Medical Recollections of the Army of the Potomac.* New York: D. Appleton and Company, 1866.

Quarstein, John V. and Dennis Mroczkowski. *Fort Monroe: Key to the South.* Charleston: Arcadia Publishing, 2000.

Schultz, Jane E. *Women at the Front: Hospital Workers in Civil War America.* Chapel Hill: The University of North Caroline Press, 2004.

Stansell, Christine. *City of Women: Sex and Class in New York 1789–1860.* Chicago: University of Illinois Press, 1982.

Stille, Charles. *The History of the United States Sanitary Commission: Being the General Report of Its Work during the War of the Rebellion.* Philadelphia: J. B. Lippincott, 1866.

Wilbur, C. Keith. *Civil War Medicine.* Guilford, Connecticut: The Globe Pequot Press, 1998.

Woodward, Joseph Janvier. *Outlines of the Chief Camp Diseases of the United States Armies.* Philadelphia: Lippincott, 1863.

Wormeley, Katharine Prescott. *The Other Side of War: On the Hospital Transports with the Army of the Potomac.* Gansevoort, New York: Corner House Historical Publications, 1998.

Discussion Guide

1. Charlotte's father left a lasting impression on her even as she continued to live life without him. His priorities for his own life became Charlotte's guiding priorities. What priorities and principles do you want your loved ones to remember you by? How are you exemplifying these in your life today? What can you do differently to further emphasize what is important to you?

2. Charlotte experiences resistance from those closest to her when she decides to become a nurse. How do you know who to listen to when making your own decisions? Have well-meaning people given you bad advice before? Have you ever been the well-meaning person who gave bad advice?

3. Ruby's crooked posture from outworker sewing, as well as her internal scars from the hardships in her life, become her identity. Have you ever known anyone personally whose scars became their identity? How did that affect their outlook on life?

4. Why does Charlotte spend so much time in a relationship with Phineas? What are some reasons that women stay in the wrong relationships today?

5. Fashionable women in Victorian America sought to achieve a fifteen-inch waist with tightly laced corsets that commonly caused women to faint. The skirts that covered their hoops were usually between four and six feet in diameter. One of Mary Lincoln's dresses was eighteen feet in circumference and used twenty-five yards of fabric. If you had to wear this type of wardrobe every day, how would it affect your view of yourself—your purpose and your capabilities? What role do you think the hoopless nursing uniforms had in helping reshape Charlotte's view of herself? How did Ruby's various dresses affect her? Does what you wear make a difference in how you feel?

6. At the ball near the beginning of the story, Caleb says to Charlotte, "What if your stepping out of formation was actually a step in the right direction? What a shame it would be if you were always confined to a prescribed number and pattern of steps." Have you ever stepped out of the expected pattern for your life? Did you feel like you

were going in the wrong direction at first? How do you view those steps now?

7. Throughout the book, Ruby either has to make "a new start" for herself, or respond to a dramatic life change that feels more like "the end" for her. Can you recall a point in your life which you initially thought was a turn for the worse, but which ended up growing into a new start for you?

8. What insecurities fuel Phineas's behavior throughout the novel? How do our own insecurities affect how we interact with people?

9. Shoddy uniforms fell apart even before the first battle, leaving soldiers exposed to the elements and driving morale into the ground. In both North and South, many soldiers even went without suitable weapons. Has there been a time when you thought you were prepared to meet a challenge, only to discover you weren't well equipped for the task, after all? Read Ephesians 6:10–17. Now think about your spiritual challenges. What happens when we try to meet these without being properly dressed in the full armor of God?

10. During the Civil War, amputations were considered necessary to prevent the damaged

limbs from poisoning the rest of the body, claiming the life of the soldier. How does this relate to Jesus telling us to cut off the hand that causes us to sin? (See Matthew 18:7–9.)

11. Edward Goodrich's crisis of faith comes when he focuses on the casualties of war and disease. Where did Dr. Gurley place the focus of his remarks during Willie Lincoln's funeral? (page 361)

12. Today, wars and injustices happen around the world every day. Does this affect your faith in a sovereign God? Why or why not? How does your faith change when you experience your own personal battles?

13. For much of the story, Ruby is held captive to shame and guilt. Is there any sin that you feel God cannot forgive? Is it harder for you to forgive someone else, or for you to forgive yourself? Why?

14. Between August of 1861 and the following summer, the North idolized Major General George B. McClellan and believed he was the answer that would defeat the South and save the Union. What is the danger in placing too much faith in any one person or possible solution? When have you seen this happen in

our own country? In your personal life? What happened?

15. Dr. Caleb Lansing hates how many amputations he must do, because it seems in direct contradiction to his innate desire to heal—which he always thought of as putting things back together. But sometimes we must experience pain or go through conflict before there can be peace and healing. When has this been true in your life?

16. As Charlotte flexes her newfound independence, she grows to disdain many men in authority over her. Her decision to circumvent the proper procedures and authorities costs Marty her life. Is she any better than the ambulance drivers who disobeyed orders and ran away from the battlefields without carrying any patients? Have you ever been placed under authority you didn't agree with? What happened? Under which circumstances is it necessary to go against authority?

17. Edward begins to lose his way when he cares more about Charlotte's approval than he cares about God's. Can you remember a time when you valued someone else's opinion of you as more important than God's? What happened?

18. Alice's priority is to serve her husband, while Charlotte's goals take her far from home. Just before the Seven Days' Battle, Alice says to Charlotte, "Sometimes the people who most need our help are the ones God has already placed in our lives." How do you balance ministering to your own family with serving the Lord outside your home?

19. When Charlotte returns to New York after nursing, she finds that she no longer fits the life she once lived. Have you experienced a similar "outgrowing" of a previous lifestyle or relationship? What caused the change in you, and how did you respond to the growth?

20. After Ruby has Aiden, she claims the verses in John 8:31–32: "If ye continue in my word, then are ye my disciples indeed; and ye shall know the truth, and the truth shall make you free. . . . If the Son therefore shall make you free, ye shall be free indeed." What kind of freedom is Jesus offering here?

Acknowledgments

Though only my name is on the cover, there are many people whose help and support have made this book what it is. I am indebted to:

Bettina Dowell, for friendship, and hospitality on my way to Gettysburg, where I fell in love with the musty research that led to this entire series of Civil War novels.

Deborah Keiser, for giving me a chance to write fiction, and to Moody's editorial team for their skillful edits.

My agents David Sanford, for convincing my doubting heart I could actually do this, and Tim Beals, for his support along the way.

Laurie Alice Eakes, award-winning author and my book mentor, for guidance and encouragement.

Linda Montgomery, for housing me during my research trip to the Virginia Peninsula, and for her ongoing support, prayers, and enthusiasm.

Terry Reimer, Director of Research at the National Museum of Civil War Medicine in Frederick, Maryland, for showing me primary sources that strengthened my research.

Everyone who prayed for me and my family during this journey.

My parents, Peter and Pixie Falck, and my brother and sister-in-law, Jason and Audrey Falck, for countless hours of child care while I wrote this novel.

My husband Rob, for supporting my intense writing schedule without complaint, for making every Saturday with the kids a new adventure for them to treasure, and for your many insightful edits to the book.

Most of all, I want to thank God, who is the Word Himself, and the Author of Life, for inspiring and sustaining me.

About the Author

Jocelyn Green is an award-winning author of multiple books, including *Faith Deployed: Daily Encouragement for Military Wives*, and *Stories of Faith and Courage from the Home Front*. She is an active member of American Christian Fiction Writers, Military Writers Society of America, Christian Authors Network, and the Advanced Writers and Speakers Association. She lives in Cedar Falls, Iowa, with her incredibly supportive husband and two adorable children. This is her first novel. Visit her at www.jocelyngreen.com.

Center Point Large Print
600 Brooks Road / PO Box 1
Thorndike, ME 04986-0001 USA

(207) 568-3717

US & Canada:
1 800 929-9108
www.centerpointlargeprint.com